SURVIVING THE SUMMIT CONFERENCE

JON KACZKA

LOW ON INK BOOKS, LLC

for my wife and daughter

CONTENT WARNING

This book contains multiple scenes with subject matter that readers may find offensive, including dead babies, child abuse, drug use, violence, gore, racism and racial slurs, murder, cannibalism, human sacrifice, and Christianity.

1

Abigor strode through the hallway of the Beburoa Hotel, twirling his golden scepter and inspecting his domain. Two minions flanked him. They dressed in the baggy black habit of Benedictine monks with large hoods covering their faces.

Abigor stopped at the doorway to one of the Summit Conference's many sessions. The sign next to the door read, "The Value of Thought Leadership." He made sure that only three of the five buttons on his black waistcoat were fastened and then straightened the jacket of his black morning suit because appearances are everything. He entered the room and observed.

Mr. Sauber stood at a podium in the front of the room and flipped through a PowerPoint presentation. A group of fifty attendees sat in densely packed chairs and stared blankly at the presentation. The men wore solid black, gray, and blue suits. The few women wore similarly colored pantsuits.

"Some people think inside the box." Mr. Sauber flipped to a picture of an empty box with the word *think* inside. "Some people think outside the box." He flipped to another slide with the word *think* next to a box. "I prefer to think like there is no box." He flipped to the last slide that was merely the word *think* on a blank background.

Abigor smiled. Everything was as it should be. He pulled his golden watch fob from his waistcoat. It was time to meet Mr. Grenville in the lobby. His two minions followed him.

Abigor ambled into the lobby just in time to watch Mr. Grenville fall on his backside as unholy fire roared at him from the revolving doors. He still clutched an ax in his hands that dripped with blood. His face was a fearless snarl.

From behind the nearby concierge desk, Mr. Mulciber laughed. "Fourth time's a charm, Mr. Grenville?" He laughed again. Light from the fire glistened off his bald head.

Abigor's face and the text "Welcome to the 2018 Summit Conference" were on two twenty-foot-high banners that hung from the cathedral ceiling. His picture had a broad, welcoming smile.

The hacked-up body parts of five minions who tried to stop Mr. Grenville lay scattered about on the white marble tile of the expansive lobby floor. Severed limbs lay there, as did a severed head. It wasn't apparent which parts went with which body.

Abigor turned to one of the minions who accompanied him. "Fetch a mop," he said in annoyance.

The minion left without speaking.

Abigor sauntered towards Mr. Grenville, stepping over dismembered corpses and twirling his scepter with one hand. He tsked loudly; each tsk rang through the air like the chime on a church bell. The lobby fell silent.

Mr. Grenville turned to Abigor, and Mr. Grenville's face blanched. He tried to talk but only stammered.

"Mr. Grenville," Abigor spoke with the tone of a parent chastising a child. "You know how much I hate an abscotchalater."

Mr. Grenville suddenly held his ax like it was an emotional support animal rather than an instrument of death. "Abigor," his voice squeaked. "My daughter turns six tomorrow. I haven't seen her or my wife, or even stepped foot outside of this hotel, in four years. Please let me leave for just a little bit. I promise I'll come back. I'll bring back a dozen new attendees for you." A tear ran down his cheek. "No, I'll bring a hundred. I'll bring as many as you want. All I ask is that I leave for just a few days. A week at most. Please."

"Mr. Grenville, you know the rules. You can never leave the Summit Conference." Abigor gestured with his scepter around the Beburoa Hotel's lobby. "You are not permitted to leave today or any other day. Like the thousands of other permanent hotel guests, you will remain and worship me like a god until the end of time."

Mr. Grenville grimaced, and his face turned red. He chucked his ax at Abigor with such speed and force that no ordinary man could dodge. Abigor easily caught it with one hand. Mr. Grenville stared, dumbfounded.

"Your escape attempts were fun at first." Abigor now twirled the ax in one hand and his scepter in the other. "But you've become such a nannygoat."

Abigor flung the ax back at Mr. Grenville. It buried into his clavicle. He fell to the floor. Blood poured from the wound and pooled around him. Still alive, he writhed in pain.

Abigor turned towards the other minion who accompanied him. "Take him to the Chuck."

"Nooo!" Mr. Grenville screamed with a gurgle as blood filled his throat.

2

Hanna Taithangklom was trying to take a nap, but her daughter had other plans.

"Momma! Momma! Here go," Alexis said in her high-pitched voice, rousing her momma.

Hanna normally found the voice so cute that it filled her with motherly warmth, but it was the last thing she wanted to hear now. *Not yet,* Hanna thought groggily. *Maybe if I keep my eyes closed, she'll think I'm still asleep and leave me alone for a few more minutes.*

"Momma! Momma! Here go," Alexis said again, putting something in her mother's hand.

What is this little round thing? Did she hand me some Playdough?

Hanna passed it back to her daughter. "Alexis, let Momma sleep."

"No, Momma. Wake up!" Alexis shouted. She put the object back in Hanna's hand and pulled at her pant leg. "Momma, get up! Momma, get up!" Alexis grunted as she pulled repeatedly.

"Okay, okay," Hanna said, finally opening her eyes. She sat up in the guest bed at her mother's condo and looked at the object in her hand. The low afternoon sun shone through the window, glazing everything in that magical shade of yellow that comes before twilight.

Maybe I slept longer than I thought. What did Alexis give me? It looks and feels like Playdough... Wait... Does Alexis have brown Playdough?

"Mommy, play with me," Alexis shouted, nearly tugging Hanna's pants off.

Hanna squished and smelled the ball. It reeked. "Did you hand mommy poop?"

"Yeah, mommy. There go. Alexis give mommy poop." Alexis smiled at her mommy.

I thought Mother was watching her. Where is she?

Hanna flushed the poop, washed her hands, and washed Alexis's hands—never a straightforward task. She barely got through it by holding her daughter in one hand over the sink and then using her other hand to wash Alexis's—all the while fighting a toddler's screams and squirms. And then she battled her daughter again to change her diaper. When it was all done, Hanna exhaled a deep breath.

"Let's go see what Yai is up to," Hanna said. She walked down the short hallway and turned left into the kitchen, and Alexis ran right by her.

It's nice to give Alexis a change of scenery by coming here once a week. This small two-bedroom condo still gives her more room to run around than my one-bedroom apartment.

Mother stood at the stove, cooking. The smell of fish sauce, chicken broth, and spices filled the air. Her short salt and pepper hair was cropped at the neck. She wore a loose-fitting green shirt and baggy blue sweatpants. She turned to look at Hanna and pushed her thick glasses, which were sliding down her face, back up her nose.

"How's potty training going?" Mother asked, trying to hide a smirk.

"Great," Hanna responded. "Just peachy."

Alexis dashed down the hall again before running back with a bright green ball in her hand. Her tiny feet made big noises on the hardwood floor. *Good thing Mother's on the ground floor. Any downstairs neighbors would be pissed at hearing Alexis tear through here.*

"Mommy, play with me," Alexis shouted again. "Yai, play with me! Come play with me! Come play Alexis!" She beamed from ear to ear.

Who can say no to a smile like that? One of these days, I'll catch up on sleep—just not today.

Hanna yawned and stretched before playing ball with her daughter. After fifteen minutes, Mother put a bowl of soup down on the dining room table and interrupted their game.

"Hanna," Mother said, "You're too fat. Eat this."

Fat? What the hell? "Mom, I'm not fat," Hanna sat down at the table. "I have six percent body fat." She looked down at her stomach and tried to see how much fat she could pinch. *Slightly more than yesterday. Am I at seven? Am I getting fat?*

"Six percent!" Mother exclaimed. "You're too skinny." She put chopsticks next to the bowl of noodle soup. "Eat this." She picked up Alexis and put her at the table, too. "Alexis, Yai has fruit for you."

Hanna grabbed her chopsticks and sifted through the soup. Noodles. Basil. Bean sprouts. Meat. She breathed in the soup's aroma, and her mouth watered. Even though it smelled of non-vegan foods —fish sauce, chicken, pork—Hanna wanted to ignore her values and eat it all. *Meat is so bad for the environment. Not to mention how those poor, delicious animals suffer abuse before they're slaughtered. And—is that a fish ball, too?*

"What's in this?" Hanna asked.

Mother gave Alexis a plate of freshly cut pineapple and blueberries.

"Noodles. And pork. And fish balls."

"Mom, I told you I don't eat pork," Hanna said, trying to sound stern while her stomach grumbled in anticipation of the noodle soup.

"You need to eat pork," Mother said, "or people might think you're Muslim."

"Mom! That's racist."

"Nothing is wrong with being Muslim. One of my cousins is Muslim. And she's happy being someone's third wife. Next weekend is Thod Kathin. Bring Alexis, and we'll give to the monks," Mother said, slipping into the broken English that sometimes came out even after decades in America. "Remember, we're Buddhist."

Her and all her old-world shit. I don't get religion. At the wat Thai, I sit still and mentally practice yoga moves while the monks chant some crap I don't understand.

"I'm not Muslim. I'm vegan." Hanna took another breath of the soup, and her mouth watered. *And I'm not a Buddhist either. I go to the temple with you on holidays only because it's not worth the argument. And because there's good Thai food.*

Mother sat down and started feeding Alexis a pineapple piece with a fork. Alexis smiled at Yai and then at her mommy.

"Arroy mai?" Mother asked Alexis in Thai. "Arroy mai?"

"Is it yummy, Alexis?" Hanna asked.

Alexis gave a big smile, and pineapple juice ran down her chin. "Yeah, mommy. Apple yummy."

"You need to teach her Thai," Mother said to Hanna.

Hanna gave a halfhearted smile. *Hu! I don't even speak Thai myself, other than a few words and phrases. Don't I have to learn it first?*

Alexis pointed at Hanna's soup. "Mommy, eat! Mommy, eat too!"

Hanna's stomach grumbled again. The soup looked and smelled delicious. *Maybe this can be a vegan cheat day. It's too hard to be vegan around Mother.* Hanna silently took a bite of the noodles and ate some basil. Fish sauce was too delectable a taste to be recreated using only vegan ingredients. *That vegan fish sauce I bought tastes like ass water. Maybe I'll just eat around the pork and fish ball. Oh no, I accidentally ate a small piece of pork... Damn, that's good. Well, no point in stopping now. I may as well eat a little more.* And before Hanna realized, her bowl was empty.

Mother gave Hanna a facial gesture that seemed to say, *I told you the soup was good for you. You might think you're so smart, but I'm still your mother.*

Hanna felt the tension with Mother, unsure what to say next or if she wanted to say anything at all. *I'm still a vegan. It's a struggle. Nobody's perfect.*

It was Alexis, however, who broke the awkward silence when she screamed, spasmed, and fell out of her chair. Hanna jumped and caught Alexis's head before it hit the floor, but Alexis's seizure only grew worse.

"Goddam!" Mother yelled.

Fuck! Not again! "Grab my leather purse, Mom! Quick!" Hanna held Alexis while the seizure continued to take her. As soon as Mother handed Hanna the purse, she put the leather strap in Alexis's mouth so she wouldn't bite her tongue.

No longer screaming, Alexis merely shook and flailed her arms and legs while Hanna held her close.

Tears stung Hanna's eyes, and dark spots appeared in her vision as she tried to soothe Alexis. She didn't know if her daughter could hear her, and Hanna may have merely been trying to soothe herself. "It's okay, baby. Shhh. It's okay. It's okay." She rocked back and forth until her child stopped twitching.

By then, the paramedics had arrived to take Alexis to the hospital. Hanna didn't even hear Mother call them, having been so engrossed in caring for her daughter.

Great, this is going to cost a fucking fortune...

After being in the hospital all night and getting examined by this doctor and that doctor, they finally cleared Alexis to go home. Hanna and Mother waited for an Uber in front of the hospital while Alexis slept in Hanna's arms. Her mind kept returning to the bill she was bound to get. *How am I going to pay for that?* She touched her daughter's soft cheek with her hand and then kissed her on the forehead. *At least she's okay. If I can get approved for another credit card, I'll take her to that specialist. But how will I pay off any of my credit cards? Oh, who cares about money? All that matters is trying to get her healthy. I'd pay any price.*

"I think you and Alexis should move in with me," Mother said.

Oh hell! Almost any price... "We're fine on our own, Mom."

"Your apartment is too expensive," Mother said in a caring tone. "Your daycare is too expensive. You don't make that much money. Let me help you."

I move in with you, and I'll go insane. Once a week is about all I can stand. "I like my independence, Mom. Alexis and I are fine on our own."

"Alexis's medical bills have to be very expensive. How are you going to afford everything?"

Yeah, I don't know. I have no damn idea. "I'll figure it out."

Hanna felt her phone vibrate. *I still don't see the Uber. They better not have canceled.* She pulled out the phone and checked the notification. It was an e-mail.

"I think my luck is turning around, Mom," Hanna said, relaxing as warmth seeped through her body. "I was just accepted to the Summit Conference."

"What's the Summit Conference?" Mother asked.

3

Damien Chernobog used his preacher voice to address his followers through livestream. "You know, Jesus said it's easier for a camel to eat needles than it is for a rich guy to go to heaven." He watched himself through his phone as the wind blew through his short dark hair and majestic Wyoming mountains adorned the background. A filter in the app provided him with a godlike aura, which also helped to hide his double chin. "But what does it mean, dear followers? Well, I'll tell you. It means that if a poor person gives the church five or ten dollars, that might be a lot for that person. But for a rich person to give the same portion, it could mean giving five or ten thousand dollars to the church. You can't take the money with you to heaven, but, hey, Father Damien will take it off your hands. Because giving to me helps you. Let's bow our heads." He bowed his head to pray, but the bumping of rumble strips and a honking horn abruptly interrupted him.

"Put the phone down and drive, asshole!" came a shout from a nearby car.

Damien swerved his gray rented minivan. He narrowly avoided an oncoming truck and several other vehicles, before finding his place again between the lines on the road.

"Jesus fucking Christ!" Damien exclaimed in his regular voice. He looked at his phone, still livestreaming even though it slid from his hands, ending up under the gas pedal.

"What the hell is going on?" Bob Willemsen said from the passenger seat, waking from a nap. He yawned and stretched, bulging the muscles in his form-fitting athleisure wear—a tight blue shirt and black running pants. He rubbed his eyes and strong jawline.

I was enjoying the peace, Damien thought. *With my idiot friends asleep, it seemed like the perfect opportunity for a Father Damien livestream testimonial. I thought I didn't have to worry about these two rubes chattering in the background.*

"Damien was streaming and driving and nearly crashed the car, man," Frank Dolan said from the backseat, pulling his long, greasy brown hair out of his eyes and puffing on a vape pen. His oversized PanWow T-shirt, baggy jeans, and long beard hid his scrawny frame.

"If you knew he was livestreaming while driving, why didn't you try to stop him?" Bob asked.

"I wanted to see what would happen, man," Frank responded. "You know, like to see if he could drive without crashing and shit." He took another puff from his vape.

"What the hell are you doing?" Damien demanded, scrunching his face up and gesturing at the smoke. "You can't smoke in here."

Bob also scrunched his face up and then pulled up his shirt to cover his nose, revealing his washboard abs. "Dammit, Frank! Don't you know how bad tobacco is for you? I don't want to put that poison in my body!"

"Hey, man. It's not tobacco," Frank answered. "This is weed, man. And I'm using a vaporizer, so you can't smell it at all."

"Can't smell it?" Damien scoffed. *This idiot's brain is like two beans trying to start a fire.* "I can smell it, and I don't like it!"

"Damien, hey, you can't smell a vaporizer. Frank, pass the shit here." Bob reached his hand out. He turned his head back to Damien and asked, "Why the hell didn't you ask one of us to drive if you were going to live stream?"

"Yeah, man," Frank said, leaning forward and blowing smoke into the front of the car as he passed the vape to Bob. "What's up with that shit, man?"

Dammit! I can't reach my phone, and it's still streaming. And these idiots are chattering.

"Dear followers, bear with me just a moment until I retrieve my phone," Damien said, shifting from his regular voice to his preacher's voice.

"Shit's still going, huh?" Frank asked.

"There is no god, and religion is a lie," Bob bellowed and then started laughing.

"Pay no attention to the other voices, dear followers," Damien said, voice quavering.

"Hail Satan!" Bob laughed harder.

"Hail Satan!" Frank repeated, laughing too.

Bob and Frank took turns puffing the vaporizer and chanting "Hail Satan" while Damien failed to reach his phone. More cars honked at the minivan as it swerved into other lanes.

Damien felt a pain in his chest and cold sweat on the back of his neck. *Jesus fucking Christ! These assholes are going to give me a heart attack.*

"Shut the hell up!" Damien exclaimed. "I'm pulling this car over now." He made a sharp turn and pulled onto the grass on the side of the road. The warm sun shone down on them. Damien quickly got out and squatted down to pull his phone out from behind the pedal. His friends continued laughing like hyenas.

"That's all for today, dear followers. Remember to stay strong as you walk through the valley of the shadow of death. Nonbelievers, evildoers, and temptations often surround us, but through your faith in me, you can overcome any situation. Like and subscribe if you feel the spirit. Don't forget that good Christians drink PanWow and donate to the Church of Father Damien. Last but not least, all Father Damien merchandise remains on sale at a ten percent discount for the rest of the month, including prayer magnets and immaculate conception prophylactics. Peace be with you."

Damien ended the livestream with a press of his finger and then faced Bob and Frank.

"What the hell is wrong with you two assholes?" Damien erupted like a geyser. "That's my bread and butter! Don't fuck with my persona when I'm fleecing the rubes. I don't fuck with you, Bob, when you're jumping off buildings or eating weird shit! Or with you, Frank, when you're smoking pots or whatever the hell you do on your streams!"

Frank and Bob also exited the vehicle, and the three found themselves huddled next to the car on the side of the road.

"Bull fucking shit, man!" Frank exclaimed. "Just last week, I was in the middle of shooting a video for my followers, doing one of my trademark giraffe bong hits from a new glass bong I just unveiled, when you burst all up in the scene and threw a can of PanWow at me."

"That's different," Damien said. "You'd smoked so many pots that the house was filling with smoke. I came to tell you to open a goddam window. I felt like I was walking through a Snoop Dogg concert."

"Damien," Bob chimed in, "You threw a can of PanWow at me two weeks ago when I was livestreaming my new recipe for elk meat sashimi."

I can't believe I've been living with these two idiots for the past year. Did I make a mistake when I agreed to live with two other influencers, whom I'd never previously met, in a house for free, in exchange for shilling PanWow? No way! That was a smart business decision. It's just like Jesus said: You need to lift yourself up by your bootstraps. I racked up so much debt that it was hard to find spare cash for things like rent. Besides, now I have two friends whom I get along with from time to time.

"Recipe?" Damien scoffed, scrunching up his face. "You chopped up an elk with a chainsaw, sprinkled salt on it, and ate it raw. You splattered blood on everything—the counter, the walls, the floor. I slipped in a puddle of blood and fell on my ass. Our kitchen looked like the scene of a horror movie!"

Bob browsed through his phone and smirked. "Let's call it even. If anything, you owe us after that stunt. Check out your social. You're blowing up. Tons of positive comments."

Damien checked his phone, and all the tension he carried suddenly evaporated. "Jesus fucking Christ! I've never had this many views before!"

"Where are we, man?" Frank looked up and down the road. "How much further to the Barbie hotel?"

"It's the Beburoa Hotel, and it's about eighty more miles to Sheol, Wyoming." Damien continued reading comments on his latest live stream. *@FatherDamien I'm going to donate to help you fight the unrighteous ones. @FatherDamien resist temptation. @FatherDamien you are God's instrument.*

"We still have eighty miles to go?" Bob groaned. He rearranged his long blond hair into a stereotypical millennial man bun, and then he yawned and stretched again.

"Eighty miles! Man, it's taking forever to get to this hotel!" Frank whined with bloodshot eyes. "Maybe we should just turn around and go home. It's such a hassle to get out to the middle of nowhere. And what the hell do we get when we get there?"

"Need I remind you that PanWow is paying for this trip and our home?" Damien asserted. "They said we have to spend a weekend at the abandoned Beburoa Hotel, generating content for our channels. We have a week to post it after we get back. Anyone who doesn't like it can find alternative living arrangements."

"I don't like it," Frank said. "Not one bit, man. This sounds like the setup to a horror movie. What if there's some crazy guy in there who wants to kill and eat us?"

"Eat us?" Damien scoffed. "You smoked too many pots. Your brain is nothing but smoke now."

Bob giggled. "You know what? I was thinking..." He trailed off, looking at the clouds.

They sat in silence for a few minutes before Damien asked, "Bob, are you going to say something?"

Bob didn't move or respond.

"Bob! Bob!" Damien barked and tapped him on the shoulder, finally getting his attention. "Bob, what were you going to say?"

"What was I going to say about what?" Bob asked, his eyes fully bloodshot. "What the hell are you talking about?"

Frank laughed. "He's a real lightweight. This shit hit him too hard, man."

If I wanted to, I could fleece these two rubes for every cent they have. Damien took a deep breath. "Get in the goddam car. I'm the only one sober enough to drive, and I'm taking us to the hotel."

THE TRIO DROVE in silence for the next hour until Bob finally spoke. "What the hell is that?"

After making a turn on the road, they spotted a 150-foot art deco statue of an old man with a mischievous grin towering over a hill. He was posed like Christ the Redeemer, and his bronze had turned green like the Statue of Liberty.

"That's one big ass statue, man," Frank said. "And it looks creepy as hell, even his smile. I mean, when most people smile, they look happy. But he looks like he just tricked you out of your soul."

"Jesus fucking Christ!" Damien exclaimed. "It's on top of a skyscraper! It's a sinister man, just as big as the Statue of Liberty, on top of a skyscraper, in the middle of nowhere." Damien glanced at his phone. "Hey, that's where the GPS is taking me. I think it's the Beburoa Hotel."

"Holy shit!" Bob tapped Frank on the shoulder. "Hey, what did you find out about the hotel when you did your research?"

"What are you talking about, man? I didn't do any research. Damien was supposed to research shit, man."

"What?" Damien said in a tone that made it clear he wasn't asking a question. "I wasn't supposed to do the research. Bob, you were supposed to do the research. Wait—did nobody research the Beburoa Hotel before we left?"

They sat in silence for a full minute before Damien exclaimed, "Goddammit!"

The statue was a strange juxtaposition with the surrounding barren area. A dirt road to the hotel cut through patches of grass and rocks. A small mountain sat unusually close to the back of the building.

Damien parked in front of the hotel. The bright sun and clear weather made it easy for Damien, Bob, and Frank to inspect the decrepit building up close. The exterior was mostly concrete, brownish, and discolored, with darker patches of brown here and there. Art deco relief sculptures of demons, whose bronze color had long ago turned green, covered the exterior. Many of the demons were rounding up or eating people. A third of the windows were cracked or missing, and no light was visible inside the windows.

Damien had parked the van next to a giant revolving door with rusty metal and glass so caked with dirt that they couldn't see inside.

Frank examined the hotel uneasily, using his hand to block the sun from his eyes. "Is it even safe to go in, man? This place looks like it's falling apart."

Bob moved with a bounce in his step as he inspected the hotel. He touched one of the demon relief sculptures and smiled. "I can't wait to climb this thing. I've climbed loads of skyscrapers but nothing like this before. It reminds me of the Woolworth Building—this neo-Gothic skyscraper that was built around 1910. I climbed it, and BASE jumped off last year. Like this building, the style resembles a European Gothic cathedral, but it didn't have these relief sculptures of demons eating people." Bob gazed in awe. "Those weird ledges jut out. And instead of gargoyles—they used to put gargoyles on these old buildings to keep evil spirits out—but instead of gargoyles, this creepy, evil-looking building has demons. And then... Man, who do you think that old guy on top is?"

"Is it safe to go inside, man?" Frank repeated.

"Yeah," Bob said. "I mean, I think we'll be okay. Most of the damage looks cosmetic. This building seems pretty strong and won't collapse, probably. But, still, be careful in there. Some shit might be broken. You won't want to fall and get injured here."

Damien checked his cell phone. "I don't have any reception. Yeah, let's be very careful. Who knows how long it will take to get help if we need it?"

Bob pushed hard on the revolving door, and it moved a foot. "The door still works. Let's go check out the inside."

"Wait, I see an inscription over the doorway." Damien read aloud, "Lasciate ogne speranza, voi ch'entrate. Huh, what language is that?"

"Sounds French, man," Frank said.

"What does it mean?" Damien asked.

Frank shrugged.

"Probably, 'Ooh la la, let's eat more baguettes.'" Bob opened the back of the van. He pulled out a large backpack with so much rock-climbing gear that shoes, carabiners, and slings dangled on the outside. He reached into a duffel bag and pulled out his flashlight headband, which he wore and turned on, and then he slung his duffel bag over his shoulder. Last, he grabbed his camera equipment. After gathering all his supplies, he ran for the door and pushed his way inside the building. The door made a loud screech as it turned.

"Hey man, wait for us." Frank grabbed a backpack, duffel bag, and flashlight from the car. He turned on the flashlight. "How long do you figure this place has been abandoned?" He asked Damien.

"I don't know," Damien responded. "Decades, it looks like."

The revolving door stopped turning. Damien and Frank couldn't see inside. They no longer saw or heard Bob.

"Bob," Damien shouted. "How does it look inside?" No response. "Bob! Bob!"

"Do you think anything happened to him?" Damien asked Frank.

"I think he's ignoring you, man," Frank said. "That or he's planning to hide somewhere so that he can jump out and scare us once we're inside. You said you're sure nobody is waiting in there to kill us, right?"

"That was something I said," Damien responded. "But I'm not so sure anymore."

"Fuck it. I'll see you on the other side, man." Frank ran through the revolving door, and it screeched again. The door stopped moving after he disappeared inside the building.

"Frank, how does it look inside?" Damien shouted.

No response.

"Bob, are you there?"

Still no response.

"Bob, Frank, can you guys hear me?"

Nothing but silence.

I have a bad feeling about this. But so many bookies are after me now. I can't turn tail and run empty handed.

Damien grabbed a backpack, a suitcase, and a flashlight from the minivan. He locked the door, and then he noticed his Bible sitting on the dashboard.

I can't leave without my most important prop. Damien unlocked the car, packed his Bible, and locked the car again. He looked up at the sky and then straight ahead to the hotel. "Fuck it!" He ran and pushed hard on the stubborn revolving door. It screeched again.

Damien was dumbstruck when he entered the hotel. It looked nothing like he'd imagined. Immaculately clean tiles of white marble stretched across the lobby. Bright electric lights illuminated everything. A pair of enormous banners hung from the ceiling with the text "Welcome to the 2019 Summit Conference" superimposed over the face of an elderly man—the same man who stood atop the hotel.

A row of three check-in desks was on the right. A smiling bald man in a clean suit stood behind the center desk.

"Misters Chernobog, Willemsen, and Dolan," the man shouted. "I'm Paul Mulciber. Welcome to the Beburoa Hotel. Please step up to the desk, and I will check you into your rooms."

Bob and Frank stood about five feet away from Damien. They looked equally surprised, and they stared at their newfound surroundings slack jawed.

"Am I high right now?" Bob rubbed his eyes. "Or do you guys see this, too?"

"Oh shit, man." Frank stepped backward. "Did we just walk into the hotel from *The Shining*? We're never leaving here, are we?"

Damien's chest tightened once again. "This is too weird. Let's get the hell out of here!" He turned tail and ran for the door.

4

Lew Starek stood at the check-in desk for the Beburoa Hotel. His eyes drifted to the nearby hotel gift shop, and his mind wandered. *I need to pick up a gift for Juliana and baby Anika while I'm here,* he thought. He turned his attention to the twin banners of Abigor greeting the attendees of the 2019 Summit Conference. *Why would the Summit Conference admit someone like me? I don't belong here. They deny over 90 percent of people who apply every year.* Acid reflux bubbled in his stomach. *I shouldn't think so negatively. They liked the paper I submitted. Be confident. I'm here because I belong here.* He took a deep breath, and his stomach calmed down.

"Here is your room key," Paul said. "You're in room 6660. The elevators are right over there."

Lew jolted back to reality. He picked up the key and turned towards the elevator but abruptly returned to face Paul.

"I'm a little superstitious," Lew said. "Some would call 666 an unlucky number—the mark of the beast. Is it possible to switch rooms?"

"Unfortunately, no," Paul said. "We're full for the conference. If there's anything else we can do to help you, dial zero from the phone in your room."

"Thanks anyway," Lew said politely before going to the elevator.

Lew settled into his hotel room. *This place is baller—way too nice for me. I have two queen beds. What am I, royalty?* He thought about how cold and empty the bed would feel without his wife, but he tried to think about the positives, like how he could stretch out in every direction and not wake up freezing in the middle of the night because Juliana had taken all the blankets in her sleep. *This will be the first night since the baby was born that I won't wake up to crying in the middle of the night.*

Curtains covered the windows. He opened them, expecting to see a beautiful view from the sixty-sixth floor, but it was pitch-black outside. *Huh, there must be a storm coming.* He closed the curtains without giving it another thought.

Lew carefully hung his secondhand suits and dress shirts in the closet. Juliana had helped him pick out his clothes and pack. He tried to learn fashion, but comprehension was always just out of reach.

"I put on a shirt, pants, and a tie. I'm dressed," he had told his wife more than once, only for her to respond with, "The shirt is plaid. The pants are pinstripe, and the tie is polka dot. None of these things go together. Let me help you." He needed all the help he could get. *First impressions are very important, and I need to look like I have my shit together.*

"Do you really need to wear a suit every day?" Juliana asked him while he packed. "I hear a lot of these corporate conferences are business casual."

"You need to dress for the job you want," Lew retorted with a smile. "Not the job you have. That's why I'm going to wake up every morning and dress like Superman."

"You dress like Clark Kent."

"They're the same guy."

Why is finding a good job so much harder than I expected? Hudnam, Howe & Hartell fired me because I left work early for Anika's birth. There were only two hours left to the workday, and nothing was urgent. I would have gone back to work the next day if... No, the hell with that. I need to forget about the past and start thinking about the future. It's nice that

Juliana's parents help us out with money, but I can't take it anymore. I'm sick of the handouts. The Notorious BIG never received handouts. He used to slang rock to feed his daughter before he blew up. The Summit Conference is my chance to blow up, too.

Acid reflux bubbled in Lew's stomach once more. His shirt collar felt tight. *Oh shit, not again.* He ate a few Tums and swigged ginger ale.

Lew checked the time—4:00 p.m. in Wyoming, making it 6:00 p.m. back in Maryland. He pulled out his laptop to connect to the Wi-Fi so he could video chat with his wife and daughter. It booted up slowly. *I'll buy myself a new laptop as a treat when I land a job.* After several minutes of waiting, it was up and running, but he couldn't connect to the hotel Wi-Fi. His phone didn't have reception and couldn't connect to the Wi-Fi either. Frustrated, he dialed zero on the hotel phone to resolve his internet connectivity problems.

"I'm sorry, sir," Paul said. "The Wi-Fi is down at the moment, and cell phone providers don't have service out here. The location is too remote."

"That's okay," Lew said. "These things happen. How do I get an outside line? I want to call my wife back in Maryland."

"I'm sorry once again, sir. The internet and phone lines are down. We hope to have the problem resolved soon."

"Thanks anyway," Lew said politely and hung up. He'd promised to call after he arrived at the hotel, and he hoped Juliana wasn't worried about him. This was his first time away from her since the baby was born. It was hard to leave his family when his daughter was only a few months old, but the Summit Conference was too good an opportunity to pass up.

Lew still had a few hours before the welcome reception. *I should practice my presentation.* He dug through his suitcase for his flash drive, and he could have sworn he saw his reflection in the mirror, out of the corner of his eye, moving independently from him. He thought it stood while he crouched, or it turned one way when he turned in the opposite direction. But every time he stared directly at the mirror and moved, his reflection matched his movements perfectly like a regular reflection. He saw only himself in a white dress shirt, blue and orange striped tie, blue striped boxers, and thick black glasses. *My mind is playing tricks on me.* When he finally found the flash drive, he closed the suitcase, and the flash drive slipped from his hands.

"Whoops, you dropped something," Lew heard a voice say.

A chill ran down his spine. He searched in every direction but found nobody.

"Hello?" Lew's voice quavered and his hands shook. "Is somebody there?"

"Nobody's there. It's just me, the voice in your head." This time Lew saw his Reflection in the mirror talk to him in his own voice.

"This isn't real," Lew told himself out loud. "I'm tired from traveling and nervous from stress. I'm going to close my eyes and count down from ten, and when I open them, you'll be gone." He closed his eyes. "Ten, nine—"

Lew felt a hand squeeze his throat. He opened his eyes to see his Reflection had extended its hand from the mirror and was strangling him. The Reflection stood with legs as firm as tree trunks on the other side of the looking glass. It leaned forward. From the chest up, the Reflection had come through the plane of the mirror and in Lew's room. Lew's neck felt like it was stuck in a vise that was slowly being tightened. The pain was overwhelming. Lew tried to pry his Reflection's hands off his throat, but its fingers felt like iron.

"Eight, seven, six," the Reflection said before laughing at him. "You try to hide who you are by wearing a suit and changing your accent, but you're still redneck West Virginia trailer trash. What will you say around these upper-class people to make conversation? Are you going to tell them about your pappy's summer teeth? Som're here, som're there!"

Lew froze, eyes wide open. His mind raced, wondering if this was real or a hallucination. The Reflection's grip tightened on his throat. Lew tried again to break free. But the Reflection was much stronger than the real Lew. He couldn't pull the Reflection's hand from his throat, even using both of his hands. The room was going black, as if someone were turning down a dimmer.

Lew lashed out and threw elbows at his Reflection's arm, but it felt like striking an iron girder. Then he threw a quick kick to the Reflection's chin that broke the death grip. Lew followed up with a strong kick to the chest with his right leg that knocked the Reflection into the mirror and onto its back.

"You have more fight than I expected," the Reflection said as it got back to its feet. "But you still don't look or sound like who you want to be. You think you lost your accent? The more you try, the more apparent it'll be that you don't belong among the civilized people who run corporations. Trailer park oozes from your every word. You may as well attend the conference barefoot in a sleeveless T-shirt and carry around a jug of moonshine." It slipped into a mock West Virginia accent. "Gee by Gawd, cap'ain! You can take the boy outta the hills, but you can't take the hills outta the boy!" Its voice boomed as it mocked Lew, and the words echoed in his ears.

Lew vomited on the floor. Puke burned his throat and nostrils on the way out. He saw stars. His neck hurt on the inside and out. He inhaled in large gulps, and his gray world grew lighter with each breath he took.

Doppelgangers aren't real. This is a figment of my imagination. Maybe I'm haunted by my past of scrapping with the other kids in the trailer park.

Lew looked back at the mirror. His Reflection was gone. His hotel room was in the mirror but vacant. *Or maybe I've gone insane.* Lew walked up to the mirror, but he still had no Reflection. He carefully tried to touch it with his right hand. It passed through where there should have been a pane of glass and disappeared. When he pulled his hand back, it was unharmed. Lew wasn't sure what he'd expected. Maybe he thought his hand would melt off when it passed through the mirror, but he was okay. He repeated the process a few times. Each time he brought his hand back unscathed.

"Hello?" Lew called out in a cracking voice. "Reflection, are you still there?" He waited for a response but received none.

Lew put his head through the plane of the mirror to find out what was on the other side. He expected to walk into a mirror world that matched his own—another hotel room with his Reflection standing there, waiting to pounce. Instead, he found nothing but darkness. The other side of the looking glass was an empty abyss. He looked left, right, up, and down...but saw nothing. He looked back towards his room, and it appeared to be floating in darkness. His legs grew weak. *This is nuts. I'm hallucinating. This is a visual manifestation of my anxiety and nothing more.* He pulled out his cellphone and turned on the flashlight. He waved it around, hoping to illuminate something but finding nothing. And then the phone slipped out of his fingers.

"No!" Lew reached after his phone, but it fell further and further until its light faded away into the darkness.

Lew backed away from the mirror. *I'm too stressed out. My anxiety is getting the best of me. I should lie down and sleep. I just need rest.* As he stepped back, he bumped into something—or someone. Lew's Reflection seized him from behind in a bear hug. It squeezed with the force of a hydraulic press. The wind left his lungs. His ribs broke. He screamed in pain. Stars danced before his eyes yet again. The Reflection lifted Lew off the ground. He uselessly tried to run. His feet kicked air, never touching the ground.

"Where do you think you're going?" the Reflection asked.

Lew's pulse pounded. Waves of pain radiated from his chest. He squirmed but couldn't break free. "Let me go, you horse fucker!"

"You don't belong in the world of light," the Reflection told him. "You belong to the darkness. Don't fight the inevitable." It ran through the mirror, carrying Lew. They plunged into darkness together. As they fell, the Reflection pushed Lew away and disappeared.

Lew plummeted into the abyss, and his stomach leaped into his chest. He screamed until his voice was hoarse. But he continued to fall for several minutes until he finally splashed into water. His face and stomach hurt from the mammoth bellyflop he'd just performed. Lew wondered how he was still conscious. He sunk deep into the water. And then he kicked and swam to the surface. A small pinprick of light that was his hotel room floated far above him in the abyss, giving him a reference point to know which way was up. *How far did I fall? Should I be dead from the impact even if I did land in water?* He treaded water, looking for a way out, but saw nothing. Pain emanated from his broken ribs. *Is this how I die? By treading water until my body runs out of energy and I sink below the surface and drown?*

And then there was light! It shone from below the water, so bright that it hurt Lew's eyes. He hoped the light would show him where he was, but there was nothing except for water. The light flickered a few times, and then it began to whir mechanically like an old air conditioner. The water turned into a whirlpool. He tried to swim away, but the whirlpool pulled him down into the light, towards the whirring. He sank into the depths below. *Is there even a bottom?* He held his breath until his lungs burned, and he grew lightheaded. He feared he would never see his wife and daughter again. Finally, when he could bear it no longer, he screamed. Water filled his lungs. The bright light engulfed him.

5

Bob Willemsen shaved his face carefully with a sharp razor. Line after line took away shaving cream and today's stubble. He rinsed it off and then touched up his neck in a couple places where he'd missed a spare hair. He patted his face dry with a towel and then redid his millennial man bun, pulling his blond hair tight.

Bob admired his body in the mirror. He flexed his pecs, which bulged through his shirt, and then flexed his biceps and traps. He flashed himself a handsome smile and ran his fingers along his freshly shaven, chiseled jaw. *I'm a goddam perfect specimen,* Bob thought.

"Jesus fucking Christ!" Fatty shouted. "Will you stop flexing and help us think? We need to figure out how to escape!"

"Yeah, man," Skinny added. "Let's put our heads together and shit. You know, it's like they say, three heads are better than one...or two."

Bob turned away from his own beauty to look at the bland dystopian hell that is a modern hotel room. Fatty sat on a queen bed, and Skinny stood near a wooden dresser next to the bathroom. The carpet was a bizarre pattern of curvy yellow lines over puke green squares that was an affront to eyesight.

We couldn't open the revolving door at the entrance. Even with the three of us pushing together and trying to smash through the glass, we couldn't move the door or break the glass. We searched the ground floor but didn't find another door. I told the asshole at the front to let us out or I'd rip his head off. But he just laughed at us, and then he somehow convinced us to go up to our rooms. What the hell is this? Unless...

"Listen up, pea brains," Bob said. "I figured this out. It's painfully obvious. We're on a hidden camera prank show. PanWow set us up. Do you think we'll be Netflix famous now? Or will we be on a regular TV channel? They're going to pull all kinds of tricks to scare us. Let's play along. Try to act surprised whenever they scare you. If this goes right, I could get my own show."

"Really? You think so, man?" Skinny said with a smirk.

"You don't think I'm TV material?" Bob asked. He flexed in the mirror again. "I set the speed record for climbing El Sendero Luminoso in Mexico. My life was made for TV. Also, this body should be seen by as many people as possible. PanWow Presents: Bob Willemsen's Most Extreme Hour of Power. Watch me free solo mountains and skyscrapers, BASE jump, and eat the freshest meat you could sink your teeth into."

Fatty went to the window and pulled open the maroon drapes. The outside was pitch black.

"I'm not sure what's going on," Fatty said. "But I think it's something else. Have you guys looked out the window? I couldn't see through the glass revolving door in the lobby either."

He's fat, paranoid, and stupid.

"They probably spray painted the windows from the outside," Bob said. "Just like how they had a crew of people rush to block off the door from the outside after we entered."

Fatty ran his fingers along the glass and the windowsill, inspecting both closely.

"What are you doing?" Skinny asked.

"I'm trying to see if I can open the window, but it doesn't look like the kind that opens," Fatty responded.

"We're on the 60th floor," Bob said. "Windows don't always open in buildings that are this high up."

Skinny joined Fatty and started pressing against the glass.

"Come on, guys," Bob said. "Don't break shit. I don't want to upset the producers."

"If you're right about the prank show," Skinny said, "they probably have cameras watching us right now, man. Maybe we should do something crazy to stand out and shit. After all, it's all about generating the most interesting TV moment, isn't it?"

Is that stoner trying to manipulate me? Bob wondered. *Let's see where it goes.*

"That's a good point," Bob said. "What are you thinking?"

"Stand back," Skinny said to Fatty, who promptly took two steps back from the window.

Skinny slowly unplugged the lamp from the wall, picked it up, and swung it through the window. *CRASH!* The glass shattered into thousands of pieces. Some fell in the room; some fell outside. Skinny lost his grip on the lamp, and it slipped out the window.

"What the hell?" Bob shouted. "Why did you do that? If you're going to smash things, why don't you do it in your own room?"

Fatty's eyes were wide, but he still quickly pulled his arms over his face to protect himself from being cut by shards of broken glass.

Skinny poked his head out the window. "This is weird, man," he said. "I don't see anything. It's still pitch black in every direction. Check it out."

Bob and Fatty joined Skinny, and all three stuck their heads out the window. A black abyss lay before them. *It was a bright day when we parked here, less than an hour ago.* Bob looked to the left and right; the exterior of the building was visible. Some windows had their lights on; others didn't. Then Bob looked up and down. The ledges blocked the view of the building, but the sky and ground were nowhere to be seen. Nothing but darkness was in sight.

"You still think we're on a prank TV show?" Fatty asked.

"I...um..." Bob trailed off. *What the hell is this?*

Skinny left the window but quickly returned with a chair over his head, which he threw out.

"Why do you keep throwing things out the window?" Bob asked.

"And how about some warning first?" Fatty added.

"Shhh. Listen for a crash, man," Skinny said. But no crash came.

"The chair looked pretty soft," Fatty said. "And we're high up. Maybe that's why we didn't hear a noise."

"Yeah, man," Skinny said. "Let's try something louder."

"You know a good place to try something louder?" Bob's voice quavered as he stared into the darkness outside his window. "From your own room."

Skinny unplugged the TV from the wall and took it off the dresser. "Watch out!" he yelled as he ran to the window. Bob and Fatty stepped back, and Skinny tossed the TV out the window. The trio watched the TV disappear into the darkness. But there was no crash —no noise at all. It was eerily silent.

Goddammit. I was looking forward to watching TV later.

"This is weird, man," Skinny said. "Really, really weird."

"Yeah," Bob responded. "You and I are switching rooms. I don't want to sleep in a hotel room full of broken glass with no window and no TV."

"Yeah, sure, man," Skinny said.

"Do you believe in ghosts?" Fatty asked. "Or spirits?"

"I don't know what I believe anymore, man," Skinny said. "But maybe. Do you think this is the hotel from *The Shining*? Was that based on a true story?"

"No, don't be a dumbass," Bob said. "*The Shining* wasn't a true story. That was a Stephen King. And there's no such thing as ghosts. This is all an elaborate prank. They'll explain how they did all this when they do the big reveal. We'll find a perfectly reasonable explanation for everything. Hollywood producers have CGI and crazy special effects."

"My grandmother's house was haunted," Fatty said. "She died when I was in middle school. But I remember staying at her house when I was younger. She lived alone; my grandfather died before I was born. But sometimes, I would see him standing in my bedroom, watching me when I tried to sleep at night. I knew it was him because I recognized him from my grandmother's and mother's pictures. He didn't move. He just stood there, staring at me. I would hide under the covers every few minutes until he went away. And he usually went away. But one night, he didn't. He stood there all night, staring at me until the sun came up. He disappeared when the morning light came in through my window. I told my grandmother about it, and she told me he always wanted a son, but he had two daughters—my mom and her sister. He probably just wanted to see me because he would have loved to have had a grandson. She told me that sometimes when people leave this world, a bit of them remains. That is what ghosts are. They are people who aren't ready to move on to the next world." Fatty stopped to think. "Do any of you know what happened to this hotel? Why was it abandoned? Did many people die here? It looked so dirty from the outside. Maybe there was a fire?"

Spirits? Ghosts? I didn't think Fatty actually believed in any of that mumbo jumbo. I thought it was just an act so he could shill a shitty energy drink to the mindless masses who bought his religious bullshit.

"You sure you saw ghosts when you were a kid?" Bob asked. "Are you sure you didn't dream it since you only saw it when you were in bed?"

"There is more to the universe than what we see, hear, and feel," Fatty said.

"You know what, man?" Skinny said, "I think we're in a simulation. Like in *The Matrix*. Our bodies are lying somewhere asleep while a scientist has us plugged into a computer. This here." He pointed at the hotel room and the empty black expanse outside the window. "None of this is real. This is like a video game or something. Did you ever see that movie *The Matrix*? We have to find a Morpheus and take the red pill. Or was it the blue pill? Maybe it was a green pill... I haven't seen it in a long time. There is definitely a pill we have to take, but I don't know what color it is."

"A simulation?" Bob asked. "You think we're in a fancy video game?"

"A very fancy video game, man," Skinny responded. "Or," he paused to think. "Or maybe this is like the *Evil Dead* movies? Did you guys see those?"

Bob and Fatty shook their heads.

"Well, shit, you need to experience more classic American cinema and shit. There's a fucking chainsaw hand, man. Anyway, in *Evil Dead* and *Evil Dead II*, these people are trapped in a cabin out in the woods while an evil dead is after them. It comes from a magic book called the Necronomicon. Maybe all this is caused by a magic book, too. We just have to find the right spell from the book to break the curse." Skinny turned to Fatty. "Don't you have a magic book with you? Can I try to read some spells from it?"

"Jesus fucking Christ!" Fatty exclaimed. "It's not a magic book full of spells. It's a Bible, you stupid asshole."

"Whatever, man." Skinny shrugged it off. "You know, we probably are in the Matrix, man. I'm switching my answer back to the Matrix."

"I want to find out more about the history of the hotel," Fatty said. He pulled out his phone. "Still no reception and no Wi-Fi. I'm going to explore and see if I can find any other ghosts to give me some clues. That Paul ghost at the front didn't reveal much. If I can figure out why they're stuck here, maybe I can help them pass on, so we can get out of here."

"I'm going to explore, too, man," Skinny said. "I'm going to look for a wise old Black man who can tell me how to play this video game. And if I can't find a Morpheus, I'm going to hit up the bar. I think I saw one in the lobby. Oh, and hey, man, if you see that autistic kid from *The Shining*, ask him to use his magic powers to free us."

"I don't think that kid was autistic," Fatty said.

"You guys do you," Bob said. "I'm going to hit up the gym. We still have a few hours before tonight's reception, and it's leg day."

"The gym?" Fatty said. "Are you joking?"

"I never joke about leg day," Bob responded. "Do you think I maintain such a high-performance body by neglecting my legs? Sturdy legs and good footwork are essential for expert rock climbers."

"Why don't we all split up and then meet at the bar in an hour?" Fatty suggested. "We can compare notes about what we found. If we split up and combine our knowledge, we can figure this out much more quickly."

"Hell yeah, man," Skinny said. "I'll be there."

"Make it ninety minutes. We still have to swap rooms," Bob said, pointing at Skinny. "And then I don't want to shorten my leg day workout. I hope the bar has protein shakes."

"Okay," Fatty said. "It's a plan."

BOB WAS DOING lunges in the hotel gym when someone knocked him to the ground. He tried to talk, but the person who knocked him over was lying on top of his head. Bob could scarcely breathe with his face pressed into the gym floor. The pressure on him was constant, and it grew harder and harder to breathe. Each breath took in less and less oxygen. He felt like he was being smothered. He smelled the rubber mat pressed against his face, and he felt like he was lying in a pool of sweat. Bob tried to talk again, but he screamed in anger instead. The person on top of his head finally moved off him. Bob got to his feet and gasped.

"What the hell was that?" Bob yelled. One look at his surroundings, and Bob knew exactly what happened. The pear-shaped middle-aged man on the treadmill tried to take off his hoodie while jogging, but it got stuck on his head. The man fell over when he couldn't see, and the treadmill threw him into Bob, who was doing lunges several feet behind the treadmill.

The gym was immense for a hotel. There were six treadmills, just as many ellipticals, a dozen weight machines, and a row of dumbbells against a wall of glass mirrors. Bob was going back and forth across the floor doing lunges with a sixty-pound dumbbell in each hand, the heaviest weights available. He lost count of how many times he had gone back and forth, but his legs were burning, and he had worked up a good sweat.

"Help! I can't see," the pear-shaped man said. "I think I'm stuck." He sat on the ground and squirmed, trying to get out of his hoodie that was twisted into a knot on his head.

"Hold still," Bob said. "I'll help you out." Reluctantly, Bob stood and walked to the pear-shaped man, untangled the hoodie, and pulled it off his head.

The man who had fallen was a tall, balding redhead with a thick mustache and several pounds of extra weight around his midsection.

"I'm sorry about that," Baldy said.

"I'm guessing you don't use the treadmill often?" Bob asked.

"I don't get to the gym much. I have five kids, so the only time I have to myself is when I'm away on a business trip."

"Next time you want to take your shirt off on the treadmill, either stop it first, or hop off and then hop back on."

"Right, so sorry. I'll remember that." Baldy stood up and turned off the treadmill. "Are you here for the conference?"

The conference! This must be another actor. I bet there are cameras hidden behind the mirror and in the corners. "Yeah, I came here for the conference," Bob lied.

Baldy introduced himself and held his hand out, expecting a handshake.

"Nice to meet you," Bob said as he shook Baldy's hand. "I'm Bob Willemsen." *I bet the producers told this guy to jump on top of me when I wasn't looking. What assholes! No, no. Don't get mad. I need to smile and grin. Grit my teeth and hide the frustration. They're trying to push my buttons. If I come across as charming, I should be a fan favorite, and I'll get my show. I'll start each episode by BASE jumping.*

"So, have you been to this conference before?" Bob asked.

"No," Baldy answered. "This is my first time here, but I go to loads of these things. I travel all the time for work. Check this out." Baldy took out his cell phone and pulled up a picture of himself standing in a hotel meeting room. He was smiling, wearing a suit and tie. "Here I am in Baltimore, Miami, Houston, New York, Seattle, New Orleans..."

Baldy flipped through his photos and named each city, but each photo was nearly identical. He looked to be in the same room wearing the same suit, even wearing the same smile. The only difference between each photo was the tie he wore.

"Amazing," Bob said. "This is my first time at this conference, too. What do you know about it?"

"Well," Baldy said, "The Summit Conference is the most selective conference I know about. This is the hundredth year. They say the people who run it are kingmakers. If you impress the right people, you'll land your dream job. I think nearly every Fortune 500 company has a board member who attends the Summit Conference."

"So, who comes to this thing? What do you do for work?"

"This is my first time here, so I don't know all the types of people who attend. I only know that many important people who rule from behind the curtain come here. CEOs like Elon Musk and Bill Gates get a lot of attention, but the front man isn't always the one making the big decisions. There are people behind the scenes who pull the strings." Baldy smiled and looked sure of himself. His body language shifted, and Bob could tell he was about to say an elevator pitch he had repeated hundreds of times before. "I'm a management consultant. The next big trend will be a business philosophy I developed. I'm sure you've heard about Kaizen and Six Sigma, right?"

"No, is that what you created?" Bob didn't know what Baldy was talking about.

"No, and don't even bother to learn what those things are. They're old news, antiquated. I developed a business philosophy known as BJJB, which stands for—"

"Blowjob job blow?" Bob guessed.

"No, it stands for Brazilian Jiu-Jitsu Business," Baldy said with a smile.

"Oh, okay." Bob returned the smile. *This is the dumbest fucking thing I've heard in my life.*

"I suppose you want to know how it works or how I developed it?" Baldy asked.

"I'm guessing you used to do Brazilian jiu-jitsu until an injury made you stop, and then you figured out how to transfer your knowledge to another arena?"

"No, but that's pretty good. I should make that my new backstory. I never actually did Brazilian jiu-jitsu—I watched a lot of UFC while I was in business school, and then..."

Bob really didn't want to hear anymore, but he was doing his best to act polite. He put a big grin on his face and thought about climbing while Baldy talked. *The outside of this building has some exciting features. I should hop out a window and climb it. Maybe when I get to the top, I'll see what tricks they're using to make it look dark outside the windows. Should I climb the hotel now or... No, no. I need to keep interacting with these actors for longer. Maybe I'll climb the hotel after the reception. Oh, shit. Baldy's mouth stopped moving. What did he say?* "That's very interesting," Bob said with a big smile. *I hope that was a suitable response. Baldy said nothing. Did it work? Did he think I was listening?*

"You think so?" Baldy smiled. "It *is* interesting. I hope I can rope in some big clients while I'm here and sell more copies of my book. If I can pull in a big enough client, I'll be able to put all five of my daughters through college and take nice vacations." Baldy used his hoodie as a towel and dabbed sweat off his arms, neck, and chin. "What do you do, Bob?"

"I'm a climber. I'm most famous for urban climbing, but I do a lot of rock climbing, too. And I'm also something like a foodie-chef." Bob smiled and turned his head to mimic one of his most popular Instagram photos.

"Famous? You're famous?" Baldy wrinkled his forehead.

How does this guy not know who I am? The producers certainly put him up to this. Those sons of bitches! They're trying to push my buttons and piss me off. "I'm not a household name, but I have thousands of followers. Maybe you know my antics if you don't know me by name. Last year I was in the news because I got arrested climbing the Space Needle." Bob resisted the urge to smack Baldy and tell him how lucky he was to meet a celebrity like Bob Willemsen. He put on his biggest grin. *Nice try, asshole! Everybody knows the crazy guy who scales and jumps off buildings while chugging an energy drink!*

"I only keep up with business news," Baldy said apologetically. "I read a lot for work, and, at home, the TV only ever plays Sesame Street or cartoons for my kids."

"You don't have social media?" Bob asked.

"I have LinkedIn," Baldy answered. "But I don't use it often. I don't even know how to change my profile photo. I don't have the time to figure out how to post a Tweet and poke a photo. My eldest daughter tried to show me how to use Instagram, but I didn't have the patience to waste my time with it."

"No social media? How do people know if you're alive or dead? How do they know what you're doing?" Bob couldn't believe it. *This has to be a prank. There's no way anybody could live in the world today without social media. If he's telling the truth, this is even crazier than being trapped in an abandoned hotel full of ghosts. No, there are no ghosts here, and this son of a bitch is an actor doing a character.*

Baldy blinked his eyes rapidly a few times. "I make phone calls and send text messages to my wife and kids. I email clients or talk to them on conference calls. Why would I need any other way to communicate?"

Bob put a hand on Baldy's shoulder and stared into his eyes. "I parachute off skyscrapers into traffic while chugging an energy drink that causes vomiting and diarrhea, and you are, without a doubt, the craziest son of a bitch I have ever met in my life."

6

Hanna Taithangklom sat in the corner of the Beburoa Hotel's Big Oak Square Bar. She buried her head in *Ulysses* by James Joyce, sipped white wine, and nibbled on a veggie platter.

I can't remember the last time I had enough time to myself to read in the middle of the day, Hanna thought. *How is it I've been reading* Ulysses *for two years, but I'm only on page twelve?*

"Hey, do you know where I can find a wise old Black man?" A scrawny white guy with unkempt brown hair emerged from nowhere and jarred Hanna from her Joycean revelry. His bloodshot eyes stared at her from above a PanWow T-shirt.

PanWow! Those bastards are among the worst animal cruelty offenders. How can anyone in their right mind decide they want to flavor energy drinks by squishing live pangolins in a press, draining the fluids, and boiling it?

"Why do you think I know where to find an old Black man?" Hanna asked. "Because I'm Thai, you think I know where to find other minorities? Try looking in a nursing home."

"Oh, whoa," the stoner said. "No, I didn't mean it like that, man. I'm only asking you because you're the only other person I saw so far

—other than the folks I came to the hotel with. I'm sorry. I need to work on my people skills. My name is Frank. What's your name?" His eyes shifted down to look at his toes in an act of contrition.

Hanna put on her best fake smile in response. "My name is Hanna." Each word sharply bit the air. "I don't know where to find an old Black man. I would like to return to my book, if you don't mind."

"Oh, yeah," Frank said. "My bad, man. Hey, I don't mean to take up too much more of your time, but I had a couple of quick questions for you."

Is the fastest way to get rid of this stoner to answer his questions quickly?

Hanna slid her bookmark into page twelve of *Ulysses* and closed it.

"Okay," Hanna said. "A couple of questions but be quick."

"Thanks, man," Frank said. "Much appreciated. So, when did you get to this hotel?"

"This morning."

"How did you get here?"

"In a car."

"Have you tried to leave the hotel since you got here?"

"No, why would I leave? There's nothing around."

"Why did you come to the hotel?"

"For the conference."

"How did—"

Hanna waved her hand and silenced Frank. *I won't waste any more energy talking to this dope. Talking to people is exhausting enough. I need to save my energy for networking at this evening's reception.* "I answered more than a couple of questions. Now, how about you let me get back to my book?"

"Oh, man." Frank took a small step back. "I'm sorry. Thanks so much for your time, man. I'll leave you be."

Frank slid away from Hanna until he reached the next corner of the bar. He flagged down the bartender and ordered a beer. Hanna wished he had left the bar altogether, but at least he was giving her some space.

Hanna reopened her book and resumed *Ulysses,* but she didn't get much further. The elevator door opened, and a meathead approached the bar. He wore tight clothes that accented his muscles. When their eyes met, he flashed a quick smile and flexed his muscles —but not overtly like a bodybuilder. Instead, he tried to subtly tighten his muscles and walk casually, even though it was painfully obvious he was holding in his breath and flexing.

He looks vaguely familiar, but where do I know him from?

The meathead sat next to her, flexed his chest three quick times without looking at her, and then ordered a drink. However, Frank knew him and shouted.

"Bob, what are you doing sitting down there, man? I'm over here."

"Yeah, I see you," the meathead responded in annoyance. "I'll be there in a minute."

Bob. Hanna realized she knew Bob. Well, they had never met, but she had seen Bob's antics on social media. He was the idiot who liked to climb and then parachute off things. And he ate so much meat. And peddled that awful energy drink.

"I wasn't expecting to see another influencer here," Bob said. "I'm a big fan of your videos. From time to time, I try your yoga routines, and they helped my flexibility. I'm a climber, you see. My name is—"

"I know who you are, Bob," Hanna said.

Bob smiled, and it made Hanna uneasy. "My reputation proceeds me. I always like to meet a fan."

"I'm not a fan," Hanna responded sharply. "I know you. You post all those Insta photos of eating meat. Meat is murder. I show people how to live a healthy and cruelty-free lifestyle with a vegan diet and yoga. But you hawk that awful energy drink. Do you know how many pangolins that company kills every year? Pangolins are the most majestic creatures."

"Meat is part of a healthy lifestyle. It has essential vitamins and minerals that helped my body reach perfection." Bob flexed his arms like a douchebag. "You don't get muscles like this by eating celery."

Hanna closed her book and downed her glass of wine in one gulp. "I'll charge this to my room." She gestured to the bartender, who handed her a black pleather book that she opened, and she quickly signed the receipt inside.

"I hope this is a big conference so I don't have to see either of you the rest of the week!" Hanna stormed off to the elevator.

THE INDOOR POOL was the least impressive part of the Beburoa Hotel that Hanna had seen so far. It was so...so...small. It might take a dozen laps in this pool to equal one lap in an Olympic-sized pool. Fluorescent lights hung from the white stucco ceiling. A small hot tub rested next to the pool. The concrete around the pool had only enough space for seven white lounge chairs. Fortunately, it was nearly empty, except for one very thin woman who sat in the middle chair. She had shoulder-length brown hair and tortoiseshell glasses, and she wore a one-piece light blue swimming suit with neon stripes. Although dressed for the pool, she was completely dry and scribbling furiously with a pen on a yellow legal pad.

Hanna settled into the rightmost chair. She had come straight from the bar, so she wasn't dressed for the pool. However, Hanna was only there to find a quiet place outside her room to read. The woman with the legal pad barely even looked at Hanna when she walked by.

Hanna stretched her legs out, leaned back, and settled into *Ulysses* as the smell of chlorine filled her lungs. However, she didn't read more than a couple of pages before being interrupted again.

"Think you're escaping and run into yourself," said the woman in blue. "Longest way round is the shortest way home."

"Huh?" Hanna responded.

"It's from *Ulysses*. The book you're reading." She had a youthful face and looked about twenty years old.

"Oh, I wouldn't know. I've been reading this for years, and I've barely made a dent in it." Hanna buried her face in the book again, hoping her new acquaintance would take a hint.

"You'll enjoy it," the woman said. "It's gnarly. Do you read a lot?"

Why do I even bother trying to read for fun? Hanna wondered.

"No," Hanna said. "Well, not fiction. I read a lot about diet, food, cooking, and exercise—mostly yoga. I used to read fiction for fun, but I haven't been able to find the time for pleasure reading in years."

"You really should read more fiction. It's healthy to let your mind veg out and escape into a good story now and then." The woman put down her pen and pad and turned to Hanna. "I take it you're not here to focus on writing. I'm Camilla, by the way. What's your name?"

"I'm Hanna." She closed her book. "I didn't realize writers came to this conference. Isn't the Summit Conference about business? I'm an influencer."

"An influencer," Camilla said with a blank look. "What's that?"

Hanna restrained a gasp. *How does she not know what a social media influencer is? Has she been living under a rock?*

"I use social media to offer advice and help people make smart decisions about how to lead a healthy vegan lifestyle, how to stay balanced with yoga, and which products can help."

"You make money that way?" Camilla asked.

"A little. Not enough. Some people make a lot." Hanna shrugged. "Does the Summit Conference have writing workshops?"

"The Summit Conference has everything. I've been here for a very long time, and it's the secret of my success. You might know me better from one of my pen names, N. D. Farmer or H. T. Huddleston."

"You're N. D. Farmer!" Hanna was sitting next to a best-selling romance author, and she didn't even know it.

"Are you a fan?" Camilla raised her eyebrows.

"I'm a little embarrassed to say I haven't read one of your books before. But I see ads all the time. You put out a lot of bestsellers!"

Camilla smiled.

I thought artists were temperamental people who explode if you aren't familiar with their work.

"I'm doing a reading of my latest novel on Tuesday afternoon. You should come by." Camilla made an inviting gesture. "The session is called Deflowering the Mystery of Romance. It'll be radical. Make some time for some fun while you're here."

"What's the other pen name—Huddleston? I'm not familiar with that one."

"Business philosophy. I examine the economics and administration of ancient empires and apply lessons learned to modern business situations. You may have heard of *Mayan Multitasking* or *Better Business Strategies from Ancient Babylon*?"

"No, I can't say that I have." Hanna sat in awe. "How do you find time to write books under two different names?"

"It's amazing what you can do when you prioritize your life. I used to never find time to do the things I want, either." Camilla packed up her notepad and pen. "Let me guess, you have a little one?"

Hanna nodded.

"I have to motor, Hanna, but it was a pleasure to meet you. Enjoy the Summit Conference. I'll see you again soon."

"Goodbye, N. D.—I mean Camilla." *Stupid, stupid Hanna! This is someone I need to impress.* "It was very nice to meet you. I hope I run into you again."

"I look forward to it," Camilla said with a smile and a wink before she walked away.

Was that really N. D. Farmer? No, can't be. N. D. Farmer has been writing books since the '80s! She looks much too young. That had to be a joke. When I get back to my room, I'll check the agenda to see if Deflowering the Mystery of Romance is even an actual session.

7

"**D**oes anything about this seem strange to you?" Damien asked in between bites. He hit the appetizers hard, and he had a plate full of junk food—mini hot dogs, nachos, bacon-wrapped dates, pork sliders, foie gras, fried chicken, waffles, cheese fries, deep-fried Oreos, and mini cheeseburgers. *I need to make a second pass later. By the time I saw the deep-fried ice cream, my plate was too full to fit it.*

"Yeah, the cooks didn't salt the food," Bob said with a frown. He ate pork from the sliders, but not the bun. "I brought plenty of salt, but I left it in my suitcase. Who doesn't salt their food?"

"Totally weird, man," Frank said while munching on baby carrots and ranch. "You know they have fruits and vegetables, too? Eating some carrots won't kill you." He also had a few bacon-wrapped dates and a half-dozen fries, but the rest of his plate was filled with pineapple, watermelon, strawberry, celery, cauliflower, and broccoli.

The three friends ate at a standing table on the side of the expansive ballroom, decked out with four bars, two buffet tables, and dozens of standing tables scattered throughout. Servers in black ties and Incan masks—flat gold plates with a three-dimensional nose, ovoid eye cutouts, and three vertical red stripes—roamed the floor with trays of appetizers and drinks. Thousands of attendees milled about the ballroom, eating, drinking, and mingling.

"No, I'm not talking about my diet," Damien said.

"Or lack thereof," Bob interjected.

Frank's eyes pointed towards Bob's meat plate in response.

"Hey!" Bob shouted. "Eating nothing but meat is a very traditional diet that has been used for thousands of years. Many Indian tribes and aborigines were only introduced to grains in the last hundred years. Thanks to my all-meat diet, I was able to climb Silence in Flatanger, Norway. Pork is natural. Deep-fried Oreos aren't. The human body isn't made to digest that crap. That's what makes people fat."

Jesus fucking Christ! I'm not that fat! "Look. I'm talking about that guy," Damien pointed to the man from the banners in the lobby and the statue above the hotel, who appeared to be in his sixties and stood at about five foot six. "He's a creepy old man who moves around like a young man. And he's dressed in those weird old timey clothes. It's just like Jesus said: You can easily recognize evil because it looks creepy as fuck!"

The old man walked while spritely twirling a golden scepter decorated with rubies and gems. He was flanked on his left and right by two mysterious figures wearing baggy black habits with hoods pulled over their heads to hide their faces.

"Hey, man," Frank said. "That's the guy from the invitation in the hotel room. Abigor."

Abigor... Abigor... I've heard that name somewhere before, Damien thought to himself. *But where?* Damien studied Abigor carefully as he made his rounds, stopping randomly at groups of people to chat or picking up a bite of food or a drink from a server.

"That guy has to be the big boss," Bob said. "The producers who set this thing up have creative minds. And the direction they gave to the extras. Did you guys try to talk to any of the people here? They're weird as fuck."

"Yeah, there's something off about them, but I can't tell exactly what." Damien bit into another hotdog and thought about his failed attempts to strike up conversations with other people at the reception. Whatever question he asked—how are you, where are you from, why did you come to the conference—was answered in a monotone voice with a strange cadence.

"I am living the success I have always aspired to thanks to the Summit Conference," one person had said.

"It doesn't matter where any of us came from. Now that we are here with Abigor, we are at home forever," another had said.

Damien shuddered. "They all have this bizarre way of speaking, and it's like they were given talking points. And everyone has these strange dead eyes—like they look in my direction, but not at me."

"Yeah, it's almost as bad as community theater," Bob said. "You think they would have found better actors? Totally unbelievable."

"Really?" Frank said, surprised. "I met this cool guy who was telling me all about Brazilian jiu-jitsu and business. This corporate stuff always seemed so boring to me before, but this guy made it sound really cool, man. Like you have to hit the competition with a flying armbar." Frank waved his arms around in mock karate moves. "Hi-yah!"

"Careful with those moves, my dear boy," Abigor said. "You don't want to hurt anyone."

Damien, Frank, and Bob all turned abruptly to find Abigor standing next to them, still flanked by the two figures. *I didn't even notice him walk up to us. I shouldn't have let Frank distract me.* Abigor grabbed a carbonated beverage from a server walking by, and he put his scepter down on the table where the three friends were eating.

"You're a real live wire, aren't you, Mr. Dolan?" Abigor asked.

"Yeah, man. I guess so," Frank responded. He thought for a minute and then asked, "Hey, how do you know my name, man?"

Abigor gave an enormous smile. He had a head of thick white hair that was carefully parted on the side. "Well, I know about all the guests of the Beburoa Hotel. I'm delighted you could join us. This is the first time social media influencers have graced the Summit Conference. I daresay that everyone here could stand to learn a great deal from you lot. We all look forward to your presentation."

"Presentation?" Damien asked. *What is he talking about?*

"You haven't been to the registration desk yet? Visit level B1 to pick up your meeting materials. You'll find yourselves listed in the program."

This is the head ghost. How is he keeping us here? "How long does the conference last? I was hoping to leave tomorrow."

"Why are you in such a rush to leave, my dear boy?" Abigor responded. "Nothing is waiting for you. I know you're not in a rush to make more videos about that peculiar concoction you call an energy drink. Your only friends are by your side. Spend some time with us and chew the rag. I daresay you'll be quite happy here."

If I can figure out how to free him, we can all escape. What unfinished business does he have? "Abigor, what did you do before you came to the Summit Conference?"

"What a hawkshaw you are, Mr. Chernobog. Why are you so interested in my history?" Abigor laughed. "Before the Summit Conference, I was a traveling salesman and then a business executive at National Cash Register. I worked with John H. Patterson himself."

What is that company? Who is John Patterson? If only I could use Google! "I noticed the Wi-Fi is down at the hotel. Do you know if the connection will be repaired soon?"

"Unfortunately, our connection to the outside world comes and goes," Abigor said. "It may be down for a while."

"Well, I, for one, think you have an amazing conference," Bob chimed in.

Oh yes, Bob thinks he can get a TV show if he puts on a good show for the cameras.

Bob gestured with his hand like a magician. "How did you do the trick with the window? It looks like there's nothing outside, and when we throw things out, we don't hear them hit the ground."

"Not all buildings are meant to be climbed, Mr. Willemsen," Abigor said. "Some are meant to be inhabited."

"Hey, man," Frank said, "Why can't we leave the hotel?"

Abigor chuckled, a strange juxtaposition to the two figures next to him who stood motionless. "My dear boy, you need to visit the registration desk. All of your questions will be answered in the meeting materials."

What does he want? If I can help him achieve his goal, he'll cross over, and all this will disappear. "Abigor, what do you want more than anything?"

"My, my, my, Mr. Chernobog," Abigor responded. "Aren't you curious? It's quite simple, really. What I want more than anything is to learn from you and help you reach your full potential. I have an eye for talent, and I am quite impressed by how you use religion to sell useless belly wash to goneys. They say a good salesman could sell sand to an Arab. I believe all three of you possess that skill. You sell a foul-tasting potable that gives the person who drinks it a boost of energy before casting up their accounts. Business is all about creating demand for your product and then manufacturing and selling as much of it as possible. Social media influencers—you are this era's version of a snake-oil salesman. You offer entertainment and false wisdom—whether by saying prayers, climbing buildings, or taking big bong hits—but it's really all a clever guise for you to sell to an easy mark. Mr. Chernobog, Mr. Willemsen, and Mr. Dolan—you understand people and know how to motivate them to do what you want. That is a remarkable skill. You have just as much to teach me as I have to teach you. The participants of the Summit Conference are lucky to be in your presence."

"Some people knew they were coming to a conference when they came here," Bob said. "But we received a message telling us we could make a lot of money by shooting footage in an abandoned hotel. Why did we get a message about shooting a viral video when everyone else was invited to a conference? Was this a mistake?"

"Nobody ever comes to the Beburoa Hotel by accident." Abigor waved a finger. "Every guest at the hotel is brought here by hearing exactly what they need to get them to come. Your friend Hanna was invited to a conference because she would come to a conference. On the other hand, you three would never have willingly traveled to a corporate conference. So, you were—"

"Tricked," Damien interjected. "They tricked us. Fucking PanWow! We don't belong here. I don't belong here."

Abigor chuckled again. "That's where you're wrong, my dear boy. Everything happens for a reason. You three are exactly where you need to be, as am I, as is everyone at the Summit Conference."

"Hey, man," Frank said. "How do we get out of here?"

"Go to meeting registration. All your questions will be answered by reading the meeting materials. Well, if you gentlemen will excuse me, I am needed elsewhere now. I look forward to seeing you tomorrow. And you don't want to miss the Centennial Celebration tomorrow evening." Abigor began to walk off and then turned back to the table and reached for his scepter.

Damien grabbed the scepter and tried to pick it up, but the scepter was too heavy. It rolled from the table to the floor and pulled him with it. He let go of the scepter and got back to his feet.

"Careful, my dear boy," Abigor said. "My scepter is heavier than it looks. Have a good evening." He picked it up and adeptly twirled the scepter once again, flipping it into the air and catching it with one hand.

Abigor gave Damien a friendly pat on the shoulder with a smile. At the touch, Damien smelled smoke and felt a cold shiver run through his entire body. The hair on the back of his neck stood up. Abigor turned and resumed his stroll, still followed by the two hooded figures.

"Are you okay?" Bob asked. "You're more out of shape than I realized."

"The scepter is only about three feet long," Damien said. "It shouldn't be that heavy. It felt like it weighed a couple hundred pounds." *And when he touched me... What the hell happened when he touched me?*

"No way, man," Frank said. "That's crazy."

"I bet it was a magnet," Bob said.

"Magnet?" Damien asked.

"Yeah, the scepter is probably iron or another ferromagnetic metal."

Bob stuck his chest out as he explained while Damien and Frank watched him. "Iron is already heavy. But they positioned an electromagnet underneath the floor and turned it on as soon as you tried to pick it up." Bob nodded his head, happy with his explanation. "But I'm suspecting that we're not the only people here who aren't actors. Abigor is obviously an actor. But I follow that Asian chick—who, by the way, is a solid nine and wants to throw herself at me—and I know she is a horrible actor. She does skits sometimes, and every line of dialogue she delivers is unbelievable."

"Hmm," Frank said. "Okay, let's go."

"Go where?" Bob asked.

"Go to meeting registration and shit. I want to see what Abigor has for us there, man."

At the meeting registration desk, Damien, Bob, and Frank each received a name badge on a lanyard and a tote bag with identical contents—two candy bars, a small blank notebook, two pens, a small booklet titled *2019 Summit Conference Program*, and a thick book titled *Rule Book*. The Summit Conference logo emblazoned each item.

Damien opened the rule book and randomly flipped through pages. His throat went dry, and he shook. "Do your rule books say the same thing as mine?" He flipped through page after page. The words were the same, though the font style and size changed. The same sentence was repeated over and over again.

There is no escape. There is no escape. There is no escape. There is no escape. There is...

8

Lew Starek awoke to the sound of a blaring alarm clock. He lay in his hotel room's bed. *What happened?* Memories swirled of a fight with his Reflection and falling into darkness and drowning while being pulled into a bright light. *Was it all just a dream? It felt so real.*

Lew put on his glasses and turned off the alarm. The bed squished when he moved. Only then did he realize he was soaking wet from head to toe, still in yesterday's clothes. Shivering, he sprung out of bed and fell onto the floor. *Am I still all in one piece?* Lew checked his body for injuries, but he felt fine. No broken ribs, no sore neck.

After getting to his feet, Lew scanned the room and found his Reflection standing inside, two feet away from the mirror. Lew hesitated, unsure if he should run or try to fight again. *Oh, fuck! Oh, fuck! Oh, fuck! It all really fucking happened. It wasn't a dream.*

The Reflection hunched forward and put one finger in front of its mouth. "Shhhhhh." And then it smiled at Lew and turned and jumped into the mirror.

Lew froze and waited for the Reflection to return. But it didn't. So, he crept towards the mirror and peered into it. Lew found his Reflection staring back at him. He clenched his jaw and went catatonic.

Oh shit! It's back.

But the Reflection was motionless as well. After a few minutes, Lew found the courage to perform some test movements—a hand wave here, a kick there—and it appeared to be a genuine reflection. Still unsure, he tried to reach through the mirror again, only to have his fingers press against the glass and leave smudges.

It's only glass.

He grabbed the mirror and lifted it off the wall, expecting to find a trapdoor or a hidden passage behind it. But there was nothing—only the wallpaper. Lew ran his fingers across the wall, checking for hidden bumps that might reveal a secret door, but it was completely smooth.

Have I really gone crazy?

He wanted to check his phone, but he couldn't find it.

I wish I could hear Juliana tell me everything will be okay. Maybe I'm still dreaming.

Lew looked down to see water dripping from his soaking wet body onto the floor.

It's just the stress. The stress is driving me crazy. I had a stressful dream, and then I pissed myself in my sleep. It's normal to piss five gallons of clear liquid in your sleep, right?

He sucked on his soggy sleeve to see if it tasted like piss.

No, it's only water. At least, I think. I never actually drank piss before, so I'm not sure what it tastes like. Maybe piss only tastes and smells like water. Should I piss in a cup and taste it to check?

Lew noticed an invitation to the welcome reception sitting on his nightstand. "Shit! I missed the reception!"

He looked again at the mirror, which was now on the floor, leaning against the wall. As a precaution, he wrapped it with a sheet and then leaned it back against the wall, facing the other direction. Not wanting to miss any more of the conference, Lew hopped in the shower and then dressed himself in a secondhand, faded-gray double-breasted Hugo Boss suit, blue pinstripe shirt, and black-and-gold patterned tie. He slicked his hair back and checked himself in the mirror. *I look like I'm ready to dominate Wall Street in the '80s. Maybe I'll bring a sense of nostalgia to an executive here and make him want to hire me.*

Lew took the elevator to the conference registration. Acid reflux started with a rumble and then turned into a maelstrom in his stomach.

No, not now! I need to exude confidence to impress these people. And why should I worry? It's not like I'm gambling by spending most of my paltry savings to attend a conference, hoping to land a job by the end of the week. It's not like I'm an unemployed temp with a baby and barely enough savings to last two more months.

He felt so queasy that he thought he might vomit. He reached into his left jacket pocket and popped some Tums.

Calm down, Lew. Relax. You can do this. Ten...nine...eight...seven...

Ding! The elevator door opened, and Lew ambled into the conference.

I'm here because I belong.

A fresh Navy-blue carpet adorned with a golden Summit Conference logo welcomed visitors from the elevator. The logo was simple but elegant. The S in Summit stood tall like the peak of a mountain, and Conference was written in calligraphy in the shape of an inverted diamond—flat and thick at the bottom, pointy at the top. Large banners hung from a high ceiling, with Abigor's picture and the text "Welcome to the 2019 Summit Conference!" Straight ahead was the registration desk—three large tables pressed against each other, covered in bright blue cloth. The Summit Conference logo adorned the front of each desk and the truss above.

Lew approached the registration desk.

Huh, I thought there would be a crowd. Maybe most people registered yesterday before the reception?

Only two people were there. A balding, middle-aged man was at a nearby standing table. A dead-eyed woman with a slight smile greeted Lew from behind the desk.

"Hello, and welcome to the Summit Conference," she said with a strange cadence. "Name, please."

"Lew Starek."

She rummaged underneath the desk and then handed Lew his name tag and a blue tote bag with the Summit Conference logo. "Here is your badge, Mr. Stark. And your meeting materials are in the bag. You'll find the summit's program, rule book, and—"

"My name is misspelled," Lew interjected. "It's spelled L-E-W S-T-A-R-E-K." He pointed at the badge that read *Lou Stark*. "Is there another badge there with my name?"

"Unfortunately, no," she responded.

Lew tried his best to sound polite. "Can you print me another badge with my name spelled the right way?"

"I'm sorry, sir. The printer is broken." She handed Lew a black marker. "This is the best I can do for now. Use this to correct your badge. Check back later, and we'll see if the printer is working. You can write at that table over there."

"Thanks." Lew took the marker and joined the balding man at the standing table.

"They misspelled your name, too?" the man asked. He had a thick red mustache.

"Yeah." Lew crossed out the typo and printed his name in large block letters. "I'm Lew Starek. And you're...." He read the man's name badge. "Anus?"

The man made a sour face. "That's a typo. My name is Inias Christensen, not Anus." He jotted down his name and hung his badge around his neck. Inias gave a smile and extended his hand.

Lew shook Inias's hand. "Nice to meet you, Inias."

Inias took his hand back and noticed it was covered in Lew's sweat. "You look nervous. Don't be scared. I won't put you in a wristlock."

Inias wiped his hand on his dark blue Canali Siena Pinstripe Classic Fit Suit. He also wore a crisp white shirt, bright-orange tie, and matching brown leather shoes and belt.

That suit costs ten times what I have in my bank account.

Lew's face felt hot. "I'm so sorry!"

He wiped his sweaty palms on the jacket of his secondhand suit. It was ripped at the armpits and crotch when he bought it, but he patched it to not be noticeable—as long as you didn't inspect up close.

Maybe after I get my first paycheck, I can buy some clothes to look like this guy.

Lew looked at the two of them in a nearby mirror. He was embarrassed by how raggedy his suit looked compared to Inias's.

To avoid spreading his sweat any further, Lew put his hands in his pockets. "This is my first time at the Summit Conference. First time at any professional conference, actually. I didn't realize I was sweating. Have you come to the Summit Conference before?"

"It's not a big deal." Inias wrinkled his nose. "I've never been to the Summit Conference before, but I go to loads of these things. No need to be nervous. In most sessions, you simply sit and listen. It's not like when you see an insult comic at a comedy club. At a conference, you can relax and observe."

"You must travel a lot," Lew said.

"Check this out." Inias pulled out his phone and showed several pictures of himself standing in what looked like the same room wearing different ties, but he explained to Lew that those pictures were all taken in other cities at conferences like this one.

"I can't imagine being gone from my family that much," Lew said. "It was tough enough to leave for this week."

"They get used to it. And so do you. I think my wife and kids are happier when I'm away. How many kids do you have?"

"Just one."

"Boy or girl?"

"Girl. She's only three months old."

Inias gave a big smile. "Oh, you're a new father. They're so cute at that age. When they get older and become teenagers, they can turn into little monsters. I have five daughters myself." Inias flipped to a picture of him with a red-headed woman his age and five red-headed daughters. "The youngest is five; the oldest is fifteen. Do you have any pictures of your kid?"

Lew reached for his phone and then realized he didn't have it. "I have a bunch on my phone, but I must have left it in my room."

Or did I really drop it into the abyss behind the mirror while I battled my Reflection? No, that was just a dream. It must be somewhere in my room.

"No big deal. It was nice to meet you, Lew. I'm sure I'll see you throughout the week."

"Yeah, it was nice to meet you too, Inias."

Lew returned the marker to the registration desk, and the lady there told him where to find breakfast and the meeting sessions.

At the breakfast bar, Lew loaded up on eggs, bacon, and fruit, and then he grabbed a full cup of coffee. White tablecloths covered the dining tables, which were set up throughout the room, and there were seats for seven or eight people at each. Many tables were full. But he went to a table where only three people were seated.

"Do you mind if I join you?" Lew asked.

"We don't mind at all, man," said a casually dressed man with long hair, who smelled like a reggae concert. "Please join us."

The three had been whispering in a private conversation before Lew arrived, but their murmurs ceased when Lew approached. The long-haired man looked ready to smoke another bowl of weed and play hacky sack. A second man looked like he was on his way to the gym. Only the fat one was dressed to attend a professional conference. Lew began eating, and the trio watched him like scientists observing a new species.

This food all tastes so bland.

Lew looked for salt, but he didn't see it at the table or back at the breakfast bar. "Excuse me. Do you know if there's salt anywhere?"

"A man after my own heart," said the athletic one. "I hate unsalted food, too. It's weird. I asked the people that work here, but they don't have any salt—not even in the kitchen."

"Oh," said Lew, crestfallen. "That's too bad."

"It's okay." The athletic man reached into his pocket and pulled out a small salt grinder. "I always come prepared." He handed it to Lew.

"Thanks!" Lew took the salt and ground some onto his food. He took a bite. *Much better.* He tried to hand the salt grinder back.

"You can keep that one," the man said. "I have more."

"Thanks a bunch." Lew placed it in his jacket pocket.

"I'm Bob, by the way," the man said. "Bob Willemsen. My sharply dressed friend is Damien Chernobog. And this guy in the T-shirt is Frank Dolan."

"It's nice to meet y'all. My name is Lew Starek."

Shit. I need to drop the y'alls and ain'ts.

"It's nice to meet you, too," Damien said. "We were hoping you could help us."

"Anything for folks who freely share their salt," Lew said.

"It's like Jesus said in Commandment Number Seven: Sharing is caring." Damien waved his arm in a benevolent gesture and spoke in a relaxed tone. "How long have you been here at the Beburoa Hotel?"

"Since yesterday," Lew answered.

"How did you get here?" Damien asked, folding his hands together.

"I flew into Salt Lake City from BWI, and then I drove a rental from there. It was a long drive. This hotel is in the middle of nowhere."

"Why did you come to the Summit Conference? And how did you find out about it?" Damien asked with a sudden sense of urgency.

Is something wrong with this guy?

"Well," Lew shifted in his seat. "I'm here to learn about business management, network, and show my value to business executives. I know this is a very selective conference. I've heard rumors about the Summit Conference since business school, and then I heard more rumors at some companies where I worked. At the last place—Hudnam, Howe & Hartell—they say Mr. Hudnam attended the Summit Conference shortly after he started his firm, and that's how he learned to grow it into a billion-dollar multinational corporation. I submitted a paper on 'Authentic Values and Leadership' to the conference, and I get to present it during the session on Corporate Leadership."

Damien, Bob, and Frank huddled again and whispered to each other. The three then resumed their previous positions and stared at Lew.

"Hey, man," Frank said. "What do you think about the giant evil statue on top of the hotel? Does it at all seem strange to you that someone would build that shit?"

Lew shrugged. "I heard Jeff Bezos erected a similar statue of himself over Amazon headquarters."

"Lew," Damien said, "are you a ghost?"

"What?" Lew laughed and then shook his head. "I'm not a ghost."

Who the hell are these assholes?

"Interesting," said Damien. "That's exactly what a ghost would say."

"Don't listen to him," Bob said. "He's a little crazy. I know that you're an actor, like everyone else here, right?" He winked and then dropped his voice to a whisper. "We're on a hidden camera show, aren't we?"

"Huh? I'm not an actor. I don't even like public speaking." Lew started eating faster.

"What does the engraving on the door to the hotel say?" Bob asked.

"I don't know. I got a C in Spanish," Lew replied.

"0100111100001011010101010!" Frank yelled.

"I'm afraid I don't understand." Lew felt the onset of a headache.

"It's binary," Frank said. "I know you're part of the Matrix, man."

Is he talking about a math thing or the movie?

"You know binary?" Damien asked.

"No," Frank answered, "I just said ones and zeros randomly. But I'm sure he knows what I said because he's a computer program!"

"Thank you for the salt." Lew wolfed down the last food on his plate and then chugged his remaining coffee. "But I must get going. I don't want to be late for the first session. It was a pleasure to meet you all."

Lew left the table in a hurry. He glanced back to see Bob, Damien, and Frank huddled and whispering to each other again.

Those three are lunatics. How did they even end up at this conference? I thought the Summit Conference was much more selective. Hopefully, I won't run into them again for the rest of the week.

9

In the front row at a meeting session, Bob Willemsen fidgeted in a chair between Fatty and Skinny. Boring business people wearing bland business attire filled all seventy chairs in the room. Bob proudly stuck out from the crowd in his athletic clothes—a bright blue shirt and dark green climbing pants. Skinny wore a T-shirt and jeans, and both had holes. Fatty wore another gray suit and a white shirt with no tie, and he blended into the crowd.

A small light illuminated the podium. The rest of the room was dimly lit. A projector displayed the Summit Conference logo.

A middle-aged hag approached the podium and announced, "Welcome to Sexual Harassment and the Workplace: How to Respect Boundaries during Times of Change."

The crowd erupted in slow, rhythmic clapping for five solid minutes, which sounded more like an evil heartbeat than applause.

She looks like an uptight bitch who sucks the fun out of a room the minute she enters, Bob thought. *She's barely a two. I haven't seen a single ten at this stupid conference yet.*

Hag said her name and then added, "This is my fiftieth year at the Summit Conference."

Fifty years at this conference—she would have come here as a toddler if that were true. The actors here are dialing up the weird. Let's get this boring video over with. I bet this bitch will scold us for the slightest transgression—never glance at a woman's chest or bottom. Never point your finger at a woman; it's just as unacceptable as waving your penis in the air. I can't help being so damned handsome that women throw themselves at me.

Hag said, "Thank you. Let's begin by playing a short film."

An old film reel played a movie. On the screen, an overweight bald man in a drab suit sat at a desk and punched away at a typewriter. Hag approached the man from behind.

The man turned in his chair and caught Hag standing behind him.

"I'm nearly done with the reports," he said. "You'll have them in an hour."

Hag went intimately close to the man and grabbed his crotch.

"I want sex," she said. "Now."

She cleared his desk, throwing his typewriter and papers on the floor in one swoop of her hand. He stood up and ripped his clothes off. She tore her clothes off just as fast.

Well, this isn't what I was expecting at all. But if they were going to show us porno, I wish they picked hotter actors. She's not a two—she's not even a one. Ick. She's a negative ten. Damn, these people are so ugly. It looks like a walrus fucking a manatee.

Bob squished his face up and tried to look away, but his eyes kept drifting back to the movie on the screen. The man lay back on his cubicle desk and displayed a fluffy mound of unkempt pubic hairs at the base of his erect penis. Hag climbed on top of him. Her huge ass sagged as she mounted him and rode. Everything everywhere jiggled. Bob felt sick. He covered his eyes.

"Let me know when it's done," he whispered to his friends. "I can't watch this anymore, or I'll fucking puke."

He sat with his hands covering his eyes for what felt like an eternity, listening to the sounds of moaning and fat slapping against fat.

"It's over," Skinny said.

Bob looked back at the screen. In the film, Hag and the man got dressed. The movie stopped, and the lights in the room came on.

Hag retook her place at the podium. "Do we have questions?"

A hand shot up from the last row.

"Yes." Hag pointed at the hand.

A man stood up, the same man from the sex video. "Can we watch that again?"

"Yes, we can," she responded.

The lights dimmed. Hag took a seat, and the film played again in its entirety.

Bob once again covered his eyes, peeking up from time to time to check if the movie was over. When it ended, the lights came back on.

Hag returned to the podium. "Do we have questions?"

Skinny raised his hand. "Hey, man. What the hell was the point of the video?"

"Let's figure it out together," Hag answered. "Play it again."

The lights dimmed, she took her seat, and the film played once more. Though Bob kept his eyes closed on this play through, each slap and moan was an assault on his ears, and he could vividly see the movie in his mind.

Bob opened his eyes. Hag stood at the podium once more, asking for questions.

"Is anything else going to happen in the session?" Fatty asked.

No, you bastard. Don't ask her questions. She's just going to—

"Let's play the film again and find out," Hag answered.

The lights dimmed, and the movie played again.

Bob said to his friends, "I'm getting the fuck out of here before I puke. I can't take this anymore."

He bolted from the room and ran down the hallway until he could no longer hear the sex sounds. He put his hands on his head and paced back and forth, staring at the ceiling.

Are the sons of bitches running this prank show trying to gross us out? It's all about the reactions, right? Well, I'll give them a fucking reaction.

Fatty and Skinny caught up to him.

"Hey, man. Are you alright?" Skinny asked.

"Didn't that gross you guys out?" Bob asked. "That was nasty!"

"Yeah, man. That was like the third grossest porno I have ever seen," Skinny said.

"What were the first two?" Fatty asked.

"The second grossest had a lot of poop," Skinny answered. "And the grossest involved a donkey."

Bob closed his eyes. "Please don't bring up even nastier things. I'm trying to clean my eyes of those images, not replace them with more disgusting ones. Ugly people just shouldn't have sex. At least not on camera." He looked at Fatty. "Sorry."

"Why would I be offended?" Fatty asked. After a beat, he said, "Hey, wait a minute! Do you think I'm ugly? I'm not ugly."

"Yeah, man," Skinny said. "I've definitely seen uglier people than you. Like in the video, for instance."

"You're beautiful where it counts," Bob said.

Fatty furrowed his eyebrows and glared at Bob.

"Alright, I can't take this anymore," Bob said. "I played their stupid game for long enough. We've been trapped in this hotel for too fucking many days."

"This is only our second day here," Skinny interjected.

Bob ignored Skinny and talked over him. "And we can't seem to find a door to get out. I'm going to do what I should have done when we first arrived. I'm going to bust out of here, Big Bob Style! That's what they really want to watch. It was the whole point of trying to spook us with the ridiculous rule book. That's why they brought me here. It will be my greatest urban climbing exploit since I climbed Landmark 81 in Ho Chi Minh City."

"What the hell is Big Bob style?" Fatty said. "I've literally never heard you say that phrase before."

"Follow me if you want to find out," Bob said.

Fatty and Skinny followed Bob back to his hotel room. Bob checked his parachute and secured it onto his back. He buckled a chalk bag around his waist and changed into rock climbing shoes. Last, he secured a GoPro onto his head.

"I'm going to climb to the top of the hotel and then parachute off.

I connected the GoPro to my iPad." Bob pulled his iPad from a bag and tossed it to Skinny. "Once I touch down outside, the camera crews will come out of hiding and greet us. I bet they have a celebrity host, too."

"Hey, man," Skinny said, "I don't know if this is a good idea. I don't think we're on a prank show. Something isn't right. If you die in the Matrix, you die in real life too, and shit."

"Jesus fucking Christ!" Fatty said. "Don't climb up. Climb down. And for God's sake, be careful. You'll probably become another ghost trapped at the hotel if you die here. It's like Jesus said: The only thing we have to fear is ghosts."

"Fuck that. Ghosts aren't real. Neither is God. Neither is the Matrix, even though it was a badass movie." Bob opened the curtain in his room, revealing the darkness outside. He grabbed a lamp, smashed the glass window, and climbed onto the ledge. "I'll see you fellas soon."

Bob was greeted on the hotel's exterior by a relief sculpture of demons eating people.

The little glutton is gobbling them down by the fistful. This is like a fucked-up Garfield cartoon.

Bob looked up and noticed the ledge jutting out, which blocked his view of Abigor's statue on top.

I should climb up there and pull Abigor's eyes from his head. If this doesn't work, I'm going to find that old bastard and shove his scepter up his ass until the producers let us out.

He looked down at the ledge he was standing on and studied it. The relief sculpture went halfway up to the next ledge. He grabbed a demon's horns and tried to shake it, but it didn't budge.

I could climb the relief—the features seem sturdy enough.

Bob walked along the ledge, and halfway to the other side of the building, a small bronze demon took up the width of the ledge. He grabbed and tried to shake it, but it was secure. The climber leaned out and tried to peek at the ledge over him, and he could see a bump.

I bet that's another demon statue.

He stood on the tips of his toes and tried to grab directly overhead but couldn't reach the next ledge.

I'm pretty sure I can catch it if I jump.

Bob looked down into the darkness below. Every direction was nothing but a black void. Only the building was visible, illuminated by lights from hotel windows.

Well, no time like the present.

The climber jumped up and away from the building to get a clear view of the ledge above him. He spotted the demon and reached for it with both hands.

"Holy fucking shit!" Skinny shouted from the hotel room window.

"Jesus fucking Christ!" Fatty exclaimed. "Don't die yet! It's only been a minute!"

The most challenging part about climbing was often determining how to do the move. Bob spent hours repeatedly falling on mountains and in rock climbing gyms until he figured out where to put his hands and feet and how to sequence moves, but he always took more risks when protected by a rope. One time, when climbing in Yosemite with Sasha, his sometimes girlfriend and frequent climbing partner, he was near the top of the third pitch of a five-pitch climb. He thought the easiest way to grab the next hold was to leap into the air —or dyno—and grab onto a big bulge of rock. He dynoed and grabbed it with both hands, but when his weight came down, his legs swung out, and his hand slipped. When Bob fell, his first and second pieces of protection popped out of the rock—he hadn't properly secured them. He took a big-ass whipper, flipped upside down, and flew into the side of the mountain face first. The climber broke his nose that day. Luckily, his last couple pieces of protection held, and Sasha caught Bob with her belay device so that he didn't fall all the way down the mountain.

Sasha, I need to pay you another visit. Bob thought about her curly brown hair, cute laugh, and soft skin. *After I leave this damned hotel, I'll come be with you again. We can spend days climbing in the Tetons, and then... Who knows? Maybe I won't even head back to the PanWow house*

after meeting you. Let's buy a van and hit the road, climbing the best moun-
tains in the States. #vanlife.

The climber was ordinarily cautious when he free-soloed skyscrapers. Without a rope and belayer, a fall could mean his death. The second time he climbed a skyscraper, he was cocky and careless. Bob slipped when he was only fifteen feet up—fortunately, not far enough to die—but he sprained his ankle. He had to go months without climbing until it healed. He hated not being able to climb, but he was glad that he fell when he did. Fear made him pay extra attention when a fall meant an injury or death. One month after his ankle healed, the climber tried again and made it to the building's roof.

When Bob leaped up to the next ledge of the Beburoa Hotel in Sheol, Wyoming, he caught the demon statue in his grip. When his weight came down on it, his legs swung out. The climber nearly slipped off. But he kept his hold. Bob swung his right leg up and hooked it onto the same ledge, and then he pulled up the rest of his body. The view here was just like it was on the lower ledge, except one floor higher.

Bob lay down on his belly and hung his right arm over the ledge. He extended a thumbs up. Skinny and Fatty cheered.

"I'm okay," Bob said. He stood up and looked at the next ledge.

The move is a backward dyno to a heel hook. Okay, now only thirty-three more dynos to get to the top. I'm pretty sure I'm high enough that I could use the parachute if I fall...as long as I fall away from the hotel.

By the time Bob reached the eighty-second floor of the Beburoa Hotel, the weather turned to a mix of snow, freezing rain, and blustery winds. He moved more slowly up here, but not from fatigue or weakness. The climber was being cautious. Every surface felt slick. Most people wouldn't climb in these conditions, but Bob wasn't most people. He walked along the ledge to the corner of the building, hoping to find more features he could use to ascend without jumping. Bob didn't want to risk falling.

The climber looked at the relief sculpture.

I don't want to touch that thing.

This sculpture wasn't static like on the lower floors. Here, the demon moved through a crowd of screaming humans and devoured them.

The demon took a break from eating to talk to Bob. "Give up, Bob. There is no escape. I'll help you inside." Its voice echoed, even though there was nothing around that should have caused an echo.

A window to this floor opened on its own.

"Return to the Summit Conference," the demon said. "Let Abigor help you realize your full potential."

"Real fucking funny!" Bob yelled up to where he thought cameras might be. "Trying to dial up the weather just to fuck with me? And then you have this stupid trash-talking puppet. Do you think you can scare me? You can't! I climbed Lunag Ri in Tibet during a goddam snowstorm!"

Bob took a step and slipped on the ice. He fell onto his face and slid. The climber came to a stop with his head and arm dangling over the edge.

Okay, that's it. I'm going to BASE jump off this bitch.

The extreme sports enthusiast stood up, flipped the camera down to his face, and screamed, "Big Bob Style!"

He flipped the camera back up and then jumped off the building. It was nothing but darkness in every direction, even from this height.

No sky.

No ground.

Nothing.

The Beburoa Hotel, snow, and rain were the only things in existence. The wind blew Bob's face and hair. He pulled the cord, and his parachute opened. The extreme sports enthusiast steered away from the hotel, searching to find something, anything. But there was nothing but the abyss.

Suddenly, a large hand came from above and caught Bob in its palm. It pulled the climber up higher into the sky so quickly that his ears popped like he was on an airplane. He soon found himself face to face with the giant Abigor statue that perched atop the Beburoa Hotel.

"Let me out of here, you bastard!" the extreme sports enthusiast screamed at the statue.

The statue opened its mouth, and Bob thought he was about to be eaten. But Abigor roared laughter out of his giant jaws with the force of massive speakers at a concert. The statue brought his other hand up and yanked the parachute off Bob. And then it pinched Bob's legs, crushing every bone below his hips. The climber howled in agony like a dying cat. Tears streamed from his cheeks. Bile leaked from his mouth.

Abigor smiled and said, "There is no escape from the Summit Conference."

The statue stretched its arm out horizontally away from the hotel and then dropped Bob. The climber wailed as he plummeted into the abyss. He wondered if he would ever hit bottom or if he would fall for eternity.

10

Lew Starek pressed a revolver against his own temple. He shook. He didn't want to pull the trigger, not at all.

On the floor nearby lay Montana Sorenson. That was the name printed on his badge. He was a tall, gangly, young blond man with a buzz cut, dressed in a light-green collared shirt with brown pants, blue socks with pink fleur-de-lis, and brown leather shoes. Montana was belly down, and he had his ass in the air and head turned sideways. His lifeless, clear blue eyes were wide. A look of shock permanently covered his face.

Lew's stomach turned, and his skin ran cold while he gaped at the dead body. Montana's eyes looked off into the distance.

Did he open his eyes so wide because he knew he was dying? Lew asked himself. *Did he see Saint Peter waiting for him at the gate? Or did he watch his soul leave his body behind?*

Blood pooled on the floor from the gunshot wound to Montana's head, and it reached Lew's only pair of dress shoes.

"I don't want to fucking do this," Lew pleaded. "I quit. I give up. Let me leave."

"You'll do it, and no more bellyaching," Brendan O'Hannigan warned Lew.

Brendan was in his early forties with slicked-back brown hair, great posture, and a stern face that looked weathered by the elements. He wore a dark-brown suit with a patterned pocket square, a white shirt, and a green tie. Brendan had a hard stare that could put fear into a man, but what Lew feared the most was the Tommy gun Brendan held.

How the fuck did this happen in a session about agile project management?

Lew's mind flashed back to the start of the session. He noticed the setup was different the moment he entered the room. It was another carpeted meeting room in the Beburoa Hotel. *There aren't any chairs for us to sit in,* he thought when he first arrived.

Brendan stood behind a single table covered with a blue cloth. On either side stood a mysterious figure wearing a habit with a large hood that covered their face. A couple of feet to the left and right of his table were two empty wooden podiums, and each had the 2019 Summit Conference logo on the front. Thirty attendees, including Lew, entered the meeting room.

"Welcome to Agile Project Management versus Traditional Project Management," Brendan announced. "My name is Brendan O'Hannigan, and this is my sixty-first year at the Summit Conference." He waved his hand, and one of the hooded figures rushed to the only door and locked it. "The door will remain locked until the session is over. We're going to play a little game today. Break yourselves up into two teams. Team One will line up behind the podium to my left and represent Agile Project Management. Team Two will line up behind the podium to my right and represent Traditional Project Management. Everyone will remain standing the entire time. Only lazy people sit. And don't think of slouching! That's almost as bad as sitting."

The attendees split themselves into two groups of fifteen and lined up behind each podium. Lew was in the Agile group.

I want to quietly sit in the back. I don't want to talk in front of a bunch of people. It's bad enough that I have to present this week. Although maybe it's better this way. There aren't many people here. Maybe this will help build my confidence. But I don't even know what we're going to talk about. I wish I knew what I had to say to practice.

Lew noticed a familiar face in line with him. "Inias, nice to see you again."

Inias wore a sky-blue Brioni textured wool-blend suit, which was worth more than Lew's car.

"The new father," Inias said. "So tell me, did you sleep better than usual without a baby waking you up every other hour?"

Did I sleep well? I don't even remember falling asleep, but I had a crazy dream where my Reflection attacked me, and then I drowned. I would have rather had my daughter wake me with her crying than deal with that nightmare.

"Yeah, I slept great," Lew responded. "I feel bad for my wife for dealing with the baby all by herself. I wish I could have called or texted her at least. Is it hard for you to be away from your wife and children?"

Inias laughed. "Yeah, it's really hard," he said sarcastically. "Thank God the Wi-Fi is out. Whenever I call my wife from a business trip, I cross my fingers that she doesn't answer. And if she doesn't and calls me back, I don't answer, even if I'm free. It's great to prove that I called her without actually having to talk to her. I've taken multiple screenshots of no cell connection on my phone so that when I get home, I have proof that I couldn't call her. It's nice to not have to deal with that this week. Do you know what I mean?"

Lew responded with a confused look.

"Oh, I forgot," Inias said. "You've been married for only a minute and just had your first kid. You probably still enjoy being around your wife and daughter. I used to be like you, too. It was so long ago that it's sometimes hard to remember. After a few more children and years, you'll be thankful for every opportunity you get to not talk to your wife."

No, that won't be me. I love Juliana and baby Anika. How could I ever get sick of them?

Lew wasn't sure how to respond to Inias, whose face had turned red.

Lew tried to change the subject. "Is this how these meeting sessions normally go?"

"No," Inias said. "Normally, all the attendees sit in rows while a long table of panelists sits at the front of the room. And then there is a podium and a screen that shows a PowerPoint presentation. The lights are dim, and the presenters take turns talking at the podium while they flip through boring slideshows. Nearly every session at every meeting is like that. After one session, you normally feel like sleeping, like you're in a rear naked choke. They may as well hang bricks onto your eyelids and have each presenter sing lullabies. After eight, ten, or twelve hours of sessions, you wish you were dead. You end up shoving so much sugar and caffeine down your throat, trying to stay awake, that when it's over, you sometimes go to your room and shit your pants." Inias turned redder. "Or at least that's what some people do."

"Traditional Project Management, you're up first." Brendan pointed to a woman from that group who was standing near the podium.

Hanna Taithangklom was printed on her name badge. She wore a blue pantsuit and matching blue high heels.

Brendan told the room, "Each of you will step up to the podium and make a statement about why your style of project management— traditional or agile—is better than the other. Then you grab this gun. Hanna...something foreign. We'll start with you." He pulled out a revolver, spun the barrel, and placed it on Hanna's podium. "Take the gun, put it against your temple, and pull the trigger. It's a six-shooter with only one bullet. If you hear a click, your team gets the point. If you shoot yourself, your team loses a point. Whichever team has the most points at the end wins."

"What the fuck is going on?" Lew whispered to Inias. "Is he trying to kill us?"

"Oh, you young people," Inias whispered back. "That's not a real gun. Or if it is, there's no way it's loaded. Oh, man. This is good. This is why the Summit Conference is the best."

"How is this good?" Lew asked. "This is insane."

"Have you ever heard the expression, 'gun to your head'?" Inias asked. "This takes the metaphor to another level. It's about overcoming a fear of public speaking, decision making, and thinking on your feet."

Hanna took small, slow steps towards the podium and placed her hand on the gun. Her hands shook. "Is this a joke? I don't know shit about project management. Aren't you supposed to teach us something? I don't want to die." She breathed heavily.

"Make a statement about traditional project management, grab the gun, place it against your temple, and pull the trigger!" Brendan barked. "Every second you delay wastes my time and the time of everyone else in the room. Now!"

"This is crazy." Hanna looked at the gun. Sweat dripped down her brow.

"It's okay," Inias shouted to Hanna. "It's not loaded. Trust me."

Hanna looked at Inias and then back at the gun. She aimed at Inias and pulled the trigger. He dove to the floor. Lew jumped back.

CLICK!

Hanna instantly looked more relaxed. She pressed the gun against her temple. "Traditional project management is better because it's more traditional."

Hanna pulled the trigger.

CLICK!

"Point traditional," Brendan shouted. "Agile, you're up next."

A hooded figure took the gun from Hannah, spun the cylinder, and passed it to the next person.

Inias got back to his feet. He whispered to Lew, "Did you see her shoot at me to test if it was loaded?"

"Yeah." Lew breathed a gigantic sigh of relief. *And I watched you dive to the floor in fear.* "You sounded pretty confident the gun wasn't loaded when you shouted at her."

Not so confident when your life is on the line, huh?

For a while, the session went similarly. Each person stepped up to the podium, made a bland statement about their project management style, pulled the trigger, heard a click, and moved to the back of the line. Most of the subsequent attendees who took the podium after Hanna had similarly strange mannerisms. They all spoke in the same cadence—a cross between Hal from *2001: A Space Odyssey* and chanting monks. And their eyes...their eyes were wide open but void of emotion.

Do those fuckers even blink?

But everything changed when Montana Sorenson took the podium. After hearing so many clicks come from the revolver, he showboated. Montana twirled the pistol around his finger. He performed multiple quick draws, like he was in a Western.

Brendan chastised him. "Stop dilly dallying! Make a statement, pull the trigger, and move on!"

"Traditional is better because I said so." Montana placed the gun against his temple, and with a big smile on his face, he pulled the trigger.

BANG!

The sound echoed in Lew's ears. He was at the next podium, directly across from Montana. It was Lew's turn next. He watched the life leave Montana's eyes as blood sprayed out of the other side of his temple. Montana fell forwards, and he landed with his head turned to the side and his ass in the air.

Lew stood frozen. His acid reflux kicked into high gear, and his stomach churned and churned.

Hanna screamed.

Inias whispered, "Holy fuck!"

"Reload the gun." Brendan pointed to one of the cloaked figures on his side.

The mysterious figure pried the gun from Montana's fingers, emptied the shell, and placed a new bullet inside the barrel. The figure approached Lew, spun the barrel, and put the revolver on Lew's podium.

"Take one point away from Team Traditional," Brendan said. "Team Agile, you're next."

"Fuck this. I won't shoot myself." Lew's mouth moved, but barely any sound came out.

"Louder, my boy," Brendan said. "We can't hear you."

Lew cleared his throat and tried again. "I'm not gonna shoot myself. I forfeit."

"Forfeit!" Brendan sounded like an angry parent about to smack a child. "No, you do not forfeit! I won't allow anyone to be a corner turner."

He reached under his table and pulled out a Tommy gun, and he aimed it directly at Lew. "You'll grab your revolver, say something about agile project management, place it against your temple, and pull the trigger. If you refuse, I'll shoot you myself. And I assure you that my chatterbox is full of bullets."

"I don't want to fucking do this," Lew pleaded. "I quit. I give up. Let me leave."

"You'll do it, and no more bellyaching." Brendan's right eye and trigger finger both twitched.

Like Biggie said: You're nobody until somebody kills you.

Lew reached for the revolver slowly, like he was pushing through syrup. He shook as he picked up the gun. "Agile is—"

Lew vomited all over his podium. Stomach acid burned his throat and erupted from his nose and mouth. Blood and vomit covered the floor. The smell was so foul Lew was worried he would vomit again. He coughed and hacked, and he wiped the puke and snot from his face.

"You disgust me," Brendan said, arms akimbo. "What kind of man has so little control over his body? You're a pathetic little baby dressed in a man's clothes. Now, do what I said!"

Lew pressed the gun against his temple. "Agile project management is better because it's more flexible."

Is this how I die? Juliana, Anika, I'll miss you.

Lew stared into Brendan's eyes and pulled the trigger.

11

Damien Chernobog's blood curdled as he listened to Bob scream.

I've seen Bob climb and jump off buildings before, but he never looked scared. I didn't even know he could get scared.

"Jesus fucking Christ!" Damien exclaimed.

He and Frank watched Bob's point of view on the iPad, which was paired with his GoPro. They caught a brief glimpse of their friend as he passed their window. His screaming grew louder as he got close and then fainter as he fell below. They didn't hear him hit the ground or anything else. But Bob soon disappeared from their view. The iPad disconnected from Bob's camera. And his screaming faded away.

"Shit, man." Frank shook. "What the fuck? Is he dead, or is he still falling? Are we totally fucked? How the fuck do we get out of here, man?" He pulled his vape pen out and took a long, long hit.

"I don't know." Damien's pulse beat so fast that he thought his heart might jump out of his chest.

Think of a plan to escape! I don't want to die. Dammit, Damien. Think! Why can't I think of anything?

"Hey, man." Frank paced back and forth. "Do you have an idea or some shit? Because I have one."

"Alright, Frank. What's your idea?" *Dumb fucking stoner. Let's hear about the Matrix.*

"Let's go to the second floor, smash a window, and try to bust out from there. If there is a bottom, man, we'll be able to see."

"Huh." Damien's heartbeat calmed. "That's actually not a bad idea."

"What do you mean, 'actually,' man?" Frank asked accusingly.

"Nothing. Let's go. It's a good plan."

Maybe this will work. But... Poor Bob. I can only hope he's in a better place now. Unless he's still falling. Or his ghost comes back to the hotel.

Frank's plan was easier said than done. You didn't need a keycard to go to the lobby or conference meeting rooms, but a keycard was required for every floor above the lobby. Your keycard only took you to the floor of your room. Bob and Frank went to the lobby, and then they took the stairs to the second floor. But they ran into the same problem. The duo needed a keycard to get onto a floor from the stairwell. The door from the stairway had a small pane of glass that let you see through, and the hallway was empty.

"We should wait here until we see someone," Damien said. "We'll knock, and hopefully, they let us in."

"Okay, man." Frank leaned against the door and stared at his shoes. "I never watched someone die before, and I never thought I would watch a friend die in front of my eyes."

Damien's mind drifted. He never watched someone die before either, but he was the first to find his grandma. Damien had been looking forward to seeing her. He was still a boy, and he loved spending time with grandma, particularly her Sunday dinners. They were the best. She cooked everything from scratch. It was much better than the slop his mother prepared. Damien was convinced his mother was the worst cook in her family. He arrived on a Sunday afternoon with his parents and his little brother. His mother thought it was weird that grandma didn't greet them, and even stranger that she hadn't started dinner. Young Damien ran through the house shouting, "Grandma! Grandma!" until he reached her bedroom. He found her naked, laying half on the bed, half on the floor, with a bath towel only covering her pubic region. "Grandma! Grandma! Mom, Dad! Something's wrong with Grandma!" Her face was turned to the window, and her eyes were open—her expression frozen in one of curiosity, like she heard a strange sound and had turned to find out what it was. Her eyes looked like cloudy marbles. Damien put his hand on her old, wrinkly arm and shook her. "Grandma! Grandma!" She was cold, like meat from the fridge, and her face didn't move. He felt a pain in his chest, like a piece of his heart broke off and fell away, never to return. His eyes stung. He thought he was about to cry, but he forced his tears back because his dad taught him that men don't cry.

"We don't know that Bob's dead." Damien's voice quavered.

"Living and falling forever, that's even worse than dying, man. I would rather be put out of my misery than fall for eternity and shit." Frank stared through the glass, but the hallway was still empty. "Bob was the brave one. He was the adventurer, the hero. I thought he would save us. What can we do without him? I'm not so sure any more about us being in the Matrix. I don't know what this is, but I don't think it's a computer program. And I don't think it's a prank show either, like Bob thought. I don't know what this is, but it's something supernatural, man."

"I'm telling you—these are ghosts. This place is haunted. We can still find a way out of the hotel. We can still escape." Damien stared through the glass in the door.

"Maybe we are in some setup like the *Evil Dead*," Frank pondered.

"How do you figure?"

"So, there are these college kids that go to a cabin in the woods. But they don't realize there's an evil book in the cabin called the Necronomicon. It's got magic spells and shit. And then—"

Damien cut him off. "You said that already. What's your point?"

"Maybe there's some kind of magic book, man. We could read some spells out of it to kill the evil dead and go free. You have that magic book you always use for your videos."

"Jesus fucking Christ!" Damien raised his voice. "I told you. It's a Bible, not a book of magic spells. It's a religious textbook. Jesus wrote it himself while he was nailed to the cross. Billions of people around the world have been reading this book for millennia. If it had magic powers, everyone would know."

"Okay, maybe it's not *Evil Dead*." Frank sat on the floor and ran his fingers through his long hair, working out the tangles. "Let's talk about a different book. What about the rule book, man? It said, 'There is no escape,' over and over on every page. That's the one rule to this place, man. We can try whatever we want, but we can't get out."

"You can't believe everything you read. Abigor, or whoever, printed that sentence on every page because they want us to think escape is impossible. There's always a way out. Ghosts are only trapped in this world because they have unfinished business. If the ghosts don't let us out, we'll just have to figure out what unfinished business they have so that we can finish it." Damien stepped away from the glass and closed his eyes. *A pious man would pray now. Should I maybe try...*

Frank pounded on the door. "Somebody's there."

Damien looked up and almost said something, but he changed his mind and pounded on the door with Frank.

A woman in her mid-twenties walked through the hallway. She wore a red pantsuit and had a keycard in her hand.

"Help! Let us in," Damien shouted. "We forgot our key, and we got locked out in the hallway."

Upon noticing the duo in the hallway, she opened the door and let them in.

Damien and Frank rushed out of the stairwell.

"Thanks so much, man," Frank said. "You can't get back in without a keycard."

"It's okay. No problem." Paying them no further attention, she used her keycard to enter a nearby room and closed the door behind her.

"Alright." Damien rubbed his hands together. "Let's find a window."

"Hey, man. Maybe this will come in handy." Frank pointed to a fire ax behind a wall of glass, next to a fire extinguisher and a fire alarm.

He tried to open the glass, but noticed you had to use a little metal hammer that hung from the window to smash the glass. So, naturally, Frank used the fire extinguisher to smash the glass and get the ax.

"You know," Damien said, "there was a little hammer for the glass."

"Fuck that, man. This was quicker. You'll thank me later."

They wandered the hallway, looking for a window. After they made a full figure eight and returned to the stairwell entrance, they realized the hallway had no windows. At the center of the floor plan was a bay with eight elevators and vending and ice machines. Sleeping rooms were around the perimeter.

"Awe, man," Frank said. "I should have checked on our floor first, you know, to see if our hallway had a window before we came all the way down here."

You moronic fucking stoner. Although, maybe I'm dumber for going along with your plan because I didn't know any better either.

"It's okay. We just have to get into one of these rooms, and then we can access a window." Damien knocked at the door to the nearest room. "Room service." There were no sounds from within, and nobody answered. "Nobody is there. Let's try another one."

Bam! Frank swung his ax into the door. It was sturdy, and only the point made it through. "I told you that you would thank me, man." Frank pulled the ax from the door.

"Frank, what the hell are you doing?"

The stoner took another swing—this time cracking a big enough hole to see through. Lights were on in the room. "You found out that nobody was here, so I'm getting us inside."

"What the hell is going on?" a man bellowed from within.

Oh shit. Frank, what the hell did you do?

The door swung open. Damien and Frank met a short old man with thick glasses, a white shirt, black pants, a white mustache, and white hair coming out of his ears. "What is the meaning of this?"

"Why aren't you at the conference?" Damien asked.

"I needed to relieve my bowels, and I prefer to do so in privacy," the man answered. "But why must I explain myself to you? Why in the hell are you swinging an ax into my door?"

What the fuck do we say to that?

"Abigor sent us," Frank answered. "He said he needs to see you in the ballroom immediately."

The old man frowned and grunted. "Fine. Let me grab my coat, and I'll be on my way. I better have a new door by the time I get back."

Is Frank an intelligent person who occasionally does dumb things or an idiot who has flashes of brilliance? I can never seem to figure it out.

"Yes, of course," Damien replied.

He and Frank waited in the hallway while the old man grabbed his coat and walked out of his room. As the door closed, Damien slid his foot in the doorway so that it didn't shut. After the old man rounded the corner, Damien and Frank slipped into his room and shut the door behind them.

This room looked just like all the rest. Damien pulled open the curtains. The darkness outside the window greeted them.

Frank took another puff from his vape pen. "Okay, stand back." Smoke came out of Frank's mouth and faded away into the air.

Damien moved near the bed. Frank picked up his ax, adjusted his grip, and swung it into the window just like a lumberjack.

CRACK!

The ax was stuck in the glass. It made a small crack and let water in. In a second, the crack spread across the entire window. In another second, the glass shattered and fell into a thousand pieces. A massive rush of water poured from the window into the room. It was like they had just opened a window in a submarine. Water hit Frank with the force of a firehose, and it threw him back. He dropped the ax.

The rush of water also knocked Damien back, and he fell and slid across the floor. The next thing Damien knew, he was over Frank with his back pressed against the closed door. The water was knee-high and rising. Damien grabbed the doorknob and tried to pull it open, but he couldn't get it to budge.

"Frank," Damien said. "Get up and help open the door. It's stuck."

Frank pulled himself to his feet. He tried to open the door too, but he couldn't budge it either. They both pulled on the door and shouted, but it didn't move. The water was waist high, and it continued to rise.

Damien slipped and fell, and he found his legs tangled around the ax. He picked it up and handed it to Frank. "Use this!"

Frank held the ax high above his head and swung it at the door, like his life depended on it.

12

In the hotel lobby, Lew Starek addressed Paul Mulciber. "Call the police! Someone's been murdered!"

"Murdered? I highly doubt that." Paul covered his nose and eyed the vomit on Lew's clothes.

"They made this guy Montana shoot himself in the head. It was room B137. Call the police." *Why the fuck isn't he taking this seriously?* "I fucking watched him die myself."

Paul shrugged. "No need for profanity, sir. I'll tell security. They'll arrive soon. If they discover a murder took place, which would be amazing, they'll call the police."

"I'll meet them there." Lew sprinted back to the meeting room.

Thank God I heard a click when I pulled that trigger. Inias damned near shit himself when it was his turn, but the session ended before he had to shoot. Lucky bastard. What the fuck is wrong with Brendan? I thought he would execute everyone, but the second the session ended, he stopped everything. He took the gun from Inias, smiled, and thanked everyone for attending.

At the door to the meeting room, Lew met two of the mysterious figures wearing Benedictine monk habits. They were also headed into the meeting room.

Lew felt something in his stomach bubble. "You guys are security?"

They nodded without saying a word.

Lew went into the meeting room, and the hooded figures followed him. "This way. He's right over here." He gasped when he found Montana standing next to Brendan. "What the fuck?"

The room was nearly empty, but Inias still stood frozen at the other podium. Montana stood in the pool of blood that came from his gunshot wound. He looked groggy but very much alive. Blood covered his head and clothes. Brendan, flanked by two other hooded figures, conversed with Montana.

"This... He's... You're alive!" Lew struggled to talk.

"He...he just stood up." Inias spoke softly—his body still frozen, his lips barely moving as his words crept out of his mouth. "After you ran out the door, he stood up like nothing happened."

"Man, my head is killing me." Montana rubbed the blood on his head.

"Get this man some laudanum for his headache," Brendan said to the hooded figures who accompanied Lew.

They nodded and led Montana away by his arm.

"Lauda... what the hell is that?" Montana asked with a yawn as he was escorted away.

Lew confronted Brendan. "What the fuck is this? You murdered him!"

Brendan scowled at Lew. "He looks alive to me."

"He... You... What the fuck?"

"Profanity is the crutch of the inarticulate. You think you're a BTO, but you act like a gink. You need to understand the situation before you make conclusions. Everything is not as it first appears. How many times today has your body and mind betrayed you? Clean yourself up before you go to another session. You smell atrocious." Brendan turned and left, and the remaining hooded figures followed him out.

"Holy shit!" Inias finally came out of his catatonic stupor and moved around like a football player celebrating a touchdown. "The Summit Conference is the greatest!"

"What the fuck are you talking about?" Lew asked.

Fuck. Is profanity a crutch? Fu... Am I as dumb as he thinks?

"Don't you see?" Inias asked, wide-eyed and full of enthusiasm. "Brendan staged the whole thing! Montana was acting. The gun was fake. The blood was fake. He got a headache from lying on the ground for so long. Oh, shit! They take everything up another notch around here!"

Lew caught a whiff of something that reminded him of his daughter. "Inias, I think you...you might have... Maybe you should also go change before the next session?"

Inias shit himself.

Inias's skin turned red. "I think you have puke in your nostrils. That must be the stench you notice. But you may have splattered some on me, so I need to change my clothes. But only because of your vomit!"

"Yeah, sorry about the puke. That was my fault." Lew nodded and spoke in a soothing voice.

Inias backed out of the meeting room like he was performing the worst moonwalk dance. He made sure to hide the back of his pants.

Lew was left alone in the empty meeting room, covered in his own vomit, standing in a pool of blood and vomit. He leaned down and touched the blood with his fingertips. Lew rubbed his fingers together and examined the blood, bringing his fingers close to his nose and smelling the red liquid.

It looks, feels, and smells just like blood. Should I taste it? No, fuck that. I won't taste a stranger's blood off the floor. How did they make it so realistic? Am I as naïve as Brendan thinks? Is it possible that I don't really know what's going on here?

Lew returned to his room to shower and put on clean clothes.

How much does dry cleaning cost in a hotel? Is it going to put me over to clean my suit? I can't let this sit in a bag all week or carry it back in my suitcase. It will make all my clothes stink. It might leak on my other clothes, too.

He stripped to his boxers and tried to scrub the blood out of his shoes in the sink.

Why did I bring only one pair of dress shoes? The same reason I own only one pair of dress shoes. Because I'm fucking broke.

Lew used a washcloth to scrub the blood out. One of the Beburoa Hotel's complimentary Q-Tips helped clean the blood from the creases in the shoes' soles. He couldn't get the blood out of every nook and cranny, but he got enough. Lew got ready to hop in the shower when he heard a baby crying in the central part of his hotel room.

"Shhhhhh, quiet honey. Dada has to work," a feminine voice said in a soothing tone.

Is that Juliana?

Lew ran out of the bathroom, wearing nothing but his glasses. The full-length mirror was back on the wall.

Was it room service? No, they hadn't made the bed yet. Is there any chance room service would fix the mirror and leave the bed?

Lew looked into the mirror and jumped back. The mirror showed the inside of his room, but instead of his reflection, he saw his wife, Juliana, holding his daughter, Anika. The baby cried and cried, streaming tears down her cheeks. Her cute black hair framed her face —Lew couldn't believe how much hair she already had at an age when some babies had hardly any. She wore a white onesie, and her tiny baby hands thrashed the air.

Juliana sat cross-legged on the floor, wearing sweatpants, a white T-shirt, and a gray cardigan. Her long black hair hung down, covering her face. The baby lay in her lap.

"Juliana! Anika!" Lew felt dizzy. "I missed you so much. What are you doing here?"

Juliana faced Lew, but she didn't have her own eyes. Lew found his own face staring back at him on Juliana's body. Lew's reflection cried just like baby Anika. And then Juliana or Lew—whatever the mirror creature was—stood up and lifted Anika over its head. It threw the baby over Lew like a soccer player doing a throw in.

"Baby Anika!" Lew dove and caught his daughter like a wide

receiver catching a touchdown pass, absorbing the impact of the fall with his chest and stomach. Once secure, Lew looked at Anika's face, only to once again find his own face staring back at him from the baby's body.

"Wah! Wah! Wah!" his daughter cried.

"Wah! Wah! Wah!" his wife cried.

"This isn't real! It's another trick!" Lew thought he might vomit again. He shut his eyes and chanted. "This isn't real! This isn't real! This isn't real!"

Lew heard the door to the room open, and he opened his eyes.

Another mysterious figure in a habit, face hidden under a large hood, stood in the doorway with clean towels in hand. "Room service," the figure said in a woman's voice.

Lew noticed he was naked, standing in front of the mirror, and holding a pillow in his hands instead of his daughter. His wife was nowhere to be seen—nothing in the mirror but his own naked reflection. He felt embarrassed when he realized he was thrashing his body and flopping his dick around in every direction. He covered his genitals with the pillow in his hands.

"Come back later!" Lew shouted. "Don't you knock?"

"I knocked," the mysterious figure said. "But you screamed, 'This isn't real. This isn't real.' I opened the door to see if you needed help, and I saw you naked and swinging your balls around. If you don't want housekeeping to come in, you need to put this Do Not Disturb tag on the outside of the door, and I'll come back later." She hung the sign on the door.

"Okay. Fine. Thanks. Now get out! Please!" Lew put his hand on her back and forced her out the door. He shut the door, turned the deadbolt, and closed the latch so that nobody outside could move their way in again.

Those fucking mysterious people. Who are they? Some are security. Some are housekeeping. She's the first one who spoke. Are they all women? Are some of them men?

Lew checked the mirror again, but it was merely a piece of glass on wood hanging against the wall. He couldn't find any hidden doors or secret passages.

I've gone insane. Or is there something else going on here, something I can't quite figure out? What don't I notice? What's strange about this place? No, no, I can't distract myself or get psyched out now. My presentation is what I need to focus on. It's time to clean up and get dressed. I need to clear my head and get confident. I will exude confidence. My presentation will be fucking perfect.

13

Hanna Taithangklom sat in the back row of the dimly lit meeting room.

That last session was...weird, she thought. *I'm glad it's over. Something seems off about this place. I hope this session doesn't turn out to be a bizarre mind fuck, too.*

Hanna examined her gray dress, black belt, black blazer, silver high heels, and silver watch.

Blood ruined my last outfit, but the outfit change was nice. I look ultra-chic. I hope these clothes don't get dirty.

The only light in the room shone on the podium where Camilla stood in a bright-orange skirt suit with matching colorful orange earrings. She had a stack of printed pages.

"Today, I'm going to do a reading from my latest novel, *And Then They Banged: An Erotic Tale*," Camilla said.

Hanna thought she might have heard it wrong. *Is that the actual title?* She couldn't imagine seeing a book with that title in a store.

Flipping her book open to the first page, Camilla read her story aloud.

Joanie heard the good news about her ex-husband, Richard, before her vacation. After leaving her for a younger woman, Richard developed dick cancer, and his penis shriveled up and fell off. Richard's new wife left the dickless asshole, and then he was struck by lightning and disintegrated.

Even though Richard received his comeuppance, Joanie's love life was as dry as the Sahara Desert. She had hoped this trip would help her relax and give her a renewed sense of life. She walked into the stable to find a horse to ride. The wood was brown and wooden, and hay was on the floor. Sergio greeted her. He was tall, rawboned, beardless, with an ingenuously appealing face. His muscles, rippling under his white shirt, quickened Joanie's pulse.

"Good morning, ma'am," Sergio said as he gave her body a raking gaze.

"Good morning, Sergio," Joanie responded. She noticed he was watching her intently.

"Would you like a good ride," he asked. There was a maddening hint of arrogance about him. "Nothing pleases me more than watching a beautiful woman enjoy a good ride."

"Are you talking about horses?" she inquired.

Joanie's reaction seemed to amuse Sergio. There was something warm and enchanting about him.

"I can talk about horses if you wish," he answered. "Anything that pleases you will make me happy." The smile in his eyes contained a sensuous flame. A wan shaft of sun struck his hair, and it gleamed like dark gold.

"I don't think you know what you are saying," Joanie said. "I'm a woman approaching middle age... You look like you're barely—"

"I'm twenty-five," Sergio interjected.

Sergio stood there, devilishly handsome. He looked very powerful; his chest was broad and muscular. Joanie took in his tempting, attractive male physique. She wondered how it would feel intertwined with her slender body and slim hips.

"Just a horse," she said. "For now."

"As you please," he said. "I will saddle Gingersnap for you. Find me in the back of the stable when you finish."

As Joanie rode Gingersnap, the wind whipped color into her face. She was on a beautiful ranch with a big, beautiful green field. Trees were further off, near the edge of the field. It was very beautiful. A bright clear blue sky was overhead, and mountains stood at the horizon, almost surreal. She felt like she was in a painting of the Westward Expansion, not in a real place.

But it was hard for Joanie to focus on the beautiful scenery while she rode. Her mind kept drifting off to Sergio. She imagined her lips touching his like a whisper. Being swept up, weightless, in his arms. His hands slid across her silken belly. She found her thoughts very satisfying.

When Joanie returned to the stable, she could no longer deny herself his touch. She found Sergio shirtless in the back, hunched over, pulling at some equipment. His shoulders looked a yard wide and like molded bronze. She wondered if his broad shoulders ever tired of the burden they carried.

"How was your ride?" Sergio asked as he stood up and turned to face her.

"It was quite pleasant," Joanie answered. "Gingersnap is very strong but gentle. It's a unique feeling to feel that much power between your legs while still feeling perfectly safe."

Hanna laughed. She looked around and saw that nobody else was laughing. She tried to stop and covered her mouth with both hands. *This is ridiculous!*

"Yes, I know what you're talking about," Sergio responded. "May I do anything else to please you?"

"Yes, you may," Joanie responded.

Joanie reached out, lacing Sergio's fingers with her own. He lightly fingered a loose tendril of hair on her cheek as she gazed at his handsome face with dark eyes and a secret expression. His eyes had a sheen of purpose. His mouth covered hers hungrily, but his kiss was surprisingly gentle. His tongue explored the recesses of her mouth and sent spirals of ecstasy through her.

Oh, and did I mention that Sergio is a ghost? Because he is! Yeah, it's time for some erotic mysticism.

"Let's bang," Joanie said.

Hanna laughed harder and harder, her hands hiding her mouth. Anyone looking at her could see her body shake in laughter, and she struggled to muffle the sounds.

How does anyone put these words together in a book that people spend money on? Hanna bent forward and put her head down. *Hopefully, nobody can see I'm laughing if I stay low enough.*

"As you wish," he responded.

Joanie smiled with an air of pleasure. Sergio reached for her clothes, and her smile broadened in approval. He ripped her bodice open and tore her bra off. His lips touched her nipple with tantalizing possessiveness. He fondled one small globe, its pink nipple marble hard. He took her hands, encouraging them to explore. She tore his clothes off his body.

And then they banged. And it was awesome.

Joanie gasped as bare chest met bare chest. Slowly, Sergio's hands moved downward, skimming either side of her body, to her thighs. He explored her thighs and moved up to her taut stomach. She snuggled against him as their legs intertwined. Passion pounded the blood through her heart, chest, and head. Joanie's body felt as if it were half ice and half flame. She breathed in deep, soul-drenching drafts, and his expert touch sent her to even higher levels of ecstasy. Together, they found the tempo that bound their bodies together. She cried out for release. Waves of ecstasy throbbed through her, and love flowed in her like warm honey.

Camilla fondled an imaginary breast in the air. She stroked an imaginary penis. She grinded her pelvis on an imaginary God knows what.

Joanie and Sergio separated their intertwined bodies.

"Did that please you, milady?" Sergio asked.

"It did," Joanie said.

"Then my purpose on this plane of existence is complete. Thank you," he thanked. "I can finally cross over to the other world."

Sergio closed his eyes, and his body faded away into nothingness while his soul departed our world. Joanie was left alone. Her body still tingled from the passion, but she wondered how much longer she would have to wait until she found another spirit who could satisfy her desires.

Camilla flipped through the last page on the podium. "Thank you."

The room promptly gave her a standing ovation, but something was strange about the way they clapped. It was a steady beat with a clap every other second, and the entire room kept the same rhythm.

This is weird. Hanna didn't know what she found stranger—that the worst story she ever heard in her life received a standing ovation or the bizarre way everyone in the room clapped. She stood and looked around. Every man and woman was staring straight ahead and clapping the same way.

Camilla scanned the crowd with a giant smile on her face. She noticed Hanna and gave her a wink.

How the hell can anyone be so confident about such garbage?

At the end, when the room cleared, Hanna was one of the last attendees to leave.

"I see you found time for something fun," Camilla said to Hanna.

"Yeah, without a toddler to keep me busy, I have a few more hours in the day. I never heard your writing before. It's really, really..." Hanna struggled to find positive words to say. *It's really, really shitty. I've heard some shitty shit before, but that was the shittiest shitty shit that anyone ever shat out of their mouths.* "Really beautiful. Are all your books like that?"

Camilla's smile broadened, and her eyes gleamed. "Thank you. I try to make each book unique, but I do my best to maintain the signature style that my readers crave." She walked towards the door. "Are you hungry? There is a private dining room for Board members. Would you like to be my guest?"

Private dining room! Luxury! "Yeah, that sounds—" Hanna stopped as she realized the words that nearly slipped by her. "Are you on the Summit Conference's Board of Directors?"

How does anyone fly so high from such crap? Maybe she's gotten lazy, and only her recent work is terrible. I've heard about writers who churn out good and bad books. I should try to find some of her early work.

The private dining room had a dozen tables with ample space between, and each table had seats for two or four people. Half the tables were empty. Potted ferns and flowers decorated the room. Every table had a vase with a single tulip. When Camilla and Hanna took their seats, a waitress immediately met them. She wore a white jacket and black pants, and her hair was pulled back in a tight ponytail. None of the other Board members in the room paid any attention to Camilla or Hanna.

"How may I help you?" the waitress asked in the same strange tone and cadence as many conference attendees.

"Oh, I haven't even seen a menu," Hanna said.

Camilla laughed. "You don't need a menu. I kid you not. Ask for anything you want, and they'll make it. I'll have foie gras, a beet salad with walnuts and blue cheese, gazpacho, and sparkling mineral water."

"You know, you almost had a vegan, cruelty-free meal." *Is this how rich people live? They can ask for anything at all, and they receive it?* "Um, I'll have a vegan Greek salad and a fruit smoothie...and a side of roasted carrots...and half a roasted avocado...and a glass of ice water."

"I'll be back shortly with your beverages," the waitress said before disappearing into the kitchen.

This is fancy. I could get used to this. Much better than waiting in line to pick up vegan carry-out while I'm out running errands, only to eat cold food at night after my daughter has fallen asleep.

"What's vegan?" Camilla asked.

"Vegan food doesn't have any animal products at all," Hanna said.

"So, no animals have to suffer for you to have your meal. Foie gras is one of the cruelest meat products there is. You seem like a good person. I'm sure you don't want animals to suffer just for you to enjoy a meal."

"Hmm." Camilla shrugged. "Whatever you eat or drink, I guarantee someone suffered. You know, many people come to the Summit Conference, but you seem different from most of them."

"How so?" *Oh, it all makes sense now. She wants a token minority friend she can tote around with her. If I could look her up online, I bet I would find a viral video of her on a racist rant. She'll probably want me to plug her on my Insta as my new BFF. "See, I don't hate Asians. You people love me. Now buy my books." Then she just needs to hire a Black friend and a Jewish friend.*

"Look around," Camilla said. "How would you describe the other people in this room?"

"They're all…" Hanna once again struggled to find the words to articulate herself. *Is there any other way to say this?* "White men who look like they're from another era."

The waitress returned with Camilla's sparkling water and Hanna's smoothie and water.

"You got it," Camilla said. "I'm not the only woman on the Board. There are a few of us, but we're certainly outnumbered. It's a group of old white men and a few white women, all led by Abigor." Camilla sipped her water, leaned forward, and whispered, "He squashes any dissent. We're all mired in groupthink. Well, I've grown tired of how things are, but Abigor is very resistant to change. He's done an amazing job over the years, but I think it's time for a new era to begin. I want to replace Abigor as the leader of this organization and become the first woman chair of the Summit Conference."

Hanna took a sip of her smoothie. *This is delicious! Tastes like fresh, never frozen fruit. A girl could get used to this.* "That's good."

"Yes, it would be good to have a woman leader." Camilla straightened her neck and tilted her head up. "I'm so glad you agree with me." She put her fist in the air. "Girl power."

Hanna took another sip. *I meant the smoothie, but I'll just go with it.*

"Yup." *And she'll want to appoint me to some high-profile position with no real responsibility to prove she isn't racist. I hope that would lead to money for me and Alexis—and her doctors.*

Camilla leaned in closer. "I want you to help me. There aren't many people here I trust. They're all under Abigor's influence. As much as we disagree, he heeds my council on many small things. If I nominate you to the Board, he will almost certainly agree to put you there. He'll want to interview you first, though."

"Look, you seem really nice and all, but we only just met. Why would you confide in me like this? Why do you already trust me?" *Does she want someone she can blame if everything falls apart? "It wasn't me. That tricky oriental put me up to it. It was all her idea. Don't trust them Asians, Abigor. I never did. She pulled the wool over my eyes."*

"Have you spoken to Abigor yet?" Camilla asked.

"No."

Camilla let out a small laugh. "I'll arrange a meeting. Let me know how he treats you, and tell me if you think someone with such an antiquated worldview has any business leading an organization in this day and age. After one encounter, you may want to get rid of him even more than I do." Camilla turned her head. "Oh, the food is here."

The waitress placed their food on their table. Hanna sniffed the freshly roasted fruits and vegetables. It smelled like a cookout on a warm summer evening. She devoured her meal and savored every bite.

14

Squish. Squish.

Dripping wet, Damien Chernobog and Frank Dolan stood in the elevator. They shifted in their soggy shoes. Each shift made a squishing sound. There were many squishing sounds.

Damien shivered.

Jesus fucking Christ! I feel like I just took the polar bear plunge. I hate being cold and wet.

"What does all this shit mean, man?" Frank asked.

"I don't know," Damien muttered. "I don't fucking know. I want to dry off and wear fresh clothes and maybe drink a hot cup of tea. I can't think like this."

Ding.

Damien got off on his floor and went back to his hotel room. Frank followed.

"Don't you want to change in your own hotel room?" Damien asked.

"I don't know, man," Frank responded. "I feel like it's better to stick together and shit. Who knows what they'll do to us if we split up? Maybe they'll try to pick us off one by one."

"Whatever." Damien opened the closet door to select fresh

clothes. "What the hell is this?" He pulled a new tuxedo out. "I didn't pack this. This wasn't here when I left."

"Hey, man. Look at this shit." Frank grabbed a small rectangle of eggshell cardstock from the nightstand and read a message written in ornate golden calligraphy. "Abigor cordially invites you to the Summit Conference's Centennial Celebration. 7:00 p.m. Hotel Ballroom."

"Jesus fucking Christ! I can't think cold and wet. I'm going to take a hot shower and change into dry clothes." Damien hung the tuxedo back in the closet, grabbed some clothes, and went into the bathroom.

"Do you think I also have a card and tuxedo in my room, man?" Frank asked.

But Damien wasn't listening anymore. He stepped into a nice hot shower and let the steam clean his nose and open his pores.

This is nice.

He washed away the cold and the filth. He felt fresh. Damien exited the bathroom wearing a plain-white V-neck undershirt and blue and white striped boxers.

"Do you think we should go to the ball, man?" Frank asked.

"Yes, I do," Damien responded.

"Aren't you worried it might be a trap and shit?"

"Jesus fucking Christ! This entire hotel is a trap," Damien snapped. "But so what? The ghosts want us to go to the ballroom, so we should go. Maybe we'll learn how we can free them. I don't think we'll be able to leave here until we put the ghosts to rest."

Damien examined the tuxedo before putting on a gray suit that he brought from home. "I miss Bob, but we lost him because he was stupid and reckless." His voice trembled. "He tried to escape by climbing up—he didn't even try to climb down. He went up! And he thought he could get away without helping the ghosts with their unfinished business. If we work smart and stop trying to climb things, we'll be safe and out of here soon." He looked in the mirror and wiped tears away from his eyes. "We have to try. It's like Jesus said: You miss one hundred percent of the shots you don't take."

"Not wearing Abigor's suit?" Frank asked.

"I'd rather wear my own clothes."

"Okay, man. I'm with you. Let's go to the ball and see what's up. Whether it's ghosts or *The Matrix* or *Evil Dead*, we should get a step closer to figuring out a way out of here. But let's stop by my hotel room on the way down."

"Do you plan to wear one of Abigor's monkey suits?" Damien asked.

"Fuck that shit!" Frank said with indignation. "I just don't want to stay soaking wet, man."

15

Abigor twirled his scepter while studying Hanna Taithangklom.

She squirmed in her chair. She felt like she was being undressed with his eyes. But she knew he was rich and influential, and he could help her career.

He's not touching me. He's only looking at me while we talk, Hannah thought. *I shouldn't feel so violated, but I do. I feel like a bowl of food set before a starving wolf, and I'm just waiting to be eaten.*

Abigor directed his gaze towards her breasts. His eyes widened, and he twirled his scepter twice as fast.

This old man probably doesn't realize what he's doing. She gulped. *Or maybe he knows exactly what he's doing.*

"Why are you here?" Abigor asked.

"You invited me to your office," Hanna responded with trepidation. "You told me you want to discuss a business opportunity with me."

Abigor's office wasn't what Hanna expected. She envisioned ample open space and a large window with the skyscraper's impressive penthouse view. She expected a marble or granite desk with a leather reclining chair, a laptop, a giant monitor, and bottles of scotch and glass tumblers.

Instead, Abigor's office was a cozy space, barely larger than her hotel room. There were no windows. Bookshelves packed with old books and handwritten journals filled the entire wall from end to end like an antique library. A glass drink dispenser the size of two basketballs, filled with ice and green liquid, sat on a glass table with empty martini glasses on a shelf underneath. A phonograph played ragtime music from a small table near the wall—the tune sent a chill down Hanna's spine. Instead of a computer, an inkwell and quill sat on Abigor's desk next to an old-fashioned oil-burning lamp and a few framed photos that faced away from her. Abigor sat behind his desk in a simple wooden chair with a little leather padding. He wore strange clothes that she had never seen someone wear. Behind him was another door—opposite the door Hanna used to enter his office from the elevator. She assumed the door behind Abigor led to a more impressive room. Hanna sat on the other side of his desk in a wooden chair without padding, and another empty wooden chair sat beside her.

Abigor smiled, but that only made Hanna more uneasy. "Not here in my office, Ms. Tightclump. Why did you attend the Summit Conference? I watched you studiously take notes in some of the meeting sessions. What do you want in your career, in life?"

Ms. Tightclump... Is he even trying to pronounce Taithangklom? And he watched me? What a creeper. "I want to make enough money to provide a better life for my daughter. She's only three. I left her at home with my mother to attend this conference. I've been trying to grow my followers to get better sponsors. My growth has been slow but steady. My Insta, especially, is going to blow up at any minute. I noticed the Summit Conference doesn't have a social media presence. I could be a valuable asset and help you reach new attendees. I've only seen a handful of young people here. Do you know millennials now make up most of the workforce? And Gen Z is even more into social media. I can show you how to bring in—"

"Where is the girl's father?" Abigor asked, interrupting her.

The question always made Hanna sad. "He left—"

"Left you both. By Jove! Such a shame." Abigor cut her off before she could finish her sentence.

"No, he—"

"This problem happens a lot with women." Abigor interrupted her again. "It's normally caused by a foul-smelling Abraham's bosom. I'll get you some Lysol. You pour it on a towel and rub it on your Madge Howlet. Leave it for fifteen minutes. And then you rinse it off with cool water. Do this twice a day for a fortnight, and then the odor will be gone. Your quim will smell cleaner than a chub in a bath."

"No, he—" Hanna tried to talk again, only to get cut off once more.

"You'll thank me when you no longer have a foul odor between your legs that drives men away from your life, Ms. Tincancam," Abigor said with a smile.

What the hell!? Does he really think he's being helpful, or is he just fucking with me? What a disgusting old man! Either way, that's not how you talk to women—not how you talk to anyone—at least not these days. Is that how men used to talk to women in the office back in the sixties or whenever this fossil started his career? And he keeps mispronouncing my name. I doubt he could pronounce it right if he tried, but I feel like he's doing it on purpose. And why the hell does he keep cutting me off? He couldn't even let me finish a sentence when he wanted to speak! Left this world... Seth didn't walk out on us. Seth loved us. But he died, and he didn't have life insurance. He meant to get it, but he kept putting it off—always procrastinating until it was too late.

Hanna twisted her mouth into a strange shape. She could not force a smile. She was too shocked to close her mouth and too disgusted to relax her facial muscles.

Her bills had been piling up slowly. She said her social media was ready to blow up, but she had been saying that for months. Mother told her being an influencer was a waste of time because it didn't make real money and she needed to find a real job to provide for her daughter. Everyone in the world can't be an astronaut or a princess. When you have children, you need to give up on your dreams and make practical decisions. But Hanna was being realistic. She could make so much more as an influencer than she could in a regular job. Hanna just had to keep stretching her money until she reached the tipping point, and then the money would flow. Once she had enough followers, it would be easy to get bigger sponsors that would pay fat stacks of dough. The last job with a regular paycheck was as a cashier at an organic grocery coop, but it barely paid anything. By the time she left for the Summit Conference, she was already making more as an influencer than she did as a cashier, with most of the money coming from selling her used bathwater to perverts online.

But it still wasn't enough. The bills were stacking up. And with Alexis's medical problems—why does she need to see so many specialists that don't do dick to help—Hanna's financial situation was getting even worse. She closed out her savings account two months ago but still couldn't afford that one out-of-network doctor everyone seemed to rave about. She maxed-out credit card after credit card. Her system involved getting new credit cards with no interest and transferring her balance on the high-interest card there. But she did little to pay down any of the balances. Anytime she made progress paying one credit card down, others went higher and higher. Hanna had hundreds of thousands of dollars in credit card debt, and she wasn't sure if she could find another credit card to move her debt to again. *How many credit cards do I have?* She lost track, but she knew that her trip to Wyoming maxed out another card.

"Women's hygiene is a hobby of mine, Ms. Tutankhamun. But by Jove, I know you weren't expecting me to help you with that problem. It's still so strange to me to see women working outside of a kitchen or a schoolhouse, especially a colored woman like yourself. But I've always prided myself on being ahead of society. It doesn't matter to me if someone is a woman, a Negroid, or a Mongoloid—through total commitment and total devotion, we can all achieve the success we always wanted. Our wildest ambitions can become a reality." Abigor beamed as he spoke.

How much more boomer shit can I take? Are rich white people really so isolated from society that they are decades behind the times?

Hanna was so appalled by his ignorance that she could say nothing in return. She opened her mouth to speak, but no words came out. The only words Hanna could think to say were, *What the fuck is wrong with you?* But she dared not say this out loud because she knew the results would be disastrous.

"Camilla told me great things about you, Ms. Tintinclam," Abigor said. "I find her to be an excellent judge of character, and she has never once steered me wrong. She told me there is something special about you. You have a hunger, a desire, a willingness to do anything." He stopped twirling his scepter and placed it on the side of his desk. "Are you familiar with the Summit Conference's Board of Directors?"

Does this dirty old white man want me to bang him? A willingness to do anything—yuck!

"No, I can't say I am," Hanna responded.

"Well, I am the chairman of the Board, but I do not run the Summit Conference alone. I rely on a trusted group of inspired minds to help me. They make many decisions, but they're also willing to get their hands dirty. They are the people who operate in the shadows—helping the Summit Conference function as smoothly as well-oiled machinery. But make no mistake about it—this is not a democracy. Think of me as a pharaoh in ancient Egypt. I make the decisions that interest me, and I rely on the Board to take care of the rest. And in exchange for helping me, I help them."

Hanna squirmed in her seat again, and Abigor finally seemed to take notice.

"Do you know I buy five million copies of each of Camilla's books?" he said.

Hanna raised her eyebrows. "No," she responded. "I didn't. You buy five million copies?"

"Yes, that's why she's a best-selling author. Erotic mysticism. By Jove, it's all strange drivel to me. I read her business books, and they make sense. But I haven't been able to finish one of her romance novels. However, she is on the Board, and I reward those who help me." Abigor inspected Hanna's face. "What is your race? You look rather exotic. Was your father a Chinaman? Or did you grow up in a tropical mud hut on an island somewhere?"

What is wrong with this man?

"I grew up in New Jersey," Hanna answered. "But my parents are from Thailand."

"Thailand," Abigor said. "Never heard of it."

"It's in southeast Asia." *How old is this guy?* "Perhaps you know it as Siam?"

"Adzooks! Why didn't you say Siam in the first place?" Abigor smiled. "In all my years, I never met a real goo-goo rice eater before. Funny that people call you slant-eyed when your eyes don't look that slanty to me." He leaned over his desk and looked at her head from multiple angles. "Stay right here, Ms. Tinningham, and don't move."

He reached into his desk drawer and pulled out something large and metal, but Hanna couldn't see it clearly. In an instant, Abigor was behind her.

"Don't move," he repeated.

Hanna felt cold steel touch her scalp in two separate locations. The hairs on the back of her neck stood on end, and she pinched her shoulders together.

How did he move so fast? What's on my head? Is he going to kill me? Oh my god, he's going to kill me.

Hanna froze, and a tear ran down her cheek.

"Blackfriars! Oh, blackfriars! These are remarkable measurements," Abigor shouted in excitement, as if he had made an incredible scientific discovery. He moved again to stand before Hanna, and he held steel calipers in his hand. "Your cranium is quite large for a Mongoloid. Were I given these measurements and had not yet seen you, I'd have thought you were a Caucasoid."

Hanna wiped the tear away.

I ought to smack you, you racist motherfucker!

She wanted to scream, but she forced a weak smile and said, "Un-huh."

"Is it true that you moon-faces know sorcery?" Abigor took his seat again. "Because I could use a sorceress."

How ignorant is this guy? But maybe I can use his ignorance to my advantage...

"Of course, all Thai women know sorcery," Hanna answered. "Ever since I could walk and talk, my parents taught me about the secret dark arts of the far east. Before I became an influencer, I was training to be a sorceress."

"So, you must know some spells." Abigor's eyes widened, and he leaned forward.

"I know many magic spells." And then Hanna smugly recited the names of some spells from *Harry Potter*.

Abigor leaned back in his chair and tented his fingers. "Interesting. What do those spells do?"

I got him.

Hanna smiled. "You mentioned a seat on the Board. Would that make me a rich woman?"

Abigor put his hands down and smiled back. "You are a shrewd negotiator. Yes, you would be a wealthy woman. But you would have to make sacrifices. Name your price, and I will name mine."

Hanna said a number far larger than any reasonable person would pay her. And then she added, "Per year. A five percent raise every year. Healthcare. 401K. And plenty of sick and vacation days for me to spend time with my daughter. Also, all the food at the conference should be vegan from now on."

I'll finally be able to afford better specialists for Alexis.

"What's vegan?" Abigor raised his eyebrows. "I'm not familiar with that word."

"Vegan food doesn't contain any animals or animal products. That means no meat and no products such as animal milk or eggs. It's cruelty free."

"Miss Tinkle, cruelty is the best part of food preparation." Abigor licked his lips. "The more everyone suffers, the better the food tastes."

Hanna felt her skin run cold, and she gulped.

"The money is easy, but the other things are not possible. You won't see your daughter again."

Goodbye, credit card debt. Hello, bright new future for Alexis and me. Wait... What does he mean? I won't see my daughter anymore?

Hanna had heard about jobs that involved so much travel you practically lived out of your suitcase. If you were lucky, you got to spend a few days at home each month.

"That's a very enticing offer, but I have to see my child. Everything I do is for her. It's hard enough for me to be away from her this week. I can't wait to get home to her. I could never agree to spend so much time away from her."

Abigor frowned. "You don't seem to understand. Jumping Jehoshaphat! Did I make a mistake when I measured your cranium? You passed the point of no return some time ago. Leaving here is no longer an option. The only question that remains is how you will choose to spend the rest of your days. You can pay for a much better life for your daughter than you ever thought possible before—the finest schools and neighborhoods. I'll connect you to the greatest doctors in the country who can cure your daughter's medical problems. She can even attend school alongside white children. All I ask in return is total devotion."

"What do you mean I passed the point of no return? I suddenly want to leave this place, and I won't have sex with you." Hanna stood from her chair and defiantly looked Abigor square in the eye.

Abigor laughed and laughed. He laughed so hard he cried. "Sex? By Jove, Ms. Tintintin, I don't want to have sex with you." He wiped tears from his eyes as his laughter died down. "I feel quite flattered that a woman your age wants to jazz around with me, but that is not what I'm after. Especially not from a woman with an odorous petticoat."

"Then what do you want from me?" Hanna waved her arms in exasperation.

"Now you're asking the right questions," Abigor said. He opened a drawer in his desk and reached into it. "I have something to show you. You seem smart enough to agree to my deal. I'll give you more than enough to pay off your debts and cover Alexis's medical bills.

You'll be a real lally cooler—much better off than if Seth ever bothered to get a life insurance policy."

"How did you know about Seth?" Hanna asked. "I never told you his name or my daughter's. Earlier, you were... You were just toying with me, weren't you?"

"I know many things, Ms. Thailandcoup," Abigor answered with a smile.

"And your disgusting comments about Lysol and my..." Hannah was aghast. "Was that some kind of sick joke?"

"No," Abigor responded. "That was advice you should strongly consider. By Jove, I smelled you before you entered the room. Lysol will cure you of that odor. Here's some more advice. You shouldn't have paid for large hospital bills with a credit card. Hospital debt can be forgiven. Credit card companies are normally less forgiving, especially the ones that I own. But today, with a stroke of the pen, you can have $437,970.23 in debt disappear, which is how much you owe the dozen credit card companies I own. And you'll soon have enough money to pay off your other debtors."

Hanna was dumbstruck.

Abigor pulled a long sheet of paper from a desk drawer. It was the standard 8.5-inch width, but nearly three feet long and densely packed with handwritten text.

What kind of game is Abigor playing with me?

"What is that?" Hanna asked.

"A contract," Abigor answered with a huge smirk.

16

Lew Starek stood at the wooden podium, clicker in hand. His PowerPoint slideshow was on a screen nearby. The current slide showed his name and presentation title. Soon he would go through the entire deck, which had a few bullets on each slide over a generic template and a handful of pictures and charts he found online. The room was dark, other than the projector screen and a spotlight shone on him.

The audience was packed full of businessmen and business-women in business clothes. Expressionless faces stared straight ahead. All mouths were shut. All eyes were wide open, unblinking, and fixed on Lew.

I heard that people mainly brows their phones during presentations. Just my luck that I give my first big presentation at a conference when the Wi-Fi is out.

Lew adjusted his faded-black secondhand suit. He unbuttoned the single-breasted jacket, smoothed his sky-blue shirt, and tightened his thin tie, which was patterned with dark black and electric blue. He re-buttoned the jacket.

Pangs of nervousness and acid were aswarm in Lew's stomach. He reached into his jacket pocket and stuffed another couple of Tums into his mouth. He chewed rapidly and swallowed the tablets in one large gulp.

I wish I had a ginger ale.

Lew took a sip from a water bottle to wash it all down.

"In their 2012 article, 'Three Pillars of Public Leadership,' Dana Kellis and Bing Ran state that authentic values constitute an essential component of leadership," he said hesitantly into the microphone, "forming a bridge between discretion without which effective leadership is unlikely."

Lew gained confidence the more he spoke. His stomach settled. He felt more relaxed without a gun to his head and a dead body in the room.

"According to Edgar Schein's 2008 book, *Organizational Culture and Leadership*, a group can hold conflicting values that manifest themselves inconsistently while still maintaining a complete consensus on the underlying values." Lew smiled and made eye contact with audience members.

They're hanging on my every word. I'm totally nailing it. I bet I impress some executives.

Abigor stood in the back of the room, wearing a black single-breasted morning coat with a sloped front, black waistcoat, and long black trousers with French bottoms. He twirled his scepter and smiled as he watched Lew.

Is Abigor really a kingmaker? All the doors are about to open. Juliana will be so happy when I return home with multiple job offers. I'm going to buy a big-ass house with a yard—a yard that's big as fuck. I'm going to set up a jungle gym for baby Anika. All my money problems will soon be over. No, no. I'm getting much too far ahead of myself. Lew, keep both of your feet on the ground. Stay in the here and now. Focus on your presentation. Be in the moment.

Lew finished the rest of his presentation. "Thank you. Are there any questions?"

He stared into the audience. Nobody raised a hand. Nobody spoke. Nobody moved.

Why isn't anybody saying anything? Was my presentation so compre-

hensive that it answered every question that it raised? Or was everybody here so bored that they don't give a shit about what I had to say? Maybe they just want me to shut up and sit my ass—

Abigor tucked his scepter into his armpit and clapped loudly with both hands. Someone exited the room and opened the door behind Abigor. Light came in from the hallway, and he turned into a dark silhouette, which cast a long shadow into the meeting room. However, his profile was unmistakable, particularly the scepter. Abigor's shadow disconnected from his body and move towards Lew. Startled, Lew blinked twice to clear his eyes, and then Abigor's shadow looked normal once again.

Moving in unison, the audience stood and gave Lew a standing ovation.

I can't believe it. They loved it. They loved every fucking word of it.

Lew grinned from ear to ear while he soaked in the praise. He was so proud that he didn't even notice the applause came in a strange rhythmic wave. The entire audience clapped in sync, pulsing to the heartbeat of something sinister—something Lew was totally oblivious to.

He took a seat, and the next presenter, Alex Dabney, took the podium. Alex was a tall, broad-chested man with a three-piece plaid suit in shades of mustard yellow and ketchup red.

Lew's head was swimming from the standing ovation he received. He smiled so hard that it hurt. He was so engrossed in reliving his own presentation that he caught only bits and pieces of Alex saying: "... assertively visualize agile platforms...all hold hands and sing kumbaya...get too into the weeds...see the forest for the trees...appropriately seize highly efficient portals...synergistically utilize bleeding-edge data...."

Before Lew realized it, the entire audience was giving a standing ovation for Alex as well. Lew stood and clapped with everyone else.

This guy must have knocked it out of the park, just like me. What are the odds of this happening twice in a row?

Next was Colum Bell—a short, stout man with a thick black mustache. He wore a dark-blue suit with a two-button jacket, a light-blue dress shirt, and a striped tie with many shades of blue. He was followed by Jonas Chris—a tall fat man with short red hair, wearing a white dress shirt with a bright-red bowtie, black suspenders, and black trousers.

To Lew, Colum's and Jonas's presentations seemed to run together: "... can't spell success without U S...globally fabricate dynamic e-tailers...can't spell victory without T O R Y...phosfluorescently scale enterprise-wide materials...bend over and spell run, R U N...energistically orchestrate top-line strategic theme areas...oil me up and slap my bottom...holistically coordinate cutting-edge niches...can't achieve if you don't believe...monotonectally productivate robust growth strategies...thinkify the conglomerates...dress up like a clown and ask Santa for lingerie...strategically ideate phantasmagoric returns on investment...bite off more than you can chew...intrinsically restore holistic materials...more exciting than autoerotic asphyxiation...enthusiastically communicate cloud-centric e-commerce...this is very ASAP...seamless backward-compatible applications...by ASAP two Tuesdays from today...collaboratively fashion vertical methods of empowerment..."

Lew noticed a pattern. *What they said... It's nothing but generic business jargon mixed with a cacophony of bullshit.*

However, Colum and Jonas both received standing ovations.

I thought I had delivered such an excellent presentation, but these people in the audience seemed to give everyone a standing ovation. Did I impress anyone, or were they merely nice to me? Are most of the speakers in a session about organizational culture change really spewing nonsense? Did I retch as much bullshit as them? But then why did everyone clap for us? Is this like when the Down syndrome kid in high school won prom king? Are these pity claps?

When the session concluded, Lew walked out with his head hung low, trying to avoid eye contact with anyone. He nearly stumbled into Abigor, who was waiting for him in the hallway, standing and twirling his scepter while two hooded figures stood silently nearby.

"Lew, my boy," Abigor said. "That beats cockfighting. You have a rip snorting mind for business. Walk with me." He strolled down the hallway, twirling his cane.

Lew enthusiastically followed Abigor.

I was much too hard on myself earlier. My presentation wasn't bullshit. I was head and shoulders above the rest. I impressed Abigor. At least, I think I impressed him—his tone makes those words sound like compliments. Is this happening? Is the kingmaker going to make me rich?

Lew felt butterflies in his stomach. "I'm glad you enjoyed it. Organizational culture is really fascinating, particularly how organizations sometimes project one culture to outsiders through written material, like mission and vision statements, when in reality they—"

"Boy! That's hanging! Just hanging!" Abigor exclaimed, cutting Lew off. "No need to impress me any further, my dear boy. Catch on?" He flashed a big smile at Lew.

Is that good or bad? I've never heard hanging used like that before.

"Yeah," Lew said, unsure of how to respond.

"Cochunk, my boy!" Abigor said. "Then everything's just ducky! You swotted up on this—I can tell. I daresay I see a great deal of potential in you. I know you're on the make. That's why you're here, after all. That's why everyone's here, whether or not they know it. But fret not; I'm not here to mollycoddle you."

Is mollycoddle an old-timey club drug?

"Thank you," Lew said.

I think those were compliments. Did I give an apt response? Please let that have been an appropriate response.

Abigor smiled and pressed the button to call the elevator. "Would you care to join me in my office to talk about your future?"

Lew tried to keep a poker face while his mind was popping off to "Juicy" by The Notorious B.I.G. "Sure, I can take some time to chat." He struggled to suppress a smile.

Abigor took Lew and the two mysterious hooded figures to his office at the penthouse level of the hotel. Lew sat down in the guest chair, and the two hooded figures waited outside the door.

"Care for a drink?" Abigor offered to fill a martini glass from a dispenser filled with green liquid on a nearby table.

"Sure, whatever you're having," Lew replied.

Abigor filled a second tumbler and handed it to Lew, and then Abigor sat down behind his desk. Abigor took a long sip and then leaned back in his chair.

"Tell me, Lew," Abigor said, "what do you want?"

Lew took a sip of his drink. *That's bitter.* He nearly spat it out, but he swallowed it to be polite. "Hmm. This is interesting. What's in this?"

"It's a simple recipe—seltzer water, lime, and opium." Abigor took another sip of his drink and smiled. "But don't dodge the question, my boy. What do you want?"

Other than a beverage without opium? It tastes like shit.

Lew forced a smile. "It's pretty tasty. Well, Abigor, I think I offer a unique set of skills that would be useful to any organization. I'm well versed in all styles of project management and organizational structure, but I'm also very into data and analysis, particularly—"

"Lew, my boy," Abigor interjected. "I'm not asking you to describe your skills. I can tell you're well trained and well educated. You even learned to hide that hillbilly accent of yours fairly well." He smirked. "I have a nose for accents. Your native tongue only reveals itself with how you pronounce a few words. I'm asking you what you want. Think of me as your booster. I know how to help people achieve their dreams. Don't act like a pantywaist now. Spit out the truth. In all the world, what is the thing you want most?"

Oh no, I feel a little funny. That opium is some strong fucking shit. I barely had a sip. My entire life might change based on answering this question, but I can't think straight. Fuck!

Lew felt like he was floating. "I want to give my daughter a better childhood, a better life than I had."

I should have said something businessy. Should I shout ROI or agile now? He looks old. Maybe I should yell Reaganomics?

Lew grew nervous and had another sip of his drink as a reflex, forgetting it was opium until the bitter taste hit his tongue.

Abigor downed a big gulp of his drink and flashed a smile back at

Lew. "You're a real galoot and a family man. That's admirable. Many men your age are nothing more than mashers."

What is he talking about? Lew looked at the half-empty glass in his hand. *Oh, no! How much of this shit did I drink? I better put this thing down before I finish it.*

"Thank you." Lew tried to put his glass down on the edge of Abigor's desk, only to watch it fall and break on the floor.

Oh, fuck! Breaking glass during a job interview is one of those things you're definitely not supposed to do. Taking too much opium is another interview faux pas. I need to say something witty now to impress him.

"My bad, man. That looked expensive." *Perfectly smooth.* "I can buy you a new one."

Lew tried to pick up the broken pieces of glass off the floor, and he cut his finger. It was a minor cut, but blood trickled out.

"Leave the glass, my boy," Abigor said, relaxed and still happy. "You don't want to hurt yourself any further. Is everything Jake?"

Lew tried to lean back in his chair and fell onto the floor. "Yeah, man. I'm, like, totally fine. Ya feel me?"

Why do I sound like a mid-90s rapper?

"You drank a lot of opium for someone with no tolerance. How often do you visit dope joints?"

"Dope joints?" *What century is this guy from? And who offers someone opium during a job interview? Keep your shit together, Lew. Keep yourself together.* "This is the first and only time in my life I have ever seen opium."

Lew sat upright on the floor and then slumped over.

"I see," Abigor said to Lew. He turned and shouted a command towards the door. "Get in here."

The two hooded figures barged into the room.

"Clean up that mess," Abigor barked. "And give him a boost."

One of the hooded figures swept up the pieces of broken glass from the floor with a dustpan. The other surprised Lew with a syringe injection in his hip.

"Is this supposed to hurt?" Lew asked. "Because I don't feel a thing."

"Skedaddle," Abigor said.

The two hooded figures obeyed. They left and closed the door behind them.

Lew suddenly had more energy. His head still wasn't quite right, but he no longer felt like he was going to fall over.

I feel like I could run ten marathons right now.

He jumped to his feet and briskly paced back and forth. "I'm so sorry about the glass. I can assure you that I'm not normally so clumsy. And I'm not a user. I think you'll find I could be a valuable asset to any organization. I have a bad habit of sipping on anything in my hands when I get nervous. It's a nervous tick. I completely forgot the beverage I held had opium." Lew spoke as rapidly as an auctioneer on cocaine. "No more drugs for me. No, don't you worry. Nothing but water and caffeine. Hahaha! Hey, what was in that stuff the lady in the robe stuck me with? They're all ladies, right? Haha! I feel better than I have ever felt before."

"Think of it as a vitamin to help you focus so we can continue to talk about your future, my boy." Abigor walked from behind his desk and leaned on his scepter.

Lew continued to pace back and forth and rambled on like a junkie having a head rush. "Yeah, yeah, yeah, my future. I tell you, yeah, I can help you or anyone do anything you want. Reorganize to improve output. Bam! Examine supply chains to make throughput more efficient. Boom! I can help you maximize your efficiency. Kapow!"

I'm totally nailing this job interview. I feel like a trillion dollars.

Lew paced back and forth, moving faster and faster. He yelled Batman sound effects and karate chopped the air whenever he wanted to add emphasis. He even jumped onto the chair and hopped up and down. "The point is, I am very professional and very business oriented. If you need something done, I'll take care of it. Zpaf!"

"Spanking!" Abigor responded. "That's what I like to hear. You're not a grouser, and you're not goopy. You're someone who will do what I want when I want. Aren't you, my boy?"

"Yes, sir! As long as the price is right," Lew responded.

Abigor laughed and slapped his knee. "I like your ambition. Money isn't an issue for me, and I'm no welcher. I want you to work for me and join the Board of the Summit Conference. Name your price."

In Lew's head, The Notorious B.I.G. was back and rapping "Juicy" again to celebrate. The news was enough to sober Lew. He stared at Abigor in ecstatic disbelief. "Is this real? Is this a serious offer?"

Abigor sat behind his desk and put his scepter down. "Very serious. I'm the real McCoy. Work for me. I'll make you as rich as you want, as long as you do what I say."

Lew almost had tears in his eyes. "I... It's... This... I can't wait until I get home to Juliana and Anika to tell them the news."

"Lew, my boy," Abigor responded, his tone more serious. "That's one thing that can't happen. Unfortunately, you'll never go home to your wife or daughter."

"Oh," Lew responded with disappointment. "Is this one of those gigs where I spend most of the time on the road and barely any time at home? When do you need an answer? I need to talk to my wife about this when I get home before I could accept."

"No, my boy. You don't seem to understand. You can't skidoo out of here. You're going to remain in the Beburoa Hotel forever, whether or not you accept my job offer. You're long past the point of no return. You'll never get home to your wife or daughter. The only options before you are if you'll agree to work for me to enrich your family, who will receive as much money as you want them to have, or if you'll remain poor and give them nothing."

"How could I ever agree to such a thing?" *What kind of trick is this guy trying to pull on me?* "I'm sincerely flattered, but I reject both offers. I'm going home as soon as the conference is over."

Abigor muttered under his breath, "As soon as the conference is over. That's a tickle." He chuckled. "Take some time to think it over, but don't be a lunkhead. You'll find that my offer is your best chance to give your family a better life. You'll be loony if you turn me down."

17

Damien Chernobog felt dizzy, and he had pressure in his chest.

The horror! The horror! Jesus fucking Christ! This place is too much.

He didn't think Abigor was a ghost anymore. He thought he was something far, far worse.

The Summit Conference Centennial Celebration started much like the reception. Crowds of businesspeople mingled, and servers carried trays of food and drinks. The servers wore the crisp black and white outfits standard of caterers, and they covered their faces with ancient Incan masks of gold, which had ovoid holes cut out for the eyes. And long, radiant zig zags extended from the face like how sunbeams look after taking hallucinogens.

Damien and Frank were already terrified and unsure what to expect next.

"I can still hear Bob's screaming, and every time I close my eyes, I watch him fall," Damien said to himself when the duo entered the ballroom. "Is it a good idea to stay here and play Abigor's game? We've seen what happens when we try to get out."

"Do you think he's dead, man?" Frank asked. "We saw Bob fall and heard him scream, but we never heard him hit the ground and shit. Is he still falling? Will he ever stop?"

"I don't know. I just don't know." Damien hung his head and whispered, "Maybe we'll see him soon. If he died, he'd probably show up in the hotel as another ghost."

If he died. What if he never stops falling? What does it feel like to drop into a bottomless pit for all eternity? No, he won't fall for eternity. At some point, he'll die from starvation or dehydration.

"Well, let's fucking mingle, man," Frank said.

"Yeah." Damien perused the delectable smorgasbord that surrounded them—foie gras, pigs in a blanket, nacho cheese fountain, bacon-wrapped fried dates, deep-fried Oreos, cured ham, pizza, raw oysters on the half-shell, pulled pork sliders, cheeseburgers, shrimp po'boys, fried chicken, waffles, and freshly cut cheeses of every color and shape—but he didn't have an appetite for once. His stomach ached, and the pain was worse every time he thought of Bob.

The duo wandered the ballroom together, talking to people at random. Though all the attendees wore suits, their outfits varied to a degree—bell-bottom suits, flared lapels, thick ties, skinny ties, and bow ties. Nearly every conversation, however, was the same.

"Why are you here?" Frank or Damien would ask.

"I'm here to achieve greatness," the person would respond in a voice with a strange tone and cadence. "Through Abigor, we can achieve anything."

"Do you have any unfinished business?"

"Abigor will help me realize my full potential for business."

"What the fuck, man? What do you want out of this place? How do you get out of here?"

"Why would anyone ever want to leave the Summit Conference?"

Eventually, they grew exasperated and took a break on the side while drinking bottled water.

"Fuck this shit, man!" Frank exclaimed. "None of these assholes are helpful at all. They're like some broken programs or some shit, stuck in an endless loop."

"Jesus fucking Christ," Damien said in frustration. "I mean, I didn't think the ghosts would give us instructions about how to help them and leave. But I thought they would at least give us hints or something. They're like mindless zombies. Do ghosts have expiration dates? Because these bastards look long past theirs. They're completely useless."

"Okay, man," Frank said. "The talking-to-people strategy doesn't seem to work. Maybe we should explore the ballroom? What looks different about this place than the last time we were here?"

Not a bad idea. Damien closed his eyes, took a deep breath, opened his eyes, and scanned the room. *Groups of mindless moronic ghosts. Servers walking around in Incan masks, carrying food. Pyramids made of empty champagne coupes, which look like they'll be filled with champagne later. Something appears to be hidden behind the curtain on that balcony.*

"Frank, look at that." Damien pointed to the balcony. "Does anything about that look weird to you?"

"Yeah, man. Now you're onto something. If you look just under the curtain, you can see feet moving around on the floor and shit. Let's check it out."

Frank walked towards the balcony, and Damien followed. Although it was high above them, underneath, they could see the outline of a door on the ground level. It was the same color felt as the wall, and it could only be seen if you were near.

"Thank you, Jesus," Damien said as he reached for the doorknob. "Hmm. It's locked."

"Watch out, man. Let me try." Frank grabbed the knob with both hands, put one foot on the wall, and pulled. "Come on, man! Fucking come on!"

But no matter how hard Frank pulled and strained, the door didn't budge.

"Let's charge at it," Damien said.

"Shit yeah, man!" Frank responded. "Now we're talking."

The two backed up about ten feet and then ran towards the door like linebackers about to tackle someone. Frank, naturally, went faster.

BAM! BAM!

A pair of hooded figures knocked Damien and Frank to the ground.

"You idiots can't go up there," one hooded figure said in a gruff, masculine voice. "They locked the door for a reason."

"Hey, man!" Frank yelled. "How do we get out of this shithole?"

"You don't," the second hooded figure replied.

The lights dimmed, and a spotlight shone on the balcony.

"Try to get a good view," the first hooded figure said. The show is about to start."

Damien and Frank got to their feet and took a few steps back to better see the balcony. The curtain pulled back a little, and Abigor stepped out.

Jesus fucking Christ! I don't want to sit through another one of Abigor's mindless speeches. He's one of those guys who talks a lot without actually saying anything. Oh, hello. This is going in a new direction... What... What the fuck... What the fuck...

"Damien." Frank's voice trembled. "This is fucked up. Are we next? Are we next, man? What the fuck do we do, man?"

"It's like Jesus said," Damien said. "When everything else fails, run like hell or hide."

He ran away. His stomach turned in knots. Frank followed close behind.

The horror! The horror!

18

Hanna Taithangklom lay flat on her back on top of a large stone block. It was about the size of a refrigerator and cut from a single piece of marble. A relief carving decorated each side of the marble block, and they all depicted a version of hell in the style of Fra Angelico's *The Last Judgment*. Demons forced packs of naked, frightened people into fiery pits and pots. The damned faces showed anguish and pain as they stared above, hoping for God to come down and rescue them. Serpents ran over their bodies and around their necks. Demons wielded pokers to put the doomed souls into their places. Each relief featured a giant demon with a big mouth that ate hell's guests by the fistful—pieces of bodies and limbs dangled from the demon's lips. The top of the block had a large square section carved out—almost like a pool table—but the middle was slightly raised, and tiny grooves ran from the center to the sides. From there, holes along the inside disappeared into the table.

It looks like a drain, Hanna thought. *But what kind of table needs a drain? Does Abigor use this in the shower? Is his old body so feeble that he can't even stand in the shower?*

"Is the rope really necessary?" Hanna nodded towards the black rope that bound her.

A team of four hooded figures had tied each of Hanna's limbs to a hitch at a different corner of the table. None of the hooded figures spoke a word as they finished their knots. It seemed like a waste to wear her sleeveless pink floor-length evening gown with a high collar if she were to lay on her back in front of everyone. They had to hike the dress up to her shins to tie up each ankle, exposing her white high heels and revealing the silver anklet with an "A" she wore for Alexis. She felt like a Vitruvian woman.

When I walk, I look pretty stunning in this dress. I could turn heads. I feel like a fool.

"Yes, Ms. Hanna." Abigor twirled his scepter and paced back and forth. "Per your contract, you agreed to help me with my presentation."

"You still didn't explain the presentation to me. Don't we need to rehearse?" The rope hurt Hanna's wrists and ankles, which were turning red from the tight knots. "Hey, loosen the knots. This is just for show, right? You're cutting off my circulation."

"All I need you to do is act surprised," Abigor said. "The less you know about what will happen, the better."

Hanna was on a small balcony hidden behind a red velvet curtain. Darkness engulfed her. Bits of light trickled in from the sides of the curtain. Down below was the Summit Conference's Centennial Celebration. Everyone at the conference was in the ballroom. She could hear the faint sounds of many conversations happening at once.

I would much rather be down there, sipping on champagne and living the high life. But if I just help Abigor with his presentation, he'll give me a seat on the Board. And then I'll start my lucrative new career. Alexis will have the life I always wanted her to have. I'll pay for however many doctors it takes to cure her. Maybe I can even buy her way into an excellent school, just like a rich white person... No, what am I saying? She'll be able to get into an excellent school on her own. Alexis is smart; she can already speak and count in three languages. But it's good to know that I'll have the option.

"I should undertake the ceremony," Abigor said.

He left Hanna and then walked to the other side of the curtain. He addressed the crowd through a microphone, and his voice boomed from speakers all around the ballroom.

How long do I have to sit here like this before he does his stupid skit, or whatever the hell he has planned? I'm nothing more than a prop to him. And I feel like everyone at the conference is merely his plaything.

Suddenly, the hooded figures pulled the curtains away and put Hanna under a literal spotlight. She had to squint because it was so bright. She tried to put a hand over her eyes, but with bound arms and legs, she couldn't move a limb more than a couple of inches in any direction.

"When I look at you all tonight," Abigor's voice reverberated throughout the room, "I see the fromage of the business world. Each one of you is a high-stepping cookie. All others envy your brilliance. Tonight marks exactly one hundred years since I kicked off the Summit Conference. To commemorate the occasion, I have arranged a special treat. If you want to make a killing in business, you need to make sacrifices. Tonight, we will sacrifice this young woman—a Siamese sorceress with unholy powers." He handed his scepter to one of the hooded figures who gave him a dagger with a foot-long blade of gold and a hilt of ivory and engraved in an unknown language. "It's hog killing time!" Abigor added with glee.

Why the fuck does he have that big ass dagger?

Hanna writhed and tried to get off the table, but her bonds were too tight.

"Fight," Abigor whispered to Hanna. "We all want to see how much vigor you have. You are a very ambitious woman, especially for a slant eyed. You are about to see the price you pay to achieve the success you want."

"That's a prop knife, right?" Hanna whispered back.

Abigor pressed the flat side of the blade against Hanna's throat. It felt cold. She shuddered and turned her head away. He drifted the knife down from her throat to her chest, stopping at the collar of her dress. The point poked her and drew a single drop of blood.

Holy fucking shit! That's a real knife.

Hanna's eyes went wide. She wanted to scream, but the breath left her lungs. She watched helplessly. Abigor grabbed her collar with his left hand. With his right hand, he cut off her entire dress in one smooth motion. She was left wearing nothing but her pink and black lace bra and matching panties. Cold air nipped at her skin. Goosebumps crept across her flesh.

"Hey!" Hanna floundered. "You're taking this too far. I don't want to be part of your skit anymore. Untie me. You can't do this to a vegan! Let me out of here!"

"That's the ginger," Abigor whispered and licked his lips. "I know all about your and Camilla's plan to overthrow me. I want you to know that I will never be replaced."

"What the hell are you talking about?" *That fucking cunt was caught and tried to pin the whole thing on me.* "None of this was my idea. I never agreed to anything!"

One of the hooded figures came close and pulled her hood back. It was Camilla.

"I told Abigor that you tried to get me to go into cahoots with you to overthrow him," she said with a smile. "I told him all about how you called him an old misogynist and a racist."

She's enjoying this. God fucking damn her!

"You fucking bitch!" Hanna hollered. "You goddam liar! I never agreed to anything! Abigor, I never said I would help to overthrow you. I only agreed to meet you. None of this was my idea. It was all her idea. It wasn't my idea!"

"Oh, I know it wasn't your idea, Miss Taithangklom," Abigor said, perfectly pronouncing her name. "Because it was my idea. All of it."

He added a few sentences in Thai—only it didn't sound how a farang normally sounds when they try to speak Thai. The language has five distinct tones, each of which can change the meaning of a word. A farang will ignore or jumble the different tones when they speak, which often results in inadvertently speaking the wrong word or speaking complete gibberish. Abigor, however, had the perfect intonation and accent of a native Thai speaker. Hanna would have understood him if she knew more than some simple phrases that you use at the dinner table.

All Hanna could do in response was raise her eyebrows and say, "Huh?"

Abigor gently adjusted her chin with his hand to make eye contact. His hands were so cold they gave her frostbite. A shiver ran through Hanna's spine, and the smell of smoke filled her nostrils.

"You're such a disappointment to your mother," Abigor replied in English.

This was a goddam setup. I knew they were toying with me. Fucking damn them both! Damn them straight to hell!

Abigor slid his knife under her bra and cut through it in one swift motion that went straight through her underwire. The bra pieces fell to either side. Her breasts flopped out, perky and exposed. He stared at her bare breasts and licked his lips again.

"You're fucking crazy!" Hanna screamed. "Both of you. Cut this shit out! Let me out of here."

This motherfucker is going to... Oh my fucking God. I know what that look in a man's eyes means. Why isn't anybody trying to stop him? Why are they all just watching?

Abigor moved down to Hanna's panties. He inserted the knife from the top and slightly pulled at the elastic. She tried to pull her knees together. She shifted her hips away as far as she could with the limited range of motion that came with bound hands and feet.

Nononononononononononono! I can't let him... I can't let him...

Abigor sniffed the air and then pulled the knife back carefully without cutting her panties.

"I wish you would have used the Lysol," he said. "I'll leave this on."

Although Hanna's vulva remained covered, she still felt fully exposed. The ballroom was silent. Multiple videos of her naked body were being projected onto the walls around the room so everyone could see her.

Camilla gave a crooked smile. She was close and leaned her body over Hanna to inspect her.

I think she's close enough to...

Hanna kicked a leg. She couldn't move much, but she managed to knee Camilla in the face, smashing her nose. Camilla fell over backward and hit the floor. But she stood back up a moment later. Blood ran down her nose.

"No hard feelings, Hanna," Camilla said. "You might not believe me, but I do really like you."

"You fucking cunt-faced bitch! I'll get you for this, goddammit! And Abigor, you goddam fucking piece of shit dickhole! You fucking bastard! This isn't funny. Cut it out! Let me go! Fucking cut it out!" Hanna flailed. The ropes were tied tight. She couldn't break free. "Help! Help! Somebody help me! Help! Cut it out!"

Why isn't anybody helping? There are thousands of people here. Why isn't anybody helping?

"I will cut it out," Abigor said. "Right now."

He raised the golden knife over his head and plunged it down into her chest, close to her throat. Hanna bawled louder than she ever had before—louder than that time in seventh grade when she broke her arm playing soccer, louder than when she birthed her daughter, even louder than when her husband died. Abigor dug the knife deep. He sawed straight down to below her navel. He then made two horizontal cuts. The first was near the top of her chest. A second was below her navel. Abigor reached his hands inside her and pulled her body open like he was opening a cabinet to her organs.

With each knife movement, Hanna shrieked. She was still alive through all the cutting. Tears rolled down her cheeks. Blood spilled out of her mouth. She thought of Alexis and how she would never see her ever again. The will to fight and the ability to move slowly left her body. She gibbered.

Abigor reached into Hanna's chest. He pulled out her beating heart. Somehow, Hanna was still alive. He handed his knife to Camilla. She gave him an empty champagne coupe. He squeezed the blood from Hanna's still-beating heart into the coupe until it was nearly full. And then he carelessly flung her heart onto the floor below the balcony.

The world of the living faded away. Hanna slipped into nothingness. Her soul left the lifeless corpse that her body had become.

19

Lew unbuttoned his secondhand double-breasted teal-blue pinstripe Victory suit. The color popped when new, but the suit was old and faded now. He loosened his purple tie and then unbuttoned the collar on his white shirt. Lew pulled out a light purple microfiber cloth that was tucked into his breast pocket. It came free with the last pair of glasses he bought and matched this ensemble nicely. He used it to wipe spit away from his mouth. At first glance, you might think Lew could remove his thick black Clark Kent glasses and turn into Superman to save the day, but he didn't feel super at all. The acid in his stomach tossed like the ocean in a storm.

In through the nose...and out through the mouth...in through the nose... and out through the mouth. Calm down, Lew. Relax. It's time to keep a cool head. You need to keep it together. This is the big event at the Summit Conference. Everyone is watching. Don't do something else stupid to embarrass yourself. You know, these people are all about pageantry. Don't act surprised. Fit in!

On the balcony, and projected onto the screen throughout the ballroom, Abigor smiled with a champagne coupe in hand, filled to the brim with blood from a human heart. From the ceiling overhead, a large rectangular marble block lowered towards the table. It was the same type of marble as the table. The block was completely smooth on every side but the bottom, which had grooves that fit perfectly into the grooves on the table. Abigor waved his arm, and the block came down slowly and squished Hanna's body. It worked like a press squeezer, designed to squeeze every drop of blood from Hanna, like she was an orange, and he was making juice.

Lew watched tiny tubes underneath the balcony fill with blood as the block came down. He hadn't noticed before because they were clear, but an entire network of tiny tubes ran through the air, partially hiding behind balloons and decorations. Bright red blood now filled the tubes, which went over the entire ballroom, and then each tube emptied over a pyramid of champagne coupes. Blood gushed until each coupe was full.

"Everyone, grab a glass," Abigor said.

The servers promptly sprang into action to assist, filling their trays with these coupes of blood and then passing them to the attendees in the crowd.

What the fuck is happening? Lew wondered. *Should I run for... Oh no, that's how they got me last time. I was the first to freak out when someone was murdered. Not this time. I watched, and nobody else freaked out down here. I'm not falling for that bullshit again. If I run into Hanna later, I'll have to commend her on her performance. It was so realistic. I almost thought Abigor really murdered her. Almost.*

A server handed Lew a coupe, and he took it into his hands. He held it up to his nose and smelled it.

Smells like blood.

He tilted the coupe side to side, and he watched how the liquid moved.

It even looks like blood. How do they make it so realistic?

Abigor raised his coupe high in the air, and everyone in the ballroom raised their glass to him. "Here's to one hundred years of excellence. We all made this possible together. With your help, we can continue to grow the Summit Conference and rule the corporate world from the shadows. Let's feed our greed."

He put the coupe to his mouth and downed it in one gulp. A trickle of blood dripped down his chin and onto the floor.

Nearly all the attendees similarly downed their coupes at once. Lew awkwardly stared at the coupe in his hand. He looked around and watched the others drink, unsure if he had the nerve to drink his as well. Brendan was nearby and dressed just like Lew—only the fabric in Brendan's suit was a bright-teal blue, nothing old or faded about it. Brendan raised his coupe to Lew before taking a sip and placing the coupe on a nearby table.

I won't let that fucker see me fall apart again. I'm not a baby. I'm a goddam man. Lew put the coupe to his lips and took a small sip. *Strange, it even tastes like...*

"Why does this taste like blood?" Lew asked Brendan.

"Because it's not bottled sunshine," Brendan responded. "Have you finally learned to trust your senses?"

But where did they get the... No, they couldn't... It can't be... "This is pig's blood or cow's blood, right?"

"No, this is human blood," Brendan said matter-of-factly. "Only a little is from the girl up there, though. Abigor had to make sure everything would work perfectly for the big event. He even practiced with other attendees first. After squishing a few people, he realized he couldn't fill all the coupes with the blood of a single individual, so he had the block up there hollowed out so that it could store blood to be pumped throughout the ballroom at the proper time."

"Abigor really killed that girl to drink her blood?" Lew asked, hoping he had misunderstood.

"Counting the practice people," Brendan said, bored with the conversation, "Abigor killed and squished a couple of dozen attendees, including the girl up there, so everyone could drink their blood."

This is... No fucking way...

Acid reflux hit Lew in the stomach like a lightning strike that hits just before a downpour in a thunderstorm. He reached into his pocket for some Tums, but his hand tore through his homemade pockets. When he bought this suit secondhand, the pocket had a large rip. Lew replaced the pocket himself—sewing a new one out of an old white t-shirt. However, the t-shirt fabric was old and worn. The roll of Tums fell into the lining of his jacket.

What the fuck?

Lew took off his jacket and reached into the jacket lining, trying his best to locate the Tums.

Not now...not now...

His stomach was in such turmoil that he began sweating. His stomach felt tight, and it seemed like all his clothes were squeezing his body.

Lew vomited a little, but he kept it in his mouth. He looked at Brendan, who stared back at Lew judgingly.

Don't let this motherfucker see me squirm!

He walked briskly to the restroom—too embarrassed to run, too worried about throwing up all over himself to stroll.

Nobody was in the restroom when he entered, so he ran to the nearest sink and spit the puke out of his mouth. He took in a big gulp of air, and then he vomited his guts out. Stomach acid and chunks of food gushed out of his mouth, burning his throat on the way.

I think I feel better now, and...

Another rush of vomit spewed out of Lew into the sink. He puked and puked until his stomach was empty, and then he used water from the faucet to clean his mouth. The chunks of vomit were so thick it clogged the drain, so he had to move to another sink to continue to wash his mouth out.

What the fuck is going on? How could they really murder someone and drink her blood? No, how could they murder dozens of people and drink their blood? Why didn't anyone else seem surprised? I thought this was a professional conference! Do they murder all the attendees? Are they going to murder me next? I need to get the fuck out of here!

Lew stared at himself in the mirror—jacket off, tie covered in water and puke, water splashed on his face.

I look like shit.

Energy and frustration built up inside of him. He shook with emotion and closed his eyes.

Ten. Nine. Eight. Count down. Calm down. Seven. Six. Let the fear and anger leave your body. Five. Four. I am calm. Three. I am relaxed. Two. I am...

Lew opened his eyes and something in him snapped. He had puked out all his fear. Nothing was left but rage and an insatiable urge for violence. He wanted to find everyone responsible for murdering the attendees and for fucking with him so that he could beat the shit out of them. Lew let the rage flow. He screamed in anger, "Wu-Tang Clan ain't nothing to fuck with!" He hit the counter with his fists until it cracked.

FLUSH!

What was that?

Behind Lew was a row of five stalls. The partitions were royal-blue steel, and the doors were all shut. A toilet in one of the middle stalls suddenly flushed again. Lew turned around and looked for feet under the stalls, but he didn't see any.

Is someone hiding in here? Am I next? Do these people plan to murder me?

"Hello, is anyone there?"

Nobody answered, but Lew heard whispers from one of the middle stalls.

I'm next. They're going to get me next. Well, I won't sit around like a target.

Some people have a button on them—it's difficult to find, but when you find this button and press it just right, they become a machine with the singular focus of exacting violence on the world. They've sometimes been called berserkers. Lew was ready to go berserk.

"Helloooooooooo," Lew said as he approached the stall on the very left.

Bam!

Lew kicked in the door. The stall was empty. Focused and methodically, Lew moved one stall to the right.

"Oh no. You followed me in here. I'm so afraid," Lew barked in a gruff voice that could make your skin crawl.

Bam!

Lew kicked the next door open. This stall was empty as well. He moved one more stall to the right.

Bam!

Lew kicked the next door open. It was empty, too. But when the door swung in and banged against the right side of the stall, he heard someone yell from the next one.

Lew grinned from ear to ear as he squared himself up to open the next stall. "I guess there's nobody here. I'll just turn around and leave."

Lew moved his feet in place with a rhythm to sound like he was moving further and further away, and then he slowly came to a complete stop.

"Did he leave?" a voice from the stall said.

"Shhh!" another voice from the same stall whispered. "I didn't hear the door open; I think he's—"

Lew exploded in rage. He kicked the door so hard that it flew off the hinges and into two men who hid standing on a toilet. One man fell onto the floor. The door landed at an angle so that one end was on top of the man on the floor and the other end had the man on the toilet pressed against the back wall.

Lew wasted no time and jumped on the door, pinning both men. The one on the toilet tried to push the door off. Lew used the opportunity to beat his fists into the man's head. The man on the toilet tried to block Lew's punches and hit Lew back but to no avail. Lew peppered the man with a flurry of punches to the face, chest, and neck until he went limp. Lew slowed his pace and threw three hard punches directly into the man's head, each time causing his skull to bounce off the wall behind him, leaving a splatter of blood that looked like a Rorschach test.

Lew turned to find the man under the door was trying to squirm away. The man turned towards the restroom's exit, but he was still on his belly and pinned under the stall door. Lew jumped high in the air and landed on the man's head, stomping both of his feet down. The impact made a loud crack, and blood leaked out of the man's head.

I recognize these two from breakfast.

Lew scowled at the bodies of Damien Chernobog slumped backward over the toilet and Frank Dolan lying face down in a pool of his own blood.

He spat at them. "Motherfuckers! Tell your friends they'll get the same if they don't stay away from me. I'm getting the fuck out of here."

Lew didn't know if they heard him. He didn't care. It needed to be said. He grabbed his jacket from the sink and left the restroom.

20

D amien opened his eyes. He was lying backward on the toilet. His head and feet were on the floor. His back was arched, and his hips rested atop the toilet bowl. His head ached. Blood had run down his nose and mouth, staining his white shirt and gray suit. He felt the back of his head. Thick, sticky blood matted his hair together. He looked up to see cracked tiles on the bathroom wall surrounded by splattered blood—clues that told the tale of the ass-kicking he received.

Jesus fucking Christ! I thought that son of a bitch was going to kill me. He must have only knocked me out. Thank God.

Damien got to his feet with the speed and grace of a drunk fighting a hangover. He found Frank faced down on the bathroom floor in a large pool of his own blood.

"Frank! Frank!" Damien scrambled to get to his last surviving friend. "Are you okay?" He put his hand on Frank's shoulder and shook him, but Frank didn't respond. Damien shook harder. Tears welled in his eyes. "Frank, you can't die, too. Get up, Frank. Get up! Dear Jesus, please get up!"

"Five more minutes, man," Frank responded. "Let me sleep five more minutes, and then I'll get up."

"Thank you, God!" Damien exclaimed. "Frank, you're alive! Are you okay?"

Frank pushed himself to his knees with the slow speed of an old man trying yoga for the first time. He stood up. Blood soaked the front of his T-shirt and jeans, and it covered his face. Dry clumps of blood were stuck here and there in his long hair.

"Fuck, man. I think I feel okay. Just exhausted and shit. Is this all my blood? What happened? That was Lew, right? The guy we ran into at breakfast. Was he another one of the vampires, man? Do I have teeth marks on my neck? Did I get bit?" Frank pulled the collar of his T-shirt away from his neck while he felt for bite marks.

"Yeah, that was Lew," Damien responded. "Sweet Jesus! That son of a bitch looked crazy as hell. I don't see any bite marks. What about me? Do I have any?" He did the same with his shirt's collar and felt his own neck.

"I don't see any bite marks, man," Frank said. "Maybe that guy wasn't a vampire like the others."

"I think you're right," Damien said. "I saw him drink blood from a glass, so I thought he was one. But maybe he didn't think it was real?"

"Yeah, man. It could have been he thought it was fake and tasted the blood to find out if it was real. Like Bob, you know. He thought this shit was part of some crazy-ass prank TV show. Bob... Damn. Anyway, when I heard Lew puke, man, I thought he just drank too much blood and got sick. Like, you know, how when you drink too much alcohol, you puke. Maybe it's like the same for vampires. I bet it was he thought we were vampires, too, man. Trying to sneak up on him and drink his blood and shit." Frank walked to the sink and bent forward to wash blood out of his face and hair. "Hey, man, do you know how long we've been out?"

Damien checked his watch. It was smashed but still on his wrist. The hour hand was missing, but the minute hand was on the three. "No, no idea." Damien looked at the large pool of blood on the floor where Frank had been unconscious. "Are you sure you feel okay? You look like you lost a lot of blood."

"Yeah, man. I feel alright." Frank paused. "I mean, I feel like shit, but I'm not about to die or anything like that." He had washed most of the blood off his face, and he turned around and bent over backward to wash his hair in the sink. He used a lot of soap and worked up a good lather. "Weird, right? You see all that blood, man, and you think I should probably be dead or in a coma. But I feel only tired and groggy. I had a headache when I first woke up, but it already feels a lot better."

Damien sauntered over to the bathroom door and quietly opened it a crack. No lights were on in the ballroom. It was completely dark. "I think we've been out for a while. All the lights are out. I think everyone went to sleep."

Frank walked behind Damien and peeked out the door, too. Frank's wet hair dripped water on the floor. "You really think those vampires forgot about us, man? Or do you think they're out there, waiting, hiding? Trying to sneak up on us and shit?"

They pushed the door the rest of the way open. The light spilled out of the restroom onto the ballroom carpet. The room looked clean, pristine, and totally empty—not a table in sight, not a speck of dirt, not another person.

"Huh, maybe they did all go to sleep?" Damien said.

"So, what do we do now, man?" Frank asked.

A single light was on near the elevator. "Let's go up to our rooms," Damien said as he walked towards the elevator. "Now that we know we're up against vampires, we have to get ready to fight them. What did you bring that we can use against a vampire?"

"I have an acrylic bong, a couple vape pens, some edibles—"

"Anything with garlic?" Damien asked.

"No, man. Nothing with garlic. But I have a multi-tool. And I think the coat hangers in the room are wood. I could try to cut some of them up and turn them into stakes, you know, like in the movies. A stake in the heart kills a vampire, right?" Frank pressed the button to call the elevator.

"Yeah. That's great. We can stab a couple of these undead sons of bitches."

"What about you, Damien? What do you have that we can use to fight a vampire?"

Damien reached under his shirt and pulled up a crucifix necklace. It was a thin gold chain with a white ivory cross. "I have this crucifix. I think these things work on vampires. And I have some holy water. And a Bible."

"Where did you get holy water, man?"

"From the faucet back at our house. I filled a few little vials and blessed them myself, using one of Father Damien's prayers for everyday blessings." *I can probably bless all kinds of stuff and make it holy. That should help fuck up these undead beasts.*

"I don't know, man. That ain't real holy water. I'm pretty sure you have to be a priest or a holy man or something to make regular water all holy and shit." Frank shivered. His wet hair dripped onto his blood-soaked shirt. He crossed his arms and rubbed them together.

"Hey, a lot of my fans know me as Father Damien. I'm a holy man. I sell a lot of prayers and religious trinkets. Christ is behind me."

"Look, Damien, man. We get along well and all. But you're a con man who sells pseudo-religion to idiots on the internet. Your gimmicks might work on morons. But I, like, don't think it's going to stop a vampire. You're not a monk or a priest. You're not a real holy man, man."

"Oh, so just because I haven't been ordained by a bunch of child molesters and given magic robes and a special collar, it means that I can't bless shit? Jesus fucking Christ!" Damien worked himself up into a fervor. "Anybody can bless anything as long as you believe in it and pray. I ordained myself because I have just as much spiritual power as the Catholic Church or any other church. So do you! So does everyone! It's like Jesus said: Anyone who believeth in me has my powers and is a God among men."

"I guess we'll just have to wait and see, man," Frank responded calmly. Damien's emotional outburst didn't rile him up.

"Yeah, I guess we will." Damien calmed himself.

Ding!

The elevator arrived. The duo got on, and it took them up towards their rooms.

"Let's be on the lookout as we head back," Damien said. "I have a feeling the vampires went into a feeding frenzy after the reception."

"Yeah, man," Frank said. "For sure. I bet every floor on the hotel is full of blood and crazy-ass vampires and shit. They're probably covered in blood and banging each other and doing all kinds of weird ass evil shit."

Ding!

The elevator stopped at the lobby. The two guys tried to find a place to hide, but there was none in the elevator. Damien crouched down on the ground with his hands up. Frank put his hands up in a karate position to defend himself.

The elevator doors opened. They were greeted by a thin woman dressed in a loose gray Mickey Mouse T-shirt, blue sweatpants, and the old-school Adidas shoes that Run-DMC used to sport. She held a plastic bag with bottled water and chocolate milk from the hotel convenience store. She sipped from another small bottle of chocolate milk in her other hand.

"Good evening," she calmly said as she stepped onto the elevator and pressed the button for her floor.

Oh shit! This chick is going to kill us! Jesus, save me!

After the elevator doors closed, Damien and Frank held their positions for a few seconds. They waited for the woman to strike, but she ignored them and sipped her chocolate milk as the elevator went up. The guys hesitated for a beat before relaxing and dropping their guards.

Is she another guest like us? Did she miss everything? Maybe she doesn't know what's going on either. I should probably warn her.

"Did you guys enjoy the reception?" she asked. Her voice was relaxed and upbeat.

"Um," Damien said. He wanted to say something, but his mind couldn't find any words. His vocabulary was suddenly as empty as grocery store shelves after the panic buying that comes before a big storm.

"Not really, man," Frank said. "That shit was crazy."

"Yeah, it's not for everyone." The elevator stopped on her floor, and she exited. "I have to motor. Have a good night."

The elevator doors closed again. It resumed going up.

"What the fuck was that shit, man?" Frank exclaimed. "Did she… It's like she… So does she know about all the shit going down here, and, like, it doesn't even bother her?"

"Jesus fucking Christ! I wasn't expecting that at all. At first, I thought she would murder us and drink our blood. And then I thought they cluelessly trapped her here like us, so I was about to warn her. But yeah, it seems like she knows exactly what's happening and doesn't care. Holy hell! What's going on in this place?"

21

Hanna Taithangklom floated through the ether. She didn't have a body—no eyes to see, no ears to hear, no nose to smell, no tongue to taste, and no fingers to touch. Yet, there was a consciousness. A religious person would call it a soul, but Hanna didn't give it a name. She floated without control like a leaf being blown by the wind.

Is this it? Is my life over? What happens now? Will I be reincarnated? Or float along forever? I hope my mother will take good care of Alexis.

Hanna drifted from nothingness to nothingness, and then a world faded in around her. She found herself in a familiar room. A light-brown carpet covered the floor. A blue- and white-striped love seat sat against the wall. A window was open behind the couch, and it let in the bright sunlight that filled the room. And then Hanna watched herself enter the room—well, a younger version of herself holding a younger version of Alexis, who was only a year old. Alexis's body was much smaller, but her head was nearly the same size. She looked like an adorable baby bobble head.

This was the house Seth and I lived in together. Hanna tried to reach out and touch Alexis, but she couldn't. She still didn't have a body. She was an unseen observer, unable to interact with her surroundings, but with the freedom to move around within the space, like an invisible Hollywood cameraman.

Young Hanna sat down on the floor. She placed Alexis on her belly.

"Stand up, Alexis," Young Hanna said. "Stand up for mommy. Stand up." Young Hanna stood up and sat back down a few times in a row. "Look. Move just like mommy. You can do it."

Alexis tried to stand up on her own by moving her little arms up. But when the rest of her body didn't follow, she turned red and started screaming.

"Come on, Alexis. You can do it," Young Hanna said with encouragement. She grabbed Alexis's tiny hands and then helped her to stand up and sit down repeatedly as if she was doing cute baby squats. "Alexis, when are you ever going to stand? Or walk?" Young Hanna asked with worry.

"It might frustrate you now," Hanna said to her younger self, "but you should enjoy this time. In a few months, she'll run everywhere, and she'll get into everything."

But Young Hanna couldn't hear the advice of her older self.

The front door flew open. Seth, her husband, trudged in and slammed the door behind him. He wore his brown State Trooper's uniform and dark sunglasses.

"Dada! Dada!" Alexis called.

"Seth," Young Hanna asked with trepidation, "is everything alright?"

"Yeah, Han-chan," Seth answered with a raspy voice. He took off his sunglasses. His eyes were red and wet as if he had just been crying. He tried to hide it by wiping the tears away. "I'm just peachy."

Oh, no. I remember this day. I don't want to be here now. I don't want to see this again.

Hanna tried to close her eyes, but she had no eyelids. She tried to cover her eyes, but she had no hands. "I'm done here! I've seen enough. Let's move on to something else," she commanded to no one in particular, hoping someone would hear her and take her to re-experience a happier memory.

"Hi, Ale-chan." Seth picked up Alexis and kissed her on the cheek. He then pressed her little face against his and rubbed her baby cheek against his beard.

"Dada," Alexis said with a laugh and a tone that seemed to say *I'm too old for kisses on the cheek.*

"Daddy is always going to protect you, Ale-chan," Seth said with grave seriousness. "I'm never going to let anyone hurt you. Okay? I'll always keep you safe." He sat on the couch and placed Alexis on his lap.

"Seth," Young Hanna said. "Can you tell me what's going on? Or would you like a vegan cupcake to calm down?"

"No!" Hanna shouted at her younger self. "You don't want to hear this story. I don't want to hear this story."

"I had a rough fucking day," Seth said.

"Hey," Young Hanna said. "She can only say Momma and Dada now, but she'll start repeating other words soon. Do you really want her to walk around saying the f-word?"

"Fuck!" Seth exclaimed before covering his mouth in realization that he just did it again. "I'm sorry. It's just... It's just... Something real fu—something real bad happened today. Also, I was suspended."

"Suspended! What happened?" Young Hanna asked.

I'm not listening. Lalala. I'm not listening. Lalalala. Hanna tried to drown out the sound of the memory with her own yammering, but it didn't work. Every word was crystal clear.

"Okay. So, earlier today, I pulled someone over. It was a white pickup truck that was doing twenty over and swerving. I approached the car, and when I got to the driver, I saw..." Seth stopped talking and stared at Alexis. He rubbed her cheek and ran his fingers through her short, black hair. A pink hair clip fell out and onto the couch. He tried to clip it back on, but his fingers didn't cooperate. It kept slipping out of his hands. Eventually, he turned and threw it against the wall so hard that it shattered.

Alexis cried. Young Hanna picked her up. She sat down on the couch next to Seth and held their daughter.

"And then what happened?" Young Hanna asked.

"It was..." Seth looked like he was trying to talk but struggling to find the words. Whenever he was overcome by emotion while telling a story, he had a hard time pulling his mind out of his memory and turning the memory into words.

"What did you see when you looked in the car?" Young Hanna asked.

"I saw the sheriff," Seth said. "Only I didn't know it was the sheriff when I pulled him over. It wasn't a marked police car, but as soon as I saw his face, I knew who it was."

"So, the sheriff got mad that you gave him a ticket?" Young Hanna asked.

"No," Seth said, staring at the blank wall. "There's more. Inside the truck, there was a girl. She was a young thing with light brown hair—maybe about twelve. She had her hands and feet zip tied together. She was stark naked. Bruises covered her face and body, and she was crying.

"She looked right at me. I could see from her eyes just how scared she was. She said, 'Help me. Help me, please. Don't let him hurt me anymore.'

"So, I grabbed my gun and pointed it at the sheriff. I made him get out of the vehicle.

"'Do you know who I am?' he said to me in a condescending tone that let me know he thought I was a minor annoyance.

"And I said, 'Yeah, Sheriff Rickabaugh, I know who you are. Why is there a naked child tied up in your truck?'

"And he said, 'How 'bout you mind your own damned business, Taka—' He couldn't even pronounce Takagawa. He gave up halfway through and told me all yellow names sound the same. And then he told me that if I let him get back in his car and if I get back in my car, I wouldn't get in any more trouble. Can you believe that? The fucking —" Seth caught himself again. "Sorry, Ale-chan. The audacity of this guy. He kidnapped a girl, stripped her naked, tied her up, did God knows what else to her, called me a slur, and then... And then he tells me I won't get in any more trouble if I let him go?" Seth's voice grew louder and louder as he spoke. He stood up and started shouting.

"Like he wasn't the one breaking laws and harming a child. He's just such a..." The next few words seemed to evade him. He looked at Young Hanna, then at Alexis, and then at the wall again before getting exasperated.

Young Hanna put her hand on Seth's arm. "And then what happened?"

"So anyway," Seth continued, still standing. "I put him in handcuffs. I cut the girl out of her zip ties, and I gave her my jacket to cover herself. I radioed in for backup, an EMT, child services, the whole nine yards—and while we're waiting there and the sheriff is in cuffs, he keeps talking shit to me.

"'You're making a big mistake,' he says. 'We should have nuked you all instead of leaving any left. Now you dirty cockroaches come over here and ruin my country.' And he said more, too. I don't remember it all. And then he looked right at the girl and said, 'Let me have what's mine and fuck off.'

"And then the girl shook in fear and shouted, 'No! No! Don't let him touch me again!' And then she cried and cried—that kind of crying where someone is so scared, they don't know how to make the crying stop.

"And then I just lost it. I kicked the sheriff in the head—a rough kick with my heel that knocked teeth out and made him spit blood. And then I made him get up on his feet. And then I shot him in the dick five times.

"And of course, that's the time when the other units, EMT, child services, and everyone else shows up—just in time to see me shoot the unarmed, handcuffed sheriff in the dick. But what he... But what he..."

Unable to continue talking, Seth broke into tears. Sickened to her stomach and overwhelmed with empathy, Young Hanna cried. Alexis cried, even though she didn't understand the story. She cried because her parents cried. The family wept together.

If Hanna had eyes with tear ducts, she would have cried, too. Instead, she felt a great sorrow and a sinking feeling in the stomach she didn't have. As the crying continued, the world faded into something else.

Hanna was still a floating cameraman, and she was still in the living room at their old house. However, more time had passed. Alexis was two. She ran all around the living room. Young Hanna was a few months pregnant, showing only the slightest baby bump. Seth was in his state trooper uniform again, ready to leave for work.

Oh no! Not this memory. This is even worse than the last one. Not this fucking memory!

Seth picked up Alexis and kissed her on the cheek. "Be good for Mommy. Daddy will be home later."

"Okay, daddy!" Alexis said.

"See you later, Mommy," Seth said.

"Bye-bye," Young Hanna said. "Be safe out there."

"I always am." Seth left through the front door and walked towards his patrol car parked in the driveway.

Young Hanna and Alexis walked up to the door to wave goodbye to Seth.

Nonononononono! I don't want to be here anymore. I want to leave. I don't want to see this again. "Stop! Don't make me relive this shit!"

A light-blue, rusty sedan zoomed down the street and ran through their yard. The sedan hit Seth and then crashed into the patrol car. He was sandwiched between the two cars. He coughed blood.

Young Hanna screamed. Alexis screamed. Young Hanna opened the door to run to Seth, but he waved her away.

"Take Alexis in the house! Lock the door and call 911. Now! Go!" Seth shouted, with blood leaking out of his mouth.

The sedan door opened. A lanky man with a revolver exited the vehicle. Young Hanna ran inside and closed the door.

Hanna rushed at the man to stop him, but she was a spirit without a body. She could do nothing but watch.

"Fuck you, Takagawa!" the man bellowed. He drunkenly staggered and pointed a pistol directly at Seth's head.

Seth tried to grab his own gun, but it was pinched between the two cars.

"My daughter's dead. And it's all your fault, motherfucker!"

Noooooooooooooo!

From point blank range, the man shot Seth in the head over and over until the revolver was empty. And then he stood there, continuing to pull the trigger again and again while the revolver clicked hollowly.

I didn't want to see that. I didn't want to see that at all. Take me away! Take me away from this place!

"Who was that man who shot your husband?" Abigor's voice asked.

"Who said that?" Hanna said.

"Did you forget me already, Ms. Taithangklom?" Abigor's voice said. "Who was the man who shot your husband?"

"Abigor, you're here, too?" Hanna asked in annoyance. "Are you the Ghost of Christmas Past? Well, that's just peachy."

"I'm many places, Ms. Taithangklom. Now answer the question. Who was that man?"

"That was the father of the girl Seth rescued from the sheriff. His name is slipping my mind. I tried my best to forget about this, but I still remember too much. I hid inside, called 911, and watched from the window as he killed Seth. It's hard to forget something like that."

"But why did he kill Seth?"

"He was confused and overwhelmed with grief. He was a drunk. His wife obtained custody of their daughter after he divorced her. She got a new boyfriend who molested the girl, and then the girl ran away. Sheriff Rickabaugh found her, but instead of taking her home, he had his way with her. There was a rumor the sheriff was moving her to a more secure location where he didn't have to worry about her being found. There was another rumor he was going to sell her off to an interested party. He might have been going to kill her and hide the body. I don't know for sure. All I know is that he had evil plans for her. Seth saved her life...at least for a time. She died a few months later."

"How did she die?" Abigor asked.

"Sheriff Rickabaugh, the bastard, said he picked up the girl for hooking. He really said a twelve-year-old girl was out trying to turn tricks. The nerve of that guy. He said she was coming onto him, asking if he would let her go if she sucked him off. He said he had to tie her up to stop her sexual advances. That motherfucker! So anyway, she was convicted of prostitution and sentenced to a juvenile detention facility. She committed suicide while she was there."

"But why did the father kill Seth?"

"He had all his facts wrong. The sheriff spread misinformation to the press. He tried to get Seth fired, but Seth worked for the state, not the sheriff. The State Troopers didn't want to give Seth more than a slap on the wrist for castrating a child molester, but the sheriff tried to blame Seth for everything. The local news rag ate up the sheriff's version of the story. Sheriff Rickabaugh even won reelection. Apparently, he was quite involved in his church, and the congregation was very influential in the community."

"Gawdstruth," Abigor said. "Another question—Why does your husband have a different last name? Did you change your last name back to your maiden name after he died?"

"No," Hanna responded. "I never changed my name when I married."

"Well now, I'm skunked," Abigor said. "That's the wizziest thing I ever heard. There's something strange about your generation."

22

Lew Starek woke to the sound of baby Anika crying from another room—the high-pitched cry that instantly wakes any parent.

"Shhhhh," Juliana said to soothe their child.

It's good to be home. What time is it?

The clock read 4:00 a.m. What's wrong with Anika? Why isn't she here in the room with us?

Lew stretched his body, grabbed his glasses from the nightstand, and flipped the lamp on. He was still in his hotel.

Did I fall asleep? Am I dreaming again? What happened after I beat those guys in the bathroom? Everything went kind of fuzzy...and then...and then...

"Juliana?" Lew called. "Is everything okay?"

"No, I can't take her goddam crying anymore!" Juliana's voice boomed with the special tone of anger women reserve for their husbands. A faucet squeaked on, and a deluge of water rushed out.

Lew sat up in bed. Juliana and Anika were in the bathroom. The door was only open a crack. Anika screamed louder, a wordless shriek that Lew interpreted as, "I want my daddy."

Juliana sniped at the child. "You're such a little... I can't fucking take your shit anymore... I can't fucking take it."

Lew sprinted from the bed to the bathroom. He threw the door open and found Juliana sitting on the edge of the hotel bathtub with Anika in her arms. Juliana's hair was a mess. She wore a gray T-shirt and black pants covered with stains and baby puke. Anika wore nothing but a diaper, which overflowed with shit that ran down her legs. Tears filled her eyes and ran down her cute cheeks. Her little tuft of black hair was still adorable, even in this shit show of a scene. The hair on the back of Lew's neck stood on end.

What's going on? Something doesn't seem right.

The tub was full of water. It overflowed onto the floor.

"Juliana, what's wrong?" Lew asked, in a soothing tone. He crept towards her and the baby. "Can I see baby Anika?"

"Why do you want to see her now?" Juliana turned away from Lew and put her body between him and Anika. "All she wants is Dada, Dada. But you're not here. You're never here. It's just her and me. And she fucking hates me. All she does is scream and shit and puke. I'm so fucking tired. And I feel like a goddam cow, between filling bottles with the breast pump and this little monster sucking the goddam life out of my tits. She has a tooth now, and it fucking hurts when she bites me!" Juliana's face turned red. She alternated back and forth between staring at the floor and staring daggers into Lew's eyes. "I can't take her fucking shit anymore. Why did you leave me with her for so fucking long?"

She would never do anything to... No, there's no way... She loves Anika too much. We both do.

"I'm here now." A tear ran down Lew's cheek. He reached to hug Juliana and Anika.

Juliana threw an elbow into Lew's ribs. It knocked the wind right out of him. He dropped to the wet bathroom floor.

"Fuck you, Lew." Juliana looked down at him. "You're a real piece of shit, you know that? You said you would always be there for us. But you left after only a few months. And you're never coming back.

Anika is such an ungrateful little bitch. She fucking hates me. She fucking hates everything about me. And I've grown sick of her, too."

She climbed onto the edge of the tub and lifted the baby high over her head. Anika yowled. Her high-pitched voice cut through the air like a knife.

No, Juliana! Not Anika! You would never do such a thing. She's your daughter! She's my daughter!

"Juliana," Lew pleaded. "No, don't! Didn't your mother help with the baby while I was gone?"

"My mother is a cunt, Lew." Juliana's arms shook with the baby over her head. "You know that. She drove me insane after two days, and I had to ask her to get the hell out. I couldn't take her criticizing every little thing I do anymore. Drove me up the fucking wall. Well, I shouldn't have needed her help for so long. You should have been here. You're nothing but a deadbeat dad with delusions of grandeur. Do you think you're going to become some fancy business bigshot with your MBA? I can't throw a stick in any direction without hitting someone who has one of those degrees. People like you are a dime a dozen. Do you think you're destined for greatness because of your ideas? You're just another asshole who left his family because he couldn't stand being a dad. You're a fucking piece of shit, and I hate you!"

"No, no, no, no, no! Juliana." Lew spoke in a soothing tone. He fought back a scream. Emotions swirled. He was unsure if he was about to faint from panic or explode into anger. Lew didn't know what to do, but he knew he didn't want to do anything to upset Juliana more, not when she held baby Anika like that. "I'm here now, Juliana. And I'm never leaving you or Anika again." He tried to get to his feet, but he slipped and fell on the slick bathroom floor. The bathroom tile hit his face like a punch. "I love you and baby Anika so much. The only reason I left was to get enough money to take care of us. I love you, Juliana. And I love Anika. And you love her, too. I'm here now. I'm back. And I'm never leaving again."

Juliana snarled her lip in disgust. "You're not here, Lew. Don't you understand? You're not here. You're not with us. And you're never coming back. I can't take it anymore!"

Anika cried harder. Tears streamed down her cheeks.

"I was gone only a couple of days. It wasn't even a week! You're overreacting. I'll be home in a few more days!"

"I'm overreacting?" Juliana stared at Lew, and her breathing grew heavy. "Don't talk down to me, you piece of shit. Days? You've been gone for months! Don't tell me I'm overreacting! I can't do this on my own. Goodbye, Lew. Forever. Burn in hell, motherfucker."

She jumped high into the air and repositioned her body into a swan dive into the tub, putting the baby down first.

"Nooo!" Lew screamed with so much force that it hurt his throat. He jumped to his feet and reached into the tub, but Juliana and Anika were nowhere to be seen. The tub was empty and still overflowing with water. "What the fuck is happening?" he shouted to nobody in particular. "What the fuck is happening? What the fuck is happening? What the fuck is happening?"

Lew reached for the faucet and turned off the water. He went into the tub to pull the plug out, hoping it would drain. But when he pulled the plug, blood gushed from the drain and mixed in with the water in the tub.

What is going on? Am I insane? Did I go crazy? Where did Juliana and Anika go? Am I still dreaming? Or was this a premonition? Is this a sign of things to come? Maybe this is a future that I can stop from happening.

"Juliana! Anika! I'm coming. I'm coming home!"

Lew trudged out of the bathroom, water and blood still flowing behind him and overflowing into the main part of his hotel room. He pulled out his computer to recheck the Wi-Fi while water and blood continued to rise, this mixture of liquid now at bed level.

Please work. Please, please, please. Baby Anika, I hope you're okay. Juliana, you would never really do anything to hurt Anika, right?

Unsurprisingly, the Wi-Fi was still down. He picked up the phone and dialed zero.

"Beburoa Hotel," Paul said. "How may I help you this morning?"

"How do I place an outside line? I need to call my wife."

"I'm sorry, Mr. Starek, but all lines are down at the moment."

"Alright. Have the valet bring my car around. I'm leaving now."

"I'm sorry again, Mr. Starek, but we—"

Lew hung up before Paul could say another word. The liquid from the bathroom was more blood than water now. There was so much that the bed floated. Lew's suitcase floated by. He grabbed and carried it with him to the closet. He opened the suitcase and stuffed his suits inside, some still on the hangers, others floating in the blood and water. He left one jacket out, and he put it on. Lew closed the suitcase and grabbed his shoes, which were floating by. The blood and water were up to his chest.

The door to exit the room didn't budge when he first grabbed it. So, he put one foot up on the wall and pulled back with a strain that flexed his muscles and caused his veins to bulge.

As easy as doing a one-handed deadlift.

Lew opened the door just enough to squeeze himself through the doorway. He spilled into the hallway, followed by a wave of water and blood. Then the pressure of the liquid slammed the door shut. He couldn't bring his suitcase through. He had only one dark-blue suit jacket, the soaking wet boxers and T-shirt he was wearing, and his shoes—but no socks.

Screw it. I'll buy new shit later. I'll get a job somewhere else doing something else. Even if I end up driving a bus or calling bingo games, it's got to be better than dealing with this mind fuck.

Lew left a trail of bloody footprints as he went to the elevator and down to the lobby. He called to Paul as he got close to the front door. "Just charge everything to my card." *Maybe one day, I'll be able to afford to pay the balance off.* "Is my car ready?"

"Mr. Starek," Paul said. "You can't leave."

"You don't understand," Lew said, without stopping his stride for the door. "It's an emergency. I have a bad feeling about something. I need to get home to check on my wife and daughter."

"Mr. Starek, you don't understand," Paul said sternly. "You cannot leave the hotel."

"Fuck it! I'll walk if I can't get my car. I'm leaving now." The view out of the glass revolving door was pitch black.

I guess I'm up before the sun. It will be a long walk, but I'll get back somehow.

Lew pushed the revolving door and made his way outside.

BOOM! CRACK!

Lew backtracked in a flash and jumped backward. He sprawled out on the lobby floor. Flames rushed into the hotel, booming and cracking over his head. Outside, fire burned in every direction. He went back into the hotel to escape the flames. Flames covered the glass on the revolving door.

"Holy shit!" Lew ran towards Paul. "Paul! The hotel is on fire. Is there another door? You have to pull the fire alarm and get everyone out before the hotel burns down! Is there another door? We're all going to die if we stay."

"Mr. Starek," Paul said. "I can assure you that the hotel won't burn down. You're not going to die today."

Lew felt someone tap his shoulder. He turned around to find a tall thin man with slicked-back brown hair. His name badge read Seymour Grenville.

"I was once like you." Seymour spoke in a monotone voice with a strange cadence. "I used to want to leave the hotel more than anything. But then Abigor helped me see the light. He helped me realize that the Summit Conference is the only place I want to be. He helped me realize my full potential and achieve more greatness than I ever thought possible. Abigor can help you, too. Didn't you read the rule book?" He handed the hefty rule book to Lew.

I didn't read the thing. I only want to get out of here. Will the rule book tell me how? Can it be all so simple?

Lew opened the rule book and flipped through pages randomly. He saw only one sentence printed over and over again. The only thing that changed from page to page was the size of the text and the font.

Lew read aloud, "There is no escape. There is no escape. There is no escape."

23

"Jesus fucking Christ, I'm tired." Damien looked in his empty coffee mug. "There's no more coffee?"

"No, man." Frank yawned. "We drank it all. All the tea, too. Do you want some weed?"

"Doesn't that stuff make you sleepy?" Damien rubbed his eyes.

"It makes some people sleepy, man." Frank yawned again. "Not everyone. I mean, yeah, I'm one of those people who get sleepy from weed, but, like, you might not be. Won't know unless you try."

Damien and Frank were sitting on the floor in Frank's hotel room. Frank leaned with his back against the bed, puffing on a vape pen and whittling away at wooden clothes hangers to make wooden stakes. The wooden hangers were brittle. Frank broke the first two hangers, accidentally shattering them into tiny pieces. By the third hanger, Frank learned how to separate the wood at the joints and then carefully carve away at the wood until it was sharp enough to pierce skin. He tested each stake on his fingertip, pressing just hard enough to draw a single drop of blood, which he sucked into his mouth as soon as it was visible.

"Do you know if vampires can smell blood, man? Are these bastards like great white sharks in the sea?" Frank asked.

"I don't know." Damien shrugged. *Like I'm a vampire expert...*

"I have some PanWow," Frank said.

"I don't want to have diarrhea when the vampires attack."

The clock read 4:56 a.m.

The vampires haven't attacked us yet. I only hope we'll be able to finish our preparations before they come. Maybe we can stand a chance. Just maybe.

Damien was sitting across from Frank with his back leaning against the wall. The bathroom door was just to his right. Damien had taken a sheet off the bed and ripped it into strips. He had also taken the wooden hanger pieces Frank couldn't turn into stakes and was using the strips of cloth to tie the broken hanger pieces into makeshift crucifixes—the Bible on his lap serving as his worktable.

"Frank, can I ask you something?" Damien said. *I'm not the best craftworker. All these crucifixes look like shit. Will these really stop vampires? Can you even tell they're crucifixes?*

"Do you want me to show you how to tie a knot, man?" Frank didn't raise his eyes. He was slow and deliberate with each stroke of his knife as he turned those hangers into weapons.

Are my knots really that bad?

Frank picked up one of Damien's finished crucifixes by the vertical piece, and the horizontal part slid onto the floor.

"Jesus fucking Christ," Damien mumbled. He picked up the pieces and began rebinding them. "No, about something else."

"Shoot."

"What do you think hell is like?" Damien tied two pieces of wood together with a strip of the bedsheet.

"Hell is other people." Frank began shaving down another wooden stake.

"What do you mean?"

Frank raised his head to look Damien in the eye. "Christians tell me to go to church and follow their interpretation of the Bible, and if I'm good, when I die, I go to a place where I'm surrounded by people like Jerry Falwell and Phyllis Schlafly. I can't think of a worse way to end up than surrounded by self-righteous, judgmental assholes like them, man. I bet you can't even get good weed where the Christians end up."

"That's the worst thing you can think of? Is it worse than being trapped in a hotel with vampires?"

"It's up there. I mean, yeah, man, the situation we're in now fucking sucks and shit, but at least I don't have some asshole preacher yelling at me about how bad my life choices are."

Damien shifted. *Asshole preacher? Jesus Christ! Does this bastard think I'm an asshole preacher?* "An asshole preacher like me?"

Frank laughed. "No, man. You're not a real preacher. I can tell you don't really believe in that stuff, man. I mean, that Bible on your lap that you like to carry with you, you've had it since I met you, and it looks brand new because you never open it and read. It's just a prop to you, but that's fine. It doesn't matter to me because I don't believe in that shit either, man."

"Well... I..." Damien was speechless. He wasn't sure why. "It's more than a prop. It's a symbol of the meaning of life."

"It's like Jean-Paul Sartre said, 'Life has no meaning... It's up to you to give it meaning, and value is nothing but the meaning that you choose.'"

"Is Jean-Paul the Haitian guy who lives down the street from us?"

"No, he's a famous French writer."

Damien took a beat to compose his thoughts. "Where did you learn that?"

"Princeton." Frank yawned.

"You went to Princeton?" Damien momentarily opened his eyes wide.

"Yeah, I went to a lot of colleges. Princeton, Harvard, Yale, MIT..."

"Wait—you went to so many Ivy League schools? How many degrees do you have?"

"Degrees? I don't have any degrees."

"What happened? Did you drop out?"

"No, I didn't enroll in any of those places. I used to go there to sell weed. Those rich kids will pay four- and five-times normal prices. I made a killing. There was a literature professor that liked to buy my stuff, too. I sold to him for regular prices, and he let me sit in some of his lectures in exchange. I learned about Sartre, Kafka, Nietzsche, and other writers. It was interesting stuff, man."

Damien laughed, and it turned into a yawn. "Went to Princeton to sell weed at a hell of a markup... You're just as much of a profiteer as I am."

Frank smiled. "Maybe that's why we get along. How about you, man? What do you think hell is like? Is this your hell?"

Damien examined his Bible. *It looks brand new even though it's five years old.* "The absence of pleasure."

"What do you mean, man? Like permanent lent?" Frank stretched his arms and blinked his eyes several times.

"Kind of." Damien yawned. "I used to envision hell like Dante's Inferno—all the fire and brimstone of an angry church sermon, being punished for the seven deadly sins in eternal torment. Jesus fucking Christ. It was enough to keep me in line when I was a kid. I lived in fear of committing the slightest sin, worried that would doom me to eternal damnation—a never-ending stint in a burning lake of fire, but as I grew older, I learned about the pleasures of life—food, drink, drugs, sex. Any attempt to abstain from pleasure for a long period turned into torture. It's like Jesus said, 'If it feels good, it's probably a sin.'"

"Hold the fuck up, man. You're a hedonist? Since when do you do drugs? You're always bitching about my pot."

"I don't touch marijuana—tried it before and just didn't like it. I grew way too paranoid. I enjoy stimulants from time to time—a little cocaine here, occasional amphetamines there. Sometimes I want more of a boost than I get from coffee or a little help to focus. PanWow gives me a quick burst of energy before sending me to the toilet. I normally drink apple juice out of a PanWow can for those videos now."

"Alright. Let's back up, man. Hell for you is abstaining from every sin and living like a goddam Mormon teenager and shit?"

"Yeah, plenty of people really need to get their fix. Junkies come in all shapes and forms. Not all addicts are hooked on booze and drugs. Some are hooked on fast food or soda. Bob was hooked on adrenaline."

"Bob, man. That was a fucking shame. I still hear him screaming sometimes. When it's quiet and shit. I know it's in my head, but it sounds like he's just around the corner."

"Holy fucking shit..." Damien yawned. "Yeah, that was scary. Hey, what if our hells were combined?"

"Eternal life as a celibate Mormon." Frank stared off into the distance. "Shit, man. It doesn't get any worse than that. Can't enjoy a blunt, a brew, or even a latte. I'd probably have to get up early to ride a bicycle and then eat nothing but carrots for lunch."

The sound of footsteps came from the hallway. Damien and Frank promptly stopped their conversation and waited with bated breath. Frank quietly picked up his wooden stakes—he had six. He held one in his right hand, drawn up, ready to stab at whoever came at him. He held the other five in his left hand. He stood up, moving slow as molasses in January, careful to not make a sound.

The footsteps came closer and closer, and then they stopped right outside the door. Damien shakily stood up. He clutched a Bible in his right hand and held a crudely made crucifix in his left hand. *I'll slap the motherfucking vampire with the word of God if he comes in here.*

Damien and Frank waited for their attacker to come at them. They were too afraid to move, lest they make noise and draw the attention of another vampire. But after a few minutes, the footsteps went further down the hall until they were so far away that Damien and Frank couldn't hear them walk anymore.

"Jesus fucking Christ!" Damien exclaimed in a whisper before he sat down on the floor again. "I thought a vampire was about to attack us."

"Shit, man," Frank whispered back as he sat down on the floor. "Me too."

They waited in silence for a few minutes, both on guard, until they grew tired once again.

"Hey, man." Frank yawned. "Do you feel sleepy?"

Damien responded with an enormous yawn. "Just a little."

"Okay, man." Frank yawned again. "I'm going to close my eyes for a few minutes to get some rest. Wake me up in fifteen minutes, tops, man."

"Sure, no problem," Damien responded.

Frank shut his eyes and leaned back against the bed. He was sound asleep in less than a minute.

Okay, I'm on guard. Stay awake in case vampires come. I feel sleepy, but it's only fifteen minutes. I can do it. Are my blinks getting longer than normal? Huh. I need to be careful. But taking a slightly longer blink won't...

24

Hanna Taithangklom continued to float through the ether until a new scene faded in around her. She was back at the house where she lived with her husband. She floated outside. A crescent moon and stars hung in the heavens. A beige Honda Civic sat parked where the patrol car once was.

"No! Not this! Not this either!" Hanna howled. "Take me away! Take me away! I don't deserve this! I'm a good person. I'm vegan."

Abigor did not respond.

Young Hanna exited the house with Alexis and walked to the car. Her stomach was bigger—six months pregnant now. Alexis was a little bigger, too. Young Hanna buckled Alexis into her car seat in the back. Before she could close the door, a man wearing a black ski mask and dressed in all black snuck up on her. He tasered her in the belly.

"You were hiding on the other side of the car, you motherfucker!" Hanna shouted, even though he couldn't hear.

Young Hanna wailed as she fell to the ground. Alexis cried.

"No! Stop!" Young Hanna positioned her arms around her belly in a protective gesture. "I'm pregnant."

The man proceeded to taser her in the belly again and again. She shrieked and then fell limp. The man kicked her stomach. He turned to Alexis crying in her car seat.

"No!" Young Hanna yelled. "Not her. Not her, too."

The man kicked Young Hanna's pregnant belly. "Fucking chink bitch! Drop your lawsuit and leave town or that one," he pointed the taser at Alexis, "will be next."

"Why are you doing this to us?"

"Nobody will investigate if you die. Do you understand that? But I hate digging. I don't want to dig two graves, even if one would be small. This way is easier for both of us. Drop the lawsuit and leave town, or I'll kill you and your only remaining child. Do you understand?"

Alexis cried harder.

"I said do you understand?" He held the taser near Alexis's face, and she had a seizure—her first, but not her last.

"Yes! Yes!" Young Hanna cried from the ground. "Please don't hurt her. I understand. I understand."

The world faded away until Hanna was once again floating through nothingness. Even though she didn't have eyes or tear ducts, Hanna somehow sobbed.

"Who was that man?" Abigor asked.

"I think he was one of Sheriff Rickabaugh's sons," Hanna answered. "But it could have been a nephew or cousin. He had a big family."

"And what lawsuit was he referring to?"

"I was suing Sheriff Rickabaugh for defaming Seth. He didn't have life insurance. I mean, what police officer with a wife and child doesn't have life insurance? I was running low on money, and I kept seeing Sheriff Rickabaugh in the news, calling Seth a pedo or a sex trafficker—even a satanist. The sheriff was a real motherfucker. I needed money, and I wanted to punish him. A lawsuit seemed like the best course of action."

"Up an alley!" Abigor exclaimed. "You should have just killed him."

"Not everyone can get away with murder," Hanna replied. "The sheriff had many powerful allies. I had none."

Abigor didn't reply.

"So, what happens next?" Hanna asked. "Do you show me the present or the future?"

Again, Abigor didn't reply.

"If you could have anything...," a new voice said. It was powerful and feminine but also shrill, like nails on a chalkboard. It would have made Hanna's skin crawl if she had skin.

"Who said that?" Hanna asked. "Who else is here?"

"If you could have anything," the voice resumed her question, "what would it be?"

"I just want Alexis to be safe, healthy, and happy," Hanna said.

"And what else?" the voice asked.

"Things are so peachy for me now that I don't think I'd change a thing," Hanna said with sarcasm. "I mean, I suppose I'd like to stop floating through a never-ending void for eternity and being forced to rewatch all the worst experiences of my life. What's next? Are you going to make me watch the time in elementary school I accidentally peed myself during show and tell?"

"What else do you want?" the voice asked.

"There's nothing," Hanna said.

"There's always something," the voice said. "What else do you want?"

"If I could have anything else?" Hanna asked.

"Anything."

Hanna revealed her deepest desires.

A beat passed without a response.

"Hello," Hanna called. "Are you still there?"

Hanna waited for a response, but none came. She continued to float through the ether.

25

Lew Starek was face to face with Abigor. *This is the man—if he is a man; maybe he's something supernatural, something cursed, or something unholy—this is the entity keeping me here. Why the fuck am I trying to reason with him? I saw what he did to that woman. What did she ever do to him? What will he do to me? I might not leave this room alive, but I must try for Juliana and Anika.*

Abigor sat behind his large wooden desk. He wore a black waistcoat, white shirt, and black tie. His morning coat was on a hanger nearby. He invited Lew to sit in the guest chair on the other side of his desk, but Lew didn't feel like sitting. Instead, he stood, still wearing a suit jacket over a wet T-shirt and wet boxers, with soggy shoes but no socks. Lew fidgeted. His wet clothes were uncomfortable and cold, but at least he was drying out.

Juliana had been crying more than usual since the baby was born. I thought it was just temporary because she was so tired. We were both so tired. Anika was constantly screaming and eating and shitting. And puking. Why does she puke so much?

Lew thought back to a night last month when he woke up to the sound of Anika crying.

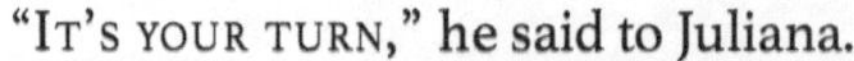

"IT'S YOUR TURN," he said to Juliana.

"Fuck Anika," she responded. "She fucking hates me."

Tired as he was, he sat up in bed and turned the light on.

It was her turn to take the baby, but I knew something was wrong.

Juliana sat wide awake, arms crossed, with a bitter scowl on her face. Tears welled in her eyes. "That thing fucking hates me. I don't want to be her mom anymore. You take care of her. I don't care. I'm done."

Lew picked up Anika from her bassinet. After checking her diaper, he shook up a quick bottle of instant formula and screwed a rubber nipple on it. He stuck it in Anika's mouth, and she started chugging. She was teeny and adorable. She put one of her little hands on her daddy's finger. His body filled with warmth and love. Her big dark eyes stared at Lew as she chugged her milk. Some people thought she looked like a little Juliana—others a little Lew.

She looks like the best of both of us. How can anyone be angry at a baby, especially one that looks like this?

"What are you talking about?" Lew asked. "Baby Anika loves you. Anika, don't you love your mom?" Lew walked around to Juliana's side of the bed with Anika in her arms. "Anika, you love Momma, right?" Lew changed his voice into a high falsetto to sound like a baby, "I sure do, Dada! I love Momma a lot!"

But Juliana turned away and pulled the pillow over her face. "I said I don't want to see her!" Her voice was filled with pain, and it cracked when she spoke.

Juliana was such a loving person. She never said anything bad about anyone. Not a bad word about my dad, who didn't come to our wedding or even call after Anika was born. No sour words for my boss, who fired me for leaving work early when Juliana was in labor. Juliana always told me that life is too short to hate. She hated no one. I was so lucky to find someone like her. I don't know how I did it, and I'm sure I don't deserve her. After all, how could she love trash like me? She was so loving.

But more than once when dealing with the baby, Juliana would spout off about how Anika hated her. Sometimes she even said she hated Anika.

"How can you hate a baby?" Lew asked.

He honestly didn't know. Juliana's bad feelings would eventually pass though. It was only a matter of time until she warmed up to Anika again. But sometimes, Juliana needed a lot of time. He once took care of Anika for two full days while Juliana ignored her. Juliana had spent most of those two days crying in bed.

I begged and begged her to talk to someone—to see a therapist, a psychiatrist, anyone. I did my best to help, but I don't understand psychology. All I did was type her symptoms into Google and follow suggestions I found online. She said she doesn't like to take medicine, so she didn't want to see a real psychiatrist. Not to mention she always said she didn't have enough time to see a shrink.

"You're enough help," she would say. "You're all I need."

BUT I'M NOT THERE NOW. *Why did I leave her alone when she needed me? I thought she would be safe with her mother, but I should have known that she would get sick of her mother and kick her out eventually. She couldn't even last a whole week? What the hell? How did I get into this situation? I should have never left for this trip. This entire conference is fucked. The only person who can get me out sits before me now, and he might kill me— and drink my blood.*

"I really need to leave here," Lew said. "My wife is... I have a bad feeling about... Are you familiar with postpartum depression?"

Does this monster have a soft spot? Will he let me out?

"It's nothing for a man to worry about, my boy," Abigor said. "A man's responsibility is to provide for his family, and that's why you're here. Depression and looniness are feminine problems. Women have a weak temperament. It's scientific. A little laudanum will normally do the trick to make a woman right again. Cocaine can also be a great help if laudanum doesn't work."

"Mr. Abigor—"

"Just Abigor, no need to add a mister, my boy."

"Abigor," Lew said, "I'm very worried about my wife and my daughter. I think my daughter is in danger. My wife has had a tough time since our baby was born, and I think that being away has only made things more difficult."

"Lew, a man shouldn't waste his time thinking about female things like raising a child. Their bodies are made to birth children and feed them. What can a man do? Does your chest produce milk? You gave your wife your seed, and nature did the rest. Now your responsibility is to provide them with scads of money to give them the best life possible." Abigor spoke with little emotion, like he was discussing something as mundane as what color socks to wear. "Worst case, your wife ends up in an asylum while you send your daughter to a fancy boarding school. The problem will be solved. That sounds hunky-dory to me."

This crazy fucker is old school as shit. Is there any convincing him?

"Is there even a way I can talk to my wife? The phone doesn't dial out, and there's no internet connection." Lew used a respectful tone. He was careful not to sound angry or demanding.

What kind of rage would I awaken if I shouted at this motherfucker? At least I'm not vomiting from acid reflux. My stomach is completely empty— I couldn't vomit if I wanted.

"Ah, now that is something I could help you with." Abigor smiled. "I can't let you leave, but you can get on the tube."

"Really?" Lew grabbed the wooden guest chair and sat down. He pulled the chair close to Abigor's desk. *Maybe he has some humanity.* "I would be very grateful."

"You remind me a lot of myself when I was younger, my boy," Abigor said. "I think you could one day take my place here when my time is done. I want to call you Son because I would like to think of you as a son. How does that sound to you?"

Take his place when he leaves? Thinks of me as a son? Is this man Satan himself? There must be perks, right? Maybe I could become that annoying rich kid who says, "Do you know who my dad is?" whenever he is seconds away from getting his ass kicked for being an asshole, but instead of

*having another bullshit lawyer for a father, I could name drop Satan.
That's got to scare the shit out of people.*

"My real father is a pretty big asshole," Lew said. "I don't think
you want to lump yourself into that company."

"Oh, I know all about Ernest Starek," Abigor said with a gleam in
his eye. "Ernest, who sometimes worked as a carpenter, sometimes a
coal miner. He was a barely functional alcoholic who blamed his son
so much for his wife's death that he refused to care for his son or take
him home from the hospital. Ernest's mother—your grandmother—
cared for you and raised you until you were twelve. You had only
occasional contact with your father until your grandmother died. You
often wondered why he agreed to take you back when he resented
you so much."

"How could you possibly know that?" Lew asked before all the air
left his lungs. He had to fight back the tears as he thought about how
much his world changed after his grandmother died. She loved Lew
so much. Grandma sent him to a Catholic school because she didn't
think the public schools in the area were good enough. She packed
him a lunch every day, and she took him to mass every Sunday. Lew
loved to have long conversations with her.

"I love you, Lew. You're my best friend," she told him many times.

Lew's dad never once said that he loved him. Earnest gave him
something like a hug on rare occasions, but it was more of a tap on
the shoulder. When Lew's grandmother died, he moved back in with
his dad. He had to switch to public school, and his dad never once
made him lunch. Ernest Starek mostly ignored his son. He provided
food and a place to sleep, and he bought Lew clothes until he was old
enough to get a part-time job and buy his own.

"I know many things, Son." Abigor smiled and leaned closer to
Lew. "I know that Ernest Starek used to be a cheerful man. He was
madly in love with your mother. Ernest had been saving up money to
buy land, and he wanted to build a house for your mother when he
could afford to. He was a carpenter, after all. But your mother's death
broke him. It crushed his spirit. He was never an alcoholic until you
were born. Every time he looked at you, he was reminded of your

mother. You look so much like her, you know. Ernest blamed you for everything. You caused his drinking and his continual sadness. He hated you since the day you were born. You ruined your father's life. I know you often wonder how anyone can hate a baby, but it happens more often than you think."

Lew felt a chill run up his spine, but he didn't think it came from his soggy shoes or bare legs.

He... How does Abigor know that? Can he read my thoughts right now? Eleven. I'm thinking of the number eleven. Abigor, what number am I thinking of? Tell me "Eleven" if you can read thoughts, motherfucker! Fuck! Fucking eleven! Fuck! Abigor, what fucking number am I thinking of? Eleven! Fucking eleven! Fucking eleven!

Lew stared daggers at Abigor as he repeated these thoughts in his head for several minutes. "What number?" He finally blurted out loud.

"What number?" Abigor said with raised eyebrows. "What are you talking about, Son?"

He can't read my mind. Then how does he know all those other things?

Abigor opened one of his desk drawers. He pulled out a long sheet of paper with densely packed calligraphy.

"What is that?" Lew asked.

"You want to talk to your wife and daughter?" Abigor said. "I can arrange that—if you sign my contract and agree to the terms and conditions. Reconsider my offer. I want you to work for me. Join the Board of the Summit Conference. You'll never see your wife and daughter in the flesh again, but you can communicate with them *if* you do what I want."

"How do I know you won't kill me like that woman last night?" Lew asked.

"You don't," Abigor responded. "But you know how rich I can make people. You've heard about how wealthy the attendees of this conference are. Send your family a scadoodle of money. Buy your wife a wet nurse, a nanny, and a maid. That should be enough to keep her out of the loony bin. If not, nothing will. Send your daughter to an excellent boarding school or a finishing school. She'll learn how to snag a rich husband and repeat the cycle. Even if she doesn't marry rich, it won't matter because she'll have as much money as you want her to have. Your family will never be in want or need again. And you'll be the provider, not your father-in-law. You can put your noodle to good use here and share your business knowledge. I want to root for you, and I want to be your booster. I can give you everything. But you must know that there is no escape from the Beburoa Hotel. While you're here, you're mine. Any attempt to skedaddle is futile. Everyone here obeys me. I have a way of changing the mind of those who don't like to listen. Catch on? Don't be a lunkhead. Many guests try to leave, but none do. One way or another, everyone falls in line."

"You tell me the sky's the limit, but I think it's really mo' money, mo' problems." Lew shifted uncomfortably in his soggy shoes. *This is fucking insane.* "I won't give up so easily. I want my family to have a good life, but I want to be there for it. I won't pick one or the other."

"Those are not your options, Son!" Abigor stood up and raised his voice. "Your choices are to make your family rich or leave them poor. Either way, you're never leaving here."

Abigor is angry. What will he do when he's angry? I need to be very careful not to do anything to upset him more... "Fuck that! And fuck you, too, old man! I'm getting the fuck out of here, with or without your help."

Lew stormed out of Abigor's office and blew past the two hooded figures standing guard outside the door. "If you won't help me to get the fuck out of here, then stay the fuck out of my way! You can't fucking keep me here. Nothing can fucking keep me here!"

"You've got a dirty mouth when you're angry," Abigor roared at Lew from his office. "I'll give you a little more time to consider your options. I would hate to waste a mind like yours, but my patience is finite. You'll acquiesce, by choice or by force!"

26

Bob Willemsen woke up to the sound of a blaring alarm clock. He opened one eye and looked around. He was in bed in a hotel room—his room in the Beburoa Hotel. Bob sat up and opened both of his eyes. Drapes covered the window, and there was no broken glass on the floor. He moved to the drapes and pulled them back. The window was in one piece, not so much as a scratch. Eternal darkness stretched on forever outside.

What the fuck happened? How am I alive? I remember climbing... I remember Abigor crushing my legs... And I remember falling for... I'm not sure how long... It felt like hours...and then everything went black... Did I die? Or was it all just a dream?

Bob shut off the alarm: 6:00 a.m. He examined himself in the mirror. He looked just as handsome as ever with a bright-blue shirt, dark green climbing pants, and rock-climbing shoes. His chalk bag still hung around his waist. The parachute wasn't on his back, though. He rummaged through his suitcase, checking for his gear. The parachute was gone. The GoPro he strapped to his head before he climbed the hotel was gone, too.

Maybe I am dead. Bob looked around at the hotel room. *Is this hell? I didn't believe in heaven or hell... Was I wrong about that? Was I wrong about everything? Is all that Christian bullshit real? Do I spend eternity in eternal damnation now?*

"What the hell is going on?" he muttered aloud.

Bob went into the bathroom and turned the lights on. He removed his shirt to inspect his face and body in the mirror. *I'm a perfect Adonis.* He saw no signs of impact—not so much as a scratch anywhere. None of his bones felt broken from the giant Abigor statue or a hard landing. In fact, he felt perfectly fine.

Bob left his hotel room. The hallway was eerily quiet. Nobody else was around.

Is the hotel empty now? Is this my eternal punishment, being trapped in an abandoned hotel?

Bob took the elevator and went to Skinny's room. He still had the keycard, so he didn't have any trouble getting in.

Bob found Fatty and Skinny lying on the floor. Skinny had a multi-tool near his hand, and it looked like he had been carving wooden stakes out of clothes hangers. Meanwhile, Fatty had made a few crucifixes out of other pieces of the clothes hangers, which he tied together with strips of cloth made from a torn bedsheet. The crucifixes rested on his chest, along with a Bible. Blood was smeared on both Fatty's and Skinny's clothes.

Are they dead? Bob gently kicked Fatty, who snored so loudly it sounded like someone using a chainsaw on a tree. *Thank fuck! They're alive.* Bob nudged Fatty more with his foot. "Hey, wake up! Wake up!"

Fatty muttered in his sleep but didn't wake up.

"Fuck it!" Bob moved to Skinny and once again tried to gently nudge him with his foot. "Wake up!"

"Five more minutes," Skinny said sleepily and covered his eyes with his arm.

"Dammit. Wake up!" Bob slapped Skinny on his cheek. Skinny opened both of his eyes and looked at Bob. He shrieked so loud that it hurt Bob's ears.

"It's a fucking ghost! It's a fucking ghost! Oh, shit! Oh, shit!"

Fatty woke up and looked at Bob. Fatty wasted no time in freaking the fuck out, too. "Ghost! I knew you would come back to haunt us if you died here! Jesus Christ, Bob. You're a goddam ghost!"

"I'm not a ghost," Bob said without confidence. "Or am I? I'm not sure." He scratched his head.

"Get out of here, Ghost Bob!" Skinny stabbed Bob in the foot with one of his wooden stakes.

"Fucking hell!" Bob screamed. "That hurt, you son of a bitch!"

"Begone, unholy beast!" Fatty yelled as he pressed a crucifix onto Bob's back. "It's like Jesus said: Two sticks tied together can defeat evil spirits!"

"That fucking hurts!" Bob screamed.

"The crucifix is working?" Fatty asked, the pitch in his voice rising.

"No, you bastard! The mini spear the other bastard stabbed me with!" Bob pushed Fatty away with one hand, and he fell onto the floor.

"Maybe he's not a ghost," Skinny said. "Maybe he's a vampire, like the others, and the only way to know for sure is to stab him in the heart with a wooden stake." Skinny wound his hand up and prepared to stab Bob in the chest.

Quick as a flash, Bob threw a gut punch at Skinny, who fell to his knees and dropped the stake. Then Bob kicked Skinny in the chest, and the force sent him sprawling backward.

"Ouch!" The stake was still in Bob's foot, and it hurt like a bitch when he kicked Skinny. "I'm not here to hurt you assholes, so stop trying to kill me!" Bob sat down on the bed and tried to pull his right shoe off. It was stuck, held in place by the wooden stake. He gave it a tug, and it shot waves of pain up his leg and into his whole body. "Oh, you bastards! Why the hell did you guys attack me? I thought you would be happy to see me." He grabbed a firm hold of the wooden stake, prepared for pain, and yanked it fast with force. "Aaaaahhhhh!" Blood gushed from the wound.

"That's a lot of blood!" Fatty exclaimed. "I don't think ghosts bleed...or vampires."

"I told you I'm not a ghost!" Bob squirmed in pain. He took his shoe off, and more and more blood gushed out of his foot. Splinters were still stuck in the foot here and there. Bob touched a splinter, and another wave of pain rushed up his leg and through his body. "You assholes!"

"Oh, shit!" Skinny said. "I'm sorry, man. I thought you were a vampire coming to kill us, like the other vampires in the hotel." He grabbed the comforter from the bed and tried to wrap it around Bob's foot. "We have to put pressure on it to stop the bleeding."

Bob screamed in pain and pushed him away. "There are splinters from your shiv stuck in my foot! It hurts too much." *Did those guys say something about...* "Did you say vampires?"

Skinny grabbed his multi-tool and readied the tweezers. "Damien, bring the lamp over and point it at his foot. I need to pull the splinters out so that we can put pressure on it to stop the bleeding, man."

Fatty tried to pull the lamp over, but the cord was too short. "Bob, spin around on the bed. Put your foot near the lamp. Put your head over that way."

Bob moved his body to comply. Blood continued to gush out of his foot. It sloppily painted the bed a horrifying shade of red like a Jackson Pollock murder scene.

Skinny issued commands. "Damien, get some towels and water from the bathroom. Bob, try not to move. I think it's only two big splinters, so this should be quick." Skinny went to work and pulled the splinters out in quick precision, only a couple seconds each. Each fragment removed sent a sharp pain up Bob's leg. "Yeah, we found out the hotel is full of vampires, man. They murdered this girl last night, and everyone drank her blood and shit. It was fucking wild, man."

Fatty returned with a glass of water and towels from the bathroom. Skinny grabbed the water from Fatty's hands and poured it on Bob's foot to rinse the blood away.

"Okay, man," Skinny said. "Here's the deal. I got those two big splinters out, no problem."

"That's good," Bob said, his voice still straining from pain, but with a tinge of relief.

"But now that I cleaned the blood away, I found five more smaller splinters."

"You asshole! Why did you stab me first and then ask questions later?"

"Sorry, man. Try not to move, and I'll get the rest as quick as I can. Damien, get some more water, man." In just two seconds, Bob felt four jabs run through his foot, up his leg, and up his spine. After a few seconds of nothing, he felt another jab of pain. And then another. And then another.

"What the hell?" Bob yelled. "I thought there were only five splinters?"

"There are," Skinny replied. "But I'm having a hell of a time trying to grab the last one, man. Hold still and stop squirming and shit."

Bob closed his eyes, held his breath, and tried not to move. He focused his mind on happy thoughts. *I'm not trapped in a hotel. I'm outside. In the sun. With the wind in my hair. Sitting on top of a mountain. With Sasha. Feeling her soft skin on mine. Hearing her laugh. Her beautiful laugh. It's enough to put a smile on my face in any situation.* One last sharp spike of pain ran up Bob's leg. He felt cold water splash on his foot, and then it was wrapped in a towel. He opened his eyes.

"I got it, man," Skinny said. "Damien, grab the belt from the bathrobe in the closet. I'll use it to tie the towel in place."

Fatty returned with the belt and handed it to Skinny. "Bob, thank God you're back. We could really use your help fighting these vampires. And...how is it you're alive? Where did you go?"

Skinny fumbled to tie a knot with the soft fabric belt.

"Give it here," Bob grabbed the belt from Skinny. "I can tie a knot." As a rock climber, he easily tied a quick, but firm knot that held the towel around this foot. "You know, you're a lot handier than I realized. You made a pretty good shiv, and you even removed the splinters rather quickly."

"Yeah, man." Skinny smiled. "Well, don't be so surprised and shit. I'm a craftsman, man."

Bob smiled for the first time since he woke up. His foot still hurt like hell, but he wasn't worried about bleeding out anymore. He sat up in bed, dangling his good foot off the edge and propping his wounded foot up on a pillow. "I don't know how I'm alive. After the statue dropped me, I fell for a very long time. I lost track of time. The next thing I know, I wake up in bed at six in the morning. I came here to check on you guys. What the hell happened last night? You guys look like shit. You both have a lot of blood on you. Only some is mine. What's all this about vampires?"

"The hotel isn't full of ghosts," Fatty said. "It's not a hidden camera prank show. And it's not the Matrix. It's vampires. There are at least a few other humans here, but it's mostly vampires."

"That's why we're making stakes and crucifixes and shit," Skinny added. "To prepare to kill vampires, like in the movies. Did you ever watch any vampire movies, man?"

"Just *Blade*," Bob answered.

"I never saw that," Skinny said. "What's it about?"

"Wesley Snipes plays a vampire that kills other vampires with karate and a samurai sword."

"Oh, shit! That sounds dope, man," Skinny said. "If we make it out of here alive, I'm going to watch it."

"Bob, what did it look like when you were out there?" Fatty asked. "Was it a feeding frenzy? How did you get in here?"

"I didn't see anyone in the hallway or the elevator," Bob said. "The hotel looked fine. Not so much as a single drop of blood or piece of trash when I walked here from my room." He looked around the room. The drapes were shut here, too. "I kept the spare keycard when I switched rooms with Skinny, so I used that to get in. Why didn't you guys put the latch on if you were worried about vampires barging in?"

"Oh, shit, man," Skinny said. "I forgot the latch."

"Did you guys notice anything different about this room?" Bob asked as he limped towards the window.

"What do you mean?" Fatty asked.

"The TV is back, and so is the lamp." Bob pointed. "The chair, too. I don't see any broken glass anywhere." He pulled back the drapes, and the window was as good as new. "Our friend smashed up the window and threw all this stuff out, but everything is back to normal. This is weirder than the time a bird landed on me when I was climbing Tribe in Cadarese, Italy." He looked into the abyss outside the window.

"Oh yeah, man," Skinny said. "I guess I didn't notice."

How the fuck didn't he notice? "You didn't think this was weird either?" Bob turned around to face his friends. *They're lucky I made it back. How the hell could they survive without me?*

"Hey," Fatty answered. "I was busy making these crucifixes and... Goddamit. They all fell apart. What happened to my Bible?" He searched and found it under the bed. "Jesus fucking Christ! Look at this!"

Bob hobbled over. What he saw made his neck stiffen and pulse race. The Bible sizzled on the floor of the hotel room. Fatty picked it up, and the floor went back to normal. He put the Bible back down, and the floor sizzled once again.

"Let me see that," Bob said.

Fatty handed Bob the Bible, and he grabbed it in his hands. He flipped through it, and it looked like a regular Bible—printed words on pages, nothing special. He pressed it against the wall, and the wall sizzled, too. Bob took the Bible away, and he pressed his hand against the wall where it sizzled, but it felt like wallpaper over drywall. It didn't feel hot or even warm.

"What the hell?" Bob said.

"It's *Evil Dead*, man," Skinny chimed in. "We have a magic book that can defeat the evil and free us. Damien, just don't fuck up and misquote Jesus, or we're all doomed."

27

Hanna Taithangklom awoke in the soft warmth of a queen-size bed with fluffy white pillows and a full comforter. She felt cozy and well-rested as if she had just finished a nap on a lazy Sunday while Alexis was at Grandma's. Hanna gently stretched her body as she stirred from her peaceful slumber.

I'm... I'm alive, she thought. *How am I alive? Was it all a dream? Did they drug me? Did I hallucinate everything? No, it felt much too real. Everything felt...*

"Good morning. Would you like some tea?" Camilla sat on a wooden chair next to Hanna's bed, sipping from a white mug with the Beburoa Hotel logo. She wore a red button-up jacket blazer with large black buttons, a matching red pencil skirt, and red stiletto high heels. One leg crossed over the other, and her right leg bobbed up and down with the shoe hanging on by only the tips of her toes.

"Is this hell?" Hanna stared up at the ceiling. Then she turned and fixed her gaze on Camilla. "Where are we?"

"I know this isn't heaven," Camilla answered. "But I'm pretty sure we're not in hell. I'm not entirely sure where we are, to be honest with you."

"I thought I died." *I remember being tied down...and cut open... That goddam Abigor... And Camilla was fucking with me, too... Floating through traumatic memories... Abigor's voice...and another voice... Who was that mystery woman? It wasn't Camilla. Now I'm back in the damned Beburoa Hotel.*

"You died, but then you got better," Camilla said with a smirk. "How do you feel?"

"Peachy." Hanna sat straight up in bed and threw the covers off. She was wearing the same dress and high heels from last night, but, strangely enough, it was in one piece. There wasn't a single cut in the fabric. She pulled at the collar of her dress and stared down at her torso. She felt her chest and stomach, and her skin was smooth—not so much as a scratch, let alone a large scar from a dagger. "You fucking bitch! You set me up and tricked me into taking the fall for your stupid coup d'état! What's going on? How am I alive? Why did you do that to me? You and Abigor toyed with me, and he promised a seat on the Board."

A glass bottle of Lysol and a stack of washcloths waited for her on the nightstand. Hanna picked up the bottle and threw it in the trash.

"The board seat and salary are genuine. The pageantry," Camilla paused for a beat and waved her hand in a mocking gesture, "was all Abigor's idea. From the plot to overthrow him, to me telling you I told Abigor you were trying to overthrow him, right before he stabbed you with a dagger and pulled your heart out—all of it, from start to finish, was carefully scripted by Abigor." She stood up and moved to a coffee machine on the table. "I'll make you some tea. The English Breakfast is quite good." She flipped the device open and then went to the bathroom and filled an empty mug with water from the sink.

Last night swirled in Hanna's mind. "Why did he... Why would he do that to me? And why would you help him?" *How am I alive? Why am I wearing my dress from last night? Why isn't it cut? Why don't I have any scars? Why is this bitch being so nice to me now? Is this another trick? Did Abigor force me to relive painful memories, or was that a dream? Is Alexis okay? Will she really get everything Abigor promised?*

"Abigor enjoys toying with women." Camilla dumped water from the mug into the coffee machine. She hit a button to bring the water to a boil. "I mean, he enjoys toying with everyone, but what he does to women is on another level. He does the human sacrifice thing to every woman who joins the Board, myself included. It's similar every time, even though a little different. At mine, he stripped me naked and used a butcher's cleaver to cut off my hands and feet before chopping my head off. The blood drinking was a new thing with you. He thought it would be a fun way to celebrate the centennial. 'Champagne is so banal. I need to do something nobody will expect.' He's never once made such a ceremony about killing a man, though. Did you know he slaughtered a couple of dozen men before you to be sure there would be enough blood for everyone to drink? But he didn't make a show out of their murders." The coffee machine spat hot water out into the empty mug. Camilla opened a packet of English Breakfast tea and put it in the mug. She handed the tea to Hanna. "Careful, it's hot."

"People drank my blood?" Hanna asked, her heart rate slowing.

"I forgot. You were dead, so you didn't see," Camilla said. "Yes, the entire conference drank a cocktail of your blood and the blood of those couple dozen dead guys—only Abigor told everyone it was all your blood." She gave an empathetic smile, as if to apologize.

Hanna blew on the tea and then took a sip. *This is good.* "How can he do this to people? I'm going to sue the shit out of him when I get out of here! We have #metoo. Boomers can't get away with stuff like this anymore. Not to mention that I don't condone drinking my blood. It's not vegan, and I want to keep my blood in my body. But...I still don't understand how I'm alive. How the hell am I alive?"

Camilla tilted her head and looked at Hanna. "Oh sweetie, did you forget? You're never getting out of this damned place. Abigor can do anything he wants to anyone he wants. Consider yourself lucky that you're getting something out of the deal. He sometimes murders people without giving them anything in return."

"In return? So, the other people who die here come back to life, too?"

"Nobody who dies here stays dead for long." Camilla gave a slight smile.

I'm never getting out of here? Damn this bitch! "Why do you help him if he did that to you? Wouldn't you want to stop him from doing this to other people? How long has he been doing this?"

Camilla sat back down and crossed her legs again. "Everyone at the Summit Conference does what Abigor wants. If you don't obey him willingly, he'll turn you into a zombie. They're around everywhere. Most people who come to the hotel end up like that. Those of us who are smart join the Board. However, even some Board members go crazy and can't take it as the years drag on. This one Board member seemed totally used to everything for his first fifty years here, only to wake up one morning and realize he couldn't stand another second of this place. He tried to escape repeatedly, so Abigor wiped his mind. As bad as being murdered is, it has to be so much better than having your mind zonked out."

"But this is..." *None of this can be real. Nothing she's saying makes sense, but at least some of it has to be true. How am I alive?* "What is this place? How is Abigor so powerful? Why do people who die here come back to life?"

Camilla stood up and put her tea mug on the desk. "Why don't you wash up and get changed so that you don't look like an expensive whore anymore? Take time to collect yourself. I'll meet you at the elevator bay on your floor in an hour, and I'll give you a tour of the Beburoa Hotel and explain all the perks that come with being a Board member. Chin up. The worst is over. You're about to reap the rewards of last night's torture." She strolled out of Hanna's hotel room and gently closed the door behind her.

An hour later, Hanna met Camilla at the elevator.

"I like your outfit." Camilla gestured to Hanna's silver pantsuit, green blouse, and green pumps. "It makes you look professional." She handed Hanna a keycard. "Hang onto this. It will take you to any floor in the hotel, and it opens nearly every door, save a few that only Abigor can open."

"Why are you doing this?" Hanna asked. *Nearly every time I see this bitch, she is all smiles and acts like my best friend, but Camilla has already tricked me once. What is she planning to do to me next? How much worse will it be?*

"I told Abigor that I wanted to take you under my wing and show you the ropes." Camilla beamed. "Think of me as your mentor. Working ladies have to stick together, right? This conference is a man's world. Girl power!"

I don't trust this bitch one bit.

Camilla led Hanna on a tour of the Beburoa Hotel. Most of the tour was bland. A lot of meeting rooms on different levels that looked nearly identical. Hanna had trouble paying attention, and she hoped there wouldn't be a test later. However, one look at the Chuck turned her stomach in knots.

"Camilla, what they're doing to those people is... It's worse than what they do to animals, and I say that as a vegan." Hanna felt a sinking feeling in her stomach, and her knees grew weak.

"It's best to keep moving." Camilla gently pulled at Hanna's sleeve. "This place isn't for the squeamish. Keep your eyes down if you can't bear to look at them. Let it serve as another reminder of why we obey Abigor's every whim."

Hanna nodded and followed Camilla out of the room, trying her best not to look at anyone else.

These people are savages.

The last stop on the tour was Abigor's office. Hanna took her seat, and Abigor dismissed Camilla. An icy chill ran down Hanna's spine when Camilla left.

Would he have done something worse to me if Camilla and all those people weren't watching us? What's worse than being gutted like a fish and having your heart pulled out?

Hanna shifted in her seat and waited for Abigor to do or say something.

But Abigor was silent for several minutes. He sat behind his desk with a drink in his hand. A black morning coat hung on a hanger nearby. Abigor wore a white-collared shirt with a black necktie and a black waistcoat. His short gray hair was impeccably combed.

"Would you like a drink, Ms. Taithangklom?" Abigor asked,

finally breaking the silence and perfectly pronouncing her name. He gave a warm smile, which made Hanna feel dizzy.

Hanna shook her head *no*, but couldn't speak a word.

Is the room closing in on me? Are the lights suddenly dimmer?

Vivid memories of last night flashed in Hanna's mind's eye—cutting her clothes off, stabbing her body, the look on his face, and the cheer of the crowd.

I feel like I should run out of here before he does something else to me, but I can't seem to move my body. Did he have Camilla drug me? No, it's merely fear.

"Are you sure? I can offer you any beverage you would like—coffee, tea, juice, soda, cocaine?"

Hanna again shook her head *no* without squeaking out a single word.

"I have something for you," Abigor said.

BANG!

The noise was loud and sudden. Hanna shut her eyes and braced for the impact. She shook. She felt hot and cold, and she had trouble breathing.

"You can open your eyes, my dear," Abigor said in a soothing tone. "I have an arky desk, and some drawers stick—this one especially."

Hanna opened her eyes to see Abigor pulling an enormous book out of a drawer. He placed it on the desk between them. A golden dagger rested atop the book. Hanna's stomach sank once again, and she found herself catatonic. Her mind went blank as she stared at the dagger. Abigor opened the book, and the knife rolled towards Hanna and stopped just at the edge of the desk. The handle hung over the edge towards Hanna and the blade directly at Abigor.

This is my chance. I can grab the dagger, stab him, and get out of here.

Only Hanna didn't stab Abigor. She didn't even reach for the knife, even though Abigor left it there for nearly a minute. She didn't move at all and barely breathed.

"I really have to find a better place to keep that." Abigor grabbed the dagger and put it back in the desk drawer. "Why are you so jiggy, my dear?"

Hanna finally found the ability to speak. "I'm fine, but I need some answers. How am I still alive?"

Abigor opened the book and flipped through it to find a particular page. He spun the book around and pushed it in front of Hanna.

"I'll put you on, but then I need your help with something," Abigor said. "And I know you have the talent to make it real hanging."

28

ew Starek walked into his room unsure what he would find. When he left, it was wetter than one of Anika's used diapers, but when he returned, it was as dry as fresh linen. Everything was clean and in its place. Dry to the touch, his suits were hanging in the closet. He took off his soggy shoes and wet jacket, and he dried his feet by wiping them on the carpet, which was soft as cotton balls and void of even a stray speck of lint. It felt good against his bare wet feet, which had turned gray and started to prune from being soaked in water for so long.

What is going on here? Am I hallucinating? Or is there some kind of magic here? Abigor is the one behind all of this, right? He must be. But what is Abigor's game? Why does he want all of us here in this conference? And what the fuck is that bullshit about thinking of me as a son?

Lew picked up his mirror from the wall and threw it through the closed window. *I'm not messing with my Reflection right now.* Glass shattered everywhere. The mirror fell outside. Bits of broken glass fell onto the carpet. For the first time, he took a good look outside. *There's nothing there.*

"What the fuck?" Lew muttered as he stared into the black abyss outside of the Beburoa Hotel. He stuck his head out and looked around. He could see the outside of the hotel, but nothing else was visible. No sky. No ground. No mountains. No roads. Only darkness.

Lew walked into the bathroom where he earlier saw Juliana take a swan dive with their baby, but there was no water or blood to be found this time. It was dry, clean, and spotless. Fresh towels hung from the towel rack.

I need to get out of here. There must be another way than the front door... Should I try to climb out the window? No, I'm not a goddam lizard. Maybe there's a back door... Kitchens usually have their own entrance—a way to bring food in and out. I'll check the kitchen and see what I find.

Lew changed out of his soggy clothes and put on a new suit—a very dark-gray check two-piece. The jacket had two hip pockets and no outside breast pocket, and it had a single button, which formed a low V. The lining was falling apart, but Lew had added enough extra stitches to hold it on—at least he hoped. His trousers were loose around his knees and tapered as they reached the ankle, but Lew had hemmed the trousers when he bought it secondhand. He guessed the previous owner must have been close to seven feet tall because of how much he had to take in to make it fit. Underneath, he wore a navy-blue shirt with a solid dark-gray tie. Lew slicked back his hair before leaving his hotel room.

Clark Kent, when are you going to turn into Superman? Lois Lane needs your help, and so does Superbaby.

Lew went down to the Summit Conference's breakfast room and filled his plate. Pancakes. Waffles. Butter. Syrup. Bacon. Sausage. Biscuits.

I'm going to need all my energy if I'm going to bust out of here. Okay, I'll just have a half cup of coffee with lots of milk after I've downed some carbs and meat to settle my stomach, and then I'll have some apple juice and water after to wash it down.

"Mind if I sit here?" Lew asked three men who were eating at a table.

He regarded their name badges and attire. The first, Philip Caspian, wore a plain gray suit. His jacket was single-breasted with three buttons, none of which were fastened, revealing a short, wide bright green-and-orange-patterned tie over a simple white shirt. A pocket square with the same print as his tie was tucked into the single breast pocket.

Daryl Balder, the second, wore a baggy gray suit that looked like it had gone through the wash. The jacket had a long lapel with a single button and visible patch pockets—one on each hip and another on the breast. Daryl wore a long, skinny dark-gray tie adorned with a silver clip.

Adam Durans, the third man, wore a suit like Daryl's, but instead of a solid gray, it was plaid and made from many shades of gray. Adam's tie was even skinnier than Daryl's and held in place with a gold tie clip.

"Please join us," Philip responded in a strange cadence typical of the many bizarre attendees here.

Lew bit into a biscuit.

Why is the food here so bland?

He checked his pocket, finding the salt grinder Bob gifted to him. He sprinkled some on his plate.

Why did that guy give me the salt? Was he somehow trying to fuck me, too? Or was he a helpless victim, trapped here like me?

Learn to observe and understand what is really happening before jumping to conclusions. Everything is not as it first appears. How many times today has your body and mind betrayed you?

Brendan's scolding still rang in Lew's ears. *What was that guy talking about? Have I jumped to conclusions too soon again? What am I missing? Three other men are seated at this table. Is there anything strange about these guys?*

Lew tried to focus his thoughts and stop his internal monologue long enough to better observe them. The men ate identical meals—eggs, bacon, and hash browns. They all seemed to be at the same point in their breakfast—halfway through the dish.

And are they... they are...

Each man cut his food, scooped it with his fork, and took a bite at the same time, as though they had rehearsed this in advance.

How many minutes have I sat here? Did nobody speak the entire time?

Their eyes were focused totally on their food.

But that can't be too unusual. I'm often so hungry in the mornings that I don't want to talk to anyone until I've eaten either.

"Hey guys, how long have you been at this conference?" Lew asked.

"I showed up the week after the Brooklyn Dodgers won the World Series," Philip said.

"As did I," said Daryl.

"Me too," said Adam.

"Brooklyn Dodgers? Aren't they in LA?" Lew asked.

"Ridiculous," said Philip. "Why would the Dodgers ever leave Brooklyn? Especially after winning the World Series."

"How many years ago was that?" Lew asked.

"Sixty-four years," Philip responded.

None of these men appeared to be geriatrics. They looked like they were in their early forties.

"You've been coming back to the hotel for sixty-four years?" Lew asked.

"No, I've been here at the Summit Conference the entire time. Why would we ever want to leave? Abigor runs the greatest conference the world has ever seen," Philip said.

"Abigor helps us achieve our full potential," said Daryl. "We are truly grateful for all he does for us."

"You should be thankful, as well, Lew," Adam said. "Abigor can give you everything you ever wanted. Nobody ever leaves the Beburoa Hotel because nobody wants to. Everything is perfect here, thanks to Abigor. This is paradise. Don't you want to stay in paradise forever with us?"

"I would rather go home to my family and relax while I listen to *Low End Theory.*" *How many people are under Abigor's spell? Is this what he meant when he told me I would obey him by choice or by force? I'll fall in line like Brendan or wind up a mindless zombie-like these poor bastards. Fuck that! I won't end up like them!*

That was when Lew noticed that the salt he sprinkled onto his plate and the table was causing both to sizzle. He scattered some more onto the table and watched it sizzle there, too.

That's weird—the absence of salt in all the food and the way the salt causes everything to sizzle. What's the extent of the relationship between the salt and this conference?

"If you'll excuse me, I need to run." Lew wiped his face with a napkin and left the table.

"There's no point in running, Lew," Philip said. "There's no escape. Embrace your new life. No need to grandstand. Stay on the beam. The Summit Conference is killer diller."

The breakfast buffet was up against a back wall in the meal room. Hot food, including pancakes and eggs, was in various chrome chafing dishes, with burning chafing fuel underneath to keep it warm. To the right of the buffet was a door to the kitchen, where two Beburoa Hotel servers ran back and forth, refilling the buffet. One was a tall man with a thick black mustache and black hair in a pompadour. The other was a thin blonde woman, hair pulled back in a ponytail.

Lew bided his time until the male server came through the door with a chafing pan full of home fries, and then he dashed through the door to sneak into the kitchen. He didn't see the woman.

I'm in. Now, where's a door to take me out of this hell hole?

The luxury of the Beburoa Hotel was largely absent here—the decorations were more utilitarian. Gray cement floors. Plain white walls. Off-white tile ceiling overhead. Lew tried to get his bearings— straight ahead was a dead end; to his right was a sink and a wall; behind him was the door to the dining area; and to his left, the hallway extended for twenty feet, ending at the staff water closet.

He turned left and moved down the hallway. A foot ahead of him, a black double swinging door was on the left side of the hallway. Another black double swinging door was on the left near the end of the hallway, just before the staff water closet.

Which door should I take—the first or the second?

The second swinging door opened, and the female server's ponytail poked out as she backed through the doors. He sprinted through the first to avoid being caught.

I hope she didn't see me.

Lew looked around again. Behind him was the swinging door. To his left was another dead end—the breakfast buffet was on the other side of the wall. Stainless steel counters and an industrial kitchen sink were straight ahead of him. To the right of the sink was a dishwashing machine. He turned right. A cart of food disappeared through the second set of swinging doors.

That was close. I must have just missed her. I should hurry.

Lew turned right and ran past the sink and dishwasher. Another swinging door was on his right. A wall was directly in front of him, and to his left was the main cooking area. He stepped into the kitchen. A grill, broiler, hot plates, hot range, and a convection oven were on the right. A large food prep area was to the left—two big tables with cutting boards, chopped vegetables and meat, and knives galore. Lew picked up a large meat cleaver.

Just in case.

Food was around in various stages of cooking, but it was unattended.

Who cooks this shit?

On the opposite side of the kitchen was another swinging door. Lew barged through.

This door led to another dead end, but there were three rooms with doors wide open—two on the right and one on the left. On the left was an office—desk, chair, an IBM computer from the '80s, shelves, filing cabinets, and menus. The room on the far right was the trash room. The space to Lew's immediate right was an industrial freezer. The chef stood inside holding a large box of bacon. He was a skinny white man with shaggy brown hair, a Baltimore Orioles' cap, and a white chef's coat.

Lew brandished his meat cleaver at the chef. "Why isn't there any salt in the food?"

"Lew, you're not supposed to be in the kitchen," the chef said in the same strange cadence as the other guests. "You belong out there, in the meeting rooms. Accept Abigor's deal so that you can realize your full potential."

"Fuck off!" Lew buried the meat cleaver in the man's head. The chef collapsed on the floor, dropping bacon everywhere. Blood gushed from the chef's skull. It covered his clothes, the bacon, and the floor. Lew pulled the meat cleaver back out. Blood coated the bottom of his shoes.

A barrage of footsteps came from the kitchen.

They're coming for me. Where do I go from here?

Lew moved to the trash room. A couple of large trash bags were on the floor, and there was a trash chute. He opened the chute and climbed in. The swinging doors opened, and three hooded figures came towards Lew. One grabbed his arm, but he chopped the figure's hand off. He threw the cleaver, burying it in the chest of another hooded figure. This gave just enough time to slide into the darkness of the trash chute.

Where does this thing go? To a dumpster outside the hotel, I hope. Anika, Juliana—Dada's coming home!

29

*W*ill *he really give us whatever we want if we impress him?* Damien Chernobog wondered.

Damien, Bob, and Frank had ventured through the hallways earlier that morning—prepared to slay any vampires that crossed their path but unprepared for what they would encounter. Frank had wooden stakes in each hand and more in his pockets. Bob was a hodgepodge of weak and strong—he limped and left a spotted trail of blood like a wounded fawn, but he gripped a wooden stake in one hand. Bob had an aura about him like he was a deadly assassin on a mission.

Jesus fucking Christ. I hope that blood doesn't draw vampires.

Damien was armed with his Bible. He touched it on the wall or floor from time to time, and the result was always the same. Whatever surface in the hotel he touched would sizzle. However, it didn't affect any of the gear they brought with them.

I wonder if... Let me find out...

"Harrah!" Damien yelled as he slapped Bob in the face with the Bible.

"What the hell was that for?" Bob barked in return as he rubbed his cheek. He tensed his muscles and then returned the favor by slapping Damien in his face.

"Ouch!" Damien shouted. His teeth hurt. "Jesus fucking Christ! You're strong." He rubbed his cheek with the Bible. "I was just testing something."

"Testing what, man?" Frank asked.

"The Bible," Damien said. "It does something to the hotel. You see it sizzle, right? But it doesn't do anything to us. Why is that? What does it mean? Jesus had a parable about someone who received a crap gift, but then it turned out to be a helpful tool for later on. How will this help us?"

"I don't know," Bob responded. "This place is crazy. I don't know what any of it means. I thought it was all special effects, but I don't know anymore. Maybe it is vampires and magic, like you guys said."

"Maybe this Bible is our ticket out of here, man," Frank said. "Somehow, we can use it to get out of the hotel. It's like the Necronomicon in the *Evil Dead* movies. We just need to say the right magic words and shit. Are there any good Bible verses about killing vampires?"

"There are tons," Damien responded. "After Jesus was resurrected, he killed five vampires before he peaced back to heaven. You just have to yell, 'The power of Christs compels you!' when you stab one."

What the hell is wrong with me?

The trio reached the elevator. Damien pressed the down button. "Let's go to the lobby, and we'll see if rubbing it on the door lets us out."

They boarded the empty elevator. Bob pressed the button for the lobby, but the elevator went up.

"Bob, did you hit a wrong button?" Damien asked. "We want to go to the lobby."

"No, I didn't." Bob pressed Lobby repeatedly while the others watched. "What the hell is this?"

"Don't worry, man." Frank pressed the buttons for other floors above them. "We'll just get out on the next floor and go back down." But none of those buttons worked either. "Try the Bible, man."

Damien felt suddenly dizzy and weak in the legs. He rubbed the Bible on all the buttons. *Maybe prayer will help.* "Our father, who art in heaven, Howard be thy name..." *Wait, how does the rest of that go?*

The elevator sizzled when the Bible touched it, but it kept going up until it stopped at the penthouse. The doors opened and stayed open, revealing Abigor casually twirling his golden scepter and standing ten feet away as if he'd been waiting for them.

"Jesus fucking Christ!" Damien exclaimed. His pulse pounded like a sledgehammer. "Let's get out of here."

The trio pressed Lobby and other floors below, but the elevator didn't move. They tried their keycards and rubbed the Bible on the elevator more, but other than sizzling, nothing happened.

"Good morning, Mr. Chernobog, Mr. Willemsen, and Mr. Dolan." Abigor stopped twirling his scepter. He was wearing another black suit that looked like it went out of style many decades ago.

"The power of Christ compels you to set us free!" Damien shouted as he opened a bottle of holy water and splashed it onto Abigor.

Annoyed, Abigor grabbed a handkerchief from his coat and used it to wipe the water off him. It had no apparent effect. "It's so nice of you to pay me a visit. Would you care to join me for breakfast?"

"I told you that shit wouldn't work, man," Frank said.

"Yeah, I feel pretty hungry," Damien responded, his stomach growling.

"What the hell are you doing?" Bob whispered to Damien. "We need to get out of here."

"He's going to eat us for breakfast, man," Frank whispered to them both. "This is going to be some shit, man."

I wasn't thinking about food, but now that he brought it up, I'm suddenly starving. I haven't eaten since yesterday.

"Being eaten alive is a chance I'm willing to take if it means I get a good breakfast, too," Damien whispered back.

"Don't think with your stomach, you stupid moron," Bob whispered back. "I'm going to end this right here and right now. I'll kill him, and we'll all be free. Trust me. I climbed Tsaranoro Massif in Madagascar."

Bob raised a stake up in an attack position. He lunged at Abigor and tried to drive the stake into Abigor's chest, like a spear fisherman stabbing a fish.

CRACK!

Abigor swung the head of his scepter into Bob's fist, shattering Bob's wooden stake and breaking Bob's hand in the process. Another quick THWACK struck the scepter into Bob's stomach and toppled him onto the floor.

How the hell did that old man move so fast?

"No point trying to attack me, Mr. Willamsen," Abigor said in an even tone, like he hadn't exerted himself in the slightest. "It's not worth a good goddam."

Bob sprung to his feet and tried to strike Abigor with his good hand, but Abigor gave him three quick whacks in the stomach with his scepter. The sound reverberated throughout the area. Bob fell over once again.

"Ow! Fuck!" Bob groaned from the floor.

"You'll be fine," Abigor said before turning to address Damien and Frank. "I mean none of you any harm. You won't be banged up unless you attack me. I don't want to sell you blind, and I don't want to do anyone in. I would enjoy your company for breakfast. You haven't shown up for your presentation yet, but I'm not in the mood to read you the riot act. I put you in another session at ten this morning. I can't wait to see what you have in store for me. Perhaps we could talk about what you have planned. If you impress me, I could help save your bacon."

"Did you say bacon?" Damien's stomach growled again.

"Yes, my boy," Abigor responded with a twinkle in his eye. "Come dine with me, and we can talk about your future. If you impress me during your session, I can help you buck the bull off a bridge."

Jesus fucking Christ! I'm so hungry. Does he have bacon or not? I'm confused.

"What the hell are you talking about, man?" Frank said. "I don't understand any of your jibber-jabber."

Abigor sighed. "If you three impress me during your presentation this morning, I'll give you anything you want."

"Anything?" Damien asked.

Will he really give us whatever we want if we impress him? This can't be true, can it?

"Yes, my boy," Abigor responded. "Anything."

Bob got up from the floor with a groan. "What kind of thing impresses you?"

"Gee!" Abigor shouted. "Now you're asking the right kind of questions, Mr. Willemsen. Join me, and we'll talk."

"Okay." Damien slipped the Bible into his suit jacket's hip pocket. "Let's eat."

Abigor led them to his private dining room. He had a simple but extensive rectangular dining table covered in white cloth. Eight tall black chairs were seated around the edge, three on either side and one on each end. Places were set for four—a glass with fruit cocktail on a doily with a fruit spoon sat atop a small plate, which sat upon a service plate. Going west from the dish was a salad fork, meat fork, fish fork, and folded cloth napkin with an embroidered picture of the Beburoa Hotel. A knife and bouillon spoon were east from the plate, and north from there was a doily with water and an empty glass. Going north from the dish was a fine china coffee cup. The spread of the table was grapefruit, codfish cakes, bacon muffins, sugar, black coffee, hard-boiled eggs, seltzer water, fried hominy, sliced peaches, raised biscuits, bacon, and maple syrup. All the dishware at the table was fine china with grisly, intricately painted scenes—coffee cup rims and plate perimeters featured demons shoving kings, priests, and common folk alike inside. The center of every plate and bottom of every coffee cup showed a giant devil in a boiling cauldron, smiling with glee as he ripped naked people to pieces and devoured their flesh. Blood dripped down his jaw and down his full belly.

Abigor sat in the middle chair on one side, and opposite him—from left to right—sat Bob, Damien, and Frank.

"Jesus fucking Christ," Damien muttered with a mouth full of bacon. "This is delicious." He had filled his plate with bacon muffins, eggs, fried hominy, raised biscuits, bacon, and maple syrup and wasted no time digging in.

Abigor smiled while he ate surprisingly little—grapefruit with sugar, black coffee, codfish cake, and seltzer water. "I'm quite pleased that you enjoy it."

Frank had taken grapefruit, peaches, a biscuit, and a piece of bacon. He lazily nibbled at his food without a care in the world.

"Do vampires eat grapefruit, man?" Frank whispered to Damien.

"I don't know," Damien whispered back. "I guess so."

Bob, meanwhile, cautiously ate bacon and sipped coffee while he watched Abigor, never taking his eyes off him for more than a second. Bob reached for his coffee cup with his right hand and winced. He silently switched to his left hand and drank.

"It will heal soon," Abigor said. "You'll notice your foot has fully healed by now. Drink some of this." He raised his glass of seltzer water for Bob to see before taking a sip. "It's an alleviator."

Bob touched his bloody bandaged foot and then raised his eyebrows. He moved his chair back from the table and pulled the bandages off.

"Jesus fucking Christ!" Damien exclaimed. "It's completely healed."

Bob examined and poked his foot. Damien was entirely right. It looked as good as new, like he had never been stabbed—and definitely not stabbed an hour ago. "I thought I was falling to my death last night, but now I'm alive. I thought my foot was severely wounded after I was attacked by my idiot friends, but it's healed now. My hand feels broken, but you tell me it will heal soon."

"It will," Abigor said.

"So, how is this possible?" Bob asked. "Why am I alive? Why are my wounds healing so fast? How are you doing this? Why are you doing this?"

"Let's not waste time with such tiddlywinking questions," Abigor responded. "You've always been so inquisitive, so curious to understand the world. Maybe that's why you spent so much time in libraries when you were younger, studying science and history."

"How do you know how much time I spent in the library?"

Abigor smirked and then took a sip of seltzer water.

"Yeah, man," Frank asked. "Like, how do you know that shit? Do you know about me, too?"

"I'm wise to a great many things." Abigor smiled and winked. "But don't waste your time trying to figure out how. Oh, I know all your numbers. Frank, I know that the first time you smoked pot was at your part-time job as a dishwasher in high school. And Damien, I know that despite your pious religious persona, you've been kicked out of two different sex parties for getting too rough with the girls when you couldn't achieve a cockstand."

Jesus fucking Christ! How did he... "That only happened because I accidentally did too much coke."

"I'm not interested in lamping your life." Abigor raised his glass. "Lap up the seltzer if you need a fix. It's loaded with cocaine."

Damien poured himself a glass and took a drink. Frank did the same.

"Hey, man," Frank said, "are you evil?"

"Good and evil." Abigor sipped his cocaine cocktail. "Morality. These are meaningless terms. Constructs invented by weak and inferior men to prevent great men from realizing their ambitions and achieving greatness. I can show you how to break free from the shackles of morality and reach a new pinnacle of success. It all starts with your presentation this morning."

"We're not businessmen," Bob said. "We don't normally give presentations."

"As social media influencers, you're all duffers," Abigor said. "You'll be naturals, especially on this topic."

"What's the topic, man?" Frank asked.

"How to be a social media star!" Abigor responded. "I'm absolutely buzzing in anticipation. Show the attendees of the Summit Conference how you manage to get round. It will be nanty narking."

30

*A*m *I going to fall forever?* Lew Starek wondered as he plummeted through the darkness of the trash chute. *Am I ever going to hit the—*

SLAM!

Lew crashed through a metal vent and then hit a wall. He fell to the floor like a sack of potatoes. It knocked the wind out of him.

Where am I?

He lay face down on the floor.

Am I finally outside?

Lew picked his head up, looked around, and then got to his feet.

No, no, no! This can't be!

Lew was back in his hotel room. The window was repaired, and the mirror was back on the wall.

"Motherfucker!" He took the mirror off the wall and threw it through the window again, shattering glass everywhere and revealing the never-ending abyss outside the hotel.

At least I don't have to deal with my Reflection again.

And then the TV turned on by itself. Reflection Lew stood in the lobby of the Beburoa Hotel, staring directly at Lew through the TV.

"You poor stupid fucking hillbilly," the Reflection said. "Did you really think you could defenestrate me so easily?"

"Fuck you!" Lew grabbed the TV and threw it out the window, too.

Cackling laughter erupted all around Lew. It was the voice of the Reflection but a higher pitch and coming from many places at once. He turned his head left and right but didn't see anyone.

"Where are you?" Lew looked around, unable to find anyone.

The laughter continued—a mocking response to Lew's question.

Lew looked down at the floor and then he jumped back. Hundreds of tiny, shattered pieces of glass were on the floor, and all of them contained a little Reflection of Lew that laughed at him. One by one, they climbed out of the broken glass and stood tall on the carpet. They ran at Lew like an army of fire ants attacking an enemy invader.

"You tiny little bastards!" Lew stomped on the incoming horde, like someone trying to stamp out a small fire.

Each squish under his shoe caused a batch of high-pitch squeals to erupt, but for every little Reflection he stomped, four jumped onto his feet and climbed up his legs. He shook his legs and feet and slapped at them, but there were just too many for Lew to fight off. In a minute, the miniature Reflections covered Lew. They scratched, pinched, and bit his skin. Pain worked its way up to his ankles and then up his calves. He jumped and hollered as he tried in vain to squish or shake them, only to hear the cackling laughter of hundreds of tiny attackers.

The miniatures had worked their way up to Lew's thighs as he sprinted to the bathroom and turned on the hot water in the tub. Most were on the outside of his clothes, working towards his face, but some were inside his pants. Steam rose from the tub as it filled with water.

"Get ready to burn and drown, you little bastards!"

Sharp lines of pain shot up and down Lew's body as he felt the miniatures attack his balls. He jumped into the tub without even taking off his suit or shoes, and he heard hundreds of high-pitched screams of pain as his feet went into the tub. But instead of hitting the bottom of the tub, Lew sank farther into the water. He looked up, and his entire body was submerged, even though he was vertical. He descended further and further into depths of an unknown body of water, and the surface grew more distant by the second. The tiny miniatures dissolved in the water. Lew tried to swim up, but he continued to go further and further down, no matter how hard he swam.

"Thought you could warsh me off, did you?" The Reflection's voice echoed in a mock West Virginia accent around Lew in the water.

Lew couldn't see anyone around him. His lungs craved air, but he was nowhere near the surface.

"You can't outsmart me, trailer trash! You can't outsmart anyone! Stay trapped here forever with the business elite. Learn to lick boots and fall in line. There's no point fighting. There's no escape!"

Lew screamed. As the air left his lungs, he gulped water. He coughed and choked on the water, which caused only more of it to go down his throat. He closed his eyes and felt his throat burn.

DING!

The elevator door opened, and Lew poured out into the hallway from the elevator. He flopped out like a fish as water gushed out around him and soaked into the carpet. He coughed out water and took several deep breaths of air.

How did I go from my tub to the elevator to the hallway? Where was that place? I'm still alive. There must be a way to escape. I have to make it to Anika and Juliana. They need me.

"Lew," a voice said. "Why are you on the floor? And how did you get so wet?"

Lew stood up, still wearing his suit, which weighed a ton now that it was soaking wet. His shoes squished with every step he took, and water squirted out of his shoes onto the floor.

Inias stood nearby, looking quite perplexed. He wore gray sweatpants and a gray sweatshirt. He had ear buds, which he took out and put in his pocket.

"Are you one of them? Tell me, Inias!" Lew demanded.

"One of who?" Inias touched the base of his own neck.

Lew rushed at Inias and shoved him against the wall. "Are you one of Abigor's minions here to mind fuck me like the rest of them? Don't tell me there's no escape! There has to be a way out of here!"

"What the hell are you talking about?" Inias tried to push Lew off him, but Lew was too strong.

"He sent you to get me, didn't he?" Lew shouted.

"I was just on my way to the gym," Inias answered with a tremulous voice. "How the hell did you get so much water in the elevator?"

Lew looked at Inias's dry gym clothes and released him.

"I'm sorry," Lew said. "Maybe you're not one of them, but how can you be so calm about everything? Didn't you see what Abigor did during the Centennial Celebration? Did you see what happened to that poor girl? I'm trying to get out of here."

"No, I skipped the reception. There's always so much junk food at those things. I overate crap yesterday." Inias patted himself on his stomach. "I thought I would put on my gym shoes and get in a workout instead."

"Inias, we have to get out of here," Lew grabbed Inias by both shoulders like he was insane, explaining how alien satellites were being used to monitor his thoughts. "It was Abigor. He... There was this girl—Hanna—and... He... Abigor killed her. He took a knife and plunged it into Hanna's chest and gutted her like she was a fish, and then he ripped out her heart and drank blood from it. And then he filled champagne glasses with her blood, and other people at the reception drank it. He's a cannibal. Most people here appear to be cannibals, too. He also has evil magic powers. He's been sending my Reflection after me to kill me. I jumped in the tub after a bunch of tiny min Lews jumped out of the mirror and attacked my nuts, and then I nearly drowned. But I fell out of the elevator, and now I'm alive."

Inias laughed so hard that he grabbed his sides with his hands and tried to stop laughing. "Cannibals killed a girl and drank her blood? And Abigor sent tiny Lews to attack your nuts? You can't be serious. Hahaha! Trying to prank me, huh?"

"Inias, this isn't a prank. Abigor killed a girl and drank her blood."

"Okay, I admit he has a strange name, the same as that demon, but I don't think he killed anyone. Why would he kill someone at the conference? Who would come back next year?"

"What do you mean, 'The same name as that demon'?" Lew's stomach fluttered.

"I know parents sometimes choose strange names for their kids. Or maybe it was a nickname he picked for himself. Abigor is the name of a Great Duke in hell. He rules sixty legions of demons and often carries a lance and a scepter. I figured he carries the scepter around with him as a nod to his namesake."

"A demon..." Lew felt dizzy. *A demon is toying with me, with all of us. The Reflection must be working for Abigor—or maybe the Reflection is merely Abigor in another form. He set up this conference to trap us here, and then he will murder us and take us to hell with him.* Lew grabbed Inias by both shoulders and looked him in the eye. "Inias, have you ever met someone from the Summit Conference before?"

"A lot of important people have been to the Summit Conference."

"No, not people who you heard about attending the Summit Conference. You travel a lot and attend a bunch of corporate conferences, right? You meet people who go to other conferences, don't you?"

"Well, I suppose I do."

"Have any of those people ever told you they had previously attended the Summit Conference?"

Inias scrunched his face up and racked his memory. "No, I mean, I met people who told me they were planning to attend, but I never met someone who told me they had attended before."

"And the people who told you they were planning to attend—did you ever see them again afterward?" Lew was frantic now, thirsting for information to confirm his fears.

"No, I can't say that I did. I figured they were just so busy with their careers taking off that they didn't have to keep grinding it out on the conference circuit like me."

"You think you never heard from them again because they died? Do you think Abigor may be a demon? That he's murdering everyone who comes here and then dragging their dead souls back to hell with him?"

"What the fuck are you talking about? Do you have any idea how loony you sound? Abigor isn't really a demon. He's just an old businessman. The thing with the scepter—it's a gimmick, nothing more." Inias looked at Lew like he had two heads.

"How do you know so much about demons, anyway?" Lew asked suspiciously.

"I went to Catholic school. Heaven and hell, angels and demons, Catholicism and the occult—it's all related—two sides to the same coin. Don't you believe in religion?"

"No... Yeah..." Lew struggled to articulate himself. "It's complicated. I used to. Or at least I thought I did. When I was a kid, I used to go to mass with my grandmother. My mother died when I was born, and my father hated me, but my grandmother loved me. She told me I was a blessing. She was a devout Catholic. I used to believe in it all, but maybe somewhere around middle school, I found it all ridiculous. You know, I kept going to mass with my grandmother, mainly because I liked to spend time with her, but I stopped going to mass after she died. I thought religion was bullshit. Heaven, hell, demons, and angels seemed about as real as Santa Claus or the Easter Bunny. But what if it's really real? What if I was wrong and stories about angels and demons are real, and there's a demon after me? Bizzy Bone said demons surround him all the time, so maybe this shit happens."

Inias sighed and gave a warm look. "Lew, the Bible is just a book of stories that teach lessons about morality. It's not a textbook that documents the history of the world. I mean, do you think two of every animal in the entire world fit on a single boat? You're too stressed out. You look like you just got out of an armbar. How much did you drink at the Centennial? Maybe you should go back to your room and lie down."

"No, I can't lie down! I have to get out." Lew ran his hands through his wet hair and shook the water off his glasses. *A fucking demon! It all makes sense now!* "Inias, do you know a lot about demons?"

Inias hesitated. "A lot? No... Well, I mean, I know a bit."

"Do you know how to kill a demon?" Lew asked with genuine inquiry.

Inias nervously laughed, but his laughter dissipated as Lew stared, awaiting an answer. "You're serious, huh?"

"I'm dead fucking serious, Inias. Do you know how to kill a demon?"

"Okay, now this is some stuff I heard as a kid in Catholic school, and I hope I remembered it right. Let me preface this by reiterating that demons aren't real, and they are just stories to—"

Lew cut Inias off. "Yeah, yeah. Stories. Come on! Out with it!"

Inias sighed again. "I don't know if a human can kill a demon, but some things can vanquish a demon or perform an exorcism. Well, three things that I know of. The first is holy objects, like a crucifix or a Bible. The second is the word of God—scripture, Bible verses. The third is crystals."

"Crystals! Where can I get magic demon-killing crystals?"

"Again, I don't know if you can kill a demon, but it should cast out a demon. Any kind of crystal will do. Even salt is a crystal."

"Salt!" *That's why there's no fucking salt anywhere in this hotel. That's why the salt causes everything to sizzle!* Lew stuck his hand in his jacket pocket, and the salt grinder Bob gifted him was still there. He gave Inias a big bear hug. "You just saved me! Get ready to bust out of the hotel. I'm going to smite this fucking demon!"

31

Hanna Taithangklom sat in the back of a crowded meeting room. All the lights were out. The session began with a projector playing a video on three panes.

In the first, Damien kneeled with his eyes closed, clutching a Bible in one hand and a cross in the other. He wore a long-sleeved black collared shirt with a white tab and black dress pants. "Dear Jesus, we turn to you in these times of weakness to ask for strength. I am your humble servant, Father Damien, asking you to lift me up. Please send me something to help me on my journey."

A bright white light shone from offscreen. The camera cut to Damien with a long brown wig, fake brown beard, and white robes. It was a half-ass Jesus costume with a filter that made it look like he was glowing and holding a glowing can of PanWow. "Father Damien, your prayers have been answered. PanWow will give you strength, energy, and absolve your sins. Whoever drinketh in me shall not perish but shall have everlasting life. Drink PanWow, the official energy drink of Jesus Christ."

The camera cut back to Father Damien—he dropped his Bible and crucifix, opened the can, and then took a sip. "PanWow is a gift from God. I'm stronger than I ever thought possible. #PanWowIsJesusApproved #FatherDamien #PanWowSavesSouls."

The camera cut back to Damien in his Jesus costume. "Buy PanWow today by clicking the link below. Save ten percent on bulk orders with the order code FatherDamien. If you order over five cases at once, we'll throw in a Father Damien golden idol for just $9.99."

The camera cut to a small golden statue of Father Damien. The fine print at the bottom read, "Not real gold."

Sweet sacrilege, what an asshole!

Hanna thought back to when a friend once dragged her to a Baptist church and made her rub shoulders with the church crowd. The people she met there were all so pushy and judgmental and annoying and fake. She shuddered.

He's the kind of jerk who probably Tebows next to the table when it's time to say grace but can't name even five of the ten commandments. For fuck's sake, he broke one of them in that heretical video.

In the next video, Frank Dolan smoked pot out of a pineapple glass pipe. He took a long hit that nearly burnt the entire bowl. The fire tore a line from the top halfway down, like wildfires marching across the Western states. He then grabbed a can of beer and took a few sips. Frank still didn't exhale. He took another long hit of the same bowl from the pipe, taking the wildfire the rest of the way through and finishing it. Frank still didn't exhale. He chugged the rest of the beer. He still didn't exhale. Then he opened a box of wine and took the bag out and slapped it and chugged half. Frank still didn't exhale. And then he opened a can of PanWow and shotgunned it in an instant. After all that, Frank finally exhaled an enormous cloud of smoke and said, "Giraffe!"

He laughed and coughed. "Check me out. You just witnessed another one of Frank Dolan's trademark giraffes. Next, I will—" He coughed harder and paused. "Excuse me, I—" He covered his mouth and looked like he might puke. "I'm okay. Sorry about that. I—" And with that, vomit sprayed from his mouth like water from a garden hose. Nothing was inside of him, but wine, beer, PanWow, and bile— not even a single chunk of food came out. He picked up the bag of wine, took another sip, and used it to rinse his mouth out. Frank pulled a joint out of his pocket, lit it, and took a puff. "Giraffe." He squinted his bloodshot eyes, smiled, and gave a stoner laugh.

That was disgusting. How does this idiot get so many followers?

In the third video, Bob stood shirtless outdoors, cooking meatballs in a pot of PanWow over a fire. "PanWow isn't just the best energy drink ever made. It's also a great marinade. Trust me. I climbed Siula Grande in Peru."

That savage glorifies eating meat. How many animals suffered to make that pot of crap that probably tastes like shit? I wish I could make the world vegan.

After a few minutes of the videos playing, the three dimwits emerged from the shadows and shouted mindless gibberish to the audience, who responded with a strange rhythmic clapping.

A spotlight came on at the front of the room, and the three amigos emerged from the shadows and then ran back and forth. A projector flashed the words "How to Be a Social Media Star" in multiple colors and flashing lights, like they were trying to elicit an epileptic seizure from the crowd.

"Do you see how easy it can be? You can do this, too, man," Frank Dolan said.

"Through the power of Jesus Christ, anything is possible," Damien said. "Even millions of views."

"Through the power of pangolins, I'll have unlimited energy," Bob Williamson said as he poured two cans of PanWow down his throat at once, spilling most of it down his shirt and chest.

This is an idiotic shit show! Hanna gritted her teeth. It took all of her strength to hold her composure and not yell out loud. *Those stupid sons of bitches. I know so much more about this than they do. They haven't even mentioned analytics or how to create an acquisition report. This is just peachy. Why didn't Abigor ask me to speak at this session?*

Hanna pulled out one of her credit cards and examined it. In the design, an art deco figure stood stoically. It didn't have a face, but Abigor's silhouette was unmistakable. She snapped it in half and discarded the pieces in a trash can.

I know so much more about social media, being an influencer, market-ing, data, and everything else than those dipshits! It should be me up there getting the glory!

Hanna inhaled and let out a deep breath.

I hope Alexis grows up to appreciate all her mommy sacrificed for her.

32

Holy shit! Is this real? Bob Willemsen wondered.

"I'll give you anything your heart desires as long as you remain within the confines of the Beburoa Hotel." Abigor stood behind the desk in his office, wearing an all-black old-timey suit. A gold watch fob on the waistcoat was the only splash of color. As usual, he spritely twirled his golden scepter in one hand as he spoke.

"Pfft!" Fatty said with his arms folded. "Anything? Anything at all?"

Skinny and Bob stood nearby, waiting to see what would happen next. Only the four of them were in Abigor's office.

"Yes, Mr. Chernobog. I won't gyp you. I'm talking straight from the shoulder. You will forever remain trapped here at the Beburoa Hotel, but this need not be hell. It can be a paradise. Besides, you have nothing waiting for you on the outside. All your family members are deceased or estranged. Your only friends are here in the room with you. Name your price. What do you want?"

"If you're talking straight, old man, answer me this," Fatty demanded. "Why the hell did PanWow send us to this hotel to be trapped here?"

Abigor smiled. "Why? Because I own PanWow."

"Bullshit, man!" Skinny shouted. "You don't own PanWow. Some Chinese guy owns it."

"What's the Chinaman's name?" Abigor asked with a grin.

The trio fell silent for a beat.

Bob answered and felt a chill in his spine. "A Chinese man named Abe Goh."

The three let out a collective sigh of disappointment.

Abigor beamed at them. "Mr. Chernobog, I ask you again to name your price. Ask for anything your heart desires. What will it take for you to obey me and accept your fate as a permanent attendee at the Summit Conference?"

"Jesus fucking Christ! You're telling me I can have a hot nun give me a blowjob whenever I want? And she can also hum the tune to *Jesus Loves Me* while she blows me?" Fatty rolled his eyes.

Abigor winked. He tapped his scepter twice on the floor and then shouted, "Send her in!" He smirked and twirled his cane as he watched the expression on Damien's face.

The office door opened, and a hooded figure in a baggy habit entered the room.

"Oh, it's just one of them," Fatty said. "Big deal."

The hooded figure held the door open, and in walked a nun in a baggy habit. She was as beautiful as a model, and her face was a solid ten. The nun stared sensuously at Fatty, and she hummed the tune to *Jesus Loves Me* as she approached him.

How does this bastard do these tricks?

Fatty gulped. He gazed at her, dumbfounded.

"What do you think, Mr. Chernobog?" Abigor asked. "How's that for a blower?"

Fatty was speechless.

Abigor used his scepter to lightly tap Fatty on the head. "Are you there? I asked you a question?"

Fatty blinked twice and jumped when he saw Abigor next to him. "Jesus fucking Christ! I forgot you were here. What was the question?"

Abigor smiled. "What do you think of your 'hot nun' blower?"

Fatty tried to act skeptical like he was dealing with a used car salesperson. "Her habit is so loose. How do I even know she's hot?"

Abigor tapped his cane. The nun's tunic shrunk to snugly hug her body, revealing her jacked tits and banging ass. She was a solid ten.

Fatty gulped. His eyes grew wide. He stared at the beautiful nun, unable to take his eyes off her. "What's your name?"

"Ruha," the nun replied in a silky, sultry voice.

Fatty smiled. "That's a pretty name."

"Sign the contract and agree to work for me at the Beburoa Hotel, and she'll satisfy your every desire," Abigor said with calm confidence.

Ruha nodded at Fatty without breaking eye contact.

"Where's the contract?" Fatty blurted out. He was salivating. "I'll sign anything. Do you have a pen?"

Abigor put his scepter down on his desk and then handed Fatty his contract and a fountain pen. Fatty hastily scribbled a signature on the contract without ever looking at it—let alone reading it—and without breaking his gaze with the nun. Abigor grinned heartily as he placed the signed contract in a desk drawer and the pen on his desk.

The nun grabbed Fatty's hand and led him to the door, out of Abigor's office. She hummed on the way out, and Damien sang along. "Jesus loves me, this I know, for the Bible tells me so. Little ones to Him belong; they are weak, but He is strong. Yes, Jesus loves me. Yes, Jesus loves me. Yes, Jesus loves me. The Bible tells me so."

After they left, the hooded figure near the door stepped back outside of the room and closed the door behind them.

Abigor picked up his scepter once again and twirled it as he casually paced back and forth behind his desk. He turned his attention to Frank. "Mr. Dolan, what do you want? Anything in the world? Name it, and it's yours as long as you sign my contract and accept that you won't ever leave the hotel."

Skinny exhaled a large cloud of smoke from a freshly lit joint. "Huh? Did you say something?"

Abigor grated his teeth. "Weren't you paying attention? Where did you get that?"

Skinny took another puff from his joint. "Where did I get what, man?"

Abigor yanked Skinny's joint from his mouth. He put it on the floor and stamped it out. "What do you want?"

Skinny belched and another cloud of smoke came out of his mouth. "Listen up, man! I want one thing and one thing only. One million doll hairs. Cash. And a bag of weed! And *Blade* on Blu-ray with Wesley Snipes doing commentary."

"Done!" Abigor said. He put his scepter back down on his desk and then reached into a desk drawer and pulled out a briefcase. He placed the briefcase down on his desk, and he went to open it but stopped short. "Dash my buttons! Did you say doll hairs or dollars? It doesn't matter. You can have both." Abigor reached into the desk drawer and pulled out another briefcase, which he placed on his desk next to the other. He opened both briefcases and spun them around so that Skinny could see the insides. One briefcase was filled with cash, and the other was filled with a bundle of loose doll hairs, a large bag of weed, and a Blu-ray of *Blade*, starring Wesley Snipes.

"Oh, shit!" Skinny exclaimed. "Hell yeah, man! I'm rich, bitch!"

"Sign my contract, Mr. Dolan, and all this is yours," Abigor said.

"Gimme a pen, man," Skinny responded.

Abigor handed Skinny a pen, who signed the contract without reading it. Skinny closed both briefcases, and he danced his way out of Abigor's office, clumsily dropping the briefcases momentarily as he struggled to open the door. The hooded figure outside the door came to Skinny's aid and helped him exit. The hooded figure stepped outside once again, closing the door.

Bob was alone with Abigor now.

"I can't believe this shit," Bob said.

"I know, Mr. Willemsen," Abigor said. "Why did he want cash? He can't leave the hotel, so the only place he can spend it is the gift shop."

Abigor sat behind his desk and offered his guest chair to Bob, who slowly sat down.

"Well, Mr. Willemsen. You have my undivided attention," Abigor said with a smirk. "What do you want more than anything? Name it, and it's yours, so long as you agree to work for me and don't waste your time trying to escape the hotel."

Is this son of a bitch Satan himself? I didn't even think Satan was real. Well, if the devil wants to dance, who am I to say no?

"What do I want?" Bob sat tall, tensing his neck and shoulder muscles. "Nothing in the hotel. I'm a climber, and I want to be outside, feeling the sun on my skin and wind in my hair. I want to be free. Being trapped inside forever? That's fucking hell for me."

Abigor frowned. "Gadsnouns, my boy. I was afraid you might say that." He tapped his cane. The door opened, and three hooded figures walked into the room and surrounded Bob. "You were the only one of the new recruits I was unsure about. Fortunately, I have less pleasant ways to make people fall in line. I must warn you—you'll never escape this place, and I demand order of all the guests up to the nines. You can fight it, but you'll lose. Everyone who opposes me loses. I'll make you obey me if you refuse to play your part peacefully, but I must warn you, you'll never be the same. It doesn't have to go this way, you know. Accept your fate to remain in the Beburoa Hotel forever, and we'll do all we can to make you as pleased as a dog with two cocks."

Bob leaned forward in his chair, and the three hooded figures each took a step closer to him. Bob sighed and sagged his shoulders. "Let me see the contract."

Abigor smiled. The hooded figures each took a step back. Abigor turned in his chair to open a drawer, and as soon as he did, Bob lunged for the scepter. It was so heavy he needed both hands to lift it.

How strong is Abigor that he twirls this damn thing with one hand?

Bob grunted as he lifted the scepter over his head and swung it down towards the crown of Abigor's skull.

33

*A*bigor *needed my talent for something important, huh?* Hanna Taithangklom thought to herself. *That misogynistic motherfucker.*

Hanna mopped blood off a tile floor. She wore the baggy black habit of a Benedictine monk, which had a large hood that hid her face.

It's such a waste that I put so much effort into diet and exercise, and then I'm stuck in these loose-fitting robes that hide the shape of my body entirely—this thing is so ugly that you can't even tell I'm a woman.

Hanna scrubbed harder with her mop.

The chef's blood is freezing to the floor. This is just peachy. I thought my place on the Board would be glamorous. Instead, Abigor named me Chair of the Committee on Departed Sanitation and said I have to clean up after the murders.

She wheeled her mop and bucket from the freezer and navigated through the kitchen to go back to the sink.

Did Abigor kill these poor bastards too? That guy is even crazier than I thought.

Hanna dumped the bucket down the drain underneath the sink and then stretched the nozzle over the bucket and filled it with hot water. She flipped her hood back while she waited, revealing her face and hair.

"Keep that thing on your head," said one of the kitchen staff in the strange cadence of Abigor's zombie attendees. She looked and sounded brain dead, but she functioned well enough to keep the buffets stocked at every meal and snack break. "We all must properly wear the uniforms Abigor gifted us. As a Board member, your clothing befits your status. Your habit is an honor."

Why the hell does she get to show her face? And wear tight pants? Because of yoga and my vegan diet, my body is beautiful. I should be able to show off my face and figure, too.

When Hanna finished scrubbing the kitchen, Abigor summoned her. At least, her new keycard let her go to any floor or room in the Beburoa Hotel—not that it really gave her any freedom yet.

Camilla talked about having free time. I only wish I could see Alexis in person and hold her again. But at least my sacrifice will give her a better life. She'll have every opportunity now. She'll be as privileged as a rich white kid. Even if she doesn't understand why I've given up so much, I know it's worth it. She'll never end up pushing a mop around for a job.

FRESHLY SPLATTERED blood decorated Abigor's office, and a dead body lay on the floor near the desk. The head was crushed so severely that no trace of the face remained. It looked like a caved-in, rotted pumpkin that someone had stepped on. Bits of brains and skull were strewn about on the floor. However, the athleisure wear on the body was a dead giveaway as to whose corpse this was.

"What the hell happened here?" Hanna asked.

"Another half-alligator guest refused to accept his place." Abigor took off his morning coat, which was splattered with blood. He used a towel to wipe specks of blood from his shirt and waistcoat. "Every year, there are a few apes who cannot adjust on their own. No matter. That's why I have other means. Take him to the Chuck. He'll get wise there."

Hanna grabbed Bob Williamson's corpse by the feet.

Only one idiot in this place walks around in stupid athletic clothes all the time, like he's always at the gym or on a mountain. It makes sense that he would also be dumb enough to fight Abigor head-on and alone. One day I'll take my revenge on Abigor and Camilla for what they did to me, but I need to wait until the time is right—after Alexis is cured, fully grown, and no longer needs my financial support. When I know she's safe and financially stable, I'll make them both pay dearly.

"Come off for a second!" Abigor waved his hand. "I almost forgot. I need your help with something more important here first."

Something more important? Is he finally going to ask me for marketing advice? I have so many ideas to help the Summit Conference grow even more.

"Yes, Abigor." Hanna dropped Bob's feet and walked directly up to Abigor.

"Fill another tumbler with elixir and bring it here," he said. "I don't want to walk all the way across the room."

You chauvinistic asshole. You can't even grab your own drink?

"Yes, sir. Right away." Hanna stepped over Bob's corpse and filled up a glass with an elixir of cocaine, seltzer, and citrus. She carried it back to him and then walked back to Bob's lifeless body.

Damned Abigor. He made me walk twice as far as he would have, just because he could.

He took a sip. "Buck up with a bucket of suds and a brush after you drop him off. I need you to clean this mess up."

"As you wish, sir." Hanna picked up Bob's feet again and dragged him out of the room.

This stupid meathead... He's heavy, but I'm vegan strong. I don't envy what's going to happen to Bob now. Maybe he deserves it because of all the animals who had to die for him to eat meat on Insta. The idiot should have signed Abigor's contract when he had the chance.

34

Lew Starek walked to Abigor's office, escorted by a figure wearing a baggy habit.

Bible verse, Bible verse, Bible verse, Lew thought to himself. *Why can't I remember a Bible verse? Thou shalt not...wait in vain? No, that's not right. Thou shalt not... Why am I drawing a blank? What is the Bible? Basic instructions before leaving earth. How is it that after years of going to mass, I can't remember a Bible verse?*

Before coming to see Abigor, Lew changed into a secondhand dark-navy pinstripe Paul Smith suit. The jacket was double-breasted with broad shoulders and four large buttons. Under his coat, Lew wore a white shirt with a pink necktie, and he also had a matching pink pocket square sticking out of his breast pocket. Walking into Abigor's lair dressed for success in a fresh suit gave him confidence. Unfortunately, he only had one pair of shoes, still soaking wet, which squeaked with each step.

And therefore, Jesus saith unto thee... Why can't I remember a single Bible verse? This is so—

Lost in thought, Lew wasn't watching his feet. He tripped over someone and fell.

"Jesus fucking Christ!" Damien shouted. "Watch where you're going!"

Lew stood up. He had tripped over a young nun. She wore something akin to the habit of Poor Clares—brown tunic, white wool cincture, white coif, and black veil—but instead of being a typical loose habit, it hugged her every curve, putting her entire body on full display. He helped her to her feet and said, "I'm sorry, sister. Are you okay?" *What is a nun doing here? Is today my lucky day?* "Do you mind telling me a short and easy-to-remember Bible verse?"

"I'm fine." The nun got to her feet, revealing pink lipstick smeared over her mouth. Her ivory face had a musk-rose flush on the cheekbones, and she had piercing blue eyes.

It was then that Lew noticed Damien's appearance. His suit was disheveled. Buttons had been ripped off his shirt. And his dick was out, smeared with the same pink lipstick the nun wore.

Damien froze for a beat. And then he stuffed his dick back in his pants and zipped up his fly. "Jesus fucking Christ, it's you again."

"So, you are one of Abigor's minions," Lew said. "What happened to your friend with the salt?"

"Ruha, let's get out of here." Damien took the nun's hand and walked towards the elevator with a sense of urgency.

He left something here on the floor. Why is it sizzling?

Lew picked up a thick black book, and he turned it over to reveal the cover—Holy Bible, gold words, and a large gold cross on a black background.

I guess it is my lucky day today.

He slipped it into his jacket hip pocket and entered Abigor's office.

When Lew arrived, Abigor was standing with his jacket off, drinking a cocktail. Fresh red blood bedazzled the office. A couple of hooded figures were scrubbing the floors. His desk and the chairs look like they had just been cleaned.

"Lew, my boy, I'm quite chirk you wanted to see me." Abigor waved at the hooded figures to leave the room, and they promptly obeyed. He took a seat behind his desk and pointed to his empty guest chair. "Excuse the hurrah's nest. Watch your step, or your shoes might get...wetter."

Lew sat down, and he felt acid reflux churn in his stomach again. *Keep it together. You can do this. For Anika. For Juliana.* "Abigor, I've given your offer careful consideration."

"Yes, and?" Abigor raised his eyebrows.

"Wu-Tang is for the children!" Lew shouted as he reached into his pocket and threw a handful of salt at Abigor and then reached into his other pocket and pulled out the Bible. He opened a page at random and read a passage aloud. "Yet she multiplied her whoredoms, in calling to remembrance the days of her youth, wherein she had played the harlot in the land of Egypt. For she doted upon their paramours, whose flesh is as the flesh of asses, and whose issue is like the issue of horses. Thus thou calledst to remembrance the lewdness of thy youth, in bruising thy teats by the Egyptians for the paps of thy youth."

What is this shit? Don't get distracted, Lew. Smite this demon!

In one swift motion, Lew closed the Bible and pressed it against Abigor's chest. He closed his eyes and repeated the passage rapidly. "Yet she multiplied her whoredoms, in calling to remembrance the days of her youth, wherein she had played the harlot in the land of Egypt. For she doted upon their paramours, whose flesh is as the flesh of asses, and whose issue is like the issue of horses. Thus thou calledst to remembrance the lewdness of thy youth, in bruising thy teats by the Egyptians for the paps of thy youth. Yet she multiplied her whoredoms, in calling to remembrance the days of her youth, wherein she had played the harlot in the land of Egypt. For she doted upon their paramours, whose flesh is as the flesh of asses, and whose issue is like the issue of horses. Thus thou calledst to remembrance the lewdness of thy youth, in bruising thy teats by the Egyptians for the paps of thy youth..."

35

In the elevator, Damien Chernobog pressed the button for his floor. "Let's go back to my hotel room," he said to Ruha.

"As you command. I exist only to serve." Her tight habit looked more like a slutty cosplay than a religious garb.

She's such a beautiful enchantress, Damien thought. *Jesus fucking Christ! This is the hottest chick I've ever seen. I could lose myself in her body for days. I should say something clever to impress her.*

"Did you know that Jesus Christ invented CrossFit?" Damien said. "That's why his abs looked shredded on all the statues."

Perfect. Nailed it.

Ruha gave him a blank stare in response.

"So, uh, where are you from?" Damien inquired.

"I was born in darkness and smoke," Ruha answered. "I am an incarnation of eternal nothingness and a gateway to the second circle of hell."

"Something about your voice is so...sultry. Anything you say just sounds so erotic. Tell me something else about yourself." Damien's pecker was rock hard, and everything about Ruha only made him hornier. It had been so long since a woman threw herself at him, and women as beautiful as Ruha rarely gave him the time of day. As much as Damien craved money and fame, a woman's soft touch was the thing he most desired.

"I will do as you command, but in doing so, I will make you a slave of the devil. You will be bound to me forever. You will do anything for my touch. Even if you were to burn your body in holy fire, you would not purge yourself of me." Ruha's voice was as sweet as honey. Even talk of doom and damnation sounds as soft as the poetry of sunshine and flowers.

"Jesus fucking Christ!" Damien exclaimed. "That...is...so...fuck-ing...hot!"

Ding! The elevator doors opened, and Damien wasted no time leading Ruha to his room.

Her hands are so soft in mine.

"Arrr, let's bang!" Damien said in a botched attempt at a seductive voice, which sounded like a pirate accent. He shut the door behind him.

"As you command. I exist only to serve."

"Say something else. Your voice really gets me going."

Holy shit! This is going to be the most incredible event in my life. I need to savor every moment and remember this forever.

"Lust indulged became habit, and habit unresisted became neces-sity." Ruha's voice was as soft as velvet.

"Jesus fucking Christ! That's so hot. That's probably the sexiest thing anybody has ever said about anything. Show me what's under your habit." Damien drooled in anticipation.

She undressed, revealing smooth ivory skin devoid of blemishes that looked too good to be real. He admired her piercing blue eyes and blonde hair, and then he marveled at her unique features—size fifteen feet, unshaven legs, and an ass tattoo of Steven Seagal. She was an amalgamation of every woman he's ever fantasized about.

How does that happen? Oh, who cares?

Damien followed suit, and they got to know each other in the biblical sense. He overflowed in ecstasy as he enjoyed release after release, but each time, he felt a little something less in himself. Some-thing drained from himself—something other than the swimmers that lived in his balls. Each discharge stole from his soul, and he felt slightly emptier than before.

"Holy fucking shit!" Damien lay on his back, panting and covered in sweat. "Let's take a brief break, okay, Ruha?"

"As you command." She cuddled up to Damien. In stark contrast to Damien's state of exhaustion, she seemed perfectly at ease. She didn't have a drop of sweat, and she breathed as though she hadn't exerted her body in the slightest.

"How did you learn how to do all that stuff, especially the feet stuff?" Damien asked. "I never could have imagined those tricks."

"As a gateway to the second circle of hell, I have complete knowledge of every act of lust ever committed. Francesca, Helen, and Cleopatra are among those whose carnal sins I can perform completely." Ruha's voice was light and sultry.

"Jesus fucking Christ! That's hot! Do you want to snort cocaine off the Bible and fuck me like an Egyptian queen?" Even though he hadn't regained his energy yet, he was already looking forward to their next erotic act.

"We cannot, for you have lost your Bible, and you have no cocaine." Ruha's nipples softly rubbed against Damien's skin while she traced her fingers across his stomach in the shape of a pentagram.

My Bible... I was going to do something with my Bible. Why the hell did it sizzle? I was going to use it to fight Abigor, I think. Maybe I should try to find it...later...after I drain my balls... I mean, what's the rush? Everything I need is right here. I don't even need to worry about my gambling debts anymore. There's no way in hell my bookie finds me here.

"Do you know where I put my Bible? Or where I can find some cocaine?" Damien's breathing was slowly returning to normal. "Holy hell, am I thirsty. I'll be right back." He went to the bathroom.

"Do not worry about the Bible. I can call room service and have them deliver cocaine. You can snort it off my tits, and then I'll show you the salacious acts Cleopatra performed on her lovers. I will use you up until you lose your entire soul to hell." Ruha sat up straight in the hotel bed, and her perky breasts hung in place, defying gravity.

I can't believe my ears. "Room service delivers cocaine? And I can snort it off your tits? Call them right away!"

"As you command," Ruha answered.

"The second circle of hell you describe sounds like an amazing place filled with the most fun people to be around." Damien stuck his head in the sink and chugged cold water from the faucet.

And if all that Christianity shit is real, my saving grace will be a Hail Mary deathbed confessional to dodge hell. It's like Jesus said: It doesn't matter what you did in life; as long as you confess your sins to him before you die, you can enter heaven.

"Now about that cocaine...."

36

Abigor awoke in bed to the sound of his wind-up alarm clock ringing. He threw his covers off and put on his slippers and stretched and walked to the window to enjoy his view of the abyss.

Abigor's penthouse suite was over three times the size of the average room in the hotel. The bedroom had an enormous bed, larger than a king, and an adjacent bathroom, twice the size of the others in the hotel. The living room had a couch, a lounge chair, and shelves to house Abigor's tomes of forgotten lore. He even had a separate dining room with a maple table and matching chairs for eight, even though he nearly always ate meals in his suite alone.

He took a seat at the dining table, which had his usual breakfast waiting for him—a halved grapefruit lightly dusted with sugar; a cup of hot black coffee; and a small tumbler filled with seltzer water, lime, and cocaine. As he dined on his breakfast, he flipped through freshly printed booklets that were also waiting for him on the table, each one containing information about the new guests who would arrive over the next few days. Even after one hundred years, he never figured out who prepared his breakfast or who assembled the dossiers, but he stopped asking those questions several decades ago. He kept his sanity these past hundred years by maintaining a steady routine and focusing his attention on keeping the guests of the Beburoa Hotel in order.

Abigor thought back to when he first arrived at the hotel. It was so small, only two stories. He could throw an object from one side to the other. But as new guests arrived over the years, the hotel continually expanded and grew enough beds for every guest. More meeting rooms appeared. The first time he woke up to find the building taller than when he went to sleep, he was shocked. But now, he was used to it.

The stimulants woke his mind and sharpened his attention as he devoured the details of the lucky few who were soon to join the Summit Conference. Abigor often wondered about the outside world. How many things stayed the same or changed? What happened to his family? He kept up with his descendants for a couple of generations, before losing interest.

Books, newspapers, and magazines were his primary method of learning what became of the outside world. He was an avid reader, and he could get any reading material he wanted. All Abigor had to do was write the name of what he wanted on a sheet of paper on his desk before he went to sleep, and when he awoke in the morning, the publications were there waiting for him. Sometimes he received other documents, as well—things he didn't even know he wanted until he came across a strange term, such as *social media influencer* in this morning's dossiers.

Abigor took a break from learning about the new guests to have his morning constitutional and use the washroom. Later, he perused his wardrobe before deciding against one of his usual morning suits, in favor of an English walking suit that was expected to become all the rage by 1915, according to the salesman who sold it to him in 1910. He started by putting on a white shirt with a wingtip collar and then tying on a black and white polka dot bowtie. He put a semi-stiff pleated front shirt over top and then a black waistcoat. He finished with gray pinstripe trousers and a black frock coat. Abigor admired himself in the mirror upon completion.

"You look tip topper today, as always," Abigor's Reflection said.

"Thank you," Abigor responded, treating this as something mundane. Sometimes the reflection was only a reflection. Other times, the Reflection shared news of the outside world or things to come.

"Did you read about all the new guests yet?" the Reflection asked.

"Only a few. Nobody seems to be a honey cooler. I don't even know what a social media influencer is—at least not yet. I'll read those books later. Is there someone I should pay particular attention to?"

"Lew Starek. Chew the cud over this one. You two have a lot in common."

"Is he another one of those influencers?"

"No, he's a young man of humble beginnings who is quite interested in traditional business. He thinks a lot like you. And he...well... you'll see when you read his file. You'll find that the apple didn't fall far from the tree."

"The name 'Starek' doesn't ring a bell. Is his father an important executive? Or did he have another family member here at the conference?"

But this time, Abigor's Reflection didn't answer. Once again, the mirror was an ordinary mirror, and the reflection was only a reflection.

Abigor sat back down at his dining table and flipped through the dossiers. He found Lew Starek's and studied it carefully.

Abigor spat salt out of his mouth in disgust and scowled at Lew Starek. "Burn you! Did you throw salt at me?" He looked around and saw salt on his desk and clothes. "It's even in my pockets! I have to change my clothes now. Damfino! Why are you holding a Bible against my chest?"

Lew felt his face become hot. *How could this plan have gone so poorly?* "Uhhh, I'm smiting you. Because you're a demon."

"Are you softheaded?" Abigor asked with an undertone of anger. "Did you really think you could blow my lights out with a Bible?" He grabbed the Bible from Lew with one hand and pushed Lew in the face with the other.

Abigor's hand felt simultaneously icy cold and burning hot. Lew fell to the ground with a thud, and he clutched at his face. His spine ran cold, and he smelled smoke. After a beat, Lew stood up again.

Abigor opened the Bible and ripped out a page at random. He reached into his desk and pulled out a pouch of tobacco and a box of matches, and he rolled a cigarette, using the Bible page as a rolling paper. He plopped the cigarette in his mouth, lit it, and puffed until smoke flowed through his nostrils.

The salt and Bible caused the desk to sizzle, but neither affected Abigor.

What the hell? Why didn't these things work on Abigor?

Abigor took the cigarette out of his mouth and blew smoke right in Lew's face. "I thought you were smart, my boy, but maybe you are just a dumb hillbilly. This was your grand plan? To scupper me with a Bible?"

"Good thing I have a backup plan." Lew pulled an ax that hid in his jacket and pants. "Thanks for keeping an ax on every floor next to the fire extinguisher."

He spun and swung the ax directly into Abigor's neck. It took five hard chops until Abigor's head fell off and rolled onto the floor. The headless body slumped backward.

Lew felt the tension throughout his body release itself and then he started to dance and then he started to sing "Woo-Hah!! Got You All in Check" by Busta Rhymes and the Ol' Dirty Bastard.

Lew smelled smoke again, but not from the cigarette. No smoke was visible, but Lew somehow knew it was the smoke of an ancient fire that had been burning for thousands of years and was now being extinguished. The room suddenly felt freezing cold. He wiped the sweat from his brow, and he pulled a couple more pages out of the Bible to wipe Abigor's blood off his suit. The blood should have felt warm but instead felt like ice. A chill ran down Lew's spine. He put the Bible back in his jacket pocket and pulled Abigor's body and chair to the side. Abigor's clothes felt like normal cloth, but his skin and blood were so cold that they burned to the touch. Lew's pulse raced.

Abigor's golden scepter was on top of his desk. Lew tried to pick it up with one hand but could hardly budge it. "What the hell?" He put down the ax and grabbed the scepter with both hands. Straining and grunting, Lew threw the scepter onto the floor.

How did he spin that thing around in one hand like he's a baton twirler?

Lew rummaged through Abigor's desk.

There must be a secret key, map, or something that will help me get out.

He opened drawer after drawer but found nothing of importance. Further confounding Lew, the same drawer didn't reveal the same contents twice. One drawer contained nothing but pens the first time he opened it, paper and pencils the second time, cocaine the third time, and the fourth time was empty.

This is ludicrous. What kind of desk is this?

Lew rummaged through Abigor's pockets, careful not to touch blood or skin as blood gushed from his neck and soaked his body. He found a worn leather wallet in Abigor's left jacket breast pocket. He opened it and saw some old, out-of-circulation cash and an unlaminated paper driver's license from New York State issued on June 19, 1919, signed by Charles Abigor Michaelson. It listed his age at the date of signature as sixty-nine years old.

"What the fuck? You're one hundred and sixty-nine years old?" Lew kicked Abigor's headless corpse in the chest, and it fell onto the floor.

"Ouch!"

Lew's stomach churned, and he started to dry heave. He looked around. "Who said that?"

That voice sounded like... No, it can't be...

Lew approached Abigor's head, which was lying on its ear and facing away. He rolled it with his shoe to look at the face, only to find Abigor very much alive, despite being decapitated.

"What the shit?" Lew screamed.

Abigor's body stood up, although it was missing the head.

Lew grabbed Abigor's head and shook it like a magic eight ball even though it burned his fingers. "What is going on, Abigor? What going on, Charles? Fucking tell me!"

"Adzooks!" Abigor shouted. "Stop shaking me, and we'll talk like civilized folk."

Lew stopped.

"You have a very foul mouth. Do you know that?" Abigor said. "Let's not lose our heads. Speaking of, why don't you hand my head to my body so that we can chew the fat?"

Lew threw Abigor's head at his body like he was trying to nail the slow kid in dodgeball. Abigor made a perfect catch and placed his head back on top of his neck. The smoke smell dissipated. Lew picked his ax up from Abigor's desk.

"Would you like some of my elixir?" Abigor said casually, as if he were greeting a guest at a party. He walked to his drink dispenser and filled a tumbler with a fizzy concoction.

"No, thank you," Lew responded. "I'm not thirsty. Now, how about you tell me what's going on here, Charles? I thought you were a demon. Are you a man? Why are you so cold? Why are you trapping us all here? What do you get out of this?"

Abigor sipped his elixir. The fluid leaked out of the hole in his neck, dripped onto his suit, mixed with blood, and dripped onto the floor, which was an utter mess now. Blood from Abigor's decapitation had pooled around his desk.

"Lew, my dear boy," Abigor said in a warm tone that would make you forget that Lew chopped off his head only a few minutes ago. "You ask a lot of questions. Why do you think the Beburoa Hotel is my sucker play? This isn't my plant."

"It's not?" Lew slumped back in his chair and stared at the ceiling. He felt dizzy.

Is Abigor lying, or was I wrong again? Am I even less observant than I thought? Brendan has my number, alright.

He rested his ax in his lap.

"I'll admit, I was the first boob to find myself stuck here. After I left National Cash Register because of a quarrel with John Patterson, I once again became a traveling salesman pushing tonic and elixirs as I plotted my return to the corporate world. But with mouths to feed—a wife and daughter—sulking wasn't a luxury I had. I came across a flyer advertising the Summit Conference in this remote part of Wyoming. It was quite a hassle to get here in my old jalopy because there wasn't even a paved road to this location. I had to come by horse. When I arrived, the Beburoa Hotel was the size of a small cottage. I wasn't sure what I expected when I entered, but I expected to see someone. However, I was alone for months, unable to leave the confines of this blazed hotel before someone else showed up here. I thought they were here to rescue me, but it was only another helpless sap stuck here like myself. I've been here for one hundred years, and I've seen the hotel gather more and more guests and grow. It gets bigger and bigger every time more people arrive."

"How the hell can you twirl that scepter with one hand when I can barely lift it with two? It must be some kind of magic!"

"There's no magic to the scepter. It used to be lighter, but I made it heavier over the years. I'm not the type to goldbrick." Abigor picked up the scepter and twirled it effortlessly with one hand. "These exercises helped me to pass the time and build my strength. If you put in the time and effort, you'll be able to twirl this as easily as me in a hundred years."

"But how did you get to be in charge? Why does everyone do what you want if you don't use magic powers?"

"I'm a management mastermind who knows how to ride herd on people. I would have taken control of National Cash Register if Patterson didn't force me out. That rocky mountain canary! I swore I would never let it happen to me again. Being here for so long helped me to learn the secrets of the Beburoa Hotel, and that, coupled with my ability to take charge and control others, meant that inevitably I would become king of the damned that are trapped here forever."

"So, this is hell?"

Abigor laughed. "Hell? Lew, my boy, we're not in heaven, but I know this isn't hell. If it were, how would I get every comfort I ever wanted in the building? And even though I never left, I figured out how to get money to my wife and child and communicate with them. They had so much cash that they were never left wanting."

"Wait, you have a family? You have a child?"

"They've all passed on a long time ago, but I had several children. My first wife, Beverly, birthed twins—Gene and Laila—who both died of scarlet fever. Beverly later died giving birth to my stillborn son, Nathan. You don't know the agony of holding your dead child or dead wife in your arms. It's enough to devastate anyone." Abigor's voice cracked, and he took a sip of elixir. "I married another woman named Meredith, and we had a son named Claude, who died of tuberculosis. Eventually, she gave me a daughter we named Bridgette, who was the only one to live past childhood. I loved Bridgette with all my heart. Unfortunately, I last held her in my arms when she was only ten months old. I promised my wife I would do anything within my power to provide for Bridgette and keep her safe, happy, and healthy. I also promised Bridgette that I would celebrate her first birthday together when I returned home from the road." Abigor wiped a tear from his eye and took another sip of elixir. "Unfortunately, I found it impossible to keep both promises. It caused me great pain and agony to never see Bridgette or Meredith again. I would have moved heaven and earth to be reunited, but, alas, it wasn't possible. Bridgette married a Polack named Ksawery Wasilewski, and they had one daughter named Christine. She married a man named Chester Westley, and they had a daughter named Katarina. She grew up to marry another Polack named Ernest Starek, and they had a son named Lew. I've called you 'my boy' many times, but perhaps a more accurate term would be great-great-grandson."

This can't be true. He's my goddam great-great-grandfather?

"What the fuck? You're shitting me, right? You're my great-great-grandfather? I thought all your kids were rich. I grew up dirt poor."

"Although I have many skills, controlling my children and grand-children from here was beyond my capabilities. I couldn't stop them from wasting their money or from marrying Polacks. It disgusts me to think the only family member I've been able to see in the flesh since coming here has mostly Polack blood running through his veins and was raised by hillbillies. Polacks, guineas, bog hoppers, and krauts—they're all a blight on this great country, coming over here in waves with their craw-thumper religion and their dirty candle shops."

"I'm not familiar with all those slurs, but I take it you're Protestant?" Lew asked.

"Hardly. My parents were Rosicrucians, but you might call them mystics or occultists. They gifted all their children with a name from Jacques Collin de Plancy's Dictionnaire Infernal. Abigor Charles Michaelson was the name they gave me. I had brothers named Moloch, Asmodeus, Stolas, and Rohovart. Of course, you could imagine how people greeted a traveling salesman named after a demon, so I simply used Charles as my first name. However, in some settings, such as this conference, having people worship me as a powerful evil demigod is quite useful. It helps to keep people afraid of me."

"So, you're part of an evil order that practices eating human flesh and drinking blood as a ritual?"

"No, you've confused Rosicrucians with Roman Catholics. You just described communion. The ritual I performed on Hanna at the Centennial Celebration was something I invented." Abigor took another sip of his elixir. "It was but a bit of fun. I'm flummoxed why anyone would follow such a whizzy religion that is focused on perpetuating and hiding the bizarre sexual deviancy of the ecclesiastical class. With your upbringing around that religion and your hillbilly education, amounting to anything should be considered a monumental achievement. It is a testament to my genes that you could become anything more than a lummox or a rummy stiff."

"Okay. Time out. Time the fuck out. This has to be bullshit, right? I don't believe a word of it."

Abigor opened a drawer and pulled out a framed family photo and placed it on his desk. "Look at the Michaelson family. Do you see a familial resemblance?" He waved for Lew to join him for a closer look.

Lew walked around to the other side of the desk where Abigor stood. He put his ax down on the desk and picked up the photo to scrutinize it. It was an old black and white with the family standing together outside a small house. Abigor looked precisely how he does now, and his wife, Meredith, appeared to be decades younger. Meredith held baby Bridgette, Lew's great grandmother.

Wow, I actually see a resemblance. Bridgette looks exactly like Anika—

the same eyes and thick black hair. I can't believe I'm really related to Abigor. Wait, is that my ax?

Lew could see a faint reflection of himself in Abigor's room from the glass covering the photo. He noticed the ax raised above his head. He tried to turn, but Abigor was much too quick. Abigor buried the ax into Lew's head, and the lights went out.

38

Bob Willemsen's head hurt like a bitch.

What the hell happened? I thought I had that old bastard. How is anyone so fast?

He tried to touch his head, but his arms were strapped into the armrests on a chair.

What the hell is this? How long have I been like this?

Bob sat in an oversized wooden chair. He could move his head just enough to see he still wore his blue shirt and green climbing pants. Only now, his clothes were covered in blood. Thick brown leather belts ran tightly across his ankles, knees, thighs, waist, wrists, elbows, chest, shoulders, neck, and head—firmly confining him to the chair. He tried to blink but couldn't. His eyes were held open with a mechanical device that slowly released eye drops so that his eyes didn't dry out and his vision didn't blur, like something out of an old movie he saw with a weird title—clocks, fruit, or something like that.

Bob tried to stand up but couldn't. He was unable to turn his body or move any part of himself away from his confines, even when he strained so hard that his veins bulged and he nearly fainted. Fighting against his restraints only made the leather tighter and more uncomfortable.

I've been in more dangerous predicaments than this. I climb mountains and skyscrapers. When I was on Thor Peak in Baffin Island, a handhold broke, and I fell thirty feet without a helmet and cracked my head on a rock. Luckily, I was on a rope then. I finished my ascent before I went to the hospital and found out I had a concussion. Sasha gave me hell for not abandoning the climb and going straight to the hospital. But I'm not a quitter. I tied a bandana to cover the bleeding, and I wouldn't even consider the hospital until I finished. When I was ice climbing in Keystone Canyon in Alaska, there was a goddam avalanche. Even though I was swept away in ice and snow, I was more worried about losing Sasha. Oh, Sasha... I have to get out of this place—this goddam hotel. Sasha, I'll see you soon. I promise.

Bob tried to look around, but there wasn't much to see from his vantage point. He faced a blank white wall in a dimly lit room. Suddenly, a light appeared, projecting a black-and-white thirty-five-millimeter silent movie of Abigor onto the wall. He wore another of his weird old suits. His projection was small enough to fit in your palm. The speckles and cracks accompanying the old film were very apparent. The sound of a film projector rolling came from behind Bob, but he couldn't see who was operating it.

"Hello?" Bob yelled even though he felt short of breath. "Who's there? What's going on?"

The black-and-white projection of Abigor looked directly at Bob and spoke, but no sound came, other than the sound of the film roll spinning on the projector.

"What the hell is going on?" Bob trembled. "Let me out of this goddam chair right now!"

A record scratched somewhere behind Bob, and then came the crackling of an old phonograph with Abigor's voice. "Welcome to the Chuck. You have proven yourself unwilling to conform to the acceptable behavior of the Summit Conference. You may feel many emotions right now. Fear. Anger. Confusion. Those feelings will all pass. Consider your wants, desires, thoughts, and every idle fancy. I am going to chuck those from you. Everything that has been you will cease to exist. Only your body will remain. Soon, I will be the only occupant of your think-box." Abigor's audio lagged about thirty seconds behind his projection.

"What the hell is this?" The muscles in Bob's chest and neck tightened uncontrollably. "Let me out of here right now, goddammit!" He fought like a rat caught in a trap, but his confines barely let him wiggle in his chair.

If I can just wiggle a little more, I might get my arm out.

He flexed and relaxed his muscles, trying to stretch out the leather by flexing so that he could slide out when he relaxed.

Abigor's projection reached his hand offscreen, and when his hand returned, he was holding a saw.

Is Abigor going to cut me up? What the hell? Maybe I should just agree to the stupid contract and play his game while plotting my escape. These walls can't hold me. They never encountered someone like me before. I free soloed Great Trango Tower in Pakistan. Sons of bitches have died climbing that goddam mountain, but not me.

Bob's attempt to wiggle free proved futile. He was sweating profusely. "What the hell? What the goddam fuck? Okay! Okay! I'll sign the goddam contract! You win! Alright, Abigor. Let me out of here, and I'll—"

Bob became speechless when Abigor's projection stepped out of the wall and landed on Bob's lap. The Abigor was only a few inches tall, but he still held his saw. The speckles and cracks still showed on this little Abigor, even though he was no longer a projection on the wall. He brought an intense chill with him that made Bob shiver.

"Let's open your box and chuck out the useless stuff from your idea pot," the mini Abigor said, no longer suffering from syncing issues between the audio and visual.

"No! No! Get off my goddam lap! Get the fuck off me! Get the fuck off me!" Bob thrashed within the little freedom of movement the restraints offered.

Little Abigor hopped up to Bob's arm and then climbed over his shoulder before making the last leap to Bob's head. Each time tiny Abigor touched his skin, Bob felt like he was getting frostbite. Wee

Abigor perched himself on Bob's coronal suture, and he began sawing into Bob's skull.

Bob shrieked as the saw dug into his head. At first, there was more fear than pain, but the more Abigor sawed, the more excruciating the pain became. Pain shot out of Bob's skull and ran in waves throughout his entire body. Blood ran down his face. He was awake and fully conscious when Abigor cut a large hole out of Bob's frontal bone.

"I tried to control you with a carrot," Abigor said. "You fought that approach. So now I will control you with a stick. Only you won't be you anymore. You'll be something far greater and superior to a social media influencer or a mountaineer. The Summit Conference has the ideal corporate culture that all strive for. You'll eat when I want. Sleep when I want. Think what I want. I will help you achieve greatness, even though you resist it. All that you lose in the process is your identity, but trust me—this will be a howling improvement. I'll even improve how you dress. You'll look much better with a haircut and a suit."

"Please, stop. Abigor, I'll fall in line. I'll sign your contract. I'll do whatever you want. Just, please, stop," Bob cried. Blood poured over his eyes, and he couldn't see anything. He could only hear Abigor's voice and feel the piercing pain of the saw cutting through his head.

I have to get out of here. Damn this hotel. I have to get to Sasha. Goddam Abigor! I can figure out how to get out of here. I set the speed solo record for the Murder Wall on the Eiger in the Bernese Alps in Switzerland. If I can figure out how to do all that, I can outsmart this stupid goddam asshole.

"It's far too late for that, my boy," Abigor said. "You've already revealed your true colors. But I'm not upset. It's your loss, really. I'm quite chirpy right now. This is fun for me."

Bob felt fun-sized Abigor rearrange the inside of his skull. Even though Bob couldn't see, he could feel things plop onto his lap and hear them splatter on the floor.

"Sasha, I'm sorry I didn't make it to you," Bob said in between his sobs. He accepted that he couldn't get out of the chair, let alone the hotel. "I never should have come to this goddam hotel. Sasha, I'm so sorry."

This was the last independent thought Bob could articulate. He screamed until his voice went hoarse, and then he lost the urge to scream. He felt different.

"I am glad to be an attendee of the Summit Conference," Bob announced in the strange cadence of the other zombies at the Beburoa Hotel, "for only through Abigor's guidance will I be able to truly achieve greatness. The success I achieve with superior business acumen will surpass any of my previous achievements in climbing. The Summit Conference is the greatest event in the business world, and it is my privilege to be one of the chosen few attendees."

39

"Do you remember Casey Anthony?" Juliana asked, her voice wavering. Her usual beautiful skin was pale and blotchy, and she had bags under her eyes. She wasn't crying now, but it was apparent she had cried recently. Her hair was an unkempt mess—clumped here and there. She wore an old gray T-shirt covered with splashes of baby puke, snot, and shit—as if their daughter were a young abstract expressionist and Juliana were the canvas.

"The name sounds familiar," Lew Starek said. "Is that your friend who likes to wear those bright neon leg warmers?"

"No, that's Cecelia. Casey Anthony was all over the news a few years ago. She was this mother who killed her baby and then hid the body." Juliana held Anika in a pile of swaddling blankets. Juliana never really got the hang of swaddling the baby, so she usually loosely wrapped Anika in a few of those blankets. "At least that was the rumor. They didn't convict her of murder, but I thought she was guilty. I used to think she was a monster. I mean, what mother would do such a thing to her baby—to her own flesh and blood? But now, I'm coming around and seeing things from her perspective. Maybe her baby was a cunt. Anika's a cunt, too."

"How can she be a cunt?" Lew asked. "She's just a baby. She doesn't even know what she's doing."

"You don't understand, Lew," Juliana said. "You're not the one taking care of her. I am."

"Why don't you hand her to me?" Lew stretched his arms out to take Anika. "You should take a shower, get something to eat, and get some rest."

"I wish I could hand her to you, but I can't." Juliana looked away from Lew.

"Why can't you? I'm right here. I love you, and I want to let you rest. And I want to spend some time with my daughter, who I love, too."

Why does Juliana get into these moods? I'll never understand it.

"Oh, Lew." Tears ran down Juliana's face. "You're not here. You're at some awful hotel attending a stupid corporate conference. It's just Anika and me, and I reached my limit of all I could take some time ago."

Lew realized he hadn't heard Anika make a noise during this entire conversation with Juliana. "Can you show me Anika? How long has she been asleep?"

"Oh, we don't have to worry about her waking up." Juliana stared straight ahead, not looking at Anika or Lew.

"Juliana, please, baby, honey, sweetheart," Lew pleaded. "Will you show me baby Anika?"

"I don't know why you act like you care now. All you seem to care about is your career and finding some hotshot corporate job. I know you don't care about us, so you don't have to worry about us anymore."

"What are you talking about? Juliana, I love you. Will you please show me the baby?"

"I should have known when you left that you would never come back home. You left me all alone with this...thing. So, I had to solve the problem myself," Juliana said with a sting.

"Solve the problem? What are you talking about? She's not a

problem; she's a baby. Will you please show me baby Anika?" Lew felt a pain in his chest.

No, no, no! It can't be.

Juliana stopped crying and held baby Anika like she was an empty piece of Tupperware. "This thing? Do you want to see this? Fine! Be my guest. But don't act like you care about her now!"

Juliana threw the bundle at Lew. The swaddling blankets fell off. Anika landed in Lew's arms. His stomach sank a million miles. He felt his heart die.

How could Juliana do this? How could anyone do this?

Anika's skin was gray and decomposing. Worms and maggots ate at her flesh, which fell apart in Lew's hands. He stared at her tiny little face, which he used to love to admire, but now it made him sick to see the flesh fall away as worms squirmed through where Anika's eyes once were. He held her tiny hands. Lew remembered the first time Anika grabbed his hand—well, it was more like grabbing his finger. She was so small. At that moment, they made an instant connection. He knew he would love Anika forever. But now—now, her hand was half bone and missing some fingers.

How did this happen?

Lew bawled his eyes out. The pain in his chest grew more intense and spread to his stomach.

"Juliana, why did you? How could you? Why the fuck did you do this?" Lew turned to look at Juliana, but she faded away into darkness. He looked back in his arms, and Anika was gone, too. "What?"

BUMP!

"Ouch! What was that?" Lew asked.

BUMP! BUMP!

"Who's hitting me in the head?" Lew shouted to no one, unable to see anything around him. Darkness surrounded him, and he was all alone.

BUMP!

Lew awoke and opened his eyes. He was lying on his back, being dragged across the floor by two mysterious robed figures. Each one held one of his legs, and his body was on the floor.

Whenever there was a step or an obstacle, they banged Lew's head right into it.

BUMP! BUMP! BUMP! BUMP! BUMP!

Lew went up two steps and then down three.

"Ouch! Why are there so many steps?" Lew grabbed his head, which was covered in bumps.

"Oh, good. You're awake," Abigor said.

Lew tried to look at Abigor, but something obstructed his view. "Why can't I see?"

"Let me help you with that," Abigor pulled the ax out of Lew's head. He then pulled a pocket square out of his jacket to wipe some of the blood off Lew's glasses. "You can take care of the rest." He dropped the bloody pocket square on Lew's face.

Lew tried to wipe the rest of the blood from his glasses, but it was caked on pretty thick. He could make a small spot to see through each lens a little, but he mostly smeared the blood around. "I could really use some running water. I can hardly see. Where the fuck are you taking me?"

"We'll have to do something about that mouth of yours, Son," Abigor said. "It's unbecoming for a businessman to swear like a sailor."

"Fuck that," Lew said. "Don't call me son. Or maybe you should call me son since I hate you just as much as I hate my dad. No, I hate you more."

"Hold it right here," Abigor said.

The robed figures dropped Lew's feet onto the floor.

"Stand up, Son." Abigor held the cleaver in one hand at his side, and he pointed his scepter towards something Lew couldn't see. "I want to introduce you to the Chuck."

Lew stood up slowly. He had a splitting headache from the ax.

"Look and see what happens to those who disobey me," Abigor said with a smile. He pointed his scepter at Bob Willemsen, who was strapped into a chair.

Even though Lew's glasses were too dirty to see the entire room, he could see Bob. "What the fuck?"

Bob had a large hole cut out of his skull. Chunks of brains were on his lap and on the floor. Something was squirming around inside his head, throwing bits of brains out. Blood ran down his entire face. An old film projection of Abigor was on the wall in front of Bob, cracked and speckled.

The hairs on the back of Lew's neck stood on end and goose-bumps crept across his skin.

Abigor's voice came from a phonograph in a projection room behind Bob, and it lagged a few seconds behind the projection on the wall. "The Summit Conference is the greatest event in the business world. It is an honor to attend this event. I will learn everything the business world offers. Thanks to Abigor's genius and guidance, I will achieve greatness and realize my full potential."

Bob repeated each word with Abigor. He had an enormous smile on his face, and he sounded like the other mindless zombies of the conference.

"If you were anyone else," Abigor said, "you would already be in a chair next to him by now. I have been lenient with you because of our familial relation, but my patience is finite. If you continue to defy me, you will experience the same fate. But chirk up. It needn't be all so bad. Follow me into the boardroom. I have something else to show you."

Abigor led the way into a spacious corporate boardroom. The walls had framed photos of Abigor posing in positions that looked like they came from Soviet propaganda campaigns. The table was a giant granite rectangle with seats for thirty people. However, there were only two people seated at the table waiting—two of those mysterious robed figures with baggy hoods that hid their faces.

"Flop and take a load off your feet." Abigor pointed his scepter towards an empty chair across from the two seated figures. Only six people were in the room: Abigor, Lew, the two seated figures, and the other two mysterious figures who followed Lew and Abigor.

Lew sat in the empty chair. A glass of water sat on the desk in front of him. He dipped his glasses into it and washed the rest of the blood off before using his shirt to dry the lenses. Only then did Lew notice two manila folders on the desk in front of him. "What is this?" He pointed at the folders.

"Your future," one of the seated figures said.

"What?" Lew asked.

"Why don't you open the folder and read what's inside?" Abigor said.

Lew did as he was told for once. "This is...an offer letter...from Hudnam, Howe & Hartell...to become Vice President of Culture Management...for one million dollars! How is this real?"

The mysterious figure who spoke earlier flipped his hood down. He was a white man in his early forties with a receding hairline and a thick brown mustache and about thirty pounds of extra fat around his midsection. "One million is only the signing bonus. There'll be a salary, too. It's real because I made the offer."

Lew looked him in the eye. *He looks familiar. Have I seen him somewhere before? On the... When I was...* "You're Mr. Hudnam! I used to work for you."

"In the flesh," Hudnam replied. "And technically, you worked for the temp company."

"How the fuck is this possible?" Lew asked, utterly aghast. "You run a billion-dollar company, and you started a charity last year when your dog died. Your firm threatened to fire me from the temp job if I didn't volunteer at your stupid charity events." *I told Juliana that if I ever met Mr. Hudnam, I would knock his teeth out for making me work a second job for him without pay. But that was before I knew he would offer me a million-dollar signing bonus.* "How long have you been here?"

"I've been here for thirty years," Hudnam answered. He was calm but commanding. "I came to the Summit Conference when Hudnam, Howe & Hartell was a small struggling firm. I was on the verge of bankruptcy, and my wife was threatening to take the kids and leave because I could hardly put food on the table. However, the Summit Conference saved my career, firm, and marriage. I learned how to run my business from afar, and my wife was quite happy with all the money she received. Our youngest goes to St. Andrew's Episcopal

School, and our oldest is at Harvard. I can show you how I achieved all these things. Abigor told me how much you impressed him, and I know that anyone important enough to capture his attention would be a valuable asset to my company."

"What's in the other fucking folder?" Lew asked suspiciously.

"Are you sure he's smart, Abigor?" Hudnam asked with a raised eyebrow.

"What in the flaxation? Why don't you open it and read?" Abigor tapped the folder with his scepter. "You seemed quite nobby earlier. Wisen up before you embarrass me further."

Lew flipped open the other folder and read the document inside. "It's a contract to join the Board of the Summit Conference...with a starting salary of a million dollars a year."

"It's everything you ever wanted," Abigor said, as smooth and confident as the best pitchman. "All the money you'll ever need to take care of your family. You'll have an important job. You can put your ideas into practice at Mr. Hudnam's company. We will worship your mind. We'll pack every room and let you lecture the attendees so that they can hear your brilliance. You can pen articles or even books on business corporate culture or whatever suits your fancy. I can get you into any publication you want and make any book an instant bestseller. The entire world will know just how valuable and important you are. I can give you anything you want." He made the possibility of attaining happiness from spending eternity in servitude in a supernatural prison sound appealing.

"You know that what I want most is to be with my wife and daughter," Lew responded. He thought about the dreams or illusions of Juliana and Anika, unsure if these were nightmares, premonitions, or glimpses of the past. *I have to make it back to them before it's too late. I hope it's not already too late. Anika needs me, and so does Juliana.* "I won't accept anything less. Help me escape this confusing fucking shithole."

"It's not so bad," the other seated hooded figure said. Inias Christensen flipped his hood down, revealing his face to Lew. "On the outside, you might spend your entire time on the road, never being sure if you could land the next big account and make enough money for your family. Abigor's deal was amazing. In the next month, a dozen Fortune 500 companies are going to adopt Brazilian Jiu-Jitsu Business. They're going to buy one of my books for each employee and enroll in my training program. I didn't have to think twice. Lew, listen to someone who has more experience parenting than you do. As a father, your most important duty is to provide for your children financially. It doesn't matter so much if you're around. When your daughter gets older and argues with you constantly, you'll realize you don't enjoy being around, anyway. Parents complain about the terrible twos, but the biggest tantrum my oldest daughter ever threw was when I didn't get her a car for her sweet sixteen. And then there are the unexpected expenses... I have five surviving girls. Our first child died of SIDS. The youngest was diagnosed with leukemia a few months ago. My HMO doesn't cover the best doctors and treatments. They only pay for the dumbest motherfuckers who have graduated medical school. Do you know what it feels like to hold your dead child in your arms? I would do anything to keep my other daughters alive. And there's no guarantee I could get enough money to pay for five college tuitions if I was on the outside, but, here, I'm able to get my family all the money they could ever want. Plus, I don't have to deal with my wife bitching at me all the time. I'll call this a win-win situation."

"Inias," Lew couldn't believe his ears. "How could you abandon your family? And when the fuck did you make a deal with Abigor? I just saw you this morning on your way to the gym. You were telling me how to fight demons. When did you find time to buy into all this shit?"

"This morning?" Inias asked with raised eyebrows. "That wasn't this morning. Do you know how many days ago that was? And I didn't abandon them. I'm taking good care of them. You're the one who will abandon your family if you can't provide for them."

"Wait! Days ago?" Acid reflux creeped into Lew's stomach. "I thought I'd only been at the hotel for a couple of days. How long have I been here? How long was I unconscious? Don't any of you motherfuckers want to leave? What kind of person wants to be stuck in a never-ending conference? This is hell! If we all work together, I'm sure we can figure a way out of this hotel."

"Don't you see?" Abigor said. "They're both quite happy with their arrangements, Son. They have everything they ever wanted. Even if they could get out, which they can't, the money would all go away. You can be happy here, too. Simply change your expectations for what you want out of life. I can teach you the hotel's many secrets."

The Bible. The salt. I'm so close to figuring this out. I can't give up now. If Abigor isn't the demon, it must be someone else. But who? "Inias, how do you spot a demon? How do you tell who's the one causing these problems?"

"I told you those are just stories. Why are you trying to go for the submission already?" Inias said. "You don't even know which grappling position you're in."

"Inias, what the fuck?" Lew said. "You're the demon expert. How do you spot a demon?"

One of the mysterious standing figures flipped the hood of his habit down. "Don't worry so much about demons," Brendan said with a scowl.

"Brendan!" Lew never thought he would be happy to see Brendan's angry face. "What am I missing here? I feel like I'm so close to figuring this shit out. You know something, don't you? Don't you?"

"Stop wasting everyone's time trying to figure a way out," Abigor said. "Change your worldview. Make the most of this situation. Many people would kill to be where you are sitting right now. Think about your future."

"You have eyes to see, ears to hear, a nose to smell, skin to touch, and a tongue to taste," Brendan said. "How many more senses do you need to make a wise decision? After decades have passed by, how will you feel when you look in the mirror and think about your life's choices?"

"Of course!" Lew shouted, feeling a boost of adrenaline. He grabbed both manila folders and spoke with the speed of someone trying to leave quickly. "Brendan, Abigor, Inias, Mr. Hudnam, other mysterious figures, thank you for this conversation. It's been very enlightening. I'd like some time to consider the offers, if you don't mind."

"Fine," Abigor said. "But cause no more problems. I'll expect an answer by this time tomorrow."

"Can it be all so simple?" Lew responded with a smile. "No problem. Hey, Grandpa, could I have the ax back?"

40

Hanna Taithangklom scrubbed the carpet with soap and water. She nearly had all the blood out. Blood dripped from the sleeves of her habit, which had become tinted red.

Another essential task from Abigor. This is just peachy. How many people get murdered at this stupid conference every day?

I thought Abigor would pick my brain for business advice. How to strategize and set up a good marketing campaign. How to build social media followers. And I thought he would help me expand my platform to teach the world the importance of being vegan and daily yoga routines. But I'm just cleaning up murder after murder. I don't know how much more of this shit I can take.

No, no, Hanna. Calm your ass down. Remember why you're doing this —for Alexis, to save her life and give her a better future. Abigor booked an appointment for Alexis with one of the top specialists in the country on Monday, and it's going to be expensive. He's just hazing me. Or maybe he's psychologically torturing me. Either way, it's all worth it for Alexis. I'd let him cut me open all over again to save her life. A lot of moms push around mops for their children, but my mop is a real lifesaver.

After she finished cleaning, Hanna changed out of her baggy

habit and into a tight-fitting dark-blue pantsuit with a light-blue blazer and periwinkle high heels and then went to the private dining room. It was one of the small perks Hanna could enjoy. She was halfway through a hot bowl of curry and rice and a freshly squeezed juice when she heard a familiar voice.

"Ching chong bing bong! Mind if I join you?" Camilla asked. She wore a brightly patterned fuchsia, royal blue, and red shimmer power suit with big shoulder pads and a fuchsia cravat. She had moussed her hair high to look like a blossoming flower.

The muscles in Hanna's neck grew tense. *What is wrong with this bitch?*

"Sure," Hanna responded.

"What are you eating?" Camilla curiously eyed Hanna's bowl. "That looks pretty rad."

"Vegan green curry with tofu and Thai eggplant." Hanna took a sip of her freshly squeezed juice of ginger, lemon, orange, and cayenne pepper. "It's a Thai dish," she added, after noticing the blank look on Camilla's face.

Camilla flagged down a server. "I'll have what she's having...and an iced tea." She turned to Hanna. "So, how is my fave Board member?"

Hanna felt hot, and not from the curry. "Honestly, being on the Board isn't quite what I thought it would be. I thought Abigor was interested in my mind and hearing my ideas about business, but he just has me serve him tonics and elixirs. And he makes me clean up murder scene after murder scene. I didn't know so many people were murdered here."

"The murders will die down after a bit, at least until the next batch of people come." The server dropped off Camilla's curry and iced tea. "There are always some people who have trouble adjusting to life here. Not everyone makes smart decisions like us." Camilla took a bite of the curry. "This is good." But she waved at her mouth when the spiciness took hold and then chugged some iced tea. "Whoa! That's some kick." Sweat ran down her face, which had turned red, and her nose was running. She grabbed her napkin and dabbed it on her face.

So, this bitch can't handle spicy food. Hanna tried to suppress her smile. "How long did you have to wait until Abigor gave you sessions and started publishing your books?"

Before answering Hanna, Camilla asked the server to replace the curry with a tuna salad sandwich and bring her two glasses of ice water. "Did you know that Mayan kings used to decapitate their enemies and wear their heads on a belt?"

Hanna nearly choked on her smoothie. "Please, I'm eating."

"These kings used priests and shamans to spread rumors that the kings were gods. Priests were also used to conduct human sacrifice ceremonies. They considered blood to be the ultimate offering to the gods. The sacrificed humans were normally high-ranking enemy captives, such as other kings. Decapitation was one method of sacrifice, but another method involved heart extraction." The server handed Camilla a tuna sandwich and her water and then took the curry away. She downed a glass of water and took a bite of the sandwich and smiled. "Mmmm. That's delicious. Does any of this sound familiar?"

They told me this was all Abigor's idea? But was it really Camilla's? Can I ever trust this bitch? Despite the big '80s clothing, she looks thin and frail, instead of vegan strong like me. I could probably take a knife from this table and stab it into her chest. Maybe I should gut her like a fish and rip out her heart—another offering for the gods.

"Very. So, you're saying that Abigor is treating me like an enemy queen? How long until he saws my head off and wears it on his belt?" Hanna took another bite of curry and chewed while she stared at Camilla in anticipation.

"Abigor's treatment of you—from your induction ceremony to the 'important tasks' that he assigns you now—it's all because he sees you as a threat. He is torturing you, but not just physically. It's all a big mind fuck." Camilla waved her fork to point at the other tables with white men. "Look around. Do you think any of those bastards can relate to what you're going through? No way. Abigor is used to dealing with men, but even after one hundred years of this conference, he's not used to interacting with women in a business setting. He'll never admit this, of course. He thinks women are best suited to birth babies, cook, and clean. The corporate business world is a man's world—at least in his mind. Abigor didn't trust me either at first. He treated me like a maid and had me clean up murders. I came to the Summit Conference with a pitch and an outline for applying the ancient world to the corporate world and a draft romance novel. But Abigor wasn't interested in hearing my pitch. However, after a couple of weeks of being his maid, I started waking up early to refine my business ideas. After three months, I had a good enough draft of Mayan Multitasking to share with him. He was so impressed that he published my book and asked me to lead a session on the topic."

Hanna soaked in every word. *Is this bitch actually trying to help me?* "I have hours of original content on my social media. Maybe I can put together a highlight reel and then show him—"

"What's original content?" Camilla asked.

Oh yes, I nearly forgot that Camilla and Abigor are from other eras. "I have text and videos. I can take some clips and put them together to show a—"

Camilla interjected. "Abigor is old school. He won't be interested in a clip show. If you want to show him something, you need to put it on paper and hand it to him. He's an avid reader. You'll be surprised how quickly he will read it."

"Interesting." Hanna took another sip of her fresh juice. "I used a lot of analytics to grow my social media followers. Metrics helped me know which posts were the most popular. So maybe I should write a business plan and put it in a little pamphlet that shows how he could grow the Summit Conference's social media presence using the same techniques that I did?"

"Don't stop there." Camilla pushed her half-eaten tuna sandwich away. "You need to think bigger and think long term. After all, you're going to be here for a while. Write an entire book about how anyone can use your strategies to build their—what did you call it—social medicine fellows, just like you did. And separately from that, put together a business plan for how Abigor can apply these techniques specifically to the Summit Conference."

"That's actually helpful," Hanna said, her voice rising.

"Actually?" Camilla repeated with a scowl.

"I was worried that you and Abigor were both toying with me, but you're really trying to help. Aren't you?" *Did I reveal too much? Should I not have voiced that fear out loud?* "It's a pleasant surprise."

"Of course, I'm trying to help you. We girls have to stick together. Girl power!" Camilla smiled.

"Yeah, girl power." Hanna held her fist out for Camilla to bump it.

Camilla moved back and fell out of her chair. "Don't punch me," she cried as she hit the floor.

"I'm not going to hit you," Hanna said as she helped Camilla to her feet.

She barely weighs anything. I feel like I could toss her into the air, or at least hold her over my head. "It's a fist bump. I hold my fist out like this, and then you take your fist and softly bump it against mine. Like this." Hanna took Camilla's wrist in her other hand and bumped it against her other fist.

Camilla laughed. Her skin turned red. "Oh, my God! I feel like such a dweeb. I don't know why I thought you wanted to hit me."

They both sat back down at their table.

"Do you mind if I ask you for a favor?" Hanna asked.

"Ask away," Camilla replied.

"Since you know Abigor so well, do you mind if I run some things by you before I present them to him?"

"I'll help you out. You know it. You feel like a bit of a noob in this setting, don't you? It must be intimidating to be in a situation like this with no formal post-secondary education." Camilla smiled.

This bitch thinks I'm not educated. "I have a degree in mathematics from MIT. I found it helpful to bounce ideas off my classmates when I was there. That's what I was hoping to do with you."

"You went to MIT!" Camilla was incredulous. "I didn't realize they let in a lot of chi—" She stopped herself mid-word, and her cheeks flushed.

And there it is. Hiding just below the surface. Hanna ground her teeth and then forced a smile. "You didn't realize they let in a lot of what?" *Say what you wanted to say. No point trying to hide it anymore.*

"I didn't realize they let in a lot of cheery young women." Camilla smiled, waiting to see how her bullshit cover would go over.

"Not really. There were lots of Asians. I was hardly the only cheery young woman there." Hanna smiled back. *So, we'll keep up the charade for a while longer. This was a good thing. Now I know what she really thinks of me.* "I sometimes look like I don't belong, but I know how to fit in."

"That's good. Because you obviously belong here, too. Abigor wouldn't have put you on the Board if he didn't think so." Camilla took another sip of her iced tea. "Unless he only put you there because he thinks it's fun to toy with you before turning you into a zombie. But don't worry. That hardly ever happens."

It looks like she bought the MIT story. It's not a complete lie. I went—I just never finished. I fell in love, got pregnant, and then had other priorities. If Seth didn't pass away, I would have gone back to finish. I just couldn't stand this racist bitch assuming I couldn't get a college education.

"Hmm." Hanna took the last sip of her juice.

Maybe I'm being too judgmental. I suppose she is helping me to an extent, but I need to be careful not to let my guard down around her again. She probably hopes a cheery young woman like me will give her business ideas that she can take to Abigor as her own.

41

Lew Starek prepared for the big showdown by dressing himself in a secondhand Sanderson two-piece suit, brightly patterned with red and pink roses and peonies. He wore a matching blue-and-white checkered tie and a red shirt underneath the suit. Never mind that he looked like a '90s couch. This was Lew's confidence suit. An inner inscription read, "At last I've found my sex machine!!!"

Okay, so I have my game plan. I'm going to summon the demon, kick the shit out of it, go home, and save my family. Piece of cake. I already took some antacids to calm my stomach.

Ax, check.

Bible, check.

Salt, check.

Let's rock and motherfucking roll.

Lew stood in front of the mirror in his hotel room. "Demon!" he shouted. "Get your bitch ass out here! I'm going to fuck you up!"

The mirror showed a reflection of the room, but Lew's Reflection wasn't present in the mirror.

"Come on! Don't pussy out now, motherfucker. Get out here and fight me." He was amped up and hyper alert.

"Geeeebygawwwd cap'n," the Reflection said in an exaggerated West Virginia accent before showing himself in the mirror. He danced into view, doing an ugly jig. The Reflection looked like Lew, but he wore cutoff jean shorts and a cutoff T-shirt with a picture of a Mountaineer and no shoes. "You want to fight a demon? How many times have you been whooped already? You want to get whooped again quicker'n a cat can lick its ass? Think yer smart? You wouldn't know beans with the sack open! You dumbass redneck trailer trash!" He flashed a big smile, which was missing half its teeth.

"Your accent sucks!" Lew shook in anger. "Go back to hell!" Lew threw the ax at the Reflection's head with the speed of a pitcher throwing a fastball.

The Reflection caught it with one hand by the handle. Lew's stomach felt like it dropped ten feet. The hairs on the back of his neck stood on end.

"Couldn't hold yer tater, huh?" The Reflection sneered. "Gave me your weapon at the beginning of the fight. I would expect nothing less from an inbred redneck."

"Fuck!" Lew exclaimed. *Not a great start. It's okay. I have other weapons. I just have to—*

Catching Lew off guard, the Reflection flung the ax back at Lew's chest. It hit him right in the breast pocket. But Lew didn't die or even suffer a wound. The ax turned into a bright flash of light and disappeared as soon as it made contact.

Lew grabbed his chest in disbelief, checking for wounds but finding none. His heart skipped a beat. He reached into his breast pocket and pulled out a Bible. He held it to his lips and gave it a kiss.

"Holy shit! It worked! Fuck yeah, Jesus!" Lew felt a sudden influx of adrenaline. He smiled and his heart raced. "Get ready for a smiting, motherfucker! Oh, and another thing—you say redneck as if it's a slur, but the name comes from striking miners who wore red bandanas during the mine wars. They were heroes who took on the coal company to fight for better rights. Shoved a foot up the coal company's ass. Now get ready to feel my foot up yours, motherfucker!"

The Reflection stepped through the mirror into Lew's room. It gave a preternatural scream, the sheer force of which hurled Lew back against the wall and knocked the wind out of him before he fell to the floor. Lew gasped for air in pain.

"You'll need more than a Bible to save you, trailer trash." The Reflection dropped the West Virginia accent.

"I know." Lew climbed to his feet. "Something like magic crystals!"

He reached his hand into his jacket pocket and flung a handful of loose salt onto the Reflection, covering its head and arms with a light dusting. The salt burned bright red like hot coals and seared its skin. The Reflection winced and roared like a lion while it stood in place.

Lew opened the Bible and read a random passage of scripture in a booming voice. "And Lot went up out of Zoar, and dwelt in the mountain, and his two daughters with him; for he feared to dwell in Zoar: and he dwelt in a cave, he and his two daughters. And the firstborn said unto the younger, Our father is old, and there is not a man in the earth to come in unto us after the manner of all the earth: Come, let us make our father drink wine, and we will lie with him, that we may preserve seed of our father. And they made their father drink wine that night: and the firstborn went in, and lay with her father; and he perceived not when she lay down, nor when she arose. And it came to pass on the morrow, that the firstborn said unto the younger, Behold, I lay yesternight with my father: let us make him drink wine this night also; and go thou in, and lie with him, that we may preserve seed of our father. And they made their father drink wine that night also: and the younger arose, and lay with him; and he perceived not when she lay down, nor when she arose. Thus were both the daughters of Lot with child by their father."

What in the Game of Thrones *is this shit?* Lew asked himself. *And people call me inbred just because I'm from West by God Virginia.*

Cracks appeared in the Reflection's skin. A bright red light shone out of these cracks, small at first before erupting without sound. Lew covered his eyes to avoid being blinded by the light. Where Lew's Reflection once stood was now a tall and handsome angel with feathered wings and long flowing hair, like something out of a Renaissance painting. However, cracks appeared again in the angel's skin. This time, instead of light shining out, only darkness was underneath. The image of the angel turned to ash and crumbled like an outer shell, revealing the true form of the demon underneath, which grew until it was ten feet tall. The demon had three heads—a bull, a man, and a ram. Fire burned in its eye sockets. He had the body of a man but the tail of a serpent. He was entirely nude, but he had a long gray beard that hung low enough to cover his genitals. For that, at least, Lew was thankful.

I really didn't want to see a demon dick.

Lew's surroundings had changed, as well. He was no longer in his hotel room. He was in a large empty cave, dimly lit with hot burning coals scattered here and there. His suitcase and suits remained, piled on the floor. Every other piece of the hotel room was gone—no bed, no lamps, no dresser, not even a bathroom. Only hard rock remained. Tunnels were dug into parts of the rock, and they led to places unknown.

The demon spoke with a deep, hoarse voice that boomed. It made Lew's bones quiver and sent chills down his spine. The demon spoke without moving his lips, communicating telepathically, directly into Lew's mind. *At last, you found my true form. Am I everything you hoped for?*

"Who the fuck are you?" Lew said with a tremble. He saw spots in his vision.

I am Balam—creator of the Summit Conference and the Beburoa Hotel, the one who brought you all here. Balam hunched over like an old man. Apart from his enormous size, he didn't look powerful. But he had a presence to him that made Lew hyperventilate.

"Why the hell did you bring us here? What do you want from us?" Lew's stomach turned into a maelstrom. *Fucking reflux. Calm down, Lew. Think of soothing thoughts, not the giant demon in front of you.*

Balam grinned mischievously like a fat man looking at an all-you-can-eat buffet. *Mortal souls vary in taste by sin. The fools who come here have the perfect mix to make their souls so delicious, but they need some special care to bring the flavor out first. You all have greed, pride, and vanity, which are coated with a lack of self-awareness of your own awful behavior.* Each of his three heads licked his lips in unison. *But things can be done to help bring the flavor out more, like what humans do to geese to make foie gras. Abigor's antics work to make most of the attendees more delicious, but everyone is different. Lew, you needed special attention to bring out your sweet flavors. You'd be surprised what helps to enrich flavor —even this conversation is making you ripe to eat. After one hundred years of preparation, I think it's finally time to feast.* Balam opened his mouths and drooled onto the floor, and the fire in his eyes flashed brighter. *You will taste just as sweet to me as ice cream with whipped cream, chocolate syrup, and a cherry on top.*

"You're talkative for a demon." Lew clutched at his Bible. *I wonder if heaven got a trailer park.*

Balam stepped closer to Lew as he spoke. *You'll soon be my meal. I know you have more questions for me. Go on and ask them. I know all things past, present, and future. This is the last kindness you will experience before I eat your soul. It will feel as though every fiber of your being is burned, crushed, and pulled apart all at once. It will last only for seconds, but, to you, the agony will feel like thousands of years.*

Lew gulped and backed up. "Those visions you showed me of Juliana and baby Anika," Lew said, voice cracking. "Tell me. Are those premonitions? What will happen if I don't leave here? Or are those things that have already happened? Am I already too late?"

Premonitions? Balam scoffed as he continued to walk towards Lew. *You stupid hillbilly trailer trash. I have shown you your deepest desires. You fear your wife and baby are holding you back from success in the corporate world. You want them to be gone so that you have no distractions from your career.*

"You're so full of fucking bullshit! I don't want my wife and baby to die! I love Juliana and Anika." Lew shouted, suddenly stepping forward to confront Balam. "Everything I do is for them. The only reason I want a good job is to provide them with a good life."

Lew, you can lie to yourself, but you cannot lie to me, for I know what your soul hungers for. Balam continued to step towards Lew. *You were so excited to escape your family for a business trip, and you hoped you would never return. They're only obstacles to your success. You yearned for a way to be rid of them. Face it. You enjoyed making a baby much better than raising one.*

"Fuck you! And fuck your bullshit!" Lew stood his ground. His pulse raced, and he no longer felt acid reflux.

You had plenty of warning signs about your wife's condition before you came here. You knew she and the baby might not be alive when you returned, and you hoped for it to be true. Why else would you risk everything to go to a conference that only gave you a chance at employment? You could have found other work back home that didn't require you to be away. There's no denying it. Balam was close enough now for Lew to feel Balam's hot breath on his face.

Lew shook his head back and forth and then jutted his head out at Balam. "No! No! No! It's not fucking true! I mean, yeah, sure, those thoughts sometimes crossed my mind. But it was never anything I hoped for. I didn't want bad things to happen to them. Fuck what you say! Why should I believe you, anyway? You're a fucking demon! Let me out of here, or I'll fucking smite you!"

Balam roared with laughter. *Your anger, self-doubt, and denial will taste especially delicious. Our time to play is nearing an end. Will you come to meet your demise willingly, or will you try to run? Fear and anxiety can be quite tasty.*

Lew slipped his right hand into his pocket and grabbed another handful of loose salt while keeping his left-hand firm on the Bible.

Balam opened his mouths wide, and he grabbed Lew.

Lew threw a handful of salt on Balam, opened the Bible to another random page, and screamed the words. "And if a woman have an issue, and her issue in her flesh be blood, she shall be put apart seven days: and whosoever toucheth her shall be unclean until the even. And every thing that she lieth upon in her separation shall be unclean: every thing also that she sitteth upon shall be unclean. And whosoever toucheth her bed shall wash his clothes, and bathe himself in water, and be unclean until the even. And whosoever toucheth any thing that she sat upon shall wash his clothes, and bathe himself in water, and be unclean until the even. And if it be on her bed, or on any thing whereon she sitteth, when he toucheth it, he shall be unclean until the even." *Who comes up with this shit?*

Balam's skin burned. He recoiled in pain and became paralyzed.

It's working! I'm going to smite him. Every word I speak burns more and more. As long as I keep reading this gibberish, he's finished.

But someone came from behind and slammed into Lew, knocking him to the ground and causing him to drop the Bible from his hands. He stopped reading scripture aloud.

Balam shook the salt from his skin and moved towards Lew again. *Every pain you make me feel will be paid back to you a millionfold. Prepare to die, Lew.*

42

Damien Chernobog caught a glimpse of himself in the mirror and saw the cocaine smeared across his face. He wasn't sure how long he had been at his fuckathon with Ruha, but he looked thinner.

I look like I've lost about thirty pounds.

Damien jumped onto the bed and lay on his back. He couldn't feel his face or his tongue. Ruha pounced on him and worked her sensuous magic. His heart beat a million times a minute, and he sweat buckets. Ruha was a fiery vixen with an insatiable appetite and limitless energy. Damien was a fat piece of shit who usually grew tired quickly, but he had plenty of energy powder to keep him alert. He closed his eyes and let his mind wander as he enjoyed the moment.

I am the smartest motherfucker in the universe. Every day for the rest of eternity, I'm going to bang my hot dream-woman. All I have to do is help Abigor with his stupid conference and give an occasional presentation about how amazing I am at social media, and then this is my reward. My life is perfect.

"Jesus fucking Christ, Ruha," Damien said with a big smile on his face. "You feel like an angel. I could—"

Damien opened his eyes to see Ruha riding him. She was no longer the beautiful woman with giant feet he had first laid eyes on. What stared back at him was a being of darkness with average-sized feet. Her form was not human. It was like someone had taken a brush and dipped it in black ink and painted the silhouette of a person and then taken a slightly darker black pen and scribbled over the profile —layers upon layers, darkness upon darkness, a two-dimensional being in a three-dimensional space. His body ran cold. His member was inside the darkness upon darkness upon darkness that was her crotch. He went from rock hard to limp worm in an instant.

Damien tried to crawl backward on the bed, away from Ruha, but the bed was also gone. He was lying on hard, uneven rock. The hotel room was gone too. He was in a small cave, along with this horrific succubus. His rod slipped out of Ruha's darkness.

"Jesus fucking Christ! What happened to you?" Damien's heart pounded in his chest like a paint mixer in a hardware store.

"You impregnated me with your children." Ruha's voice had changed. No longer sweet, it was deep and echoed but also had high-pitched screeches like nails on a chalkboard.

Damien shuddered. "Jesus fucking Christ!"

Ruha's belly grew dramatically in size, like someone was inflating a balloon. "I have birthed djinns and demons over many millennia. Let's see if your seed has sired someone great."

Father to djinn and demons... What the fuck is a djinn? Pain swelled in Damien's stomach.

"Did it not feel good inside of me? Our children will spawn in a few moments, and then I would like you to give me more." Ruha screamed while eggs shot from between her legs. Each was gray, the size of a fist, and covered in black goop. A dozen of them lay on the floor, and Ruha's belly shrunk down to its original size. She sighed in relief. "I'm ready for you again, lover. Enter me, Damien."

One egg hatched. A small gray creature that looked half Damien and half bat crawled out and screeched. It flapped its wings and was soon airborne.

What is happening?

Damien felt his throat tighten, and he had trouble breathing. "Jesus fucking Christ!" He pulled himself to his feet with the grace of a fish flopping on land. There was an opening to the cave behind her, and he sprinted out of it, sweaty and naked, dripping blood and cum from his dirty dangling plaything.

Damien found himself in a stone hallway, crudely carved as if a giant badger had clawed away at the stone to build a tunnel. The only light came from bits of fire and hot coals that ran along the hallway. He ran like a waddling penguin. He soon tripped and fell and slid on his belly. The angle of the tunnel became steep, and he slid fast like a fat guy on a water slide. He passed other little caves in his fall, some of which had other people inside.

His belly slide turned into a full tumble, with his feet rolling over his head and then his head over his feet.

I feel like I'm sliding through a honeycomb. What happened to the hotel?

He closed his eyes and prayed. "Dear God, I'm sorry for all the shit I pulled in my life. I know it was fucked up. Please help me to... FUCK!"

Damien slid out of the tunnel ass first and slammed into Lew, knocking him to the ground and sending the Bible and Lew's glasses flying. Damien landed on his bare belly, his face in the dirt and his ass in the air.

Every pain you make me feel, a reverberating voice said, *will be paid back to you a millionfold. Prepare to die, Lew.*

Damien took one look at the giant three-headed demon and then screamed as loud as a steam whistle. "Jesus fucking Christ! What the hell are you?" He shivered and stared at the demon, who stared back at him.

I am Balam, a king of hell, Balam answered in a thunderous voice that echoed in Damien's mind. *And you, Damien, are naught but another morsel of food. You should have stayed with my mother and let her extract your seed until there was no life left in your body. It's more pleasurable than the agony you will experience here with me.*

Damien pissed himself and shook in fear. "Mother? Ew!" *It's time to say my prayers.* "Dear God, please forgive me of my—"

43

Hanna Taithangklom didn't recognize her surroundings. One minute she was pushing her mop around, plotting her revenge. The next, she was in a cave, and her mop was missing. Her baggy habit was missing, too, but she still wore the gray yoga pants and green T-shirt she had on underneath.

What's happening?

The cave was enormous and dark, the only light coming from hot coals scattered around on the floor. She walked slowly, examining the surrounding cave.

She heard a man scream in the distance, and she stopped moving. A shiver ran down her spine, and goosebumps crept across her flesh.

Should I go to the scream? Or away from it?

The man's cry echoed all around her. She realized she wouldn't even know if she was moving towards or away from the scream because of the echo.

I may as well just keep walking this way.

Hanna took a deep breath to calm herself and then moved ahead, walking in the same direction as before.

Don't be scared, Hanna. You're a vegan. Nothing should scare you.

She scanned the cave for some kind of clue as to where she was but found none.

Is this another one of Abigor's tricks?

She stopped for a beat and then called aloud. "Abigor? Camilla?" She was unsure if she would feel better or worse to see them in person.

Is this more torture? What the hell is this?

A swarm of bats suddenly surrounded her head. One got caught in her hair and stuck in front of her face as it tried to fly away but was unable to break free. Hanna screamed. The creature was ugly with Damien's face on the body of a small gray bat, and it screeched like nails scraping against metal. She grabbed the bat and threw it on the ground. She stomped on it repeatedly until she heard a crack, and it stopped screeching. She swatted her hands around wildly, smacking more of the bats. The remaining swarm of bats shrieked and flew away.

Hanna stooped down and looked at the dead bat. The body was squished, but the head was in one piece.

That doesn't look like a bat. It looks like someone sewed a little Damien head on a bat's body. What the hell? Is the Summit Conference over?

Hanna noticed she had bat guts stuck on her shoe. She walked backward, scraping her feet on the ground to break the guts free. Not looking where she was going, she fell into a tunnel.

"Shit!" Hanna shouted as she fell.

What's happening? Did someone kill Abigor and set us free? Am I falling out? Maybe I'll finally get to go home to Alexis. I miss my baby so much. But how much longer will we have a home? How much money did my mother receive so far? Is it enough to pay for the doctors? Am I going to be back at the hustle? I thought I made it. I sold my soul to save my daughter and give her a better life, but was it all for naught?

A tear ran down her face as she slid down the tunnel.

Hanna landed on top of someone who screamed. She nimbly got to her feet and saw Camilla lying on the ground.

Camilla's face was red, and her cheeks were wet as if she had been crying. Her face lit up when she saw Hanna. "Hanna! Thank God it's you! This is... The hotel is... This has never happened before. I've been here for decades, and the hotel never disappeared. I don't know what's going on... What the hell is going on?"

"I don't know." Hanna had to fight back a smirk. As upset as she was at her own situation, she was happy to see Camilla squirm. "What's the last thing you remember?"

"I was writing." Camilla got to her feet. Though she looked commanding in a business setting, she looked out-of-place standing in a cave while wearing high heels and a woman's pantsuit with giant shoulder pads. The hot coals' red and orange light cast strange shadows on her face and big hair. Her eyes were wild like a junkie's. "I was getting ready to join the conference when I had the most brilliant idea for another business book, *Move the Needle Like Quetzalcoatl: The Serpent God's Guide to Improve Any Organization*. I sat down at my typewriter and typed so fast. Everything made so much sense. I could see so many parallels between Quetzalcoatl and modern business leaders. The chapters were writing themselves. My fingers moved in a flurry. And then it was all gone. My typewriter was gone. The pages I typed were gone. My hotel room was gone. I was in a little cave—all alone, with nothing but my suitcase and the things I brought to the hotel when I arrived in '83. I wandered around into the hallway, which was just a tunnel, I suppose, and I've been wandering here ever since. You're the first person I've seen so far, Hanna. What is going on? What's going to happen to us? What happened to my pages? Everything I typed was so brilliant. It was going to be my magnum opus. It was all so glorious. I have to get out of here and to a typewriter as soon as possible. You don't have a pen and paper, do you? I'd settle for pen and paper." She broke down and cried. "I'd settle for pen and paper."

The schadenfreude was strong, and Hanna stifled a smile. But she didn't have time to waste on Camilla, not now. She had to figure out what was going on first.

Or maybe I'll twist the knife a little deeper.

"I remember seeing a typewriter over there." Hanna pointed. "But you need to hurry. Someone else said they had an important business idea they needed to type up."

"Like hell they do!" Camilla stormed towards where Hanna pointed.

Hanna followed closely behind. *I literally have a human shield for whatever danger lies ahead.*

And the danger was ahead, as Camilla soon found out. Someone blindsided her, sending her flying into the wall and then falling to the ground. Hanna stopped as Camilla screamed and then crawled back to Hanna and grabbed her ankles. "Save me, homegirl!"

I knew a human shield was a good idea, but she's supposed to be the shield, not me.

A shiver ran down Hanna's spine, and her stomach hurt. Hanna saw a figure of darkness upon darkness before her—a feminine creature with long hair mixed between two and three dimensions. Its movements left trace patterns of darkness like something from a macabre mushroom trip.

"Hanna," the darkness spoke in a squeaky, shrill voice that made Hanna's skin crawl. "The Summit Conference is over. What do you want now?"

Hanna tried to walk, but Camilla hugged both ankles with the strength of someone three times her size. "Camilla, get off me! We need to leave now!"

How does this scrawny skeleton keep my legs together? I'm vegan strong! I should be able to toss her off me like nothing!

"I'm sorry," Camilla said through her tears. "I'm scared. Carry me. I can't move."

Hanna struggled but couldn't shake Camilla off her. "I can't carry you. Get off me before you kill us both! How is your grip so strong?"

"Little drones like you argue over who is more important, but it doesn't matter." The being of unnatural darkness walked towards Camilla and Hanna. "It never mattered. All bow before the queen." She screamed in a voice that sounded like sheet metal being torn apart, and a swarm of bees shot out of the darkness between her legs.

Bees flew past Camilla and Hanna, who both screamed.

"What are you waiting for, Hanna?" the darkness asked as she approached the two women. She touched her hand to Hanna's cheek. It felt smooth and cold like a stone. She whispered into Hanna's ear, "The illusion of the Summit Conference is over. So is the illusion of eternal life. This is your chance to take your revenge on Camilla—for how she tortured you, for the part she played in your sacrificial ceremony, for how she tricked you into thinking your servitude would be glamorous. She's too weak to fight you. Why don't you make her pay?" She gestured to the ground near Hanna's feet, and there were two large bowls of curry paste—one green and one red.

Hanna took a beat as she pondered the recent development. And then she grabbed the curry—green in the left hand and red in the right—and smeared both handfuls onto Camilla's face. She shoved it down Camilla's throat, up her nose, and into her eyes. Camilla wailed in pain. Her face turned red. Tears poured from her eyes, and snot ran down her nose. Camilla vomited. She let go of Hanna's ankles and tried to wipe the curry from her eyes.

"She deserves worse than this," the darkness said to Hanna. "Let the hate flow through you."

Hanna stopped, kneeling next to Camilla. Hanna helped Camilla wipe the curry paste from her eyes.

"Hanna, why did you do that?" Camilla asked, sobbing.

"I'm sorry. Let me help you." Hanna's voice had genuine concern. She used her shirt to wipe the curry out of Camilla's eyes.

Camilla blinked her bloodshot eyes and looked around.

"Can you see?" Hanna asked.

Camilla nodded.

"Good." Hanna smiled. "Because I want the face of a cheery woman like me to be the last thing you ever see."

Camilla's eyes went wide in shock.

A split-second later, Hanna hit Camilla in the face with a rock she found on the ground nearby. Camilla's nose bled. She tried to speak, but Hanna hit her with the rock again in the mouth and knocked out her teeth. Hanna pounded on Camilla's face with the rock, and it made a crunching sound as the blows broke Camilla's skull and teeth.

By the time Hanna stopped, Camilla's head had caved in. Blood and brains had splattered over Hanna's face, shirt, and clothes, as well as onto the rocks nearby. Underneath the mess, Hanna smiled.

"Now, we're even," Hanna said.

The unholy darkness stood next to Hanna and put her icy-cold hand on Hanna's shoulder. Hanna looked into the bizarre creature's strange, surreal face that was darkness upon darkness.

"She's going to come back, like I did, right?" Hanna asked.

She made a squeaking sound that made Hanna's skin crawl. It took Hanna a minute to realize she was laughing.

"She's not coming back," the darkness said before caressing Hanna's cheek. "You truly killed her. How does it feel to be a murderer?"

An icy chill ran down Hanna's spine, and her stomach sank. In the heat of the moment, she didn't think about whether the murder was truly fatal. She simply enjoyed the act. But now, she felt a pang of regret. Hanna gulped and then looked away.

"You're the voice I heard when I was dead, aren't you?" Hanna asked.

She nodded.

"What the hell are you?" Hanna asked.

"I'm Ruha," the darkness answered.

"Are you going to kill me now?" Hanna inquired. *I have a good life insurance policy. I'll be able to provide for Alexis in my death in a way I never could in life.* "Leave my body somewhere other people will quickly find it when you're done." *It will be harder to prove death without a body. I don't want to die in vain.*

"Hanna," Ruha said. "I see great things in your future. Follow me." She turned around and walked down the tunnel.

"Where are we going?" Hanna asked as she forced herself to her feet and trudged behind Ruha.

"To a sumptuous feast," Ruha said.

44

Bob Willemsen walked through the cave tunnel. Skinny greeted him.

"Bob, man," Skinny said with a smile. His eyes were dilated, and he reeked of reefer. "What happened to you? You cut your hair short and styled it like a dork. And you're wearing a suit, too. And what the hell is up with the hotel, man? We're in a cave or something now. I think this means Abigor must have died or some shit, man. Do you think we can get out of the hotel, now that the conference is over? I know we signed some shit with Abigor, but if he's dead, none of that shit matters, right? I wonder who killed him and how? Hey man, let's go see if we can find Damien, and then let's get out of here."

Bob smiled at Skinny. "Don't waste your time thinking of a life outside of the Summit Conference. Abigor helped me realize what I have been missing in my life—a sense of purpose for achieving my true potential and excelling in business. Stay with us and achieve greatness." His voice had the same strange tone and cadence as many other Summit Conference attendees.

"Oh shit, man," Frank responded. "You're a zombie. Well, ain't that some shit? Is there a way to snap you out of it?" He pulled at

Bob's eyelids and looked into his eyes. "Bob, are you in there, man? Can you hear me? It's your boy, Frank. We gotta bounce, man. The conference is over. Even the hotel is gone, man."

"Don't fight success," Bob said as he continued to walk straight ahead. His feet clumsily stepped on hot coals and caught fire. The fire ran up his pant leg, but Bob seemed to neither know nor care. "Through Abigor, we can all realize our full potential and—" Bob's was interrupted when the ground underneath him collapsed, and he fell into a hole. He didn't scream or make a sound. He simply stopped talking and fell.

Bob landed on his ass, and a moment later, Skinny landed on top of Bob. The fire on Bob's pants had gone out, and Bob noticed he was lying on top of someone else.

"Adzooks!" godlike Abigor shouted from underneath the pile. "Get off me at once. Go to Bannagher!"

Skinny and Bob got to their feet, and godlike Abigor did as well. Swift-footed, godlike Abigor pushed the two and shouted, "Watch your step, both of you. Gorblimey! This whole place is falling apart. I'm still in charge here, and I demand to be treated with respect. You will not disrespect me. I don't care if you're a dope fiend or a lunkhead." The god among men wore a black morning suit and carried his golden scepter.

"A thousand apologies, Abigor," Bob said. "For it is only through your outstanding leadership that any of us can—"

"Oh, shut it!" godlike Abigor snapped.

"Oh shit, man!" Skinny said. "You're alive!"

"Of course, I'm alive," godlike Abigor said.

"I thought you were dead because the hotel is gone, man," Skinny said. "What happened to those creepy guys in the robes that follow you everywhere? Is the conference over? Can we go home now? By the way, man, I lost my million dollars and my bag of weed. Can I have another?"

"Can you have another what?" godlike Abigor said with a sneer.

"Both, I guess, man." Skinny shrugged.

Swift-footed Abigor responded with winged words, "Aw, go soak your head!" He took his scepter and struck Frank in the face. It left a red mark on Frank's right cheek, but the scepter itself snapped in half. The spherical orb at the top detached and rolled away, bouncing and clinking along the cave.

"Ouch, man," Skinny said. "That hurt."

Godlike Abigor, for whom the sun rises and sets, froze and widened his eyes. He stared in wonder at the broken wooden shaft in his hand.

"Motherfucker!" Skinny shouted as he lunged at godlike Abigor.

But swift-footed, godlike Abigor nimbly dodged the attack and punched Skinny in the stomach with a blow that bowled him over.

After Skinny fell, the ground underneath the trio collapsed, and they plunged into another hole. They landed on someone else.

"Judas Priest!" a lesser minion shouted from under the pile. "Get off me! Tramp on it!"

Bob, Skinny, and then godlike Abigor got to their feet one by one. The lesser minion stood up last. Upon noticing he had shouted at godlike Abigor, he bowed his head in shame.

Swift-footed, godlike Abigor addressed the lesser minion, "Don't be a grouser. You goop! I ought to remind you to respect me!" He raised the broken handle of his scepter in preparation to strike.

The lesser minion braced for impact but stopped upon seeing that the broken stick was the once-powerful scepter. "You lost your power, didn't you, you old fart?" He stood tall and became bold. "That's why the hotel and the conference are gone. You'll soon feel my wrath for making me crawl under your shoe." He prepared to attack.

Swift-footed Abigor stabbed the sharp, broken handle into the lesser minion's neck. Blood spurted out and sprayed godlike Abigor.

The lesser minion collapsed and stared at godlike Abigor as life trickled from his body. The minion whimpered, "When I come back—"

"I'll be waiting!" Swift-footed, godlike Abigor stomped on the minion's head. The skull split open like a coconut, splattering brains and blood everywhere. Godlike Abigor looked like a red-and-black

Jean-Paul Riopelle painting from the front, blood splattered all over his black morning suit. He smiled.

"Where is the dope fiend?" godlike Abigor asked as he turned towards Bob.

Bob stood alone, but he stretched out his hand to point behind godlike Abigor, who turned around, ready to strike the stoner in anger. But swift-footed Abigor paused when he saw something unexpected—a giant three-headed demon holding Fatty.

The demon tore Fatty's chubby naked body in half and then sucked his soul out of his head until he withered into a wilted gray husk that collapsed into dust when it hit the floor. Fatty's bottom half, with a bloody, piss-covered ding-dong and chubby little legs, was still intact. The demon tossed it away.

"Adzooks!" godlike Abigor exclaimed. "What are you?"

Abigor, the demon said in an ear-splitting voice, *you should know me better than anyone, for you have been my livestock for the past one hundred years. I am the face that stared back at you through the mirror every day. I'm the one who pampered you with cocaine, opium, and luxury; the one who bent others to your will; the one who gave you power and riches to satisfy your every desire. Feast your eyes upon Balam, the creator of the Beburoa Hotel. Now stand aside."*

Balam swatted swift-footed Abigor with a backhand that knocked him back twenty feet. Balam then walked towards the minion's lifeless body, and he bent down and placed his hand over the minion's face. A dark light shined from his hand, and when Balam pulled it away, the minion's face was healed. The minion opened his eyes and stood up.

"What are you?" the lesser minion asked with a tremulous voice.

I am a king, Balam answered. *And a connoisseur of exquisite tastes. You look sweeter than honey.*

He snatched the minion up in one hand and sucked his soul from his body. Balam turned and tossed the lifeless husk at godlike Abigor.

The thing I put in your skull helped to keep you under control, Balam said. *But it makes you taste quite sour.* He motioned his index finger towards himself, like a mother calling her child, and he watched Bob intently.

Something pressed from the inside of Bob's skull, stretching the skin like a balloon. It pushed out once, twice, and then it exploded out and split the front of Bob's skull open. A little Abigor emerged, covered in blood and brains, and then took a bow. Little Abigor looked at real Abigor, put his hands in the air, and faded away.

Bob remained awake, though in a daze. Balam picked up Bob with one hand and Bob's face with his other hand. A dark light shone from underneath Balam's palm. And then Bob awakened from Abigor's spell and finally sensed the surrounding danger.

"What the hell?" Bob shouted, feeling like himself again. *What happened to me? Where am I now? How much time did I lose? Why am I trapped? And what is this thing?*

Bob squirmed, trying to break free from Balam's grip, but it was no use.

Balam sniffed Bob's head. He licked his lips. *Yes, that is much better. You will taste spicy and delectable. Like pizza drizzled with honey and chili peppers.*

The demon sucked Bob's soul from his body. The pain felt like being set on fire, stabbed, crushed, pulled apart, and twisted all at once.

45

Lew Starek crawled along the cave floor. Large boulders and stalagmites hid him from Balam's direct line of sight, for now. Lew felt around the floor for his glasses and the missing Bible. He was nearsighted, so he could read from the Bible without his glasses if he held it close enough to his face. If he found the Bible before he found his glasses. If he found it at all. Lew squinted and tried to look around. He saw broad shapes and colors, but everything was blurry like a Van Gogh painting.

He reached his hand forward again, and this time he felt the black frame and lenses resting on the cave floor, near a burning coal but not touching it.

I'm so lucky today.

Lew tried to grab them, but before he could, someone's foot stomped down on his hand.

CRUNCH! CRACK!

The person who stomped on his glasses fell to the ground and whimpered in a masculine voice. Lew picked up his glasses and tried to put them on. One lens had popped out. The other lens was still in the frame but scratched in several places. The glasses stayed on his face—until he spun his head quickly, which caused them to fall off again.

"Fuck!" Lew exclaimed, much louder than he wanted.

Lew! Balam shouted back in his booming voice that echoed inside Lew's head. *You can't hide from me, and you can't escape.* He stomped as he walked, shaking the cave-like a T-Rex. *I don't like to waste food, and you are one of my tastiest morsels. I seasoned you myself. Fee fi fo fum, I smell the blood of trailer trash.*

Lew put his glasses back on his face and took a gander at the guy who broke them.

Mr. Hudnam glared back at Lew from the cave floor. Hudnam's eyes were wide. He was shaking and sweating. He spoke, hushed but franticly. "Lew, you have some kind of power over that bastard, don't you? Get me out of here—before that damn monster eats me, too."

You broke my glasses, you piece of shit. You might have killed us both. "Okay, Mr. Hudnam. I'll save your life. For ten million dollars."

"Ten million dollars! Are you out of your fucking mind?" Hudnam shouted and furrowed his brow.

Scream after scream filled the cave and echoed from all around as Balam grabbed the guests of the Beburoa Hotel and sucked their souls from their bodies. The demon belched and then laughed.

As if firing me wasn't enough. "Fuck you! Pay me or get ripped in half and eaten like the others. He said the pain feels like it lasts for hundreds of years, even though it's only a few seconds, you dirty rat fuck."

"Fine. Fine!" Hudnam snapped back.

"Great," Lew said as he continued to scan the floor. "I have a plan. I just need my Bible. Balam knocked it out of my hand. Help me look."

"A Bible?" Hudnam said in disbelief. "That's your plan? A Bible? That Jesus shit doesn't work. If it did, I wouldn't have ended up in this hellhole. Do you know how much money I give to churches every year? Enough so that I don't have to pay Uncle Sam a copper cent, that's how much."

I should leave this asshole behind. No, no. If I get out of here alive, I'll need money to take care of Juliana and Anika. I can eat his shit for a little while until he pays me. I can be nice to this jerk who fired me for leaving work when my wife went into labor.

"Listen!" Lew shot back in a heated whisper. "If you hadn't broken my glasses, I might have found the Bible by now. Help me find it or say your prayers."

Hudnam didn't say a word. He rolled from his back to his stomach, and he started scooting around, searching for the Bible.

Lew crawled and searched. He paused from time to time to sit up and look all around.

Maybe I wouldn't need a Bible if I remembered a single Bible verse. How many years did I go to mass and Catholic school, and I can't remember a Bible verse to save my life? Wait, I think that's it!

Lew saw the Bible up ahead, lying open, pages down, on the dirty cave floor. He crawled towards it like a lizard, and when it was finally within arm's reach and almost in the palm of his hands, Hanna Taithangklom stepped from the shadows and scooped it up.

"Hanna." Lew gasped. He paused as he replayed Hanna's horrible murder in his mind, and then he shuddered. "You're alive! I can get us out of here and kill that demon. Just hand me the Bible."

Hanna held the Bible firm in her hand and moved it behind her back.

A being of darkness upon darkness that defied two- and three-dimensional space emerged from behind a stalagmite. It moved close to Hanna from her blind spot. *What is that thing? It's going to kill Hanna!* "Watch out! Behind you! That thing is going to—"

It put one hand on Hanna's shoulder in a gentle embrace.

"Lew, Lew, Lew," the being of darkness said in a voice that was both as deep as a bass drum and as high-pitched as nails on a chalkboard. "I'm not here to hurt Hanna. I'm not here to hurt you either, if you give me what I want. Refuse me, and you can become my son's dessert."

Her son? "You're its mother?" Lew squirmed. "What the hell are you? What do you want?"

"I'm Ruha. And I want something only men have." Ruha took her hand and grabbed Lew by the balls. "I want your seed."

A chill ran through Lew's body, radiating from his crotch. He pushed her hand away and jumped backward, falling onto his back. His stomach churned, and he thought he might vomit.

"Is it my appearance?" Ruha asked. "Because this can change." She suddenly looked like the vixen that seduced Damien. She was completely nude, and she had a sultry smile. Her voice changed to sound sweet as honey again. "Is this more your style? You remember me from the hallway." She twirled and slapped herself on her ass tattoo. "Are enormous feet and Steven Seagal tattoos not your style? No big deal." She looked at Hanna and then back at Lew. "Are you curious?" Now she looked like Hanna—still completely nude. She walked closer to Lew, and he crawled backward without breaking eye contact. "Did you like what you saw during the ceremony?" she asked in Hanna's voice. "Don't you want to experience this body? It's really quite amazing. I can contort in any way you imagine, as well as several ways you hadn't thought possible."

"Hanna," Lew said, addressing the real Hanna. "Throw me the Bible, please. Come on! Help me out. I have a wife and a daughter. I want to go home to them."

"Would you prefer something more familiar?" Ruha asked. Now she looked precisely like Juliana, and she was still completely nude. "You don't need to leave to see your wife again. My loving face is right here."

Lew stopped crawling backward. *How did she...* His loins stirred while his eyes ate up Juliana's body. *This isn't Juliana. It's a demon... But it looks just like her...*

Taking advantage of Lew's halted retreat, Ruha walked over and stood so that her feet were on either side of his hips. "I can be your anything. Say the word, and I'll turn into Bonita Applebum." She smiled sensuously at him. "Now take your pants off and put a baby in me. We can listen to 'A Tribe Called Quest' the entire time."

46

Hanna Taithangklom pondered her predicament.

Ruha is some kind of demon shapeshifter. Lew said he could save us. There's a giant demon eating people further away, and Abigor is running and hiding from that devil. Will Abigor still be able to help Alexis? Will Ruha offer me something better?

"Take your pants off," Ruha said as she bent over and grabbed Lew's belt buckle.

That bitch is showing me her asshole. Disgusting. She even turned into me earlier. I don't like the idea of someone disguising themself as me to fuck guys. Yeah, I'm really alluring—thanks to my vegan diet and intense yoga training—but I don't want some doppelgänger slanging my poontang around. I know it's not really me, but it still makes me feel violated.

Hanna looked at the Bible in her hand. It was dirty on the outside and inside.

Does this thing really have some kind of magic?

"Salt!" Ruha shouted. "Did you really throw salt on me, Lew? You think that I'm a weak demon you can easily cast out with some silly tricks? I'm the mother of demons!" She rubbed the salt off her breasts with her hands and then licked it. "Nobody can subjugate me. Nothing can stop me. Give me what I want, or I'll feed you to my son."

Can Lew really save me? Hanna flipped through the dirty Bible. *Is there something hidden in the pages? This is just a book. What the hell is so magical about it? It would be nice to see Alexis again, to hold her in my arms. I would do anything for her, even sell my soul, which I thought I already did. Was this all nothing but a pipe dream? Maybe I should go home, go back to the grind. At least I'll get to be with Alexis. Perhaps I've already gotten everything I can out of the whole influencer thing. Maybe I should give it up. I can get a job as a yoga teacher at a studio or do private yoga instruction for wealthy clients. It will be a living.*

Hanna approached Lew and Ruha. He was still on his back, scrambling, while Ruha had taken hold of his pants and was trying to pull them off his body.

Will Ruha feed me to her son, too, if I don't give her what she wants? Let's find out if Lew really can take me home.

She prepared to toss the Bible to him, hoping he would work magic with it. But before Hanna could throw it, someone tackled her. She hit the ground hard. The impact knocked the wind right out of her, and her head bounced off the rock floor.

"Take that, bitch!" Hudnam shouted from on top of Hanna. He grabbed the Bible out of her hand while she struggled to catch her breath. "I have the Bible, Lew," he said with a gleam in his eye. He sauntered towards Lew and Ruha.

What the fuck was that? I've never been tackled before... My head hurts... It sounds like the phone is ringing... And everything is blurry... But now it's clear again... Why won't somebody answer the damn phone? Well, this is just peachy.

Hanna staggered to her feet like a boxer who had been knocked down.

That bastard Hudnam—he and Abigor like to pal around together, even when he wears his baggy habit. Did he call me a bitch?

"Asshole!" Hanna shouted in a loud, commanding voice that caught the attention of everyone nearby.

Hudnam turned around to regard her. Lew and Ruha stopped their dance to look at her. Abigor popped up from behind a stalagmite to watch her. Even Balam momentarily paused with Seymour

Grenville in his hands to observe her, but then Balam sucked Seymour's soul from his body and dropped his husk on the floor while he took a steady march towards Hanna and the rest of the mayhem.

"Asshole!" Hanna shouted again. She ran at Hudnam full steam and hit him in the face with a flying knee kick. He dropped like a sack of bricks, and she tore the Bible from his hands. "Asshole!" she screamed directly into the face of his half-conscious body.

Balam continued his march towards them. He was thirty feet away and closing. The cave boomed with each step.

"Like a true queen," Ruha said with a smile. "Take your place by my side. My son won't hurt you as long as you stand with me." She turned her attention to Lew again.

Balam moved closer still. He was only twenty feet away now, and the sound of his footsteps grew louder with each step.

Who can I trust? Ruha is a demon. Can I trust her? Can I trust Lew? Fuck it!

Hanna swung the Bible like it was a bat and clobbered Ruha on the side of the head with it. There was no magical force to the impact, but it was hard enough to knock Ruha off her feet and onto the ground. Hanna held the Bible out towards Lew. "Take us home, Lew, if you really can. I want to see my daughter again."

"Insolent and foolish girl!" Ruha shouted from the ground nearby. "You dare to strike me!"

Lew grabbed the Bible from Hanna, and then she helped him to his feet.

Balam was ten feet away and closing. He would soon be on top of them.

"Now or never, Lew," Hanna said. "What kind of magic can you do?"

Lew flipped the Bible open to a random page, and his glasses slid off his face and fell. The single lens popped out when it hit the cave floor.

Balam was close and ready to attack.

Lew buried his nose in the Bible and shouted the words at the top of his lungs. "And the king said unto her, 'What aileth thee?' And she answered, 'This woman said unto me, "Give thy son, that we may eat him today, and we will eat my son tomorrow." So we boiled my son and ate him. And I said unto her on the next day, "Give thy son, that we may eat him"; and she hath hid her son.'"

Shank! Shunk! Shluk!

What the hell was that?

Balam stopped dead in his tracks. Frank Dolan had jumped onto the scene, armed with metal crucifixes with razor-sharp points, which were made from cans of PanWow. He stabbed three of them into the demon—one in Balam's left side, another in his stomach, and a third in his ram head. When Lew read the Bible aloud, the crucifixes glowed gold, and red light leaked out of Balam's wounds.

Raaahh! Balam roared so loudly that it shook the entire cave.

Frank stood near Balam, holding another crucifix in his hand. "Where's my weed, man?" he shouted at the demon. "You're out here eating everyone. Did you eat my weed, too, and shit? You even ate Bob, you fucking bastard. Where the hell is Damien, man? Did you eat him, too?"

That stoner bought us some time, Hanna thought. *I never thought he'd be useful at all. And the Bible... The Bible verses hurt the demon. It's casting a magic spell. This is some real* Harry Potter *shit.*

Lew stopped reading to turn towards Frank and Balam. He squinted his eyes and tried to figure out what was happening. "Where are my glasses?" He squinted and looked around on the ground, unable to see anything.

This blind bastard! Hanna grabbed Lew's frames and lens from the ground and handed them to Lew.

He popped the lens back into place and put the glasses on. "Thanks," Lew said. He ripped a few pages out of the Bible and stuffed all but one in his pocket.

Hanna turned to where Ruha was, only to find she was gone. *Where the hell did she go?*

Frank's screams of pain answered Hanna's question. Ruha had taken Frank's sharpened crucifix from him and stabbed it into his shoulder. He fell onto the ground and tried to pull it out with his other arm, but even putting a hand on it made him wince in agony.

Ruha pulled the other crucifixes out of Balam. She was still in the form of a nude woman with black hair. "Hush, my child," she said in a soothing tone. "You'll feel better soon. Feeding will help."

That reminds me of Alexis and me. Are all mothers the same on a deeper level? How many people would I kill to feed my daughter? Is there a limit? Or is the answer everyone? *And whose phone keeps ringing?*

Frank tried to pull the crucifix out of his shoulder again.

Idiot!

"Leave it in!" Hanna called out. "He can't touch the crucifix! Leave it in and run!"

"What did you say, man?" Frank turned around, too engrossed in his own pain to pay attention to Hanna's warning. He gave one more tug on the crucifix, and it popped out of his shoulder, fell to the ground, and broke apart into two twisted pieces of metal.

Wasting no time, Balam took Frank's arm and ripped it off his body in one motion. Blood gushed out of the empty arm socket. Balam grabbed Frank with his other hand and sucked his soul from his body.

Hanna and Lew, Balam's voice boomed. He looked at them both and licked his lips. *Shall I eat one, or shall I eat two?*

"If you're going to do something with those ripped-up pages," Hanna said to Lew, "hurry!"

47

L ew Starek poured salt into one of his ripped-up Bible pages and folded it into an origami pocket. *Nothing fancy,* he thought, *but it should hold the salt together.*

Hanna stood next to him, watching his actions.

Hudnam was slowly getting off the floor.

Abigor emerged from behind a stalagmite and approached Lew and Hanna. They recoiled, but Abigor put his empty palms up to soothe their fears.

"I mean no harm to you," Abigor said. "Begorra! You two are quite a team. Get me out of here, and I'll reward you both heartily."

"The Summit Conference is over, Gramps," Lew scoffed. "Your powers are gone."

Abigor responded with a laugh. "Go to blazes! You think a corporate conference is the extent of my domain? I've spent the past hundred years accumulating unprecedented wealth and power. I have a controlling stake in hundreds of major corporations, and I have more stocks, bonds, and cash than anyone in the world's history. You're looking at the only trillionaire that humanity has ever seen. I can give you everything I promised on the outside, but only if you get me out of here alive."

Lew's head swam. *I can get back to Juliana and Anika, and I could be rich beyond my wildest dreams!* Lew turned to Hanna, who stared at Abigor, slack jawed.

"Now get a curve on," Abigor said. "We must act fast if we—"

Abigor's words were cut short when Balam grabbed him and sucked his soul from his body. In seconds, Abigor was an empty husk that Balam tossed to the ground. Lew's stomach sank, and he felt everything around him spin.

Still as nude Juliana, Ruha patted Balam on his back. Balam belched, and the entire cave shook.

It reminds me of Juliana burping Anika, Lew thought. *Why does she still look like Juliana?*

Nothing tastes as savory as meat that has been cured for a hundred years. Balam laughed and licked his lips. *Abigor was as delicious and rare as Southern Maryland stuffed ham.* When his laughing subsided, he turned his attention to Lew and Hanna.

Lew put a hand on Hanna's shoulder to steady himself. He grabbed salt from his pocket and sprinkled it over his body.

"Hey, motherfucker," Lew bellowed. "Come get some!"

He ran straight at Balam, who grabbed Lew with one hand. Balam lifted Lew towards his mouth, but the salt burned the demon's hand. Balam dropped Lew almost instantly. However, Lew was close enough to throw his Bible origami salt bomb straight down the throat of Balam's human head.

Lew pulled out the Bible once again, flipping it open randomly and screaming the passage aloud. "And Saul said, Thus shall ye say to David, The king desireth not any dowry, but an hundred foreskins of the Philistines, to be avenged of the king's enemies. But Saul thought to make David fall by the hand of the Philistines."

Balam choked and gagged. He grabbed his throat with both hands. The burning fire that was his eyes grew dim. He coughed, and the cave shook.

Ruha slapped Balam on his back. "Spit it out! Spit it out, baby! Spit it out!" She cried as she watched her child in pain, unable to soothe him.

Lew put the Bible down on the ground so that he could cover both of his ears, shielding himself from Balam's deafening cough. He kept reading. "And when his servants told David these words, it pleased David well to be the king's son in law: and the days were not expired."

A white light came out of Balam's mouth as he choked and fell to the ground. At first, the light was soft, but it grew brighter the more Lew read. "Wherefore David arose and went, he and his men, and slew of the Philistines two hundred men; and David brought their foreskins, and they gave them in full tale to the king, that he might be the king's son in law. And Saul gave him Michal his daughter to wife."

What the fuck kind of story is this?

Balam fulminated in an enormous blast of light and sound that temporarily blinded and deafened Lew, who fell to the ground with a ringing in his ears, unable to see anything but the white afterglow of Balam's explosion. Soon the light faded, and the ringing stopped. Balam was gone—not a trace left of him. Ruha was gone, too.

"It worked," Lew said in disbelief. "It worked! We're free!" He felt warm all over. Lew high-fived Hanna, and he high-fived Hudnam. "I'm free! I'm going home! Hahaha!"

And then the cave shook. It began as a slow rumble, and it turned into a violent earthquake. Stalactites broke from the ceiling and stabbed the ground below.

Inias wandered into the cave from a tunnel, dressed in his gym clothes. "What the hell is going on? Where is the hotel?" he asked. But a falling stalactite skewered him before he could get an answer.

No, not Inias...

"Over there!" Hanna shouted. She pointed towards a tunnel that had a light at the end. "It's a way out." She took off.

Lew and Hudnam followed.

~

FROM OUTSIDE THE MOUNTAIN, Lew heard hundreds of simultaneous shrieks and squeals from the remaining Summit Conference attendees. Voices shouted out in toe-curling pain and terror and despair. It was deafening. And then, all at once, the screaming stopped. But Lew knew that the silence didn't come from their rescue—it came from their death.

Lew regarded Hudnam.

"What happened to you?" Lew asked.

Hudnam looked much older than he had inside the hotel. His hairline receded more, and the remaining hair turned gray. His jawline turned jowly, and his skin turned wrinkly and paler.

"The agelessness I experienced at the Summit Conference must have been part of the demon's magic in the cave. It doesn't work out here. I finally look and feel my age. I think I have arthritis." He softly touched his wrists and hands. "Is *Xena: Warrior Princess* still on the air? I used to love that show." He breathed deeply and stretched his legs. "Oh, it feels good to get out and get some fresh air. Lew, do you have a car here? I'm eager to get back and check on the company. It's been a long time since I've been in the office."

Eager to get back and check on this company? Does he even have any interest in seeing his wife or kids?

"I'm not sure. I drove here, but I left my car with a valet who might have been a demon. We might have to walk until we get to a town." Lew looked around and took a deep breath. "So, Mr. Hudnam, I'll accept my ten million dollars for saving your life as cash or check. I'm assuming you need to go to the office to get your checkbook?"

"Well, here's the thing, Lew," Hudnam said with a sleazy grin. "I signed nothing, so you can't prove that I owe you a cent. What's with your generation, anyway? Why are you so lazy and looking for handouts? You need to pull yourself up by the bootstraps and learn to make something of yourself."

"You dirty motherfucker," Lew said. "I never should have saved your life. You're a real piece of shit, you know that?"

"What are you going to do about it?" Hudnam said, full of false confidence. "You can't un-save my life."

"Like hell, I can't, you human jizz stain!" Lew threw a flurry of punches at Hudnam, who wasn't accustomed to his older and slower body.

Hudnam couldn't bring his hands up to protect his face before Lew broke his nose, fractured his jaw, and knocked several teeth out. He fell to the ground and spit out blood and teeth.

The top of the mountain where the Beburoa Hotel once stood exploded, and a giant sparrow flew out. It circled the mountain and then landed behind Hudnam. Lew and Hanna froze and then slowly backed away. Hudnam was too punch-drunk to even notice the ten-foot-tall bird behind him, even after it changed shape and turned into Balam.

"Yeah, that's right," Hudnam snarled at Lew. He sprayed blood when he spoke, and his teeth whistled. "Back up and fear me. I didn't see that coming, but now you'll feel my wrath."

Balam grabbed Hudnam with one hand and lifted him up. Only when face to face with Balam did Hudnam fully grasp his situation. "Lew, if you have any more magic crystals and Bible verses, now is the time. I'll give you fifteen million...twenty million...one hundred million dollars. Save me, and you can have anything you want."

Lew put his hand into his pocket and found his Bible, but then he paused. "Balam!" he called. "I bet Hudnam tastes delicious."

"Lew, you piece of shit! You'll regret this! This was a once-in-a-life-time opportunity! I could have—" Hudnam screamed as Balam sucked his soul out of his body. When it was nothing but a gray husk, Balam tossed it to the side, and it turned to dust when it hit the ground.

Balam belched and then turned towards Lew and Hanna. Lew cautiously stepped away and pulled the Bible out of his pocket. He held it between him and Balam.

Now Ruha appeared behind Hanna.

I didn't even see where she came from.

No longer in Juliana's form, Ruha was once again darkness upon darkness.

"Hanna!" Lew shouted. "Run!" But he didn't call soon enough.

Ruha put her hand on Hanna's back, but it wasn't an attack. Ruha leaned in and whispered in Hanna's ear.

What is she saying?

Hanna widened her eyes. She appeared to contemplate something, and then she whispered to Ruha. A few more exchanges went back and forth.

Hanna nodded and then stepped towards Balam.

You accept the deal? Balam asked.

Hanna nodded.

What the fuck is she doing?

Lew cried out to warn her. "Hanna, be careful! He's dangerous!"

"I know," Hanna answered without turning away from Balam.

Balam turned towards Lew and ran at him.

Lew pulled a ripped Bible page from his pocket and read it aloud. "This thy stature is like to a palm tree, and thy breasts to clusters of grapes. I said, I will go up to the palm tree, I will take hold of the boughs thereof: now also thy breasts shall be as clusters of the vine, and the smell of thy nose like apples; And the roof of thy mouth like the best wine."

This book is really weird.

Lew turned his gaze up from the Bible, expecting to see Balam stopped in pain, but Balam was gone. Lew looked back to the Bible and saw his hand was now full of worms. He jumped back and shook the worms away.

Balam's laugh echoed in Lew's ears, but he was still nowhere to be seen. Hanna and Ruha had vanished, too.

Lew, Balam's voice echoed inside of Lew's head. *Did you really think you had a magic book that could smite a demon?* Balam laughed again. *Listen to me, trailer trash. I will not eat your soul today. I will leave you alive to stew in your guilt. You left your wife and daughter hoping they would both die before you returned. For two weeks, you were my prisoner in a cave. Rush home to see if your family is alive or dead. If they are alive, you will live with the agony that you wanted them dead. If they are dead, you will live with the agony that you caused their death. I will return to eat you one day. Maybe I'll come back in a year, maybe in fifty years, or maybe in a week. The fear of not knowing when I'll eat you will make you taste oh so scrumptious.* He laughed again, and then his voice was gone.

Lew was finally all alone.

Juliana, Anika, I'm coming for you. Daddy's coming home.

LEW HAD LOST his cell phone in the Beburoa Hotel. He couldn't find any sign of his car—not that it mattered, since Lew didn't have his keys. He had to walk, and it was a long walk.

After eight hours on foot, Lew found a paved road. He tried to flag down a car to hitchhike.

It works in the movies.

But no cars stopped for him. One slowed down enough to throw a soda at him, and then it sped away. After another three and a half hours on foot, he found a gas station.

Am I glad I still have my wallet!

He bought and consumed a heap of junk food and Gatorade.

I never realized how much I would miss salty food. I'm really outside. None of this shit is an illusion.

He bought a burner phone and tried to call Juliana, but she didn't answer.

Lew called a cab and went to the nearest place to rent a car. From there, he drove to the Salt Lake City Airport. He called Juliana seven more times and sent dozens of text messages before he boarded the plane, but he never received a response. Lew fell asleep on the plane, and he had an actual dream—instead of another mind-fuck from Balam. He dreamed of Anika's smile and laugh, Juliana's warm embrace, and Anika's soft skin. Anika giggled when Lew kissed her cheeks.

When the plane landed, Lew turned his phone back on. He still didn't have a single message.

Why hasn't she responded? I hope I'm not too late. Was Balam right? Am I getting what I wanted? No, fuck that demon. They're everything to me.

Lew took a taxi home to his apartment. He called and sent several more texts on the ride, but he didn't receive a response.

Lew walked down the hallway to his apartment as pangs of pain ate at his sides. He didn't know what he would see on the other side of the door. He reached into his pocket for his key and remembered he didn't have it. He knocked on the door.

"Juliana," his voice cracked as he spoke. "It's me, Lew. I'm home. I don't have my key." After receiving no response, he knocked some more. "Juliana…" Knock, knock, knock… "Juliana…" Knock, knock, knock… Lew rapped "Kick In the Door" by the Notorious B.I.G. while he continued to knock. After twenty minutes of knocking, a baby cried from inside.

Thank God, she's alive.

Lew knocked on the door harder. "Juliana? Hello? Juliana?"

Lew pressed his ear against the door and listened.

"Shhhhhh," Juliana said to Anika inside the apartment before yawning. "Anika, why is some jerk pounding on our door and waking you up so early?"

Lew pounded even louder and shouted. "Juliana! Juliana! Open the door."

Footsteps walked up to the door in the apartment. A gasp came from the peephole.

Juliana scrambled to open the door. She was face to face with Lew, and she held baby Anika in her arms. Bags hung under Juliana's eyes. Milk and spit-up speckled her shirt. She stared at Lew, incredulous and unable to say a single word.

Lew smiled. He felt lightheaded and was once again at a loss for words.

"Dada," Anika said.

"Did she just… Did she say Dada?" Lew asked.

"She started saying Dada the first week you were gone," Juliana said. "And she has been saying it nonstop since. Where were you, Lew? You've been gone for weeks, and you haven't called once. You said you would call every day. What happened? Did you at least get the job you wanted?"

Lew hugged Juliana and Anika, and tears rolled down his cheeks. "I'm so sorry. I'm so sorry that I was gone for so long, but I'm back now. The Summit Conference was awful. I never want to go on another business trip again. I'm home, still jobless, and with even more credit card debt."

"Lew, you look like shit. Your suit's dirty and ripped." Juliana looked in the hallway. "Do you even have any luggage? What happened to all your stuff?"

"I have everything important to me in my arms right now." Lew finally stopped the hug. He took Anika from Juliana and held her in his arms. "Let's go back inside, and I'll tell you about my trip. I don't know if you'll believe a word I tell you, but it's all true. If I didn't experience it, I wouldn't believe it either."

"Dada! Dada! Dada!" Anika said.

"That's right," Lew said. "Dada's home."

48

Hanna Taithangklom walked through the lobby of the Frank Dolan Memorial Hotel. Large windows let in a thick yellow light, showing off the vast open space—classy tan and green marble floors, hanging chandeliers, and wood furniture with red velvet padding. A few large green potted plants dotted the perimeter.

A pair of enormous banners hung from the ceiling—displaying Hanna's portrait, smiling and staring up into the distance. Text on the posters read, "Welcome to the 2029 Summit Conference!" The style was modern but reminiscent of a Soviet propaganda poster of Lenin.

Hanna pressed a button to call the elevator, and she surveyed her domain while she waited.

Balam and Ruha cured Alexis, and now she has a long life ahead of her. I need to uphold my end of the bargain. I promised them I would double Abigor's attendance in just fifteen years. In ten years, I matched his numbers. Now I have five years left to meet my goal.

Hanna smiled and let out a sigh.

A young woman walked by, and she took a second glance when she noticed Hanna standing there by herself. She bit her lip and twice walked towards Hanna, only to change her mind and retreat. The third time, she finally engaged in conversation.

"Ms. Taithangklom," the young woman said, "I'm so excited to be here at the Summit Conference. I've heard that people who come here become extraordinarily successful."

"Beyond their wildest dreams," Hanna said with a huge smile. "Little Sandy and Sally will soon have everything you ever wanted to buy them."

The young woman opened her mouth to speak but bit her lip again. After a beat, she asked, "How do you know the names of my—"

"I take the time to learn about all my meeting attendees," Hanna beamed. "You have a lot to offer. Come and find me at the vegan, cruelty-free reception. I would like to discuss your future."

The young woman's eyes glistened, and she nodded with gusto.

The elevator door opened, and Hanna entered. "Excuse me."

"Thank you, Ms. Taithangklom," the young woman said.

HANNA OPENED the door to the dungeon. Sheriff Rickabaugh stood chained where she left him. Shackles held his neck, wrists, and ankles against the wall. His restraints allowed him little mobility—he couldn't even reach his hand to his face. When he was abducted from the March for Life, he weighed nearly three hundred pounds. He was now an emaciated skeleton that looked barely alive. He greeted Hanna with a glance from his sunken, unblinking eyes.

Hanna smiled. "You've been eating."

She regarded the dead baby that hung around his neck. From the bite marks and fresh blood, Hanna deduced that Sheriff Rickabaugh had grown hungry enough to eat his grandson, who was alive and crying when Hanna had last seen them.

"How do you feel now?" Hanna asked. "Are you peachy?"

He glared at her, unmoving.

"Do you still want to kill me?" she asked.

He nodded.

"Tsk tsk," Hanna responded with a frown. "That won't happen. Would you like it if I killed you and put you out of your misery?"

Sheriff Rickabaugh nodded. Tears silently streamed down his face.

Hanna smiled. "I will eventually. You have a few remaining family members who need to be dealt with first. But don't worry. You'll get to watch them die, and they'll know their deaths are entirely your fault."

He sobbed harder.

"I'll check on you again later. If you get hungry in the meantime," Hanna gestured at the dead baby on his neck, "you know where to find more food."

Hanna smiled and closed the door, leaving Sheriff Rickabaugh trapped in the darkness.

THANK YOU

Thank you for taking the time to read this novel! I hope you liked it.

Stay up to date on my latest activities at jonkaczkaauthor.com.

Did you enjoy *Surviving the Summit Conference*? Remember what Jesus said: "Support authors you like by writing honest reviews online. Honest reviews will help other readers find the book."

Thank you!

ACKNOWLEDGMENTS

I would never have published this book without the help of so many people.

Thank you to my wife and daughter for inspiring everything I do.

Thank you to Erin PT Canning for making my sentences coherent. Thank you to Katie Eagan Schenck for helping me turn a story into a published novel. Thank you to my good friend for designing this book's incredible cover. Thank you to Ari for reading early drafts of this story when it was in another format. Thank you to Brian, Mike, Steve, and Toby for helping me work through my plot problems. Thank you to everyone who read any version or draft of this story, even if you didn't like it. Thank you to the magnificent team at Low on Ink Books, LLC for taking a chance with me. And thank you to anyone else I forgot to thank by name.

I want to give a shout out to the Wu-Tang Clan, A Tribe Called Quest, Busta Rhymes, and the other titans of '90s hip hop. Rest in peace to the Ol' Dirty Bastard and the Notorious B.I.G.

REFERENCES

Collin De Plancy, J. (1844) *Dictionnaire Infernal.* [Paris, P. Mellier; etc., et] [Pdf] Retrieved from the Library of Congress, https://www.loc.gov/item/24006547/.

Edwards, L. (2020). *How to Read a Suit : A Guide to Changing Men's Fashion from the 17th to the 20th Century.* Bloomsbury Visual Arts.

Green's Dictionary of Slang. (n.d.). Greensdictofslang.com. https://greensdictofslang.com.

Holy Bible, King James Version. (n.d.). *The King James Bible.* Retrieved from https://www.biblegateway.com/.

Kellis, D. S., & Ran, B. (2012). Three pillars of public leadership: Making a difference in public organizations. *Institute of Public Governance & Management E-Bulletin, 25.*